TOMB OF THE FIRST PRIEST

A LOST ORIGINS NOVEL

A. D. DAVIES

CRATER OF THE NORTH PUBLISHING

NOVELS BY A. D. DAVIES

PART ONE

There is nothing new in the world except the history you do not know.

—Harry S Truman

Do you want to know who you are? Don't ask. Act! Action will delineate and define you.

—Thomas Jefferson

CHAPTER
ONE

PRAGUE, OLD TOWN - CZECH REPUBLIC

Four stories above the street, Jules Sibeko raced over Prague's ocean of rooftops, sprinting over one snow-dusted eave and riding the momentum to its neighbor. While his tracking beacon followed the roads at a predictable speed-limit-minus-two miles per hour—the rate at which Jules had rehearsed every likely route—he kept one eye on his phone and one on the next obstacle. The real-world exercise proved more difficult than any dry run, though.

He hadn't expected snow either, a rare sight in April.

So he adapted. Planting his rubber-soled feet more firmly, he sought out nooks and crannies protected from the weather, and although the added caution shaved between 5 and 7 percent off his speed, he was still able to traverse the skyscape in pursuit of the thieves. In these moments, whatever the conditions, all that mattered was putting one foot after the other, timing his jumps so his fingers gripped the lip of the next vent, wall, or recess just so, and progressing smoothly and silently.

It was the closest he ever came to flying.

He barely felt the cold rushing by except through the ski

mask's eyeholes. His midnight-blue bodysuit—a smooth cotton-Lycra blend he'd had custom made in China—clung to him over thermals, and with his backpack coated in the same light-absorbing material, it offered better camouflage in the city's shadows than the matte-black outfits he'd worn in the past.

Sure, he resembled a cosplay enthusiast who'd fallen on hard times, but the getup worked for him.

He glided over a ridge of terracotta like a tightrope walker, thankful for the clouds overhead; there was little danger of his silhouette betraying his position. Toward the edge, he sped up, preparing for the twelve-foot jump. As fast as he dared, he gripped the peak's edge with his foot, bent his knee, and threw his body weight forward.

The calculations used to appear to him in written form, as if he etched the formulas and trigonometric diagrams with neon ink in thin air. After years of practice measuring distance, calculating the power required, the effect of gravity along with wind resistance, answers now came to him in a split-second of probability.

This time, in addition to propelling himself over the distance, he dropped four feet before landing on a wooden balustrade, only four inches wide, where he slipped in the snow. Momentum pushed him onward faster than predicted. But he spun in midair, kicked his legs over his head, and planted both feet firmly on the balcony.

Fluidly resuming his forward motion, he scaled the penthouse skylight at half speed.

Back clear of tweaks.

Knees bending, straightening. No pain.

Neck retains full motion.

Conclusion: no injuries from the mishap.

At full speed, executing an even riskier shortcut over a series of plush apartment buildings, Jules might've been mistaken by a casual witness for a thrill-seeking free runner. But this was no pastime. His years of training with parkour masters, of honing his body and learning every trick of every trade he might need, might all pay off tonight.

The thought that he could, in a couple of days, be kicking back and consuming pizza for the first time since his fourteenth birthday, trying beer for the first time, *period*, and perhaps even indulging in a melted-in-the-middle chocolate pudding... it caused his mouth to moisten. And he lost another three seconds.

The tracking beacon halted at a street that Jules scouted two days ago, an alleyway housing a fried chicken takeout place and a bookmaker, plus a low-end knockoff designer boutique. From his rooftop perch, he couldn't quite see beyond the shadows at the back end of the narrow passage, so he sidestepped to the foot-wide slab running along the bookmaker's angled roof. Lying flat, his weight crunched down the snow and melted it into a freezing slush. He peeked over using a riflescope.

A two-year-old Range Rover, black of course, idled in the chill night.

Do these guys ever drive anything else?

Most tourists were now indoors. Even the drunks. Those snug within the 4x4 seemed in no hurry to leave.

As if assessing their position.

As if scanning for a tail.

People like these rarely looked up. If they did, they *might* spot Jules, contrasted heavily against the snow, but he was just another vague shape atop a roof in a world of CCTV cameras, covert surveillance teams, and drones. No way would they be looking for him four stories above their heads.

The passenger door opened, and out stepped a buff Caucasian dude with blond hair and a neat, trimmed beard. A dark suit, no tie. His breath misted as he scouted the scene, pretending to check his watch. The gun under his armpit flashed for less than a second, but Jules recognized the butt of a Sig Sauer P229. When the guy walked, he favored his right foot by a ratio of less than an inch, indicating a backup piece on the ankle. Barely noticeable, but it was there.

This was no amateur.

The man nodded to the Range Rover.

Wearing an emerald-green trench coat, a slender woman with shiny, copper hair climbed out carrying a metallic briefcase. Head down, age indeterminable. Jules assumed she was Lori, whose name he'd picked up during low-tech surveillance of potential antiquities middlemen.

Red hair.

Emerald-green coat.

That's a bold look.

It was a shame Jules was about to ruin her day.

He lowered his scope and returned it to his pack.

As the Range Rover departed, the woman marched into the alleyway. The blond man closed in four feet behind while her free hand remained in her pocket.

From his backpack, Jules removed an extendible baton, currently retracted into a twelve-inch tube, and a three-pronged grappling hook attached to a bungee cord. He slipped the baton into his belt loop next to three throwing knives, opposite half a dozen dime-size smoke bombs—ninja-type equipment that made his fourteen-year-old self squeal with delight. His twenty-three-year-old *current* self concentrated on the serious business of now. And there was no squealing. Of delight or otherwise.

After stashing his pack, Jules wedged the grappling hook between two steel rails atop the fire escape, fed out the correct amount of elasticated rope for the height, wound the slack around his hand, and noiselessly positioned himself above the alley, calculating his targets' pace.

Again, in years past, he'd have spent seconds writing the sums and probability factors in the air, scrawling equations in two columns; one for those under observation, the other for his own approach. It was no longer necessary, his brain now fine-tuned to the speed of any calculator. Without a need for fingers, it was faster.

Could this be the last time?

Might he soon be able to disregard this level of learning? Allow some knowledge, some skill burned into his mind to slip, to be replaced with those insignificant skills he observed in everyday people. Like small talk. Like enjoying food solely for the taste, not sustenance alone.

He was so close.

As soon as the red-haired woman passed under him, with the bodyguard maintaining his four-foot distance, Jules dropped.

Once more, his fourteen-year-old self called from the past to highlight how thrilling this should be. But all that entered modern Jules's mind was how the cord should slow his descent from 1.25 seconds to a full three, depositing him approximately four feet behind the man carrying the Sig.

Within one second, he was plummeting at ten meters per second. Half a second later, the bungee cord pulled tight around his hand, slowing him to five, and as he neared the ground, it continued to drag his speed back in fractional increments until he halted smoothly, touching down with only the tiniest scuff; closer to three feet from the target than his intended four.

It was enough to alert the bodyguard.

The Sig appeared in the man's hand as he spun in one expert motion. Jules let go of the cord, flicking it forward. The end snapped in the minder's face, snapping like a whip.

The distraction let Jules fling the baton out of its loop and into the guy's wrist, releasing the gun. Before it hit the floor, Jules caught the firearm, rolled aside, and aimed at his opponent's right ankle. Unsure which side the backup piece was on, he fired both outside and inside the limb, striking the gun on the second try —inside.

Math wasn't the only skill that infused itself to him once he'd learned it. Perhaps gunplay was a burden he could shed soon, in favor of inane chatter regarding the weather or politics.

As the bodyguard fell, clutching his lower leg and checking for damage, Jules sprinted after the woman, who had already taken flight. He caught up with her beside the bookmaker's, the raised Sig Sauer enough to halt her in her tracks.

"Hey," Jules said. "Look at that. You lose."

She glanced at the man before fixing Jules with stern, green eyes. Younger than Jules expected, between twenty-five and twenty-seven, a couple of years older than himself. Her skin looked pale, red cheeks accentuating the light shade. An English rose in appearance. But when she spoke, she was pure southern belle. Alabama, if Jules wasn't mistaken.

She held up the case. "Take it. Please. Just don't hurt me."

Her bodyguard found his feet, pointing the backup firearm from his ankle holster—a small Walther. "Put it down and back off!" Another American, his accent blander, probably West Coast, practically the polar opposite of Jules's Brooklyn tone.

Jules grinned beneath his mask. "That's a risky move, friend."

"Not your friend. And since you went for my leg instead of putting one in my head, I'm guessing you don't wanna kill anyone here. But I have orders, and I'm not so picky."

"Army guy, huh? *Ex*, I'm guessin'. But you can't shoot me."

"You won't be the first to be wrong about that."

The red-haired woman slowly retracted the case, eyes roving, lips stiff. This wasn't her regular field of work.

"I don't mean you're afraid to kill me," Jules said. "I mean... aw heck, I'll demonstrate."

He swung his gun toward the musclehead. The guy pulled his trigger once, twice, clicking dry both times.

"I wasn't aiming for your leg," Jules said. "I was taking out your backup piece."

The bodyguard tossed the Walther hard at the wall and advanced, but Jules sidestepped behind the girl and firmed his grip on the Sig, halting her would-be savior's advance.

Jules returned his attention to the redhead. "Okay. Lori, right? Let's have it."

She presented the case with a shaking hand. "I'm not Lori."

"I don't want the decoy, hon."

More calculations, more probability, all firing his synapses to one simple conclusion.

"Decoy?" Not-Lori took a single step away. A minuscule shake of her head. "I don't know what you mean."

With his free hand, Jules ruffled her sleeves, then yanked them up to her elbows, revealing two smooth, bare arms. He retreated from her and focused on the man instead.

"Clever," Jules said. "Hand it over."

"I thought they'd send more men," the minder replied.

"Where is it?"

"Where is what? This?"

The man tugged up his left sleeve to expose the item Jules had pursued across the globe for nine long years. Pinched on his forearm, the bracelet was made of stone, infused with metallic green flecks, its circumference broken only by a half-inch gap, forming a tight letter C. That gap and its fixed shape made it technically a *bangle*, not a bracelet, but Jules didn't care about the distinction. He concerned himself with one solitary factor.

It's mine.

Jules released the Sig's magazine and popped the chambered round. He tossed the gun up onto a second-floor fire escape, and charged at the bodyguard, pulling up short of a bull-like attack to prevent what was obviously a well-trained individual from countering early.

The other man had no such qualms.

He jabbed at Jules's throat. Jules twisted away and simultaneously shoved the bodyguard off balance, then kicked the guy's standing foot, dropping him on his backside.

The ex-military man rolled, popped into a crouch, and drew a knife from behind his gun holster.

"What is it with you people?" the man asked.

"Me people?" Jules said.

"These objects aren't supposed to be collected like trinkets."

"I don't know who you think I'm with, *friend*. I just want what belongs to me."

The man with Jules's property slackened faintly. "You're not one of Valerio Conchin's guys?"

Jules palmed one of the mini flashbangs from his belt. "I don't know who that is."

With a flick of his thumb, he set the smoke bomb to its shortest fuse and threw it forward. The flash of light and eruption of potassium chlorate made the guy jerk back, drop his knife, and hold his eyes. To his credit, he didn't scream.

And with the redhead frozen in his peripheral vision, Jules moved in hard. A flat hand to the man's throat and a heel to his jaw sent the musclehead tumbling, allowing Jules time to grip the bracelet and straighten the man's arm, locking the joint. A simple aikido manouevre. Like so many techniques, he'd learned and mastered the art and never forgotten.

Jules tugged and twisted, sliding the bangle as low as the wrist, but it was stuck there.

"You won't get it off," the woman said, taking a single trembling step forward.

Jules maneuvered the arm around and forced his foot into the man's shoulder blade so its owner lay facedown.

"We had to use a whole a lot of olive oil just to jam it on there," the woman insisted. "And it hurt like hell."

Jules strained, pulling up skin, causing the man on the ground to gasp in pain. "I won't lose it now. Not when I'm so close."

"Please," she said. "It belongs somewhere *safe*. You say you're not with Valerio. Then *trust* us."

Jules twisted the object. "I'm taking it with me."

"No. Please try to understand. If Valerio wants the Aradia bangle, we *have* to secure it."

Jules slackened his grip on the stone jewelry but held his subject firmly underfoot. "What did you call it?"

The woman frowned, took one step forward. "The Aradia bangle. You say you own it, but you don't know what it's called?"

A hundred questions flew through his mind. Yes, he wanted it back, but he knew little else. He wouldn't let it go again. It was his again, as it had been before.

Or, more precisely, "It was my mom's."

As the woman's frown deepened at his words, Jules rolled the ski mask up over his mouth and spat on the man's wrist, mashing the stone bangle into the saliva. He wrenched at the locked joint with all his strength, and the man gave a painful grunt. The movement drew a line of blood, but that aided in slicking the surface.

Jules spat again, and for just a second, the ornament appeared to glow, its flecks of green catching the streetlight.

And then it popped free.

Jules released the man's arm and glided away, finally holding the chunk of rock that had consumed the whole of his adulthood.

The whole of his adulthood *so far*, he reminded himself. He had plenty of life ahead of him.

The woman checked on her minder, who sat upright against the wall beneath the lit door of the fried chicken place, cradling his wrist. Both glared at Jules.

"Sorry, but the bracelet's mine," Jules said.

"My sentiments exactly," a new voice replied in a deep-throated Australian accent.

Jules turned. The newcomer was a brick wall of a man, at least six-feet-eight, almost a foot taller than Jules and twice as wide, most of it muscle. Dark-haired, he possessed a jaw the shape of a shovel. Ten local cops moved into place behind him.

He held out a hand that seemed big enough to engulf Jules's head like a baseball. "Now surrender the Aradia bangle, and Mr. Conchin promises no one else'll get hurt."

CHAPTER
TWO

Jules stepped back and gazed up at the shaved mountain gorilla. "Hand over the *what* now?"

"The trinket." The new man pointed at the object in Jules's possession. "Hand it over, and you won't get hurt."

"Oh. Okay."

Jules flicked and detonated two smoke bombs in quick succession. The man merely flinched and snorted. But the flinch let Jules duck, then sprint back past the bookmaker's shop. As he leaped and gripped the first fire escape, ten cops streamed by the big guy, ignoring the two people Jules had robbed, and headed straight for him.

If they were genuine cops, someone would have helped the injured man. Also, Prague cops typically carried the short-recoil CZ 75 pistol, or if they were feeling adventurous, an H&K MP7 submachine gun for major ops. These guys wielded a mishmash of weaponry, including Uzis and AK-47s. Jules couldn't pinpoint the exact makes because he was too busy smashing a second-floor window by the time they opened fire.

Jules dived through the jagged pane just before the slugs impacted the surrounding wall. He rolled to his feet but did not stop to apologize to the elderly man and woman sitting bolt upright in bed, instead banging through the door into the cramped apartment's exit.

The home lay above the clothes boutique, so Jules sprinted up the first staircase he came to, reasoning it must end on the roof.

Floors below, doors crashed in, voices rose, orders issued, and boots thundered on stairs.

At the top, the fourth floor, Jules found the door locked tight. Chained, in fact.

Some fire exit.

He descended to third and kicked out a window, exposing himself once again to the alley below.

As soon as he slipped out, the enormous man shouted in Czech to open fire.

Jules pushed his arm through the bangle. "You want this real bad, huh?"

Over the fire escape's wrought iron rail, he gripped the drainpipe with his hands and knees, and monkey-climbed for three seconds—the time he estimated it would take an average ex-soldier using a black-market machine gun to draw a bead on him, then pushed away from the wall before the bullets rained in.

While the gunmen repositioned below, he snagged the lip of the roof, heaving himself up to where he'd left his backpack. By the time he retrieved his grappling hook and snatched up his bag, the fake cops had shot out the chain barring the exit and poured out.

Using the building's air conditioning units as cover, treading carefully on the snow, Jules evaded yet more angles at which the bullets could pulverize him. He raced toward the edge, where a huge chasm lay between this roof and the nearest safe haven. In a flat-out sprint, he ran the numbers:

Thirty-two feet, possibly 32.5.

The world record for long jump is an inch or so shy of 29.5 feet.

My record is 25.7 feet.

The approaching lip is two feet lower than the current one.

To reach it, after the apex of my leap, I would drop at five meters per second, which is fifteen feet...

Even at optimum distance, I'm 1.5 feet short.

And no fire escape to land on below. The building is sheer.

The entire risk assessment took no longer than two seconds.

Instead of leaping to his probable death, Jules absorbed the spike of fear in his gut, controlled his breathing, and swerved left. As soon as the operatives posing as cops rounded the AC units, the lead men opened fire again.

That left Jules little choice.

Rather than take the direct route over adjacent blocks, he darted right to lose himself where more vents rose from the rooftop. The spacing and zigzag design provided no solid cover but gave no clear line of sight either; the shooters would have to be very lucky to wing him.

However, Jules was about to run out of building. The next one was over fifty feet across the boulevard.

He cursed his lax planning. Tonight's exit routes seemed ideal because most parts of the city featured those open avenues dotted with alleys, the buildings mostly close together, so he had not compensated for the wider streets. But then he'd never been ambushed by a small army before.

And that's where he threw himself next: out into the void of the night, four stories above a road that was fifty feet wide.

Jules swung his grappling hook, snagged a thick telephone cable that spanned the street, and let himself drop, plummeting as he worked out the length of the bungee cord feeding out.

The metal claws slipped along the ice-coated wire, and momentum carried him onward. The slippery sensation of being out of control felt alien, but the elasticated rope stretched as it fought with gravity to stop him from hurtling into the asphalt at inhuman speed.

It reached its limit with Jules still twice his own height off the ground, but he'd decelerated to a virtual stop. He let go, and the cord snapped upward like a rubber band flicked from a thumb.

With the swing carrying him forward, he performed a midair backflip to slow himself, landed on both feet, and rolled behind a parked car.

Another bungee lost.

Gunfire erupted from the roof, peppering the vehicle, but Jules was already assessing his body again.

Slightly jarred knee.

Ankle took more impact than intended.

A 10 to 15 percent decrease in efficiency.

"I can live with that."

He kept low, using the cars as cover, until he located an alley. As the men at ground level emerged to give chase, he ducked out of sight. The fence barring the end was no problem. He hopped it and then tuned in to his mental map of the central city blocks.

Sticking to the puddles of melted snow—less of a trail that way—he turned left, then right, not looking behind him at all. He only slowed to check his mom's bracelet was still secure.

The *Aradia bangle,* as they'd called it.

Hiking into one of Old Town's squares, dotted with tourists catching a few final drinks under the heaters at overpriced bars, Jules peeled off his mask and reduced his speed to an amble.

Snow flurries dusted across the terracotta-tiled roof of a church. Jules estimated it was from around the fourteenth century. He was unsure of the clock tower opposite, but then he never researched more than he needed, no matter how intriguing a place's history; extra facts clouded his mind.

Still, the snow on the medieval buildings reminded him of a fairy-tale book. Not a specific one, just the fantastical feeling of a childhood story revisited. A useless notion that he dismissed as soon as it formed.

He withdrew one arm from his backpack to appear more casual and ripped open the Velcro strap on his chest that released his torso from the blue bodysuit. This left a maroon Breaking Bad shirt on view, with the gloves in place as he figured he could use them. He dropped the bracelet into his pack and tied the suit's arms around his waist so he fit in with the other vacationers returning to hotels after skinfuls of beer.

Jules had played the fish-out-of-water African American student plenty of times before, though, so this wasn't difficult to pull off.

He only needed the cover for three minutes anyway as he accessed the backyard of a disused restaurant, shut down for refurbishments before the foreign trade picked up in May and June. The tarp came away from the stashed Suzuki GW250 with ease.

Jules donned the crash helmet and leather jacket he'd tucked away there and swapped his tactile gloves for thicker, more appropriate ones. He fired up the motorcycle and eased it into the square, drawing attention from various groups of exhausted revelers as he rumbled by.

Once clear of the tourist hot spot, he gunned the engine and sped up to thirty-eight miles per hour—yeah, two below the limit —and pointed his nose north.

As the streets sped by, Jules thought about pizza toppings and where to make his purchase.

Backgammon Pizza was the only real option. A small chain when he was a kid, it was now a global conglomerate to rival Pizza Hut and Dominos. It was where his parents had taken him for his fourteenth birthday, pizza from a restaurant being a true luxury in the Sibeko household. Although he'd had no clue what to order back then, he tried to look as if he knew what he was doing, relishing the independence, the opportunity to choose as he wished outside the supermarket's frozen goods aisle: pepperoni, red onions, and tuna. The waitress pulled a face but jotted it down beside with his parents' more traditional options.

None of them ate their pizza that night, though. And Jules had abstained from junk food ever since.

He turned a corner, ready to speed up the on-ramp to the freeway out of town—or "motorway" as they called them here— but found it blocked.

Two of those bad-boy black Range Rovers stood nose to nose, and an old military-style jeep was parked beyond them, manned by two more fake cops.

They guessed my escape route.

No—there are probably more of them on the other passages out of town, too.

Cop uniforms, bold enough to fire automatic weapons in public, able to block roads...

Who are *these guys?*

Jules screeched to a halt and spun the bike around, rear wheel smoking and screaming, and tore away from the roadblock. It broke up, and the 4x4s sped after him.

The Suzuki was no slouch, but here, on a broad road designed for eighteen-wheelers, it gave him little advantage against the other vehicles' brute force. If he made it to the smaller arteries in the city, he could lose them thanks to the bike's superior maneuverability.

The two Range Rovers' raw horsepower brought them level, and they raced on either side of him. He prepared to brake and branch off, but they were ready, closing in from both sides, the jeep bringing up the rear.

A limo pulled up a hundred yards ahead, lengthwise across the street. Boxing him in.

Jules opened up the throttle and shifted through the gears for maximum torque.

The limo's rear door opened and the giant from the alleyway unfolded himself to stand tall in the road, before hustling out the redhead in the green coat. He placed a handgun at her temple.

And waited.

Unmoving.

Jules had no idea who the girl was. *Not-Lori.* But she sure wasn't with the men chasing him. If he got away, they had no reason to harm her, but he'd seen people murdered for lesser objects than the one he recovered tonight. And these guys were trying to kill him for his mom's bracelet, after all. Something *not-Lori* had possessed until recently.

Maybe they blamed her.

Jules reduced his speed. The Range Rovers matched him, guiding him rather than pursuing, dropping back until he skidded to a stop six feet from the huge guy and his hostage.

Nobody moved.

The bike chugged idle.

A second man climbed from the limo. Early thirties with thick blond hair and a tan suit. The man's skin was sallow and yellow, so Jules figured the latest arrival suffered a form of liver disease, although he appeared jovial in his walk—spry, almost skipping along.

"Hey." Jules flipped up his visor. "You in charge?"

"You seem clever." The yellow man wandered around the side of the limo, hands in his trouser pockets, which rode his jacket up, crinkling at the hem. "Which is great! Clever people tend to know what I'm after. Then, after some utterly *pointless* macho posturing..." The guy smiled. "They give it to me."

Jules couldn't place the accent, almost British, but not quite. He said, "I got ten other items like the bracelet. Nicer. Older. More valuable. I'll hand 'em over at a place of your choosing. But you can't have this."

"See? Posturing. *Pointless* posturing. How sad. I thought you'd be different." The yellow man signaled to his guy. "Horse, shoot the girl in her pretty little knee, see if that loosens up our pal here."

Horse? Was that the Australian hulk's name?

"Wait." Jules removed his helmet and his pack, took off his thick riding gloves, and unlatched the backpack's flap. Opened it. "I swear, I can get you better pieces. Nothing special about this. I got a sentimental attachment is all—"

"Do you think we set up all this effort to acquire some *random* artifact? Have you mistaken me for a common *grave robber* in this business for the *money*? No. We want that *specific* trinket." The yellow man clicked his fingers. "*Now*, please."

The girl stared at Jules, arms rigid by her sides. Her stockinged feet extended on tiptoes to ease the pressure applied by... What was his name? *Horse*? The man's fingers enveloped her neck without throttling her.

Jules reached into the pack and grasped his mom's bracelet. He could virtually feel it vibrating, urging him to not let it go now they were finally reunited. His shoulder stiffened. An ache in his gut spread to his chest.

Nine years...

So close...

He locked eyes with the yellow man. "Please... there's nothing special about this. I can—"

"Horse," the yellow man said.

Horse pointed the gun at the woman's knee, and Jules averted his gaze as he removed the bracelet from his pack.

He couldn't bear to look at it. Could not watch someone take it from him the way it was stolen from his mother.

"Nothing special?" the yellow man said curiously.

Jules held still for a long moment until he realized the bracelet wasn't *virtually* vibrating. It really *was* humming between his fingers. And when Jules steeled himself enough to turn his head in that direction, the green flecks were lit up, glowing, as they had when he'd spat on it and removed it from the girl's minder.

It wasn't a trick of the light after all.

His heart raced. He struggled to keep his face neutral. The prospect of parting with it now hurt even more.

Just what was my mom into?

"Now *that's* interesting," the yellow man said. "And really quite unexpected. But whatever. Larry."

One of the fake cops from a Range Rover offered a white cloth sack and held it open. Jules released the bangle and it landed in the bag, the lights dying instantly.

"Sir?" Horse flicked his gun toward Jules.

The yellow man seized the bag. "Can we sweep the murders of a couple of Americans under the carpet here?"

"Done it before, sir."

The yellow man sighed. "Fine, do it quickly."

Horse shoved the girl forward. She stood beside Jules, frozen. The big man's gun came up.

Jules had already palmed a throwing knife, though, waiting for the girl to get clear. He snapped his hand forward and launched the blade.

It thunked into Horse's gun arm, making him drop the weapon.

Then Jules deployed two smoke bombs in Horse's face, swept the girl up, planted her behind him, and opened up the bike with a storm of wheel spin and roaring engine.

While the mercs gathered themselves, Jules dropped the remaining smoke bombs to obscure their escape. Before a single shot came their way, they were around the corner and gone.

CHAPTER
THREE

After patching up his wrist using his field kit, Dan Vincent steered the stolen van, following the sluggish GPS function on his phone to the freeway north of the city.

The only clues after the alleyway came from a drone camera intended to monitor the bangle's handover. Unfortunately, the "drone" was nothing more than a $1,000 store-bought quadcopter with a camera streaming via a jerry-rigged smartphone. It had followed their Range Rover on the roads, monitoring fore and aft for tails, but it did not possess the scope to cover rooftops with the efficiency of a $10 billion spy satellite.

"Who follows a target by rooftop, anyway?" he asked aloud.

He had no field intel beyond the direction the weird vigilante guy had fled and that Valerio Conchin's men bugged out with Bridget the same way. When the shooting started, he ushered Bridget aside, but she screamed when a second barrage opened.

They had become separated.

The drone, controlled remotely from their base of operations, stuck with Bridget's abductors for as long as possible, but it was more the sort of kit used for semi-pro filmmakers, so wasn't up to following a speeding motorcade.

He'd told Toby that Bridget wasn't ready, but with Harpal delayed, she was the only decoy available.

Damn it.

He slapped the wheel with his good hand. She was *his* responsibility.

Sure, she was a capable kid, gusty and passionate about their work. But he was almost twice her age and fifty times more experienced. He should have aborted and risked missing the handover.

Verification could've waited. Securing the item was the priority, not working out what it did. It was a luxury to enjoy once the danger passed. Then Dan could drink a beer and pretend to look interested as their faces lit up with the realization that it was far more valuable or "impossible" than they'd expected.

Everything they recovered lately seemed impossible. Until it wasn't.

This new player, though, he hadn't acted shocked when the Aradia bangle lit up. Barely even noticed. Meaning the criminal was intimately familiar with the artifact. That made him as dangerous as Valerio Conchin.

Dan risked a check on the Uzi he secured from the lone guard whom Conchin's ragtag mercs left to watch over him. It had already been fired, so although it was black market junk, he knew there was no jam, leaving the number of bullets as the only variable. He ejected the clip and weighed it in his hand.

Between five and ten rounds.

Not that it mattered much.

The guy who took the bangle was fast, and he had skills, had even caught Dan off guard. But Dan was an ex–Army Ranger. He wouldn't be sucker-punched like that again. And no amount of skill could dodge a bullet. Even a single round would be enough.

But Bridget was the priority now.

The phone sent him wrong twice, stuttering with the dodgy app, so that by the time he reached the on-ramp, the standoff was in full swing: Bridget held hostage by the lump called Horse, Valerio himself handling the negotiation, and the Spider-Man wannabe was pausing, delaying the handover.

Do it and they'll kill you both.

Damn it. Amateurs always screw things up.

Dan parked around the corner and crouch-ran up the adjoining street. In thirty seconds he was ready to launch himself from a bush, fire one round into Horse's head and another into Valerio Conchin's jaundiced heart. He'd snatch Bridget while the rent-a-bad-guys cleaned up their pants.

He'd drop the Spider-Dude too if he interfered.

Dan had faced worse odds, but Bridget hadn't. This was all new to her, and she wouldn't understand Dan's signals—when to duck, when to bite or shove or stamp on her captor's foot. And her window for escape was shortening.

Horse shoved Bridget toward the thief, and Valerio made a gesture that could only mean one thing: *kill them.*

Dan rose, adopted a shooting stance with the Uzi's folding stock planted firmly in his shoulder, and drew down on Horse.

Then it all went south.

The kid on the motorcycle—and he *was* a kid, not much older than Bridget—threw something that hurt his would-be killer, then did his trick with the mini flashbangs. Before Dan could get his bearings, they were speeding around a corner, the goons and their bosses watching them go. Conchin's men then formed a convoy and fled with their prize rather than give chase, which left Dan with a decision.

Follow the artifact or secure his friend?

He ran back to the van. The motorcycle's tire marks betrayed their route, which gave Dan the general direction where the stranger was taking Bridget.

When it was clear that Horse and the others were not following, Jules pulled up in the parking lot of a suburban bar still pumping music from within. He knocked out the kickstand, opened his visor, and ordered the girl off.

"I'm—" the girl started.

"What, you're sorry?" Jules said.

She looked down. "I'm Bridget." That Alabama twang extended her vowels, which kept Jules watching her lips as she spoke. "And yes, I'm sorry we lost the bangle. But thank you for saving me. Perhaps we can—"

"What? Perhaps we can what, *Bridget*? Work something out? You know how long I been looking for that? Nine *years*. You any idea what I gave up?"

Jules kicked the stand back up and revved the engine once, his whole body drained of energy. No anger, no frustration. Just a crushing emptiness.

A blue van trundled past; the only traffic they'd seen since stopping.

"What will you do now?" Bridget asked.

"What I always do when I get close and fail." Unable to summon the energy to leave in a huff, Jules's shoulders slackened and dropped. "I'll start all over again."

Bridget stepped up and touched his arm. Her freckles had not been apparent before, but up close she bore the character of a porcelain doll, her copper hair once again shining under halogen lights. "Let me help you."

Dan spotted them in the parking lot of a club. Bridget, ever the gentle soul, appeared to be chatting with the stranger. She had no idea of the trouble men like him could cause her, no matter their intentions, no matter how passionately they claimed to be good people. Dan knew, though. Dan knew what darkness lay beneath the most pleasant-looking shells.

Protocol dictated he should use caution since the subject hadn't used, or attempted to use, lethal force against anyone yet. But this might still count as kidnapping.

Pulling to the curb, out of sight, Dan told himself it was legitimate to take no chances with this one. That the guy with Bridget was dangerous, and lethal force was justified.

He gave the gun a final check and stalked toward them from the side.

———

"Your mother used to own the Aradia bangle?" Bridget asked. "How did she come across it?"

"I don't know. And I don't care. I just know I have to get it back."

"Why?"

Jules swallowed, forcing an acidic mix back into his chest. "Because now she's gone, and—" He was sharing too much. "That's my business."

From around the side of the club, the guy from the alley, Bridget's minder, sprang forward, an Uzi raised and pointed Jules's way.

"Bridget, get down!" the guy shouted.

Jules instinctively ducked at an angle, but before he could dive sideways and arm himself with a throwing knife, Bridget spread her hands and stood between him and the shooter, a voluntary human shield.

"What are you *doing*?" the man demanded. "Move!"

"No," Bridget said. "Let him go." Hesitation. The pair staring. "Dan, he's no threat. In fact… he's more than likely lost more than we did tonight."

Slowly, the man lowered the weapon.

Bridget relaxed.

Jules pulled the Suzuki upright, eyes holding on the gunman, the knife ready in his palm. No one moved on him. Bridget had the situation under control, and the guy—definitely a pro— seemed to respect her word.

So Jules simply nodded once to the pale redhead.

Without another word, he flipped down his visor and accelerated as hard as he could toward Prague's center, screaming his lungs out as he went.

CHAPTER
FOUR

CHATEAU CACHÉ - BRITTANY, FRANCE

When Dan transmitted confirmation of Bridget's safe retrieval, Toby Smith's legs turned to jelly, the air in his lungs grew thin, and he had to sit down. There was no chair nearby, so he planted himself on the floor in his new beige suit. He wanted to cry. If it hadn't been for Charlie's calm analysis, her firm way of monitoring the airwaves, of tracking Dan's movements... well, let's just say she kept Toby sane during that hour.

Was it a whole hour?

It felt like both minutes and several hours. The speed of events, the drawn-out uncertainty.

The youngest member of the institute, Bridget Carson was the brightest researcher and analyst he'd ever hired. But no matter her qualities, she was not a field operative. It would be his fault if she died.

When the op went wrong and Toby demanded answers he knew Charlie could not give, the concentration on her face never wavered, her expression barely altering. She'd simply placed the controller aside and fired up the Demon Server—not quite a supercomputer, but far superior to most server farms—where she hunted for any clue to Bridget's fate. She may have frowned a couple of times when nothing popped up immediately, but that was her only indication of concern.

"The police scanner, paramedic frequencies, even social media," she assured him, her Welsh tones offering no concession to failure. "The firefight in central Prague... it's already all over the net, but the cops can't respond."

"Why on earth not?"

"You know why, Toby. Please don't waste your breath yapping."

He did know, of course. They'd covered it during prep. Dozens of cops were engaged in an armed standoff in the south of the city. Plus, in a separate incident, two uniformed officers suffered gunshots to their legs, inflicted by people wearing gang colors, so they were spread far and wide hunting down the shooters.

The fact all this occurred half an hour before their handover indicated that it was no coincidence, but Toby had pressed ahead anyway. Against Charlie's advice.

Slowly, after the good news about Bridget reached them, Toby's thigh muscles reconnected to his body, so with little else for them to do, he and Charlie adjourned from the ops room in the chateau's east wing to the teak-paneled study. Here, they poured healthy measures of brandy in crystal glasses, which Bridget claimed were a gift from the Sultan of Brunei.

Neither spoke for at least a minute.

Charlie watched Toby, causing him to pace, his legs now the opposite of jelly, a need to move coursing through him. Even his fingers were jittery. Eventually, he halted and sipped the alcohol.

Charlie did likewise.

The institute's tech specialist was a head taller than him, but so were most people. At forty, she could easily have passed for early-thirties, which he put down to good living. Or maybe it was just Toby's age showing. In his mid-fifties, he found policemen and doctors and, yes, engineering savants really did look far younger than in the past.

"She should never have been there," Charlie finally said.

"I know." Toby downed his drink and poured another. "But this third party intrigues me."

The institute had never heard of another person being involved. Despite Valerio taking down the traffic cams—usually a great source of intel and a simple hack for someone like Charlie—they'd managed to snag a few partial images of the stranger's face from CCTV at the club where he released Bridget. Low-res, but it had taken Charlie a shade under thirty minutes to conjure a name while Toby was trying not to blub on the operations room floor.

She produced a phone in one hand, swirling her drink in the other. "Ready to be educated?"

Toby sat heavily on a leather couch.

The furniture reminded him of the cigar-laden gentlemen's clubs from the 1970s back in his native Britain, where Members of Parliament and heads of industry would plan the future of the country, and often the futures of other countries too. The modern world intruded on the throwback interior through a sixty-inch TV screen opposite the couch, in which Toby's reflection appeared distorted and gnomelike.

"Ready," he said.

Charlie remained standing and hit several keys, which activated the screen. Dan and Bridget appeared, congregated in a single, low-rent room. Dan was still in his ops gear with two guns close at hand, while Bridget had showered and changed into sweats and an over-size woolen pullover, her hair damp. Like Toby and Charlie, she was imbibing a large tipple, medicinal bourbon if Toby wasn't mistaken.

Toby's third drink turned his head into a thick stew. He set it down for now.

"Our gate-crasher is Julian Sibeko," Charlie announced.

"What is he?" Dan asked. "CIA? Military?"

Charlie shook her head, reading from her phone directly to the

TV's webcam. "Looks freelance. And mostly off-grid. Only pops up here and there."

"He must have a service record somewhere. No one's that good without real training."

"I concur," Toby said. "The ease with which he took out Dan… that wasn't a fluke."

Dan's lips thinned, clearly still embarrassed.

"It's true, Dan," Toby added, noting the reaction. "Anyone who can best our man-at-arms like that needs acknowledging."

"Mr. Sibeko isn't a complete ghost," Charlie continued. "Twenty-three years old, born and raised in Brooklyn, New York. He's a keen traveler. Hasn't been home much at all. The last time was two years ago when he sold his family's apartment. Netted him a half-decent cash flow, which he has almost exhausted."

"So he has family?" Toby asked.

"It'd be easier if you didn't interrupt." Charlie returned to her screen. "His parents were killed in a robbery. A pizza place on Staten Island. I can't access the full police files yet, just media reports. Julian's dad was ex-army, so I guess his alpha genes went a little wild." Charlie flicked her fingers over the screen again. "Julian Sibeko is listed as a material witness and describes a 'stone bracelet' as one of the items taken."

All paused to absorb it.

Bridget blew out her cheeks. "He was telling the truth."

"Indeed." Toby lifted his glass on instinct but held it still, not wanting to drink, but was loathe to appear indecisive. "And he's searched for the bangle ever since?"

"Looks like it." Charlie scanned more headlines on the reports for anything relevant. "His dad was a martial arts champ for the US Army, scoring gold against Israel in Krav Maga, so he was handy with his fists—"

"Sorry to interrupt," Dan said, "but an American beating the Israelis at Krav Maga is the equivalent of a Brit team beating the US at baseball."

"*But,*" Charlie continued, "his son won a few contests of his own. After his mum and dad died, there's no mention of it. He goes dark. Foster homes, but I'll work on the details." More fluttering fingers gave her a new line of interest. "Moneywise, he inherited his mum and dad's apartment after their deaths. They weren't rich, but his mother owned the property outright. The apartment went to a trust and supplied Julian with rent, which he's subsisted on until recently, when he sold it to a developer."

"But he's spent all the money?" Bridget said.

"On travel mostly." Charlie once more fiddled with her phone, intel feeding from the Demon Server on autopilot. "He's popped up all over: Syria, Iran, Pakistan, Israel. Strionia in Eastern Europe. Some South American destinations..."

Toby placed his glass down. "I'm surprised we haven't run into him before now."

"The big news, though, is there's mention of a 'Jules' on the dark web that syncs Mr. Sibeko's legit travel arrangements. A guy who..." Charlie smiled. A smile that became a laugh. All waited patiently for her to ingest what she was reading. "Oh wow. He repatriates stolen artifacts from black marketeers and grave robbers."

Bridget's grin matched Charlie's. "He's doing the same job as us?"

"Similar," Charlie corrected. "He charges a fee where he can."

"But he does it alone," Dan said.

"And low-profile." Charlie lowered her phone and nodded. "He's still wanted in Pakistan for the theft of a Persian bust of Alexander the Great, which turned up in a Teran museum four months later. The Iranians refuse to give it back, saying they obtained it legally since it was stolen from their lands in the first place during their revolution in 1979."

"So," Bridget said, "he sees his mom's antique bangle stolen and gets into freelance archeology? Toby, we should bring him in on this."

"He's more like a treasure hunter," Charlie said.

"Hmm." Toby reclined, unsmiling. He didn't share their

happiness at the coincidence. "A youngster in foster care who has trained himself to scale buildings and break into top-end security vaults? Not to mention honing his fighting skills to the point where he can take out a former US Army Ranger and evade a cadre of Valerio Conchin's mercenaries..." Toby crossed his legs, trying to ease the soreness from his body. Unfortunately, his discomfort wasn't caused by his sitting position. "If Charlie's intel is up to date, this chap is now skint. But he's got a sniff of his late mother's property." Toby pondered the risks. "That could make him dangerous. Or he could be useful."

Charlie gave a slight shake of her head. "A guy who's held an obsession so long? He must be unstable. Look at what he went through. Losing his mom, all that training, all that money thrown away just to recover a piece of jewelry."

"It's not just jewelry," Dan pointed out. "And I'm not talking sentiment. Jewelry doesn't glow."

"But he didn't know that any more than we did." Charlie emphasized each point with a chop of her hand. "Bridget said he looked surprised when the contaminants in the bangle lit up. This is *personal*. It's an *obsession*. That makes him a risk."

"We owe him the chance," Bridget said. "And he might be able to help with answers. The historical texts we've examined were vague about the Aradia bangle's properties—"

"We owe him nothing." Toby sat forward, the alcohol having thickened his head. "But indeed, he *could* be useful. Since he's been chasing this for so long."

"If the Aradia bangle belonged to his mother, that's *nine years*."

"It's a bad combination," Charlie said. "Hard to control."

Dan nodded. "He won't work well with the institute."

"And let's not forget the object *glows*." Toby leaned on his knees, his chin resting on fingers pointing upward. "Have you dispatched Harpal?"

"Of course. He's streaming imagery right now. Awaiting orders."

"Tell him to assess."

Charlie made a noise akin to an ape dismissing a pesky youngster, stood, and wandered out of the webcam's field.

"No action, though, not yet," Toby added, also standing. "Let me know when you need assistance."

"Stand by." Dan killed the feed.

Charlie folded her arms. "It's a mistake, Toby. Waifs and strays like this guy... it won't end well."

"Let's wait on Harpal," Toby said. "If we can utilize this Julian character without major risk, we will. If he won't cooperate on our terms, we cut him loose."

Almost immediately, new footage streamed onto the TV screen: Julian Sibeko sat alone in a cheap hostel bar.

CHAPTER
FIVE

HOSTEL PORBORSKI, NARODNI OBRANY DISTRICT - PRAGUE

Harpal Singh did not interrupt the audio streaming into his right ear through the bone conduction bud nestled within. Nor did he absorb everything his colleagues said. But he had full access and tuned in to the relevant points: Julian Sibeko had bested Dan Vincent without hurting him too much, and he had mad-impressive burglary and climbing skills. Harpal wanted to keep an open mind but would err toward the notion that Sibeko was dangerous.

Every situation demanded caution until all the parameters were known. Then Harpal could let loose and do his thing. Yet it was the buildup that often intrigued him the most. Asking who this person was, why he needed watching, how he should be approached. What one thing could Harpal use to turn the guy to his way of thinking? To use him?

As the institute's discussion continued, the target ate a chicken salad and drank carbonated water. A camera lens as wide as a pen was nestled in Harpal's fist as he pretended to read a novel, his body pointed away from the bar. An occasional glance at the phone in his lap kept Sibeko in frame.

The conversation between those in Prague and in the north of France eventually concluded.

"We either win big or lose big," Toby said. "Harpal, make contact."

Harpal answered too quietly for anyone close by to hear, but it was picked up by the throat mic attached to his collar. "Copy that. Stand by."

Although there were fewer than half a dozen people around at two a.m., he couldn't risk one of them being a plant from Conchin's crew. It seemed to be mostly folks arriving off planes, some returning from late-night fun, and a barman with two-day stubble and a three-day shirt. All young.

All but Harpal. And the middle-aged couple who departed for bed ten minutes ago. That said, early thirties isn't really old, but it probably seemed that way to these youngsters.

He closed his book but kept the nearly invisible earbud active along with his mic and remained seated. He'd had plenty of time to plan his approach to what appeared to be just another American backpacker. He didn't want to come across as if he were hitting on the target, who was a handsome fellow for sure, his hair closely cropped and his clothes plain, loose, and casual, yet still fashionable and... *cool*. Yeah, that was the word that Harpal stuck with. The kid looked *cool*. More than his clothes, it was the easy way he moved, a complete confidence and knowledge of what he wanted to achieve.

With a ten-second glance at the menu earlier—short as it was —he'd ordered. He kept his head down, not interacting with fellow backpackers unless he had to, and when he did, it was with a wide smile that belied his stern approach to matters when he wasn't required to interact with people.

One pair of tipsy girls—British by the sound of them—said hi, called him "Jules," and asked what he was doing up so late, to which he replied that he'd been to the opera followed by a couple of drinks. When the girls seemed impressed, he added in a heavy New York drawl that he "didn't really get it" and was planning on hitting the sack soon. The girls both touched his arm, smiling as they went, and giggled in the double doorway leading to the rooms. Jules let out a huge breath, plainly relieved at being alone again.

Approaching the bar, Harpal pocketed the camera and ordered a small Urquell beer and sat at a stool with one seat between him and Sibeko. He sipped and wished he wasn't such a lightweight when it came to alcohol.

While Dan could chug ten of these and still pilot a helicopter under the radar, Harpal would be challenged to climb into the passenger seat after three.

He let out a sigh but didn't draw Sibeko's attention the way he hoped. The guy poked at his salad as if searching for a lost diamond that he'd only just noticed was missing from his ring, but was trying not to panic. Not that he wore jewelry. Just the plain trendy T-shirt. No tattoos either, no distinguishing features at all.

Intentional?

Probably.

Harpal sipped again, the cold, crisp fizz coating his throat and landing pleasantly in his stomach. He hadn't realized how thirsty he was until the beer hit. "Damn, that's nice."

Sibeko ceased his foraging. "Talkin' to me?"

"Anyone who'll listen." Harpal moved only his head. A whole-body turn wasn't on the cards yet, and a stranger initiating conversation uninvited tended to raise suspicions. Harpal let the silence work for him.

Sibeko speared a chunk of chicken. "I'm happy for you."

"Happy?"

"Your beer." The target chewed, eyes on the liquor bottles beyond the barman, who was reading what looked like a Czech version of *Harry Potter and the Prisoner of Azkaban*, awaiting the next interruption. Sibeko swallowed. "I'm happy for you. That you're enjoying it."

Odd response. Was it sarcasm?

"Not like back home," Harpal said.

"They sell Urquell in the UK."

"Yeah, but it tastes different on holiday, right?"

"The travel screws with it." Sibeko scooped half a baby tomato along with a chunk of cucumber into his mouth. Chewed. Swallowed. "It's brewed in a town called Plzeň and exported. The more times it gets loaded on and off trucks at warehouses, the more the carbonation and sugar change the taste. Not a lot, but makes it different."

Harpal nodded, feigning interest. "You know your stuff. You in the business?"

Sibeko still hadn't looked Harpal's way. "I've tended a few bars." He searched around the salad bowl again. Gulped a couple of times at his water and set the glass down. Wiped at the condensation. "You with the redhead or the giant dog and his yellow master?"

A jolt swam through Harpal's chest.

It must have shown, as Sibeko said, "Don't sweat it. I figured there was something off, you chattin' to yourself over there. Your lips hardly moved, but I started wondering if maybe you're just a bit lonely, living in your own head and stuff. Wasn't sure until you came and sat by me. Not *right* next to me, 'cause that'd be weird. But one stool between us 'cause strangers don't snuggle up in a group of three when there's five other seats to pick from..." Sibeko faced Harpal. "I'm guessing you're with the redhead and her beefcake pal."

"Why?"

"The others don't strike me as subtle."

In Harpal's ear, Toby said, "Be honest. But don't give us away. Not fully."

Harpal smiled. He hadn't been made since his first undercover assignment when his commanding officer bailed him out by activating the sprinkler system in a Hilton. Scooting one stool over, he lowered his voice as two men holding hands passed behind them. "I work for an institute that recovers artifacts that have been... misplaced. We have an interest in the Aradia bangle."

"No kidding? You got an interest. Never woulda guessed."

"The purpose of tonight was for an expert to authenticate it. We intend to return it to the place it was taken from nearly a hundred years ago."

"It was taken from my mom *eight* years and *seven months* ago."

"That's part of the period when the artifact went dark."

"Dark?"

"It was looted from India during British rule, in and out of collections for decades, until it disappeared completely in the forties. Last known location was Berlin, in the vault of a Jewish shipping magnate who had close ties with the British royal family. Most guess it didn't look valuable, so got destroyed or lost in the Second World War, but we heard whispers of it six months ago. Valerio Conchin was making inquiries, meaning he had a clue to its location. And if he wants it, then—"

"Sounds like you know a bit about this guy. Valerio Conchin?"

"We can talk about him later."

"How about we talk now? Or I can leave."

"Go ahead," Toby said.

Harpal sighed and acquiesced. "We don't know as much as we'd like. Secretive billionaire. Family made money in the arms trade. Offices all over the world—construction, emerging tech, and a new hobby in archeology. He looks ill, but we can't find his medical records, so no way of knowing if his liver is failing or if it's another condition. But he snatches up these rare artifacts... pre-Persian, usually, often pre–written language. He's trodden on our toes before, but we've mostly stayed off his radar."

"Careful," came Charlie's voice. "Don't give him everything."

"If Valerio Conchin wanted the Aradia bangle," Harpal summarized, "then there was a good chance it was real. And a *very* good chance he'd need an illegal transaction to get his hands on it. Meaning a bribe. Or violence."

Sibeko hadn't moved since Harpal shifted stools. He just

stared at Harpal.

"Now, if you have a claim to it, we'll look into that. An independent tribunal can determine ownership, but—"

"Dude, seriously," Sibeko said. "What do you *want*?"

Toby said, "To bring you in on the search."

"To bring you in on the search," Harpal repeated.

"You just said an independent tribunal would decide who owns it."

"That's the fairest way."

Sibeko hopped off his stool, left ten euros on the bar, and stepped away. "I don't know who this Valerio asshole is, and I don't care about your institute. The bracelet's mine. I'm takin' it."

Sibeko walked toward the door.

"What's happening?" Charlie asked.

"He's leaving," Bridget said. "Isn't he?"

Harpal nodded to no one in particular. "Yeah. Sorry."

"Try money," Toby said. "And I don't mean appeal to his greed. He *needs* money. He has nothing left."

Harpal sprang up. "How's your cash flow?"

Sibeko halted just beyond the wide doorway to the reception lounge. He spun around, his face tight, like a drunk in a pub ready to strike an opponent. "Leave me alone."

"We have money." Harpal raised his hands defensively. "Not a lot, but... enough."

"Voices in your head tell you to say that? Who are they?"

Honesty seemed important to Sibeko, so Harpal pointed at his ear. "Subvocal mic and earbud combined in one unit. Four voices." He pulled his phone from his pocket and showed him the faces of Toby and Charlie on one half of the screen, Bridget and Dan on the other. Bridget waved. Harpal said, "We're the Lost Origins Recovery Institute."

"LORI. It's an acronym." Sibeko returned to the bar to face Harpal. "Yeah, I heard the name. I was tracking the expert, not the thieves."

"We're not thieves."

"Bounty hunters."

"We get rewards sometimes. But not every time."

"And you got money for me? Meaning you know I'm light on funds right now, meaning you investigated me. Pretty quick too. So now I know you got resources I don't. Hackers, logistics, spy craft like yours... but small. You're not government, so you got private backers or you wouldn't be offering cash for a piece of rock with more sentimental value than black market kudos."

Harpal nodded along, letting Sibeko talk. Was that how fast his brain was working? Who *was* this guy?

"Yet you got some yellow goon wants a look-see too, a guy who's wealthy and connected as hell. Tell me, right now, what's so special about my mom's bracelet?"

Harpal glanced at the phone as he would if Toby Smith were in the room. Toby gave his instructions, and Harpal relayed them: "Come work with us. Help us recover the Aradia bangle. If you convince us you should own it, it's yours. We just want a chance to examine it first. And if Valerio wants it, all the better if *we* take it."

Sibeko was looking sideways at Harpal, apparently suspicious and yet processing everything they'd said. His deductions spilled fast before, but now he appeared more considered.

"Maybe," Sibeko said.

Harpal listened and said, "We need more than 'maybe.'"

"I don't do anything without my own due diligence. Need to see how you operate, what chance I got of success. Then, maybe, I'll throw in with you. Until I'm convinced, that's all you're getting. *Maybe.*"

With Sibeko still out of earshot, Charlie said, "He's aggressive, intelligent, and hell-bent on possessing that object."

"True," Toby answered. "But he knows more about its recent history than any of us. And it *appears* to be his touch that made it glow. He may not only be useful. He could prove to be *essential.*" No one else spoke. "Harpal, accept his offer. Bring him to France so we can give him the grand tour. Tonight, please."

CHAPTER
SIX

BRITTANY, FRANCE

Bridget, Dan, and Harpal flew home on the institute's jet, a twenty-year-old Lear that wasn't exactly the discarded toy of some billionaire playboy. Functional and well serviced, it bestowed a semblance of respectability when palms needed greasing, yet the closest the Lear got to true luxury was the reclining seats; although fixed in place and not the swiveling cream numbers Bridget lusted after, they folded flat to function as beds. The institute had no money for a flight crew, making Dan and Harpal the only people who could pilot it, which seemed unfair to Bridget. She'd been lobbying them to give her lessons with no success to date.

Sure, it was frequently her bookwork and occasionally her on-the-spot deductions that sent the team on their way or solved a problem, but actual transactions and trades were always handled by others. She was allowed on site only when they were certain no danger would present itself. She was the group's princess, enveloped in bubble wrap for the good of the mission.

Every damn mission.

After four years of growing into her academic role, she needed something more. Hence the outing in Prague. She'd cited her need to handle the object after Dan and Harpal liberated it from a salesman, "donating" gold coins dating from the early Roman Empire in exchange. Once Bridget confirmed the stone bangle appeared authentic, they were taking it to the man they knew only as *the Curator*. He was supposed to date the find and confirm or refute Bridget's and Toby's initial discoveries relating to its provenance.

Now Valerio Conchin had taken possession of it.

Julian Sibeko, meanwhile, insisted on flying commercial, which Bridget understood, but she could not pretend it didn't disappoint her. Dan ribbed her about being "dumped," but she shot back that the "new boy" hadn't yet expressed a gender preference, meaning Dan still had a chance—a jibe she would not have dared express when she first met him. As a faintly homophobic ex-army type, he might have taken offense. Now it was second nature to her.

They touched down at an airfield outside La Rochelle at ten a.m., where Charlie played chauffeur in a minivan and drove them north through the French countryside to Chateau Caché, a property that Bridget's parents leased to them for a dollar a year.

Julian was due to land at the main airport in Nantes at midday and had refused the offer of a ride, although Harpal would tail him covertly once they confirmed the flight. He was on Valerio Conchin's radar, after all.

Charlie entered the grounds and sped along a two-hundred-meter driveway toward the house, its shape resembling a castle from the Middle Ages, albeit smaller and with a modern roof. It even had turrets, but you wouldn't know it from the inside, which incorporated a more up-to-date layout.

They all disembarked, gathered their overnight bags from the trunk, and passed through a colonnaded front door into an anteroom that was paneled in mahogany.

"Toby!" Charlie called.

"Study," came Toby's reply, echoing through the wide passageways.

Charlie led the way to the room ten meters down the corridor, followed by Dan, then Harpal. Bridget hefted her too-large bag to her shoulder and trailed behind.

Despite a massive *three* hours of sleep on the jet, and the fifteen minutes she managed during the airport connection, she was ready to flop onto her bed in fresh flannel pajamas and read a book until she dozed off, awaiting Mr. Sibeko's arrival. A hot chocolate would seal the deal. But first, she would endure Toby's debriefing, even though he already knew all he could.

As Bridget dragged herself into what people thought of as "Toby's" study, she halted at the sight of her teammates frozen in place, a look of surprise across each face. "What is it? What's wrong?"

Toby was sitting in his usual dark green leather armchair, an espresso cup in one hand, the saucer in his other. "We have a guest."

Bridget waddled all the way in, hair strewn over her face. She dumped her bag and whipped her hair out of her eyes.

Occupying the couch beside a crackling log fire, Julian Sibeko sipped a glass of iced water.

He nodded, his face stone. "Hey."

Toby explained how he found Jules in the control room on the second floor, but the new guy had refused to reveal how he (a) discovered LORI's location, (b) arrived ahead of the Lear, or (c) broke in undetected. All he said was, "Because I'm smart."

They agreed Bridget should give their guest the grand tour in an attempt to earn his trust, so she donned a thick coat and strolled the perimeter of Chateau Caché with the American, thankful for the unseasonal chill. It kept her awake. He never spoke except when responding to Bridget, and even then, only if it absolutely necessitated a reply.

"Calling it a 'chateau' makes it sound grander than it really is," she said, forcing the small talk, "but it's perfect for the five of us. A bit of privacy in a nosey world." When her comments generated not even a flicker of a smile in response, she went on. "Large enough for a fine party, my momma tells me, but small enough to be homey."

Jules nodded without looking directly at her.

"We're spread over four floors, although we only really use three. Grounds are fifteen acres. Including a two-bedroom cottage for our housekeeper, Margarete."

Jules gave that soulless nod again, but at least he spoke this time, his accent tinted with Brooklyn but not the full-on cabdriver drawl from the movies. "You keep your housekeeper isolated?"

"Actually, she *insists* on living away from the house itself. She's also our librarian, but she isn't exactly... comfortable in the main building. Partly because she's *always* lived in her cottage, but also... well, she's a lifelong catholic and lots of the books and plenty of the artifacts LORI deals with here... they're sometimes heretical."

Jules's nod was turning into a robotic head bob, his eyes roving over the landscape and architecture. "You're supposed to be filling me in about LORI. Not the house."

Bridget swallowed back a firm retort, writing his short manner off as jet lag, but exaggerated her southern roots almost to stereotype. "Okay, *yessiree*, allow me to introduce us formally. We are the Lost Origins Recovery Institute."

She led him through a yard that used to house small farmyard animals, toned back her accent.

"Essentially, we locate items that belong elsewhere and return them to their rightful place. Whether that's negotiating the sale of a Persian bust from some too-big-for-his-boots businessman or a collection of gold coins looted from a village—"

"Or digging up new relics no one thought of before," Jules added for her. "Treasure hunters."

"You've done your homework. All since you dropped me off last night?"

"I'm resourceful."

"We prefer the term 'freelance archeologists.'"

The path curved away, over a natural rise into a copse of trees, which hid the building as they walked.

"But, yes," Bridget said. "We also initiate our own explorations. We're looking for items of real significance, something to... blow the archeological community away. And I know, I know, it makes us gosh-awful egomaniacs, but all of what's known about human history currently is just scratching the surface."

"Right. So 'freelance archeologist' translates as 'conspiracy theorist.' You make those snazzy videos I seen all over YouTube with the doomsday music, banging on about lizard people and planet Nibiru?"

Bridget sighed, but contained her frustration. It was a common response to her explanation of LORI's work. "Conspiracy theorists base their assumptions on gut feelings. They figure something *must* be inaccurate because they don't trust officials. They go looking for evidence that fits their feelings and ignore everything else. We approach it from the point of view that the official record is correct, but when we find something that doesn't gel with it, we don't shoehorn the accepted version into our findings. There are gaps in history. Which is an undeniable fact. And where there are gaps, the establishment—"

"Fills the gaps with theories," Jules interrupted. "And they don't like people tearing down those theories. You don't profit from 'blowing the archeological community away,' even a bit?"

"We have to make *some* money. It keeps us going here. But what we find... it's never to hoard for ourselves. Even in the days of antiquity, there was a trade in antiques. You can imagine how old *those* things must be."

She smiled. Waited. Jules managed to chuckle at her lame joke, but it was so forced she wasn't sure whether it was sarcasm or bad acting.

She said, "We prefer to exchange them for items that mean more to that country. We use diplomacy where we can, or sometimes, if it's *very clearly* a dishonest person who's taken it recently, yeah, we resort to covert means."

"Right. So you steal it back."

Bridget left the comment hanging, allowing the cool breeze to swirl. "We're not a government agency. Charlie's got automated programs running constantly to wipe any mention or photos of us from social media or public forums, so we keep our heads down. Obviously we can't hide completely—"

"No," Jules said as they emerged from the trees to a wide view of the house. "You're Bridget Carson. Daughter to oil-rich billionaires who don't approve of you swanning 'round the world, digging up old bricks. Guessing there's some conditions attached to this property, but they ain't public record."

She frowned. "How did you—"

"Graduated from Oxford University with a double first when you were just twenty. Must've started early. Seventeen?"

"How did you get that?"

"I found your hotel in Prague and then your ID. That got me access to personal info. I ain't a hacker on the level you people play by, but I do what I gotta. Basic background, family, bit of hanging 'round the dark web. Didn't take much to locate your secret lair, either."

"It's not a 'lair.' It's our home..." Bridget tried to continue, but Jules was speaking again.

"So you guys don't just do this for fun?"

"We'll sure accept a reward if it's offered. Mainly because we don't have much choice. How about you? What's your financial interest?"

"If I can't profit from a find, I don't find it. Like you, I got no choice. But the ops where I go returning items to their owners? They're the times I failed to grab my bracelet."

"It's a bangle."

"Whatever."

They crossed a stone bridge arching over a stream that flowed through the chateau's land. Ducks splashed in the shallows, and a light mist rose from the surrounding fields.

Bridget glanced at him. "Everything you do is to track down that one thing?"

"Yeah. Mostly. So?"

"So... what will you do when you find it?"

"Eat pizza. What's your interest?"

"Not everything is as it seems when you get right down to it."

"Not everything is as it seems," Jules repeated with a roll of his eyes. "Like this place?"

They passed the section housing the Demon Server's main body.

Bridget paused to gaze out over the fields, the long grass unkempt due to budget issues. "That's why we go to the source for our intel. If we find something that veers from the historical record, we probe it until we're certain of the facts."

Again, Jules sounded divided between bored and sarcastic. "All this helps you return artifacts to where they belong?"

"That, and a few other things."

"Like my mom's bracelet," Jules said. "You think that ain't as it appears? That weird glow thing it did?"

"It's a bangle. And you don't know the half of it."

She led him back inside, past the study, which was now empty, and into a wide, tall room where dozens of bookshelves formed a claustrophobic library. "Most are first editions, from prebiblical to Louis the Fourteenth to Darwin's *On the Origin of the Species*. A lot have to be reprints or copies because the originals are owned by museums and in private collections."

Jules followed, hands in his pockets, a teenager dragged against his will to his parents' choice of venue. "Why so many?"

"Because, as you say, history is written by the victors. Many of these works are *firsthand* accounts. By people who were physically *present* at the time of events. I've had to learn so many languages, which is kind of a gift I suppose... I do that sorta thing quickly, and—"

"And you decode ancient symbols and pictographic language," Jules interrupted. "I also found the *Guardian* newspaper article from when you spoke at the British Museum. Your theory of links between Egyptian hieroglyphs and Native American cave paintings. The journalist called you 'the Human Rosetta.' True?"

"They exaggerated," she said. "A little, anyway. How'd you find that so quickly?"

"I'm smart." Jules edged out a thick black spine from the nearest shelf, the whole tome backed in matte leather, with Latin words formed of decorative gold. He said, "The Fabian Necronomicon."

"You're familiar with the work?"

He slotted it back in place. "I stole an original from a penthouse apartment in Caracas two years ago."

They moved on, up a tight spiral staircase to a mezzanine, also crammed with books, which opened to another flight of stairs to the second floor. Or the *first* floor as the Europeans called it, something Bridget had never gotten used to. She wondered if Jules ever got confused when speaking to Brits as she did. "Popping up to the first floor" seemed wrong unless you were in a basement.

"Final stop on the tour." She led him into a room that reminded her of the bridge of a starship: the control center. "This is Charlie's domain. Everything in here is connected directly to the independent banks of computers downstairs. She calls her setup the 'Demon Server.' Ninety percent of it is linked to the internet, but we keep a few air-gapped partitions. Meaning those drives have never been connected online. Can't be hacked except on site—"

"I know what 'air-gapped' means." Jules gazed around the place, seemingly impressed for the first time. "This must be expensive."

"Charlie mostly built it herself, so it's trade prices."

A bank of five terminals lined one wall, each with a twenty-inch 4K screen, one of which displayed a rolling landscape that looked like it had been processed to resemble an X-ray.

"You got a LiDAR here?" Jules said, watching the feed.

"No, 'LiDAR' is a brand we can't afford. *This* ground-penetrating radar is another of Charlie's own." Bridget stood beside him, shoulder to shoulder. "Cheaper and more efficient. You hook 'the puck' up to a drone and sweep over the land looking for anomalies. This is film taken three months ago in Derbyshire in the UK. We thought there was more to some burial mounds than the pros had worked out." She pointed at the screen as a fuzzy perpendicular shape flashed by near a stone marker. "And there *was* more. Interesting to the local society, but nothing earth shattering. A grave for a Pict king's mistress."

Jules silently scanned the rest of the room.

Bridget had insisted on seats and desks for everyone, although they were rarely all present at one time. Toby loved the curved hundred-inch glass pane in the center that acted as a holographic display, generating 3-D images without the need for those glasses from the movie theater. It was operated from the touch screen table in front of it, what Charlie called her "Demon Hub."

Charlie had a thing for demons.

"So, that's pretty much all of it," Bridget said. "What do you think?"

Jules took a long, considered moment, pacing the room. He stopped at the touch screen. "I think you guys *could* be useful. Just one thing."

"What's that?"

"You gotta tell me everything you know about my mom's *bangle*. Then I'll tell you everything *I* know. Deal?"

"Deal."

CHAPTER
SEVEN

Bridget hit an intercom, and when the little dude called Toby answered, she told him, much Jules's relief, that their guest was ready to talk.

Although she'd relayed a lot of useless information, it was polite—according to Jules's mom—to feign interest and come up with comments that convinced the boring person of your fascination.

Just tell me about my mom's bracelet.

Sorry, I mean bangle.

Jules knew plenty of trivia, though, which filled the gaps in conversation until normal folk were comfortable getting to the point—like his chat with Harpal about beer. He absorbed so much, from cultural idiosyncrasies to complex facts and figures, that experts in his childhood termed his memory "eidetic." What common language called a "photographic memory." The condition forced him to retain all instruction, all teaching, both physical and academic, and never lose it unless he chose to focus on rejecting it.

Now, as the team of strange people filed into their operations room, he tried to get a read on them all.

Bridget—researcher, professional archeologist, language expert.

Would have made a good code breaker. American, Alabama.

Toby—appeared to be in charge; classical education, with obvious experience in the echelons of diplomacy. If he turned out to be a former government minister or military officer, Jules would not be surprised. English, upper crust.

Charlie—presumably short for something (Charlotte?), engineering expert and multilingual coder and hacker. Moved well, athletic, ex–Royal Signals according to his research. Kept a knife sheathed on her thigh, which looked military but was stubby, shorter than the average Ka-Bar—out of place with the smart jeans and flowery T-shirt. Welsh, well educated.

Dan—another ex-military, this one from the US Army Rangers, an expert in close protection—a bodyguard—who took the lead on field ops. Silver Star Medal for an undisclosed incident. Unmarried, he was the epitome of an ex–military type: a thick but well-trimmed beard dressed his jaw, and his fashion sense may as well have included a hat with "I'm a veteran" printed on a flag sticking out of the top. American, West Coast.

Harpal—the hardest to pin down, but he blended in well. A recon expert, possibly a former spy, certainly trained in undercover ops. Designer labels, even when in the field, a haircut that probably set him back more than his shoes did. British, second or third generation, from Indian lineage.

Charlie and Bridget remained standing beside the big touch screen—the so-called "Demon Hub"—in the middle of the room. Toby perched on a tall chair next to them while Dan and Harpal took seats by the bank of monitors.

Toby leaned forward, adopting the manner of a teacher. "So, how much do you know about the Aradia bangle?"

Jules shrugged. "I know it belonged to my mom. She got it from Africa—Kenya, I think. I know it was lost, but found its way back to where it belonged. My mom said it was more valuable than the rock it was made of. More valuable than gold. And it'd be mine to look after one day. Your turn."

"Did she say that? 'Yours to look after?' Those words?"

"I don't know. I was a kid. Everything's kinda hazy from back then."

Totally clear since she died, though. Every memory, every incident, etched there forever.

Bridget asked, "Could she have said 'yours to guard'?"

Jules shook his head, paced, unclenched a fist he hadn't realized he'd closed. "I said I don't know. I was a kid. It could've been... I'll be *responsible* for it one day, or I gotta *look after* it. It was an ugly rock thing that she never took off, and I was thinking about the basketball tryouts and whether playing ball'd help me hook up with Sondra McKay. Then, a couple months later, someone robbed a pizza shop. My mom didn't give up the bangle, so they killed her *and* my dad. They twisted it off her wrist. Sold it for ten bucks to a pawnshop. So I'll say it again: *your turn.*"

The three at the desk exchanged solemn glances.

Dan said, "Okay, here he comes. It's Basil Exposition time."

Jules looked at him. "Who? I thought his name was Toby."

"It is," Harpal said. "It's a joke. Like in the movies. When something needs explaining—"

"I don't watch movies."

Bridget did the same as a lot of folks whenever he revealed this tidbit about himself: she opened her mouth a crack as if rendered speechless from shock. And what was going on with Dan and Harpal? Dan had been a stone-cold soldier back in Prague; now he joked like a regular guy bantering with his buddies at a barbecue.

"Basically," Dan explained, "Toby loves giving history lessons. Bridget gets a real kick out of it too. Charlie... she's happy sounding smarter than everyone."

Charlie winked. "Good reason for that, boyo."

"It's called the Aradia bangle," Bridget said, finally someone getting to the point. "And it's one of a pair."

．　．　．

A pair. Jules had never considered there might be others. But then he never considered anything not directly connected with acquiring the item. That sole, single item. He held no interest in any of that background stuff. It was all a distraction. He held no interest in this session either, frankly, but they seemed committed to it. He'd play willing and endure what was plainly their preferred method.

It was *polite.*

"First," Toby said, "let me tell you about the Cult of Aradia."

As if by a telepathic prompt, Bridget fluttered her hands over the touch screen on the tabletop. Artwork popped up on the free-standing glass pane: a group of six men hung upside down from a tree, flayed by whips wielded by two women in black robes.

Toby continued, "Conventional texts will refer to 'Aradia' concerning a group of nineteenth-century folklore witch stories, but we don't think the bangle is anything to do with witchcraft. A mere coincidence. This painting was rendered during the time the cult was active."

Bridget zoomed in on the canvas. The image pixilated slightly, but the women appeared to be wearing grayish-green bangles of the same proportions as the one stolen from Jules's mom—three inches wide with green flecks rather than jewels.

"Cult of Aradia," Jules said. "Tuscany witches?"

Bridget's voice rose an octave. "You've heard of it?"

"Vaguely. I hear a lotta stuff. There's a book outlining the Aradia rituals. Fortune telling, sacrifices, blah blah blah. If trivia helps me find something, fine. If it's legends and stories, it ain't relevant."

Toby slipped on a pair of oval spectacles and selected a thin notebook from a drawer beneath the touch screen. "Legends and stories can often point the way to genuine facts. Peel away one legend, seek out its origin, investigate that origin. Repeat."

"Yeah, but it's usually just another legend."

"So you peel that one away too. Eventually, you arrive at the truth. Elementary investigation."

Jules focused on the notebook. "Fair point. But when there's only one source, like these Aradia women, what then?"

Toby turned to the first page and thumbed half a dozen more. Stopped. "Because it's rare that we only accept one source. Here, the cult of Aradia first came to prominence thanks to the folklorist—"

"Charles Godfrey Leland," Jules finished for him. "I told you, I know about it already."

"Oh. It... sounded like a passing familiarity. The 'blah blah blah' you mentioned."

"There ain't no passing familiarity with me. Either I know it or I don't. And I know these girls popped up in this *Gospel of Witches* book published by the Leland guy. Some text he got ahold of called *il Vangelo.*"

"Indeed. Literally 'the Gospel.'"

"But it's nonsense," Jules said.

Toby gave him that smile again, a teacher impressed by a tricky student. "Why?"

"Because of the gap. Eleven years between gettin' hold a' *Vangelo* and publishing his own book."

"Good. So you understand how we do things."

"No, it's how *I* do things. Discard the useless and focus on what gets me where I wanna be."

Bridget tilted her head, her lips pouted in a vaguely smug manner. "You failed to connect this to your mom's bangle because you didn't dig further."

"And what would I have found if I dug more?"

A chuckle from Toby—the inspirational professor now a patronizing schoolteacher. "You would have found the Cult of Aradia is more accurately known as the Cult of *Herodias.* They sound similar, don't they? And who is Herodias?"

Jules sighed but cut himself off midway through—because, well... *politeness*—then mined his acquired knowledge from various hunts. There was a lot of it.

He said, "Wife of one of King Herod's sons. Bible stuff."

Dan groaned. "Damn, I hate when it gets biblical. There's always a smart-ass conclusion."

"Yeah," Harpal agreed. "Then we end up flying off somewhere to prove Toby and Bridget were right. You'll get used to it, Jules."

Jules focused on Bridget. "I ain't sticking around long enough to 'get used to' anything. And I don't mess around debunking two-thousand-year-old myths when they got no bearing on finding what I'm looking for. All I care about is *actionable intel*." Jules folded his arms and met the gaze of everyone in the room, one at a time, halting on Toby. "So. This Herodias. She gonna help find my mom's bracelet?"

Toby breathed through his nose and adjusted his spectacles, then leafed through his notebook. "Bridget, will you be so kind as to bring up our favorite *Feast of Herod* painting by Peter Paul Rubens?"

"It's a bangle," Bridget muttered as she returned to the touch screen.

The flaying image was replaced by a tightly framed scene of ancient times rich folks at a banquet or—yeah, a feast—with a serving girl in a long red dress presenting some nobleman with a silver platter. On the platter lay a severed head. It wasn't excessively gory. The king, or whoever he was, seemed positively relaxed about it.

"Herod Antipas," Bridget said. "Son of Herod the Great, he was the man who counseled Pontius Pilate on the fate of Jesus of Nazareth. He is also Herodias's second husband after Herod the Second. Also a son of Herod the Great."

"Keepin' it in the family," Jules said.

"The head on the plate belongs, or *belonged*, to John the Baptist. Not to be confused with the *Apostle* John who features in the *Gospel* of John. There's more than one John." A narrow-eyed glance at Dan suggested the clarification was for his benefit. "John the *Baptist* called Herodias marrying her brother-in-law 'incest.' And before you get on your high horse, *this* is where your actionable intel comes in."

Jules extended his hand, indicating she should continue.

"Herodias persuaded her husband to order the execution of John the Baptist. She held something of a grudge and couldn't rest until she put it right. John's head was removed during this feast and presented to her and Antipas."

"Very *Game of Thrones*," Dan said.

Jules had only the vaguest clue what Dan meant. A popular TV show? Might have been a book, too.

"Indeed," Toby said. "And it gets rather more interesting than that. What if I told you that Middle Ages folklore found Herodias transformed into a spirit, condemned to walk the sky forever as punishment for her part in John's death?"

Jules crossed his arms. "I'd say you're getting into irrelevant detail again."

Bridget leaned her hip on the table, her arms folded in a mirror of Jules. "Where do most myths come from concerning loose women?"

Jules let his arms drop and rolled his eyes as his patience once again wore thin. "Let's assume it's the church slandering her."

"She chose to leave a powerful husband for his more successful brother. She used her feminine wiles to murder a Roman Catholic icon. After that, the vacuous bitch whispered in her husband's ear to accelerate their standing within the kingdom. But when Antipas tried to lay a claim to a royal title, Herodias's actions meant both she and her husband were exiled. All the blame was laid at her door. So yeah, she was slandered. A bit."

"Okay, fine. What's the actual intel?"

Bridget hit more icons, and several windows opened containing texts written in an ancient script. "Flavius Josephus was a chronicler at the time. His writings've largely remained in the hands of the Roman Catholic Church and museums, although independent historians have been permitted a peek on occasion."

Toby turned to another page in his book. "Josephus worked at the same time as the events we are discussing here, so we can assume they're contextual. But we can also assume that much of his writing did not survive or was mistranslated, either by design or error."

Jules wound his hand around in the air in a "get on with it" gesture, his *politeness* quotient having all-but exhausted itself. "You found part of it? Some vanished writings?"

Toby's tongue played at his lips, not getting that this delaying tactic of building tension had no effect on Jules. When Jules gave no reaction, Toby went on, "Of those present during the feast, which eyewitness would know the real reason for John's execution? Herodias, surely. Herod Antipas, maybe."

"The executioner," Jules said flatly.

"The executioner." Toby turned to his dense, neat handwriting on the page. "Josephus claims the following: 'And John did confide in his murderer that the order passed from a woman of fake words and vindictive motives. That she accused the Baptist of theft, a crime of which he was innocent. But he had knowledge of the theft, and approved, and so did die with this knowledge.'"

"Meaning John knew who stole something from Herodias," Harpal said brightly, as if the knowledge surprised him.

Toby nodded. "It might not have been her narcissism that invited John's death, but a threat of what would happen if he did not talk. Shortly after the execution was carried out, Herodias grew impatient with her husband's lack of title and lands, and—as Bridget mentioned—pushed him to acquire more power—"

"Okay, I'm outa here." Jules turned from the sermon and set off toward the door.

"Where *are* you going?" Toby asked, standing.

Dan was laughing. "You finally found someone who doesn't go for your lesson plan."

"It is *not* a lesson plan. This is important information gleaned through extensive research."

Jules paused but did not turn. "Clearly we're headin' to the part where Herodias owned my mom's bangle but lost it, then she killed John the Baptist in the hope of gettin' it back. Herodias then resorted to violence in some quest to find it, and it got passed down the centuries until this witch cult got ahold of it and made copies for their followers to wear. How'm I doin'?"

He glanced over his shoulder to see Toby shuffling his feet, his cheeks a light shade of red.

Jules knew he was right. "So that's its origin. Herodias dies, her legend grows, and a bunch a' Middle Ages progressives decide to fight back and turn her into the goddess Aradia. It inspires other women to stand up to the menfolk, and because they're so insecure in their *dude*ness, they denounce the women as witches, like the church did. *Then*, I dunno, let's take a guess—the Aradia bangle symbolizes rebellion or purity or leadership or something that don't matter *one... damn... bit*."

Jules closed his eyes, breathed deeply, and listened to the noises around him.

Fans whirring.

Others' breaths.

His own heartbeat in his temples.

Someone stood from their chair—Dan, judging by the weight shift.

One of the women coughed.

Jules opened his eyes and faced them. "Last chance. Tell me how this helps. Or I walk."

Bridget stepped to Toby's shoulder. He nodded for her to proceed, plainly disappointed at not getting to conclude the story himself.

She said, "Remember we said it was one of a pair? We think the other still exists. And Valerio wants them both."

Jules started to get it.

Dan stuffed his hands in his pocket and smiled. "All this history lesson means is... we follow the trail, grab the other bangle, and Valerio comes to us."

CHAPTER
EIGHT

Jules sat in one of the seats next to Harpal and listened. If this Valerio Conchin weirdo wanted matching stone jewelry, fine. LORI could keep the twin, and Jules would walk off into the sunset with his mom's for a beer and a pizza.

Toby did most of the talking, and Jules listened.

"Because John the Baptist felt that Herodias leaving her husband for her brother-in-law was incestuous, he investigated the arrangement and discussed it with Jesus of Nazareth himself. Now, we know very little about Jesus as a man except from gospels written decades and even centuries after his death. Josephus notes many meetings between the pair, but little of the content. *However...* another chronicler—a Roman called Trelius—was also a bookkeeper and one of Jesus's more avid fans." He paused to take in Jules's nonexistent reaction. "Of course, the details here are unimportant."

Another pause to find his place in the notebook.

"Anyway, Trelius notes that he met with Jesus, and indeed Jesus's mother, on numerous occasions, intrigued by the Jew's teachings, although not yet a convert. And when Trelius learned of John's execution, he made inquiries, which ended with the apostle Philip."

Jules nodded. "Are you trying to make history cool? Why don't you just skip to the important bits?"

"History *is* cool," Bridget said. "When you actually look into it properly."

"According to the Bible," Toby continued, "Philip sought Jesus out himself. First came to him after hearing about his deeds, curious. Philip is the only apostle who did that. The others either happened across him or were introduced by another. Philip went on to assist Jesus in arranging his congregations, bringing people to him, organizing the Feast of the Five Thousand—"

Jules sat forward. "Sounds like you're *almost* at the point."

"Indeed. Trelius heard the description of the item stolen from Herodias—yes, the *bangle*—and he remembered seeing something similar years earlier. And Philip was the only man he knew who could be interested."

"Why?"

"To continue the work that Philip had made his life. Helping Jesus minister to his flock. Imagine an item of power in the hands of people opposing the Messiah. If Herodias worked out how to tap into that power, it would undermine humanity's savior."

"*Almost* interesting," Jules said. "Not quite *cool*, but interesting."

"Because Jesus's mother wore an identical piece."

Jules sat back and laughed. "Get outa here. The Virgin Mary stole the sky witch's bangle?"

"No. And there is no record of someone retrieving the other bangle. But it would not be unusual for a lot of items from the same region to end up in marketplaces after a campaign. If Agrippa had one bangle taken from a conquered tribe or people, maybe another soldier took a second?"

"Guesswork." Jules did not seem impressed.

"Sometimes that's all we have," Bridget said. "Others, we get accounts that are more specific.

Toby nodded his thanks at Bridget's intervention. "Evidence points at Philip as the instigator. Of the plan, at least, if not the actual theft itself. But he only went ahead with it because of what John the Baptist witnessed. Namely, Herodias consulting with great minds, linguists, poring over a manuscript that was brought back by her brother Agrippa from his exploits out in the Empire."

Bridget added a high-def photograph of the Aradia bangle to the big screen, a close-up in which it was arranged on a polished wooden table. "This is what Agrippa brought Herodias as a gift. A bangle with metallic seams and flecks of green. Not gold, not a title. Agrippa took it *and* the manuscript from a primitive tribe who held the bangle in high esteem. It was considered an 'ancient' object even then, so it probably dates back more than the two thousand years you mentioned."

As with Toby, when Bridget paused, it appeared to be so she could assess Jules's degree of interest.

She said, "But Herodias was furious at what she saw as a snub. The manuscript wasn't even written in a language she could understand. As wise man after wise man admitted defeat in translating it, though, she concluded there was more to this than she first thought."

"Right," Jules said. "So Philip hears about it, figures it might be important to his buddy Jesus, and organizes the theft. Where'd it go?"

"According to Trelius, and touched upon by a third chronicler named—"

"If it saves time, how about dropping the sources and just tell me what you found?"

"As you wish." Toby shut his notebook with a snap. "Essentially, Philip and John the Baptist located someone to translate the pages, then got the two bangles together—Herodias's and Mary's —and what they discovered caused them to hide their finds from everyone, including Jesus. After Jesus's death—his *second* death, if you believe that sort of thing—"

"Wait, wait, wait, back up a sec," Jules said. "What happened when the two bangles got together?"

"The translations are sketchy," Bridget said. "But one interpretation is..." She swallowed. "Magic."

"Another is 'curse,'" Toby added. "Yet another is 'power.' But the real curiosity is why would an apostle of Christ take a heretical object as proof of the apostle's own holiness? Proof he spoke on behalf of Christ?"

"They took them? Where?"

Toby welcomed the narrative baton. "Around the year 40 AD, the twelve apostles went their separate ways to preach the gospel to the world. And Christianity was born. They often took holy objects of power with them to prove their authenticity, and in two accounts, one apostle carried a handwritten translation of the manuscript, while apostles took the two bangles in other directions, hoping to return them to their rightful places in the world."

Jules thought it through. "Which apostles took them? Philip, I guess, is one."

"We think so. And he kept the original manuscript. But you know about the apostle called Thomas?"

"Doubting guy, yeah."

"Correct. '*Doubting* Thomas' is the modern term. Thomas is the disciple who refused to believe in Christ's resurrection until he saw it with his own eyes. Which, in the opinion of the only other apostle to mention this doubt—this is the *other* John, by the way—indicated Thomas was less than faithful. Or—"

"Or more practical. Like Philip. Makin' him a natural choice to trust with stuff that don't jibe with Christian teaching. Sure."

"Tradition has Thomas preaching most actively east of modern Syria, traveling as far as India, where the Marthoma and Kerala Christians, to this day, revere him as their founder. He was supposedly murdered by rival soldiers in an Indian town called Mylapore, with a spear, if memory serves. His bones allegedly lie in Santhome Church in Chennai, but as with many religious relics, no one is permitted to test them thoroughly. Other accounts suggest he survived his ordeal in Mylapore and traveled north to continue his mission."

"What other accounts? How solid is this intel?"

Toby chuckled. "Now you want to know sources?"

"Two bracelets were taken outa the Middle East at the same time as a book that's actually, what? An instruction manual?"

"Quite possibly, although I wouldn't have put it so simply."

"Nah," Harpal said, "you'd have spent half an hour talking about it."

"Shut up," Charlie said. "We're nearly done."

Toby patted the air to break up the silliness. "You are correct, though. Sources in this case are important. If the Aradia bangle surfaced out of Africa as recently as the 1990s, and your mother knew of its special properties, it probably means she was aware of its true nature."

"My mom wasn't no witch."

"Not a witch," Toby said. "A chronicler. Like Josephus. The bangles disappeared around 40 AD, and Thomas the Apostle was last heard from sometime after 52 AD, which is when it is documented that he landed in India. While it is possible the Mary bangle has been destroyed or lost in some random place, one thing is certain: if we can get them together, we may be party to something that... well, I don't wish to get too excited, but it could be rather special."

"Yeah? So how do we find it? Carthage?"

"Ah, you know your extended biblical history. Very good. Not many people do.

"Yeah, I guess I picked it up somewhere."

"Well, indeed. It is part of the trail. Carthage was Philip's ministry after Greece and Syria. One convert preserved much of Philip's writing after his death, including his personal journal. The apostles apparently each carried a transcription of the original manuscript with them, translated of course. But Thomas was the only one to send word to unite the bangles. Thomas carried one already, and Philip duly arranged transport of the other."

"Neither bangle is in Carthage," Jules said.

"Thomas found what they were looking for. And although we

don't know what it is, if Valerio Conchin wants it, he must believe it is a source of either power or wealth."

Jules felt his face slacken, and he could not temper his dismissive tone. "Seriously? Power?"

"Power, Jules," Bridget said. "When you touched the bangle, it glowed. Me and Dan—nothing. Whatever the explanation, be it an unknown branch of science or straight-up magic, we have to get there before Valerio."

Jules stood. "Man, you nearly had me for a while." He headed for the door.

Toby stood too. "Where are you going?"

This time, Jules didn't stop. "Biblical myths I can handle. Magic? Nah. You guys are either cuckoo, or you're playin' me. Whatever it is, I'm gone. For real this time."

CHAPTER
NINE

Jules's allocated room was more like a hotel suite, with deep carpet and cream walls, a decent TV, a large desk, and a king-size bed. He hadn't unpacked fully—just a change of clothes for after his planned shower—which he wouldn't need now. Predictably, though, when he closed his backpack and moved to exit, Toby was waiting alongside Bridget.

"Are you really telling us there's nothing strange about the bangle?" Bridget asked. "It *glowed* when you touched it."

"Ain't magic," Jules said. "I've seen people go gaga over sculptures and books and even rings because they thought some spirit or another lived inside. They're always wrong."

"Always?"

"I once did a job for this guy out of Gabon. A tribal leader. Been elected to the ruling party's parliament. He wanted their dancing head back from some breakaway region next door. This three-foot head and shoulders carved outa ebony. Pure black. When he got it back to the land he was born in, at the foot of this dormant volcano, guess what? It *did* dance. No one'd seen it do this before. Kinda levitated on its special altar sometimes. Wobbled others. So I stayed on. Had to figure this thing out, you know?"

Toby and Bridget stood transfixed, and Jules then understood why they talked so much. They were story junkies. They lapped this stuff up like cats did cream.

"Long story short, it turned out to be magnetized ball bearings, all negatively charged. Inside the statue. I got a portable X-ray machine out there. Geological survey revealed the volcano wasn't completely dormant, just stable. The magma beneath still flowed around a system of tunnels, and the ground was rich in iron."

Toby and Bridget shrugged as if accepting bad news. They clearly yearned for a magical explanation even though he'd telegraphed there wasn't one.

"One thing I didn't solve," Jules said, offering a crumb of mystery. "How they got the ball bearings in there. Who made it? No seam in the sculpture, so maybe they were already there. Maybe they saw a rock moving funny and carved a face in it. Million guesses, but we won't ever know the answer." He felt warmer in his gut at their smiles. "I've even seen plenty of stuff glow when the light catches it right."

Bridget offered a sympathetic glance. "You know it wasn't reflecting light."

Jules stared at the floor. "And you know more about these bangles. And you wanna hide it in all that ancient text stuff. Means I can't trust you."

Toby nodded. "We think the Aradia bangle and its counterpart are made of materials that are... not entirely uninteresting to science."

"What materials?"

Bridget shook her head. "I only handled it briefly, so it's hard to tell. Possibly quartzite. But there was metal in there. Those flecks. Could've been ionized copper. And it was magnetic, which is odd because the spectrograph picked up no steel that we could see."

"A seam running through it?"

"Maybe. But if it was an antique when Herodias received it,

they would have assumed it was supernatural."

"Or God's will," Toby said.

"Let me get the history straight since it's so important to you." Jules did not want to admit his fascination, having shown his defiance so firmly earlier, so he kept his tone even. "Agrippa brings the bangle back from Africa, gives it and some coded manuscript to his sister Herodias. She works out it has power they can't explain, and Saint Philip—"

"Just Philip," Bridget said. "Wasn't a saint at the time."

"Whatever. He steals it, and when the two bangles get together, they see something that scares 'em. After Jesus dies, the apostles make copies of the manuscript before heading out into the world. Only Thomas checks back in. He don't like what he finds, and sends Herodias's bangle back to Philip, splitting 'em up with a warnin' to stay away. Then what happened?"

Toby wobbled his flat palm back and forth. "No one can be sure. Between Philip forwarding the Aradia bangle to Thomas and Thomas returning it, Philip was killed. The other bangle, Mary's, is lost to wherever Thomas hid it."

"Or he destroyed it," Jules suggested.

"If it belonged to Jesus's mother, I do not believe for one moment he would do that."

"Plus," Bridget said, "why destroy one and not the other?"

Two bangles.

Together, apparently, they do more than just glow.

A manuscript was written to accompany them.

"It vibrates as well as glows." Jules dropped his bag and met Toby's eye. "There's more to it. But it ain't *magic.* 'Kay?"

"Okay." Toby approached, with Bridget a step behind. "We'll get it back. We'll find out what it's made of and why it does the things you say."

Jules scooped up his bag and tossed it on the bed. "To do that, we gotta find the one Thomas hid. Draw this Valerio guy out. How do we do that?"

Bridget grinned. "We?"

"Thomas's last known location is India. His manuscript still there?"

"Thomas wrote a great many things. But we're most concerned with a manuscript sacred to Christians of the Kerala region—"

"You're lecturing again," Jules said.

"Sorry. Yes, what I mean is... many of India's treasures were raided during British rule, including a repository of works from Christians in Kerala."

"British rule?"

"Queen Victoria accepted many curiosities into her personal collection and passed them down through her descendants." Toby's smile widened, a mischievous child anticipating excitement. "We need to pay a visit to my former employer."

"We gotta rob a museum?"

Bridget was not smiling. The opposite, in fact. "Toby used to be the head curator for the British royal family. Technically, he worked for Her Majesty Queen Elizabeth II. Before she fired him."

"Yes, yes, don't bore the lad with details," Toby said. "The manuscripts and books from Kerala are part of her personal collection in the catacombs of Windsor Castle. If Saint Thomas's documents are with the royals, that's where they'll be."

"Great. We're gonna rob the Queen of England." Jules pulled open his bag. "Mind if I shower first?"

PART TWO

We become just by performing just action, temperate by performing temperate actions, brave by performing brave action.

—Aristotle

Great thoughts speak only to the thoughtful mind, but great actions speak to all mankind.

—Theodore Roosevelt

CHAPTER
TEN

WINDSOR CASTLE - UNITED KINGDOM

Toby paced alone in the Round Tower's shadow which stretched across the castle's Middle Ward, while Jules's voice carried into his ear via the nearly invisible bud lodged there. "Hey, did you know Windsor Castle was built by a guy called William the Conqueror? Yeah, after the 1066 Norman Conquest. And did you know it covers 52,609 square meters? Which—*whoa*—is thirteen acres. Over one million visitors per year."

Toby watched people of dozens of nationalities milling around, reading pamphlets, taking photos. He didn't fully understand the bone-conduction technology that Charlie adapted for covert use, but understood it received and fed vibrations through the ear canal and transmitted them without the need for a microphone. It wasn't something he dwelled on, happy to adopt the tech rather than understand it.

He said, "I know what you're doing."

"Saint George's Hall is the biggest room," Jules went on. "It's 55.5 meters long and nine meters wide. Or 182 feet by thirty if you're from my part of the world. You can cram in 162 people for state banquets."

"What *is* he doing?" Charlie asked.

"He's reading from a flyer," Dan said.

Toby had split them into four parties: Jules with Dan, Bridget with Charlie, Harpal on his own, and Toby loitering here to meet Colin.

"Forty monarchs, including Her Majesty the Queen, have lived in the castle." Jules now enunciated badly, an American doing a terrible impression of an upper-class British person. "The oldest glazed window in the castle dates back to 1236 AD and is thought to be a wedding gift from King Henry III to Eleanor of Provence."

"He's making fun of yours truly," Toby said. "Thank you, Jules. I tend to talk a lot. I get it."

"Huh. Just trying to lay out some pointless detail for you while we wait. Thought you enjoyed that."

Toby paused until a Japanese family passed by. "My 'pointless detail' is rarely without point."

He'd also laid out the castle for them: the Lower Ward housing the glorious Saint George's Chapel, the Middle Ward with the old Round Tower as the central feature, and the Upper Ward where the residences lay. Also incorporated in the Upper Ward was the precinct where the Changing of the Guard took place, meaning there would be fewer tourists in every other area.

Then came the nasal plummy tones he was hoping for. "Why, Toby, look at you. You got old!"

Toby turned to find Colin Waterston smiling down at him. In a beige suit, the younger man was in his mid-forties, so not exactly a spring chicken himself. Although he was a head and a half taller than Toby, his hair was far thinner; he'd developed a widow's peak, and the stringy brushed-back sweep suggested a bald spot was likely brewing too.

One could but hope.

Toby might be short, his years inching closer to sixty than fifty, but his mane was that of a thoroughbred.

He extended a hand. "Colin, how wonderful to see you."

They shook hands firmly, smiles at full wattage, a seriously expensive watch on Colin's wrong wrist—the *right*—a frightful habit Toby had all but forgotten about. But the Patek Philippe timepiece was his only item out of place.

Colin broke away first. "I must admit I was surprised when I received your message. I'd have thought this would be the last place you'd care to visit."

"Bygones." Toby wafted the notion away as if it were a fly. "Hopefully it goes both ways."

"Of course, of course. So what the devil are you up to?"

"I was rather hoping to chat to you about that over tea. If I'm not imposing."

Colin forced a chuckle. "For you, Toby, I have laid out the best china. Or rather, the best china we staff are allowed to touch. Right this way."

Bridget mingled with the crowd alongside Charlie, positioned at the north end of the Upper Ward as the Household Troops marched into position for the traditional Changing of the Guard. Their red tunics, black trousers, and enormous bearskin hats never failed to fill Bridget with anticipation, implying something incredible could happen at any moment. This regiment had guarded the reigning monarch for nearly 350 years, making the tradition older than the modern United States.

All around, history beat down at her from every brick, every window, every speck of dirt.

While most people *read* about events, Bridget *absorbed* them. Simply taking in others' accounts was never enough, and this was one of the oldest standing castles in the world. Not quite ancient, but more had occurred here over its eight hundred years than she could comprehend. If the public displays contained such wondrous artwork, what lay beneath?

"Concentrate," Charlie said, having drifted four or five people away.

Bridget nodded. It was rare that they all came out into the field together, especially Charlie, but she insisted she'd be more useful on the ground. There was little to be accomplished remotely, having digitally reconnoitered as much as she could, and drones of the type they usually scouted with were expressly forbidden around the castle.

The troops halted, and the commander yelled his orders. Late-arriving spectators slotted in behind Bridget, some pushing through to crouch near the front with cameras.

"Okay, boys," Bridget said. "I think we're occupied."

Jules followed Dan at a distance. Toby was right. Most tourists were watching the soldiers in red perform their ceremony. In this section—the State Apartments and Gallery—there were occasional guides waiting to offer assistance who barely reacted to Dan's presence, dressed as he was in a polo shirt with the logo of Trident Facilities, the castle's contracted maintenance service. That Jules headed in the same direction—the restrooms—was normal for a tourist carrying a near-empty one-liter water bottle.

Can this even come close to working?

Jules hated trusting others. Hated that he hadn't had time to verify the secrets Toby had promised lay beneath their feet. But he'd worked here. He'd been a part of it for years.

If Jules trusted Toby was telling the truth—which, for some reason that he couldn't pinpoint yet, he did—then he also had to trust the tech and the intel.

That morning, traveling in a rented minivan—or "people carrier" as the literal Brits called them—they took ninety minutes to reach Windsor from Luton airport. Although it was quicker to pass directly through the town, they then entered the royal grounds via a route aptly named "the Long Walk," a path aiming straight at the sprawling walls of Windsor Castle itself, stationed atop a rise in the lush, mist-strewn landscape. Dozens of visitors trekked in short sleeves, carrying jackets instead of wearing them.

"Can't we just tool Dan up with a bunch of Uzis and RPGs?"

Jules had asked. "Full-frontal assault. He'll look real cool running up there, guns blazing."

Dan gave him a sideways smile. "We don't do full-frontal assaults. Much as I'd love to some days. But Toby doesn't approve."

"Okay, people, back to the matter at hand," Charlie said. "Trackers?"

"Got mine," Bridget replied, tapping the side of her jaw.

All except Jules responded the same.

Charlie's hand landed on her hip. "Jules? You set up yet?"

"I ain't bein' pegged with a tracker," he replied.

"It just means we can come get you if there's a problem," Dan said.

"Look." Charlie produced a curved tube the size of an M&M but flatter. "Take this. Bite on it to activate. You don't have to turn it on unless you need us."

Bridget took it from Charlie and held it up for Jules. "Please. It'll mean we worry less."

"Fine." Jules accepted the tracker and secured it in the back of his mouth against his gums. Addressed Toby. "You sure about the safe? Still can't believe there ain't a computer system, hand prints, pass codes."

"For the fiftieth time," Toby said, "the tunnels and catacombs are eight hundred years old. How do you think they'd get a modern system down there? And who would be trusted to install it?" He pulled himself up, reverting to a less impatient tone. "The vault was a Mancunian-Warner 83 during my time and still was as of two years ago. Barring *possibly* a few low-tech upgrades, the only modern features are on the *outskirts* of the tunnels. No one would dream of our access point."

"And you're sure there ain't a full schematic somewhere?"

"I tried," Charlie said. "But plans for eight-hundred-year-old tunnels don't tend to be kept on a computer."

"In fact," Toby told them, "the curator... he doesn't trust computers. But I have it." He tapped his head. "Up here."

Toby had even sketched a map, which Jules memorized rather than having to carry it with him.

"Who is this curator friend of yours?" Jules asked.

He hadn't asked too many questions back at the chateau, preferring to discourage irrelevant detail. But their walk was gearing up to be a long one.

"Colin Waterston," Toby said. "Actually, he and I are old friends. I was his... mentor, for want of a better word. We have a tea date since I'm in town. But I'll be wired into our comms system. You can listen in to what we say. I'll try to pry any useful information from him. Casually. Now, one more time before we split up."

Groans from everyone. Each time, their recaps got mercifully shorter. For the first briefing back in France, Toby had embarked on one of his soliloquies, which Jules was already sick of. Today, though, taking an elongated route to the castle, Toby had run through the plan once again in a shorter, simpler way that Jules wished he would use to *start* such stories: access the floor void, identify the weak spot, snake through a fissure under the foundations, and locate the vault in the heart of the catacombs. Then rob it.

Simple.

The castle bathroom Jules now entered was small: two urinals, three stalls, and a locked door set flush to the wall. The smell of flowery urinal cakes filled the place. Dan hung an "Out of Order" sign on the outside, locked them in, then gestured to the supply closet. Jules took out his lock pick's scrubbing device and inserted its proboscis into the Yale lock. The teeth whirred until the stem bit into the mechanism. Jules turned the chamber. It unlocked.

"You like?" Jules said.

"Eh, it was okay."

Jules and Dan emptied the cupboard of a mop and bucket, an industrial pack of toilet paper, and stacks of hand towels. On the floor, a manhole cover lay cemented into the surface, the date 1795 decorating the metal.

Both crouched to examine it.

"Sealed," Jules said.

Dan dug in his tool bag and removed a plastic bottle identical to contact lens solution. "Nothing's ever really sealed. Watch this." He squirted the fluid around the newer cement. It hissed and bubbled, eating away the looser stone, then a long, heavy screwdriver chipped away the remaining fragments. "Well?"

"It was okay," Jules said. "I'll get the recipe later."

Dan jammed the sturdy screwdriver into the new gap between metal and floor and strained to pry it loose.

Back at the plane, Jules had watched him pack, and they had discussed a crowbar, even a mini one, but Dan insisted he'd lifted heavier barriers than a manhole cover with this screwdriver. Plus, a crowbar might look suspicious despite his undercover persona.

Now, though, he hammered the screwdriver with the palm of his hand so it burrowed deeper, then leaned on the tool again. Something shifted. But it wasn't the cover.

The screwdriver bent under Dan's weight.

Dan swore loudly. Too loud.

Both froze, waiting for someone to enter the bathroom to investigate.

One Mississippi.

Two Mississippi.

Three Mississippi.

Nothing. No one heard.

Dan wiggled the screwdriver loose, returned to his bag, and rummaged, returning with a hammer, by which time Jules had already produced the twelve-inch crowbar he smuggled off the plane and positioned it in the acid-hewn gap.

"Asshole," Dan said.

"What's he done now?" Charlotte asked over comms.

"Nothing you need to worry about." Dan took over the crowbar and jimmied a new crack—progress at last.

The metalwork came loose, with more cement cracking and crumbling. Jules helped Dan heave it aside.

Both peered in and recoiled at the odor.

Jules pulled a cotton scarf up over his mouth and nose, prepared with Vick's ointment, and dangled his legs over. He removed his jeans and long-sleeve top, revealing his bodysuit, this time decked out with rubber-soled shoes and knee and elbow pads.

"You done this before?" Dan asked.

"Sewers? Of course. And don't worry. Royal poop is pretty much the same as working-class Bavarian poop."

"2018?" came Toby's voice.

"What?"

"2018. Is that when you were in Bavaria?"

Jules caught Dan's grin and said, "No comment."

"I'll look after these." Dan packed Jules's spare clothes into a garbage bag and set it aside for his return, then pulled out wrenches, hammers, and a handful of pipe fittings. Finally, he passed Jules another squeeze bottle of clear fluid. "Your GPS on?"

Jules tapped the adapted smartphone strapped to his wrist. All it needed was an initial GPS reading from the satellite, then he could use it offline. "Looks like."

"Good luck," Toby said.

Jules turned on his headlamp, dropped into the pipe, and bent to his hands and knees to accommodate the tight space. "You better be right about this."

CHAPTER
ELEVEN

"Are you talking to yourself?" Colin asked, returning from washing his hands.

"Not at all." Toby rose slightly from his seat, as was only polite when one's host enters the room. "Commenting on the tasteful decor."

The curator's office had changed greatly since Toby's time here, which was to be expected after more than a decade of absence. Even in Toby's day, though, it served more as a drawing room than an office. Yes, it held the same antique desk on which prime ministers had signed many a document and commanded a view of Windsor Park that swept into the middle distance like a perfectly composed painting, but it also catered for meetings of up to twelve people. The boardroom table had once—according to Colin when he showed Toby in—adorned a tsar's palace before the Russian Revolution dispatched their royals. The chairs were all modern—Ikea, if Toby wasn't mistaken.

But it was the view that roused Toby's jealousy.

Whenever confronted with a problem or dilemma, he used to lock his door and sit here, on the couch away from the desk, and simply contemplate the issue until a solution dawned. Today, he was the guest—on the sofa beside the floor-to-ceiling window, legs crossed. There was a fine china tea set on a silver tray before him, the coffee table designed to fit in but clearly a reproduction.

Colin sat opposite him on a second couch, poured two measures of milk into the delicate-looking cups, and lifted the teapot. "Actually *from* China," he said.

"Yes." Toby watched impassively. "Eighteenth century?"

"Nineteenth. But only just." After pouring two cups of tea, he offered the bowl of sugar cubes—white and brown.

Toby declined. He noted the milk going in first, a matter of etiquette frequently misunderstood. Splashing boiling tea into a thin china cup—real china, that is—can damage it, so the milk dampens the effect. Another touch of class now absent from his life.

Colin presented him with the cup and saucer and sat back with his own. "So what can the House of Windsor help the great Toby Smith with today?"

"I'm involved with a modest project," Toby said. "And I was hoping you may be willing to loan me a piece from Her Majesty's private collection. The Indian section."

"A loan?"

"Or even just a quick peek. I'd be grateful for even a few hours, supervised if necessary, but if you could see a way to instigate a full loan, I'd be ecstatic."

Colin sipped his tea, frowning as if it were pure lemon juice. He set the cup back in the saucer with a clink, expression unchanged. "Toby, I'm more than happy to have a civilized conversation with a former colleague. But after the way you left things here, you don't really think we're going to cooperate in that fashion, do you?"

Jules had explored exactly seventeen sewers in varying degrees of heat, through tunnels massively differing in size, and for vastly different lengths of time. Oddly, the sewers in the developing world, towns and cities dating back to Roman times, were easier to navigate, if infinitely more infested with rats, snakes, and other undesirable creatures; their age meant they dated from hundreds of years ago, when people needed to stand upright to conduct maintenance, while newer cities installed the cheapest, smallest pipes they could get away with. Likewise, London's main sewers were something of a treat at low tide and still in great condition.

The sewer in which Jules lay now was not one of those, but a modern installation after the advent of mass tourism.

Again, coming down here had been a matter of trust for Jules. Back in the chateau Toby had started out blathering about a conspiracy, which had some bearing on the plan, but a little guiding steered him to the point.

He didn't know how the LORI team put up with it on a permanent basis. Maybe he'd ask them some personal questions about that when he got the chance. For now, he couldn't stop his eidetic memory from replaying the briefing in full—a downside to what was, usually, a useful gift.

"The best security system in the world is secrecy," Toby had told them, settling into that wide armchair in the chateau's study. "Do you remember the great fire of Windsor in 1992?"

"Sure." Bridget perked up. "I know *of* it."

Jules nodded.

Toby said, "Ever wonder why, with all that artwork in the State Apartments, a fire was allowed to destroy over one hundred rooms while firefighters were dispatched to save Chester Tower? Why a relatively simple section of the structure was prioritized over the Crimson Drawing Room and the Queen's Private Chapel?"

Jules shrugged and applied a patient smile. "You don't 'allow' a fire to do anything. It does what it wants. But yeah, Chester Tower. That's kept me up at night."

Toby ignored the sarcasm. "The fire started in Saint George's Hall and spread quickly, mainly thanks to the huge rooms being drafty and full of air. Plus the dry voids in the floors and ceilings."

"So there's something special about Chester Tower?" Dan asked. "Or was it just a strategic spot to contain the blaze?"

On a tablet computer, Toby had pointed to the apartment section on publicly available plans. The State Apartments, Queen's Chapel, and the Crimson Drawing Room featured in the upper ward, the apartments ending at the circular section called Chester Tower. It was part of the outer wall rather than a stand-alone structure.

Toby went on, "Equipment is stored there to break out the Britishness for state visits and the like. But the mirroring subsection has supposedly been cut off and disused for three hundred years." He indicated the area around Chester Tower, stabbed his finger at the ground just before it. "There's an entrance via the kitchen, but it is never opened while regular staff are using it, and there's an emergency exit directly to the grounds in this wall. It places them in what is disguised as a CCTV center. If they get discovered, that's what they say it is. But beyond... that's where the catacombs begin."

"Catacombs?" Jules said.

Bridget blossomed with the impression that she was about to squeal and clap her hands. "I love catacombs. Especially secret ones."

There was more, of course, but the main point he danced around was a repository of plundered items from the days of the Empire, belonging to people and tribes that were wiped out in the name of progress. A long, drawn-out explanation followed as to why it didn't make the royal family assholes, but Jules managed to tune a lot of it out.

Sometimes it was easy to stay quiet. Other times, he had to focus. Like when he was playing his part in this team outing, something he almost never tolerated.

Teamwork sucks.

Yet, as a result of Toby's plan, and of the trust he was placing in the others' abilities, Jules commando-crawled along an access pipe from the public restroom, elbows and knees braced on the sides to evade the worst of the filth. Emerging into a tunnel linking the others through which he had to crouch, his rubber soles and pads gripped the sides, keeping him out of the slurry, but minor splashes could not be avoided. He checked the GPS and concentrated on his destination, ignoring the two upper-class twits in his ear.

"They talk funny," he commented, switching the Bluetooth audio through his phone to mute Toby's channel.

"Like *Downton Abbey* if it was written by stoners," Dan said.

"What's *Downton Abbey*?"

"Seriously? The TV show? Films? You never watched *Downton Abbey*?"

"I told you, television is irrelevant."

"You are one weird kid."

Jules arrived at a T-junction under the Upper Ward, and as Toby had promised, an area of shoddy repair work stained the opposite wall. Using the acidic fluid from Dan's stash, Jules squeezed the bottle, and the jet arced over the shallow stream of waste, hit the patched-up bricks, and went to work. All he could smell was the ointment on his neckerchief, but he imagined the alternative would be grim.

As the fizzing mist cleared, Jules pulled at the gap with gloved hands, and the top part of the wall fell away. An open space spread out before him.

Actually a corridor of sorts. According to Toby, it was at one time accessed by servants for transporting dirty coal from one end of the castle to the other, bypassing the monarch's pristine passageways and living quarters. Jules was now directly beneath the State Apartments.

Rather than fill in the old coal void that had spread the fire in 1992, they sealed it, sprayed the floors and walls with retardant fluid that solidified to a gel, then plastered over the access. Jules crossed this, his feet sticking occasionally, and followed the route mapped out in Toby's crude drawing, which Jules had memorized.

The going was far easier in the corridor than the sewer, and Jules pulled his neckerchief down. Aside from the remnants clinging to his pads, the place smelled like the water in which flowers had been kept too long—not vile, but off, slightly rotting. The lack of ventilation made it hot, too. Dust motes floated in his flashlight beam. No scurry of creatures, though. The gel coating must have made it an uninviting place.

At the end of the void, the farthest point from the coal storage, was the lowest section of basement floor, where the retardant fluid had settled. Because there was so much here, it made the floor moist before it could react with the air and coalesce, a discovery made when the fluid leaked into the subbasement corridors...

The *secret* subbasement corridors.

The only problem?

What Jules had to do was a long way from silent. He was directly beneath Chester Tower, where additional security was stationed at all times, but especially during the Changing of the Guard. He could hear them above in their cramped room, heavy feet shifting, voices muffled.

He had to wait on Harpal now. If he didn't do his bit, Jules—and the whole mission—was sunk.

CHAPTER
TWELVE

Harpal crouched outside Chester Tower, twenty feet back from the crowd observing the red-clad troops' synchronized marching. He wore flowing white trousers and a tunic, with sandals on his feet, and a skullcap. Essentially—much as it felt politically incorrect—anyone in the vicinity would see a Muslim watching the Changing of the Guard, along with dozens of others within Windsor Castle's walls. As Sikhs, his family had charted centuries of conflict with Muslims and now, as Islamist terrorism had cemented itself around the world, Muslims in the West had their problems, too.

It depressed him, though, to see how many predominantly white British people hated all of that faith, how they feared Muslims for the way they dressed, the bags they carried, the prayers they uttered. Such a tiny, almost insignificant portion of the population in the UK was a genuine threat, yet even before Harpal intentionally drew direct suspicion, he'd received plenty of furtive glances and people "subtly" ushering their kids away from him.

It depressed him. But that didn't mean he couldn't use it.

He slipped his backpack off, set it on the bench before him, and slid the zipper open, his body angled so the guard station could see. And what they would see was a young Muslim man checking the contents of his backpack: a small pressure cooker—an object known to serve as the base for bomb attacks in the past. The bag would ring a few bells, even though it had been scanned at the entrance.

He checked it over, zipped the pack up, then slung it on his back and took out his phone.

Jules heard a commotion above. Weight shifted; footsteps slapped back and forth. The ceiling was solid here, not simple floorboards, so the muffled words didn't carry. All he could be sure of was a change in tone, an urgency that continued with the movements.

All fell silent, so he guessed the place was empty. He pulled a hatchet from his pack.

Quietly, he said, "Okay, get ready. You're about to have company," and used the blade to scrape back the gel from the floor in the corner.

Three guards strolled out from the concealed door close to Chester Tower, trying to look casual in their dark-blue suits with walkie-talkie handsets clipped to their lapels. One was as built as Dan, two of them more so, almost struggling to move as humans due to their bulk. Two of the three sported pristinely trimmed mustaches, the third as clean-shaven on his head as his chin. They split up, circling the gravel path.

Harpal pointed his phone at the crowd watching the ceremony, although their backs were to him and he was plainly too far away to take it in. Bridget and Charlie stood near the back.

Bridget glanced his way.

He would have told her to turn back to the troops, but one of the security guys was too close. A mustachioed guard. Forties. Candidate for steroid abuse. He would have heard anything louder than a telepathic prompt.

"Sir," he said, now at Harpal's shoulder. "May I see your bag?"

Harpal dead-eyed the guard. "My bag? Sure, you can see it. Look. It's right there." He hooked a thumb behind him and turned his attention back to his video app, filming from afar.

"Inside it, please."

Harpal hit the stop button and dropped his hand to his side. "Why?"

"Because I need to see inside your bag."

Harpal flicked his phone to its contacts list. "Then I'm gonna call my lawyer first, see if that's okay."

The guard instinctively snatched Harpal's wrist and yanked it down, wresting the phone from him. The bald guard was on him in a second, initiating a choke hold so Harpal could barely breathe, presumably worried that the handset might act as a detonator.

The third struggled to remove the backpack without his bald friend breaking away, meaning the guard had to wriggle it from Harpal's shoulders and pry it from beneath his colleague's body.

"Subject neutralized," the first one said into his handset.

"Wait," Harpal said. "You've really got more people inside that tiny room?"

The mustachioed security guard just stared back.

Jules was in position, about to swing the miniature ax down on the exposed wooden floor, when he heard Harpal speak as if to the guard, but it was plainly directed at him. He froze.

A scuff and creak above indicated movement.

Charlie caught Bridget watching the mini drama unfold, listening in just as Charlie was. She shook her head, but Bridget trotted away.

"This is not what we agreed," Charlie said.

"No, it wasn't how we planned it." Bridget continued onward, her gait stiff, eyes lasering at the unfolding scene.

Charlie's choice to stay back most of the time was not a matter of skill or experience, and Bridget knew this. She always felt like such a *mum* whenever she operated in the field, even when the risk was as low as today. She accepted that she was a decent team leader on these sojourns, but she preferred to downplay her skills and make use of her experience in comms, engineering, and computing. Her mothering role wasn't necessary out here anymore, with Dan available to corral them into a cohesive unit.

Besides, Charlie had other priorities these days, priorities that trumped artifacts and dusty old bricks no matter how much they meant to Toby... or to her.

And yet.

There was always the "and yet" aspect whenever she tried to distance herself.

And yet...

The mysteries, especially those surrounding the objects they found—objects out of place or in the wrong time period—simply called to Charlie. Even when she kept her promise to Phil and prioritized her family life over LORI, these objects' presence in the world would not allow her to sleep or concentrate on anything else until the mystery was solved.

And, clearly, Bridget felt the same way.

At least Charlie had experience in hostile environments, in places where working women often weren't welcomed. Bridget had exactly two years of fieldwork behind her, and those were in university-approved risk-assessed regions. That is until Toby came a-calling.

Harpal was teaching her how to blend in, to make herself invisible. But with her flame-red hair and pale complexion, that wasn't always possible in countries where Harpal could simply alter his hairstyle and dress sense to go unnoticed. And, more problematic right now, her improvisation skills left much to be desired.

"Hey," Bridget called within earshot of the guards who were manhandling Harpal. "What are you doing?"

"No, Bridget," Charlie said quietly. "Don't over-egg the indignation."

"Ma'am." The guard's reply sounded muffled, the downside of the nearly invisible throat mics they were using. "We are dealing with the situation."

"They're official guards holding a brown-skinned suspect," Charlie added. "You go in too hot and sure he's innocent, you'll make them suspicious."

Bridget coughed. Paused. Charlie saw her halt ten feet away. Then she said, "That's my boyfriend you're hurting. Let him go."

The guard did a double take.

No, Charlie thought. *Wrong approach.*

Bridget in her skinny jeans with a designer jacket and bag. Harpal in a tunic and loose white trousers and skullcap. Not a chance in hell they'd buy that.

"Boyfriend?" the guard said. "Really?"

"Really," Harpal answered, forced to go along with Bridget's bad call. "What, she and I can't be together? This not a free country anymore?"

The guards all glanced at one another, likely waiting for someone else to take the lead. The one holding Harpal's backpack spoke into his lapel-mounted radio, but Charlie couldn't hear. A pause. Then the fourth guard emerged from the hidden door, not so hidden anymore.

"Okay, great," Bridget said, her Deep-South accent strengthening like an amateur dramatic production of *A Streetcar Named Desire*. "Any others hiding? Any more folks wanting to oppress a pair of people goin' about their business?"

The fourth guard approached—a close-cropped, clean-shaven type. Ex-military. He asked the mustachioed man to open the backpack. They both looked inside, and the guy holding it stiffened. A pressure cooker would do that. And that was the plan. The team hadn't expected the reaction to be so fast and physical.

"It's soup." Bridget stood with her hand on one hip.

The new guard indicated for his subordinate to lower the bag to the floor. Charlie heard him say, "Is this some sort of joke?"

"Clear," Charlie said. "Jules, do it now."

Jules hacked the hole in the wooden floor as planned, stared at what he'd exposed, and said, "*This* is why you needed me." A fissure lay between the man-made concrete subfloor and the bedrock beneath the castle. "I'm the slimmest."

A barely audible, "Ahem," came from Bridget, but there could be no verbal argument given her position.

He said, "You're fine, sure. But things that make you fine mean other things too. A chest. Hips."

He pictured her, had assessed her as a size six, making her size ten here in the UK, with a B-cup chest. It wasn't a sexual thing, just one of the many observations he could not help when meeting new people. Harpal had a thirty-two-inch waist and forty-inch chest; Dan was thirty-eight inches at the waist, forty-eight in the chest, which sounds big but was clearly firm; Charlie sported at least a D-cup and was a size ten US, a fourteen UK; Toby had a thirty-eight-inch waist but a thirty-four-inch chest, so his dimensions were all over the place. Jules always made subconscious assessments like that within seconds of meeting people, and found it difficult to turn off.

Careful to avoid splinters, Jules lay on the floor, switched off his lamp in case anyone happened by below, and gazed into the space. He took a moment to recall the sketch Toby drew, a crude map that the man himself admitted wasn't to scale, but having walked those catacombs many times, he was confident of it being the closest thing to a blueprint.

"Okay, I can do this. I'm going in."

CHAPTER
THIRTEEN

No matter how many of these sorts of conversations Toby held, he never got used to the difficulty of maintaining visible outward pleasantries. Especially when things weren't *quite* going to plan. Usually, the team withdrew at the first sign of a snafu, but they had progressed too far.

Bridget should have left Harpal to the security personnel. After discovering his soup was unlikely to explode, they would have simply apologized and stood back while Harpal ranted at them and accused them of racism. He might even have come away with a lifetime membership to the National Trust or some such appeasement. But the physical nature of the guards' reaction was unexpected.

"So I noticed a tad more security these days," Toby said.

"Fine tuning for a new world." Colin poured a second round of tea. "Our upgrades reflect a change in the sophistication of thieves, and more violent threats. And indeed the conspiracy theorists who think Her Majesty is a breed of lizard creature from Venus."

Toby chuckled and slapped his thigh. "That one has been around for a while. But I thought she was from a parallel dimension."

"Who knows? Her Majesty is very versatile."

Toby lifted his cup. "So, these upgrades."

Charlie's voice: "Careful, Toby."

"Costly?" Toby said, realizing he could not push for details so directly. "With the new world's desire for openness, it can't be easy pushing those things through."

Colin's cup made a louder than usual clink as it touched the saucer. "There are people with other interests." A smile—a royal lizard creature spying a fly. "Like your secret little club, for example."

Toby's stomach dropped, but he kept the shake out of his fingers. "My... club?"

Colin switched his gaze to his lap for a moment, and when he returned to Toby, the smile was gone. "I hear you must tread very lightly in Nigeria these days. If you dare return."

"An... advisory capacity, I assure you. A misunderstanding."

"Really?" One of Colin's eyebrows arched as he sat back, fingers locked over his stomach. "And Prague? How were the gyros?"

Although Jules had gotten good at blocking out irrelevant chatter, having tuned back in to Toby's channel he picked on Colin dropping significant hints toward the existence of the Lost Origins Recovery Institute. He just hadn't named it yet. But still, Jules squeezed through the gap in the foundation headfirst—an incidental crack, not a man-made escape hatch. His bodysuit stretched without tearing, although it threatened to rip several times.

He eased one shoulder out first, reached behind for his pack, and dropped it to the ground. He waited.

No alarm sounded.

No guards came running.

To squeeze the other shoulder and arm through, he had to shift his body sideways. Bracing his hands on the wall, he inched his torso and stomach down, then walked his hips out one inch at a time. When he was clinging by his toes, he listened.

Toby said, "I have advised in numerous countries, many special interest groups. Including some nice people trying to repatriate the Elgin—"

"Yes," Colin said. "We know how you feel about *our* Elgin Marbles, Toby."

Jules picked up no noise from the corridor, saw nothing, so he dropped the rest of the way, landing almost soundlessly on his feet.

"I'm in."

Toby jumped as Colin's mobile phone trilled to life, a ringtone mimicking an old-fashioned dial phone. He checked the screen. "Unknown number." He dismissed it with a swipe.

"Probably one of those sales calls asking if you've been in an accident," Toby said.

"Probably, yes." Colin placed the phone facedown beside the empty teapot. "Perhaps you'd care to explain why a man who is rumored to be operating outside of international law is asking for a favor. What, exactly, are you seeking?"

"I must say, your insinuation is rather rude—"

"And yet you do not deny it."

Toby allowed a smile. Both teacups were empty. No more props. "I wish to read one of the Kerala manuscripts."

"One of Saint Thomas's?"

"You assume correctly."

"But didn't you denounce them as fakes?"

"Reproductions." Toby raised his finger. "They were very committed people. I suggest 'transcriptions' would be accurate."

"Not a real, honest-to-God manuscript penned by Doubting Thomas himself?"

Toby frowned. "Are you suggesting they might be real?"

Colin stared, poker-faced. "One of them, perhaps. Which one, specifically, interests you?"

Toby probed his top lip with the tip of his tongue. Pulled it back. His own poker tell. He was about to inform Colin exactly which manuscript he was interested in when another *brrriiiiingggg* blared from the phone.

Again, Colin checked the display. Unknown number. He dismissed it. "My, those compensation solicitor folks are persistent."

The farther Jules proceeded through the catacombs, the more impressive they became. Lit only by the faintest of bulbs, this section was visibly curved, plastered smooth but cracked in places, the floor a skim of cement with a dark-red carpet a foot wide covering the middle to lend it an air of respectability. Not the medieval brickwork he expected.

Deathly quiet, security clearly believed they had covered the ingress and egress sufficiently.

The alcoves held a variety of treasures: vases and headdresses, weapons and armor. Occasionally he came across a relief of a noble person lying down as if the wall hid a coffin or the body of an interred royal. With the castle's foundations sunk this low, gothic architecture streaked the ceiling, the height varying between eight feet and fifteen, foundation work melding into the walls. The precise locations of the support columns seemed fortunate.

The more he saw, the odder things looked: arteries burrowing deeper, the logical layout, the fact the floor was level for the most part...

"I thought Toby said this was a natural cave system."

"He did," Dan said.

"Then why does it all seem so conveniently set up?"

"You're a big fan of relevance, right?"

"Right," Jules said.

"Then you can ask Toby questions later. Now focus. Get where you need to be."

Jules acknowledged that Dan was correct, so he followed Toby's map, matching it to the GPS unit on his wrist. If the manuscript describing the location of Thomas's second bracelet—"the Mary bangle" as they'd taken to calling it—was in the vault as expected, he couldn't waste time on trivial stuff.

He rounded the final deserted corner and stopped short. There was another reason for not having patrols here.

He said, "Uh, I got a problem."

Toby acted as naturally as he could. While he listened to the men outside returning the soup receptacle to Harpal without offering an apology, he tried to keep track of Jules, too. An open channel always brought these issues. He hoped for a reassuring word from Dan or Charlie, the most experienced of them in these binds.

"The upgrades you mentioned," Toby said. "How would you power something like that? You can't embed cables in the structure, and using visible trunking would defeat the aesthetic."

He assumed Jules was checking for wires, for a power source. Even if Colin clammed up, the message would reach the lad.

"To an old thief such as yourself," Colin replied, "let's just say we have our ways."

Jules said, "No kidding they got their ways..."

The phone rang yet again. Colin picked it up. "I'm sorry, but no one is *that* eager to represent me after an accident that never occurred. Would you excuse me?" He stepped away and answered. Listened. A long, drawn-out frown. Then he stared at his phone for a moment, the frown deepening, and held the handset toward Toby. "It's for you. He sounds Italian."

Set into a natural alcove, Jules stared at a security buffer using infrared lenses he'd selected from his bag. Before the vault door—

which was a shade bigger than the average house door—a series of lasers shot horizontally from domes in the walls two feet in front of the steel slab. He recognized the make.

Fine tuning...

One camera roved side to side in a 180-degree arc, taking in the vault, the entrance to this vestibule, and a portion of the corridors beyond stretching both ways. When it aimed toward Jules, he had time to duck behind a natural limestone outcrop, timing the sweep until it switched directions.

"Motion detectors, battery powered," he said. "One camera. Each dome is Wi-Fi enabled, so there must be a booster. Why didn't you see this?"

No answer.

"Toby?"

No answer.

"Fine, I'll do it the hard way."

Dan spoke for the first time in what seemed to be an age. "I'll hit up the control room through the kitchen."

"Two are escorting Harpal out," Charlie said. "Two heading back to their room. Bridget's going with Harps for appearances' sake. Security figured them for pranksters or troublemakers."

"That leaves two in the control room." Jules examined the domes on his left, careful not to break the beam, counting the seconds of the camera's slow pivot. "That's two people who could be a problem for you. Where are they?"

"Thirty, maybe forty seconds out."

It sounded as if Dan was already moving. "They won't be a problem."

"It ain't fair." Jules hopped back to his hidey-hole as the camera edged back his way. "Knocking 'em out, however you do it. They're innocent guys doing a job. Bit heavy-handed with Harpal, but—"

"They'll get over it. Probably get worker-comp, too."

"No." Jules assessed the gaps between the beams. "I do this my way."

"They're Wi-Fi enabled, you say?" Charlie asked.

"Yeah. Battery powered, so it can't be cut. And a remote camera too. View is up and down the passageway. I'll need to get through the beams while it's facing away, which..." He counted in his head, still out of range. "It's possible I can slip through, but I gotta time that jump just right. Go flat, then... I'll have thirty seconds to get in the safe."

"Is thirty seconds long enough?"

Jules ran through it again. "No. It's not. I can't do it in that time. The goons back in their hole?"

"Yes, they're inside. Stay away from the camera."

"Abort?"

"No," Charlie said. "I've got this. Stand by."

"You know who this is talking to you?" the person on Colin's phone asked. Specifically a *Sicilian* accent, not Italian, as Colin assumed.

"I can hazard a guess," Toby replied. "How did you get Colin Waterston's personal number? And why not call me directly?"

"It is more fun this way. Besides, you might not believe my access to certain things if I simply *told* you."

"Clever, Alfonse. No electronic trail connecting me to you. And you know I'll *have* to listen."

Alfonse laughed heartily. "Always sharp in the mind, Toby. Always."

"If that's the case, what must I listen to?"

Colin stepped closer, leaned in, trying to eavesdrop on the conversation's other end, too. Toby dared not leave the room or conceal himself completely, but he did pull away. Colin would not insist too forcefully.

More concerning was that Alfonse never called personally. Contact was always via a double-blind intermediary.

"Why so desperate to speak with me?" Toby asked. "I'm having tea with an old friend."

"Yes, yes. And my apologies for the unusual means of communication, my friend. But I must have your full attention."

"You have it. I assure you."

"You are looking for a manuscript, yes? A very old one? From approximately 60 AD, perhaps?"

"Perhaps," Toby said slowly.

"It is not where you think it is."

"What do you mean? How do you know?"

This time, Alfonse's laugh was less genuine. "Because it has already been stolen. And I know who has it. Cancel your plans, Toby. Come out to the coast. We will chat more then."

CHAPTER
FOURTEEN

"No," Charlie said. "I've got this. Stand by."

She sat on a bench opposite the CCTV room, laptop open. The device was built into the shell of a MacBook but ran military-grade hardware procured by Dan, which she had adapted. She ran a series of scans, picking up eight Wi-Fi signals, one of which was an open public facility while six others were hackable through an automated program. That left one with added oomph, which she tore into under the assumption it was the only one capable of handling the security of an übersecret network.

She was correct. Like her laptop, it was military standard.

"I can spoof myself as an admin for three minutes," she said, "but more than that risks them finding me. I'll fake a worm attack in a more important area so this section won't be observed so much. And *this* distraction won't get us kicked out of the grounds."

"Yeah," Bridget said over the network, "sorry about that. My dear boyfriend and I aren't allowed back in. We'll meet you in Windsor town center."

"Copy that."

· · ·

Toby handed Colin his phone back. Both wore frowns; Colin's one of suspicion, Toby's confused. And a little frightened.

"Is this a trick?"

"A trick?" Colin said. "Why would I be tricking you? What could I possibly *trick* you about? I thought this was just a chance to catch up with my former boss."

"Of course. Of course." Toby racked his brains to pull something together. He paced. Looked out the window.

How did Alfonse know?

"I mean, if it was a trick," Colin said, "you must have something to hide."

Toby faced Colin. "Why carry on this conversation if...?"

Colin grinned.

Jules watched the camera halt. The light did not blink out. It was still filming, but at the extreme apex of its swing, pointed away from the vault door, it froze in place. The laser domes darkened.

"Okay," Charlie said, "let's go."

Toby stormed away from Colin. The man was a snake, reveling in Toby's shock.

"Terminate this," Toby said. "Immediately."

"Oh, dear." Colin fast-walked to keep up with the older man. "Can your little band of cut-price burglars not penetrate the vault?"

Toby struggled to reply, the words threatening to spill out in a torrent but slamming into each other in this throat. He coughed the blockage away. "I came here hoping for a professional courtesy. To borrow an item to help with my research. That phone call was a contact who claims someone has, shockingly, stolen what I'm interested in."

Colin's mouth opened slightly, but he concealed his surprise with more bluster. "I believe it is *you* attempting a trick. And not a very sophisticated one."

Toby halted. Again, he directed his comments at Colin but hoped Jules twigged it was aimed at him. "*Young man*, listen very carefully. There is no point in me sending someone to steal what isn't there. And when you search your supposedly secret vault, you'll find no trace of anyone. Understand?"

An analog safe needs an analog safecracker.

Jules spun the old-fashioned dial, his audio bud flat to the Mancunian-Warner 83 safe door, listening to the gaps in the locking barrel align. "If I'm reading you right, you got some sorta anonymous tip. I ain't trusting anything that comes in anonymously."

"Pull out," Dan said. "That's an order."

"Confirmed," Charlie added. "Changing of the Guard is nearly up. Move it, Jules."

Jules hit the last of the numbers, heard the cylinders click together. "Why, exactly?"

"Because what we came for isn't here."

"We can't be sure."

"We're pulling out," Dan said. "I'm not waiting for you."

"That's cool. I don't need you people ordering me around, anyway. I told you how I do things. I never assume. And I ain't assuming Toby's mystery phone call is on the money. I need to see for myself."

Charlie sounded harried, as if she were walking fast. "You're being an idiot."

It was one minute and fifty-five seconds since Charlie called three minutes.

"I got time." Jules turned the handle.

"Time to leave," Toby said forcefully, again addressing the group but presumably talking to the man in front of him. He added, "Unless you'd care to stop me."

Jules pulled the door a crack. Air hissed out as the seal broke.

"You're either part of this team or you're not," Dan said. "Now fall in."

"I'm too *close*," Jules insisted. "The answer could be *right here.*"

"Good for you. You're on your own."

Jules stepped into what resembled a warehouse hewn out of rock, so deep and wide it was a wonder the castle above didn't crash down into it. Then he remembered the perfectly aligned foundations, meaning those who built it had used the strength of the bedrock that was already there.

The space sloped downward, a cave dropping in steady increments. Lined with modern shelving, it delved deep into the earth beyond the field of light cast by Jules's headlamp. He thought he could see the other end, but it wasn't clear. What was clear, though, despite the capacity of the place, was that the shelves were empty.

"Aw, damn."

Aboveground, in the sealed-off bathroom, Dan dumped Jules's bagged clothes at the back of the hole and replaced the toilet paper and other stock they removed from the closet earlier. He left the manhole cover unsealed and closed the door.

"You're on your own, then."

He stripped off his agency uniform and stuffed it into a bag. He was now dressed in a checkered shirt and loud shorts, slipping out of the bathroom and leaving the "Out of Order" sign in place, then scooted along the same corridors down which he had come.

Outside, he met Charlie in the precinct as the Changing of the Guard concluded with the new batch of troops marching to their posts. He greeted her with a kiss on the cheek and, as the crowd broke up, it wasn't difficult to mingle before sauntering to the exit, his loud shirt camouflaging him amid the many stereotypical American tourists around the attraction.

· · ·

Jules ran ten yards into the warehouse-like vault, yet there was still nothing but plaques and flyers left.

It looked as if Toby's informant was right, although judging by the amount of storage space that was now emptied, the word "burglary" didn't cut it. Everything of interest was gone. The place even smelled like an old cardboard box.

He sprinted to the door and was met by two uniformed guards—one with a mustache, one bald.

Damn.

"Don't move!" The bald one reached for the radio handset on his lapel.

Jules sidestepped, spun the guy's elbow down, then pushed it toward his eye. With the man's balance lost, Jules used the momentum to lever the guard over his hip, spin him the other way in midair, and thrust him into the other, who barely had time to pull his baton. Both landed in a heap.

It wouldn't hurt them too bad, and it gave Jules the chance to sprint away.

Having memorized the route, and thankful the guards didn't wield guns, he fled at full pelt, worried more about running into reinforcements than the pair of muscle bags catching up. He didn't even hear footsteps by the time he reached his access point.

He threw his bag up, then pulled himself to the aperture and squeezed through faster than he had come down, ripping the shoulder of his bodysuit in the process and scratching his skin.

No biggie.

The coal void felt more cramped this time, and he was more conscious of his footfalls, but the exit strategy was more frenetic than he was used to. He'd needed to improvise in the past, but this felt chaotic.

That the vault was a complete bust also rankled. Toby had impressed him as a details person, albeit sometimes a bit too detailed, so Jules had assumed his recon would be as thorough as his own.

Well, he'd been wrong before.

Not often. But no one's perfect.

He reached the sewer access and crawled out into the stink, then back through the tunnel and up into the public bathroom closet.

Dan had placed the goods on higher shelves, so Jules had the space to rip off his operational gear and dump it in the sewer below, before opening the bag containing his day clothes. Thirty seconds later, he was dressed.

He replaced the manhole cover, washed his hands and face, made sure he appeared to be a calm, collected student of history, then prepared to leave and join the crowds. He opened the bathroom door.

And came face-to-face with four red-coated soldiers, the two in front with their rifle bayonets pointed his way.

"Oh man," Jules said. "You guys are the real deal, huh?"

"Yes, mate," said one of those behind the bayonets. "And you're under arrest."

CHAPTER
FIFTEEN

MAIDENHEAD, WINDSOR WEST DISTRICT

It was not the worst police station Jules had ever experienced; run by the ever-so-polite Thames Valley Police, it didn't exactly fill him with dread since he was booked in under his real name.

They called him "sir."

Once he was locked in the ten-by-ten room with its PVC-covered mattress and seatless commode, they asked if he needed anything while they waited for the duty brief. Although Jules had never been arrested in Britain, he knew that "duty brief" essentially translated as "free but crappy lawyer."

After the Royal Guard apprehended him, armed anti-terror police showed up minutes later to read him his rights and whisk him away in a screaming van with blue lights flashing. They were already on alert due to Harpal's ruse, so they assumed it was a genuine emergency and acted accordingly, scaring the pants off over a hundred visitors and thrilling hundreds more in the process.

After an hour of quiet meditation, he banged on the door and called for an officer. A smiling blonde woman in a black-and-white uniform attended, and he waived his right to a lawyer. She seemed happy to help and said she'd be right back, adding, "Sir."

Within half an hour, the smiling blonde constable escorted him to an interview room with a mirror spanning one wall opposite a plain desk where a man of about fifty commenced a recording and introduced himself as Detective Sergeant Murray. His shorter, stockier colleague confirmed his name as Detective Constable Deepay. Both wore cheap suits, and both appeared as serious as doctors about to deliver a fatal prognosis. Murray issued a time check—4:22 p.m.—and asked Jules to state his name.

"Julian Sibeko," Jules answered with equal seriousness.

"And you have waived your right to counsel at this time, correct?"

"Correct. But I reserve the right to terminate the interview and request legal representation should I feel my rights are being violated." He made sure to annunciate clearly for the recording.

"Seems you know your stuff." Murray sounded casual but concentrated on the formal paperwork stacked between him and Jules. "Been in trouble before?"

"Never," Jules said. "I just read a lot."

Murray looked up. "Being clever, mate?"

Jules cast a glance at the papers. Long enough to establish them as statements taken from what he assumed were the arresting officers and the soldiers who challenged him. Jules affected a smart-ass faux-British accent. "Not at all, old chap."

Detective Constable Deepay's face tightened between a smirk and a scowl.

Murray rearranged the papers, slowly examining each one. He found what he was looking for and lifted the sheet to read so Jules couldn't see it. "You vandalized a part of Windsor Castle, then trespassed in a restricted area before assaulting two guards and attempting to flee. Wow. That's..." He made a show of counting on his fingers. "Four years minimum."

"Okay." Jules resumed his natural voice. "Except I was just using the bathroom. Or trying to."

Deepay adjusted his chair. "Perhaps you have a good reason for accessing that area. If you do, now's the time to tell us."

The trick to coming out on top of any interrogation is patience. Don't offer them anything. Don't explain your actions. Try not to deny stuff *outright* because that gives them leverage if they catch you in a lie.

Jules placed his hands flat on the table. "I'm sorry. What do you think I've done again?"

"You accessed the void under the main building," Murray said. "But we don't believe you acted alone. We think maybe you were put up to it by someone else."

"Do you? Who?"

"This person." Deepay slid a grainy CCTV screen grab featuring Harpal Singh at the entrance as he paid his fee. "He acted suspiciously to distract a number of security personnel."

Jules picked it up and held it in front of his face. "How? By being a Muslim?"

Murray took the photo from him. "You both work for this man." He replaced it with an image of Toby Smith checking his watch, again grabbed from CCTV.

Jules moved his head closer to the picture. "Why do you think I'm working for him?"

"You don't want to take the fall for this alone."

Jules formed an inkling of how to get out of here. He just needed to buy more time to process it. "You do know I'm an American, right? You really think my embassy will let me go to jail over an accusation of trespass?"

"More than an accusation," Deepay said.

"What possible evidence do you have?"

"No," Murray said. "We're not going there yet. We know what you did, and you now have a chance to explain yourself. Tell us why, tell us who put you up to it, and maybe you walk away."

Jules finished his calculations. It was really no different from judging the distance between buildings or how much strength to put into his jump to compensate for wind shear.

He sat back in his seat, legs spread, a cocky, lopsided grin aimed right at the senior detective. "The Reid interrogation system is frowned on in this country, ain't it?"

Murray sat taller. Deepay let his mouth gape for a second, but resumed his poise.

"Too many false confessions. I mean, you guys are good, workin' it with less aggression than the US feds are trained to use, but it's the same method. Hit me with the accusation—trespassing, assault, all that business. Then tell me to explain myself. That don't work, cop number two comes in with an offer to distance myself from the crime by laying it on other folks. Gives the suspect a way out. But when they start talking about their accomplices, you swoop back in and hammer 'em. Then there's all that confirmation, affirmation, consolidation that follows... But why'm I talkin' to you about this? You got the playbook. And you don't have any evidence, or you'd have dropped it on me already—"

"We have your onesie," Murray said.

"My what?"

"Your outfit. The all-in-one number you wore. Here." From a box under the table, he produced a clear plastic bag containing Jules's bodysuit and slapped it in front of Jules. "For the benefit of the recording, I am showing the suspect an item cataloged into evidence as W-three-two-four. Mr. Sibeko, would you care to explain that?"

Don't get caught in a lie.

"You didn't find that on me," Jules stated. "And it doesn't look like the kind of material that holds onto fingerprints too well."

"That's true. But it's ripped. There's a spot of blood. It'll have your DNA on it, and there will be a corresponding cut on your shoulder."

Jules extended his cocky demeanor to suck his teeth slightly, mimicking the tough gang kids he'd seen on TV when he was younger. "Thing is, this is a trespassing charge. An *accusation* of assault. But when I came in here, they only charged me with trespass, so I'm guessing there's no camera evidence of any fight.

Which is weird, don't you think? Cause every other corner of that place is covered."

He gave them a second to digest that.

"Look, your textbook Reid interrogation course was great value for money, I'm sure, but it only works when you have *evidence*. And since there's no way I'm getting charged with assaulting anyone, that leaves a bit of criminal damage and trespass. With some dubious circumstantial evidence of grazed skin, you ain't paying for DNA tests for something so trivial."

Silence.

Then Murray said, "We know you were down there in the sewer, Mr. Sibeko. In the void that's off-limits even to castle staff. And we have the evidence to prove it."

If he pushed harder for a duty brief, there was enough information on this tape already to grant even the most harried, least-interested lawyer an easy win. But the mirror intrigued Jules.

A mirror *and* a recording?

Why place him in this cell when most modern police stations in Britain no longer used such observation rooms?

A gamble suggested itself, one he didn't need to take. But it might furnish him with more information. And that was his purpose in Britain after all: to glean intel that might help recover his mom's bangle, not to mess with cops or explore secret passages. The more he dwelled on his earlier failure, the hotter it burned.

"Okay," Jules said. "Let's say it's true. Let's say I broke in. I'm guessing it'd be to explore the secret catacombs beneath Windsor Castle. Motive would have to be something worth the risk, say a vault full of artifacts stolen during the height of the British Empire? If you take me there, I'll try to show you exactly where they're rumored to be—"

Three fast bangs sounded like thunder on the door.

Murray and Deepay exchanged looks. Deepay stood and opened the door, revealing a woman in a formal police dress uniform, someone in clear authority.

Murray said, "For the benefit of the recording, Chief Superintendent Sue Clifton has entered the room."

"Interview suspended," Clifton said firmly.

"Interview suspended under the order of Chief Superintendent Clifton at... 4:35 p.m." Murray flicked off the mics.

A tall man entered. Pristine suit. Thinning hair. Wide toothy smile. "Well, gentlemen, thank you for your time here. But I think we can say the Windsor Estate has no wish to press charges."

Murray stood and addressed the chief. "Ma'am." Then he faced the new guy whose voice marked him as Colin Waterston, Toby's old pal whom Jules had listened to earlier. The cop said, "Sir, it's a misconception that the victim needs to press charges for the police to *prosecute*. The evidence and our recommendation will go to the CPS—"

"The CPS?" Colin's eyebrows popped high up on his forehead. "You mean the *Crown* Prosecution Service gets the final say on whether charges are brought? Which makes it the service that acts on behalf of Her Majesty, Queen Elizabeth the Second? Is that who you mean?"

"Err, yes. That's right." He turned to the woman in charge. "What is this?"

"This," Clifton replied curtly, "is a representative of the House of Windsor asking you to drop all charges in relation to a young man's minor infraction."

"Hardly worth bothering the taxpayer with this, is it?" Colin's eyebrows resumed normal service, but his finger rose and pointed at Jules. "On one condition. A *private* five-minute chat between myself and young Julian here."

Jules smiled. Nodded. "Sure. But this ain't me admitting to anything."

"Understood." Colin clasped his hands behind his back, chin high, and rocked on his heels. "Well?"

The woman straightened her uniform tunic. "Gentlemen. Thank you, that will be all."

Murray gathered the statements and the bodysuit and made

for the door, but Colin laid a palm on the evidence bag, halting Murray.

Colin's fingers curled into a fist so he gripped it. "I believe this was found on Windsor property."

"Yes," Murray said, not letting go.

"And if this gentleman denies it belongs to him, that makes it property of the Queen, yes?"

The chief superintendent stepped aside. "It needs logging out, Mr. Waterston. It'll be waiting for you when you get finished here."

Colin placed his other hand on the bag and ripped it open, removed the item, and relinquished the plastic. "I believe you have everything you need on that label to log it out."

The chief sighed, hard eyes leveled at the curator. "DS Murray, DC Deepay, my office, please."

The two men plodded out of the room, their heads low. The woman gave Colin another narrow-eyed stare. "*Five* minutes."

Jules watched in silence as Colin spent the first minute of the five checking the room. He ensured the recorder was inactive, then flicked off the light to illuminate a suite behind the two-way mirror. Empty. After that, he took a small box the size of a smartphone from his jacket pocket and held down a button while sweeping the walls. Satisfied, he sat opposite Jules and clasped his hands in front of him.

"Unfortunate business, the police getting involved."

Jules mimicked Colin's pose. "Lemme guess. The soldiers you ordered to intercept me weren't supposed to call the cops. You wanted to handle it yourself."

No reply.

"But the earlier alert had the police on edge. So they get wind of a trespasser picked up by the Royal Guard... They ain't gonna mess around waiting for you."

"Quite."

"So, what was your plan? Drag me to the Tower of London? Set the ravens on me?"

Colin took a breath. Let it out slowly. "I was actually going to offer you a bribe."

"Bribe?"

"You're not a member of Toby's little band of 'freelance archeologists,' or whatever they're calling themselves. You're not really known for anything except getting in trouble around wealthy people and areas of historical interest."

"Nice homework."

"So if you're only a temporary part of Toby's plans, and you were expecting to find something in the vault, you must be seeking a very specific piece."

"What happened to your collection? Wasn't all stolen, was it? You moved it, didn't you? When you realized someone broke in?"

Colin sighed. "When an item goes missing, and we are forced to dismiss three members of staff who are implicated in that disappearance, it behooves us to take certain precautions until we can be sure of the extent of the thieves' reach. *If* there was anything of value, we would have removed other items that were potentially at risk."

"That was one big room. And all those other channels... I read up on the history while I was waiting. William the Conqueror was supposed to be the first king to build a castle there, but I bet Toby will have a real long, boring way of saying there were settlements here long before the Brits."

"It's one theory. But let's not dwell." Colin slid a card over the desk with one manicured finger, stopping in front of Jules and withdrawing crisply. "This is my number."

The card held only a phone number.

Colin said, "I have far more resources than Mr. Smith. I work with people to track down artifacts much like the one I suspect you are looking for. We cooperate with institutions and governments all around the world, and we can use our diplomatic clout to get you out of sticky situations. Such as this one."

Jules read the card without touching it. "Can I go now?"

"I need an answer before I let you leave."

"No you don't. You already ordered them to let me go. So why don't you get out of my way? You want Toby, or anyone else, you're gonna have to work a lot harder than a get-out-of-jail-free card."

CHAPTER
SIXTEEN

CENTRAL LONDON

"Indeed," Toby said. "There have always been castles built on top of other castles. Churches are often built on top of other churches too, and even temples and places of worship from religions supplanted by Christianity. There's one in Mexico of particular interest, a cathedral built directly on top of what the Christians saw as a pagan site."

Jules groaned internally. He knew he shouldn't have raised the notion of the Windsor catacombs being hewn partially by nature and adapted by human hands long before the modern royal line commenced. Unfortunately, conversation in one of the many Pizza Huts in central London had died with Charlie's confirmation that they couldn't leave tonight due to their plane being impounded while the authorities searched it for anything related to terrorism or antiquity theft.

"In fact," Toby went on, "the Saint Clement Basilica in Rome was built in the twelfth century over a previous construction dating back to the fourth, and *that* one actually replaced an ancient *Roman* temple that predates Christ by a few hundred years. I forget how many exactly. I'd have to look it up."

"Philip's arranged accommodation," Charlie said, hanging up her cell phone. "Five minutes from here. I'll get the Tube home."

Jules asked who Philip was.

"My husband," Charlie replied, her hand touching the spot on her thigh where her knife would have sat; British laws forbade carrying such weapons in public. "We live in Greenwich."

"Not at the chateau?"

"No, no," Toby said. "Charlie pitches in from time to time, and Philip arranges transport and guides and such from his base here. A remote fixer, if you like."

"So what is he? Army?"

"My husband," Charlie said again. "And he parents our kids when I'm working. He's just good at arranging logistics."

"Kids?"

"Yes, why?"

"No reason." Although Jules was taken aback for a moment, he shouldn't have been. Charlie struck him as something of a single-minded type, her lush hair and athletic build not obvious pointers to motherhood. But then he wore so many disguises himself, other people's shouldn't come as a surprise. "So it's just the four of you in... LORI?"

"Most of the time," Dan said. "We all got our own things going on."

"And pizza's an acceptable diet?"

Following his release, Jules had gotten a message to Bridget, who told him they'd split up to leave Windsor. Although Toby expressed a preference to rendezvous somewhere with table-cloths, he was the only one who did.

"You don't like pizza?" Bridget asked.

"Never tried it. Ain't gonna either, not till my mom's proper-ty's back where it belongs."

"Wait." Harpal waved his menu. "You never ate pizza? How can you never have eaten pizza?"

"It's a choice."

Conversation hit another lull. Jules was an interloper and felt like it. Although he struggled to adapt to the banal niceties of everyday life, he rarely had a problem faking whatever locally acceptable mores were required for a mission. He put it down to absorbing physical cues and being able to repeat them, but did not understand them deep down. In other words, he could adopt the *how* but not the *why*, hence the reason he probed the subject of the castle maybe having stood on a prior structure.

Conversation 101: ask open questions on subjects the other person is interested in.

He needed these people, or at least would find them useful.

Jules addressed Bridget next. "So how come we missed the manuscript?"

"We'll find out tomorrow," Toby answered for her. "And no shop talk tonight. Let's eat. Everyone ready to order?"

Toby caught the waiter's attention and they all listed their pizzas and their beer or wine.

"Just the salad bar for me," Jules said. "And water."

"At least have some meat," Charlie said. "You'll need your strength."

Jules went off the menu, which the waiter was clearly confused by, but a piece of grilled chicken was not out of the question. Orders taken, the waiter departed.

"Oh, come *on*." Harpal, now dressed in jeans and a white shirt, held the menu toward Jules, a perfect pizza photoshopped on the front. "How can you resist this?"

Conversation 101, section B: when asked, offer information about yourself.

"Like I said, it's a choice," Jules replied. "I choose to only eat things that don't clog my arteries or threaten my health. High protein, low fat."

"So no sugar at all?" Dan said.

"*Some* sugar. In the form of the right sorta carbs. I'll eat pasta, rice, whole-grain bread. I enjoy *good* food too. Tasty stuff. But I steer clear of refined sugar. I don't drink alcohol and I avoid saturated fat. Unless I'm somewhere with no choice, of course. But *here*, there's a choice. And I choose salad."

Silence reigned as the waiter brought their drinks. Jules sensed they were intrigued, but no one wanted to be the first to ask him to elaborate.

Conversation 101, section B, clause 1: only offer personal information where appropriate.

When the waiter left them again, Jules said, "Doctor's got a stethoscope, plumber's got a wrench, and archeologists got their trowels. I got my brain. My body. In synch. They gotta be at the top of their game. Peak fitness. You already know my parents were murdered and robbed. In a Backgammon Pizza place, right?"

Sitting next to him, Bridget laid a hand over his. "Oh, I'm sorry, we didn't think—"

"Don't worry, it ain't PTSD or anything like that. I can handle other people eating pizza. But I always knew I had to get my mom's bracelet back. While I was bouncing around foster care, I started looking, even when the cops didn't care no more. To keep outa trouble, I needed escape routes. Best escape route is where the people chasing you can't go. That needs fitness. It needs focus. Add krav maga and aikido into that, and I ain't got room for saturated fat and sugar."

"Like in Prague," Dan said.

"Right. So, I got into the treasure-hunting game. Learned to dive, with oxygen and free diving too, shoot guns, solve incomplete clues. I funded my travel by locating sunken ships, lost paintings, even old stashes of coins. So I don't have time for... this." He circled his finger around the table. "Or TV or movies or bowling or whatever you do for hobbies."

This period of chat had gone on too long. He was volunteering too much. They knew a little of it already, so he didn't want to bore them as they did him.

He chose to finish up where they met. "When I got close to my mom's bracelet again... Prague... that was the final stop. Or was supposed to be."

The waiter delivered their orders. Jules's grilled chicken was presented alone on a white side plate, and he was directed to a salad bar. He ordered more water before heading over. No one added to their alcohol tab except Dan, who made a point of requesting something American. He got Bud.

When Jules returned from overloading a second plate with veg, pasta, and rice, they were all into their fat-and-grease-soaked dough.

"No time for TV or movies. Does that mean no time for friends?" Dan asked. "No girlfriend? Must be lonely."

"Another choice," Jules said.

"How do you *choose* to be lonely?"

From everything Jules had read about social situations, he concluded Dan was being a bit rude. Or "pushy." He hadn't over-stepped any line, though, and no one else in the group called him on it, so Jules resumed the brief personal disclosures. "It's called a disconnect. You know how when overweight people say they *can't* lose weight? Well, there's a disconnect between how much they wanna lose weight and how much they wanna eat pizza."

Toby paused, a slice three inches from his mouth.

"They want the pizza more than they wanna lose weight. So pizza wins. They switch that around, wanting to lose weight more than eat a pizza, they break out the grilled chicken salad instead. Me, I want my mom's bangle more than I want friends. More than I wanna watch a superhero movie and more than want a regular girl in my life. I ain't lonely."

Bridget bit into her ham and mushroom. A small bite. Chewed. Swallowed. "You're alone because you have something more important to work for. That's not the same as choosing not to be lonely."

"How?"

"She's right," Dan said. "Think about it. The fatty choosing between pizza and salad is hungry. He might choose pizza over salad because the fat and sugar fires more pleasure synapses in the brain. But if he chooses the salad, he still *wants* the pizza, even if he's not hungry no more."

"*Any*more," Toby corrected.

"Shut up. My point is, you're not choosing to *eliminate* loneliness. You're choosing to *be* lonely. Big difference."

Again, Jules detected an awkwardness in the lull. He figured it was time to tie off this chapter. "Same result. I'm better off this way. I'll eat my pizza when I don't need to be so fit."

"What flavor?" Bridget asked.

"Pepperoni, red onions, and tuna."

"Eew." Harpal made a gagging gesture.

Dan smirked. "You really never ate pizza before, huh?"

"It's what I was ordering on the night... you know what night." Jules was beginning to bore himself. "Someone else's turn to speak. Like how about the boss tells us what's next?"

Through a mouthful of dough and cheese, Toby said, "Sicily. When they release the plane, we're flying to Sicily."

After Charlie departed for the Tube home and the guys discussed a final beer in a pub around the corner, Bridget asked Jules if he'd take a walk with her, citing a need to stretch her legs before hitting the sack. Minutes later, they were strolling beside the Thames on a wide sidewalk known as the Embankment, accompanied by joggers and cyclists enjoying the final glow of daylight.

"All major rivers have rich histories," Bridget said, conscious of her southern drawl extending her vowels as she lectured. "Rivers were where the first major settlements grew from. Both farming and fishing were early man's greatest resources."

"Yeah," Jules said.

"Over the years, as man started asking questions like 'Where did we come from?' and 'What's it all about?' rivers were one of the things revered the world over, even worshipped. From the

Britons all the way to early Asians and South Americans. The Thames was no different."

As they passed Cleopatra's Needle amid the hundreds of commuters and tourists, the glow of streetlights reminded her of the passage of time and how it waits for no one, no matter how much they wish to hit the pause button.

But she'd seen how Jules grew frustrated about conversations that led nowhere and held no purpose, so instead of regaling him with a multitude of tales featuring Mesolithic man, she inquired after something more relevant. "We heard about the bangle through Valerio's interest, which came from one of Toby's old friends in Russia. How'd you come to it? How'd you track us in Prague?"

"I got lucky too. Traced a bronze belt buckle to a private stash, stolen ten years ago from a guy I done a few jobs for. Needed this item verifying, and he knew I got a rep for asking about an ugly stone bangle that crops up now and again. So he asks if I wanna see it. He wanted me to double his fee, but I couldn't afford it even with the belt buckle, so I said no. But I listened around the black market. Traced it back to your seller. Couldn't believe it when I cracked their double-blind drop and found—"

"Us." Bridget couldn't help a smile. How both had gotten lucky, their paths crossing purely by chance. Or *fate*, as Toby would have it. The word actually slipped out: "Fate."

Jules shook his head and she blushed. She didn't believe in fate, nor would someone such as Jules.

He said, "When you look long enough, spend enough time in this game, the same names and faces show up. Ain't fate. It's hard work plus intelligence plus logical deduction. But what I don't get is the things I saw with my mom's bangle. What makes it glow like that? The metal?"

Glad for the change of tack, Bridget put her hands in her pockets and found herself walking closer to Jules as she explained. "We didn't know about the light effect until we saw it that night. None of this is an exact science."

"I thought you only dealt in certainty."

"We only *act* on certainty," Bridget corrected. "'Actionable intel,' you called it. But *un*like you, we think the history is important. Where something came *from* can indicate where it's going *to*."

"Shame there's no actual instruction manual, eh?" He cracked a smile.

Was that his attempt at a joke?

Jules's comments about events staying with him no matter what perhaps pointed to an eidetic memory or a mild, highly functional form of Asperger's—he retained vast quantities of information while struggling socially. Last night, after Jules insisted on heading to bed early, Toby suggested the man might have savant syndrome rather than Asperger's. Neurological trauma—often physical but not always—could alter a person's ability to learn, whereby they demonstrated profound skills in areas in which they'd seen little training, such as playing a musical instrument or computing. It would mean that Jules fell into the small numbers on the autism spectrum, but Bridget was keen to point out that autism wasn't a superpower. Savant syndrome would allow Jules to do some things extremely well, but in other areas, he would be distinctly lacking.

Such as interacting with large groups. Such as obsessing over issues that most people would let go of once they became seemingly impossible to overcome. Issues like a loved one's missing jewelry...

Utterly disconnected from normality, his life had been consumed with locating this singular object, leading to fanatical attention to keeping his body fit and his mind sharp. What he did to Dan's guns in Prague was off-the-charts focused.

Cool in one way.

Worrying in another.

Bridget grew up in a household where anything "wrong" with someone was their own fault. The poor needed to stop being lazy to get jobs, the sick needed to work harder to obtain insurance, and the depressed, anxious, and delusional needed to *just snap out of it*. Only recently had Bridget understood that certain shortcomings in the brain, like the inability to connect to others, were as easy to "snap out of" as a broken leg or the flu.

But did Jules really have an illness? Because, when it came down it, some people were just jerks.

And that was the odd thing: most of the time Jules closed himself off, while other times he appeared to be making an effort, either with conversation like back in Pizza Hut or with his act of banter and chitchat, of almost joshing with Dan during the raid in Windsor.

I'll get the recipe later.

So what did it mean?

His quirks, she decided, overrode any physical appeal he possessed. And there was plenty of physical appeal, so those quirks must be huge.

But he'd still made *a joke*, no matter how lame. Perhaps there was no savantism. Maybe he *was* putting on an act.

"Books are more reliable than people," she said. "Toby can draw on his experience and tell you your mom's bangle is three thousand years old based on drawings, writings, and vague references that might be related or might just be something similar. I mean, how many items like this must've been made? Hundreds? Thousands? But firsthand accounts of real events, journals like Plato's, Marco Polo's stories of his journeys, still exist, kept in the Vatican, sealed away."

Jules was watching her closely, weaving between passersby with what must've been remarkable peripheral vision.

She said, "What?"

"There's a phrase I heard, but never seen it in real life."

"What phrase?"

"Your eyes're sparklin'. Like for real."

"You're making fun of me." Her cheeks flushed again. She looked away until they cooled, waiting for the punch line. When it didn't come, she hooked a strand of hair behind her ear and returned his gaze. "They really... sparkle?"

"You go for old books, huh?"

She nodded. Swallowed. Searched for the words. "Genocide, war, violence. Those are constants throughout humanity's time on this planet. But one of the greatest tragedies ever, in my opinion anyway, is the destruction of the Library of Alexandria."

"Which one?"

"What do you mean, which one?"

"I had sniffs and rumors of relics folks wanted, stuff they thought was saved from the fire. I never verified the objects, but I know there was more than one fire. At least three, maybe four."

"Well, yes, but most accounts were written long after the events. The last one was when the Moors took over the region, but the only version of that was written five hundred years later. The first we know of was 48 BC, Caesar's siege. Accidentally destroyed great works dating back hundreds of years."

"What works?"

"Lots. A guy called Berossus is said to have chronicled world history, including the great biblical flood, and dated the Earth at four hundred thirty-two *thousand* years. Which is about ten times older than the Old Testament says. Sappho was a female poet and musician, so talented men often called her a goddess. But the biggest loss is probably the works of Aristarchus of Samos. In the third century *BC*, he calculated that the *Earth* orbits the *sun*. Not the other way round, as most folks believed at the time... and for the next couple thousand years. He also figured the solar system was way, *way* bigger than other astronomers, *and* he worked out the right order of the visible planets."

She absorbed and accepted that her cheeks were stretched and her eyes were wide... *sparkling*... as Jules continued to watch her and smile.

"Just think where we would be if Aristarchus had been recognized as the genius he was or if scientists down the line had access to his work instead of waiting for Copernicus to conclude the exact same thing eighteen hundred years later."

Jules stopped and leaned on the wall, gazing out at the river. Bridget joined him, her shoulder leaning against his arm. She still wasn't sure whether she wanted him to wrap it around her.

He didn't do it.

He simply said, "Even if the astronomy book survived, you think the Christians woulda let folks believe it?"

"Impossible to tell. If the knowledge was widespread, they may have had to incorporate it in the same way they incorporated other religions and bent theirs to keep the locals in line. You know there's a goddess whose birthday is the 25th of December? The early Christians built churches on top of temples dedicated to her existence and—"

"Thank you, Toby," Jules said.

Bridget stopped. She could talk for hours about how Christianity, Judaism, and Islam had spread so effectively due to the fluid nature of their hierarchies. "Books are more reliable than people."

"Yeah, people say a lotta stuff they don't mean. 'Anything you need, just ask' and 'Stay in touch' or 'I'll be back one day.'" He swallowed. The wind blew in from the river, setting the spring leaves overhead fluttering and a line of lights on a boat dancing. "Let's head to the hotel. It's nine o'clock. Sleep's as important as diet."

It was as if Bridget had poked a hole in his armor, but he'd patched it up almost instantly, shutting out his amusement at her enthusiasm for old lost tomes. She fell in step beside him and played along, changing the subject. "Sure. Big day tomorrow."

"So, who is this guy? Alfonse?"

"Oh, Alfonse is a sweetie. You'll love him."

PART THREE

Basically, we are a whole world of people desperately trying to figure out what is the dark side of our natures and how much can we explore without becoming something else.

—William Peterson

If ignorant both of your enemy and yourself, you are certain to be in peril.

—Sun Tzu

CHAPTER
SEVENTEEN

SICILY

Alfonse Luca was a big man. As tall as Jules but rotund, meaning he filled the doorway of the villa, which gaped atop white stone steps at the peak of his vineyard. A light shade of brown with thick curly hair, he exuded Moorish ancestry with Caucasian genes just about dominating, and his open manner gave him the air of a retired game-show host.

"Bridget, my dear!" he called as the team—minus Charlie, who felt she wasn't needed at this stage—stepped from the mini-van. "You look ravishing, as always. Tell me these men are not ogling you too much!"

Bridget beamed right back at Alfonse, not shyly as Jules had come to expect of her. While the men wore the sort of casual gear they carried over from the day before, Bridget had donned a light summer dress for the Mediterranean sun. It was not quite summer, but Sicily was far warmer than the UK or northern Brittany and positively hot compared with the cold snap embracing Eastern Europe. Her hair shone in the early afternoon haze.

As Alfonse strode past the three men ahead of Bridget and embraced her with three kisses on the cheek, Jules adopted the expression he practiced for such occasions as meeting gregarious benefactors and potential clients: relaxed shoulders, a high but not surprised brow, and a smile exhibiting a gap to glimpse between five and seven millimeters of teeth.

Holding Bridget's shoulders, Alfonse focused on Jules. "And is this the young man responsible for your radiance?"

"Oh!" Bridget gestured to Jules. "No, no. This is... this is Jules. Jules Sibeko. He's partnering with us on our expedition."

Alfonse threw his head back and laughed. "Expedition! Ha! I love your words." He thrust a hand at Jules, who grasped it and pumped it in a mirror of the man's enthusiasm. "Alfonse Luca. Delighted to meet you, sir."

"Likewise," Jules said, waiting for the other man to disengage.

Alfonse let go with a slap to Jules's arm and spun to the trio of men higher up. "So, Toby. I hope I did not rain too badly on your plans."

Toby stood with his hands in his trouser pockets. "Was it you, Alfonse? Did you take the manuscript?"

Alfonse shook his head. "Sadly, no. Otherwise, I would give it to you with my compliments. Please. Step inside. Let us talk."

Jules was never great at reading people until he spent four months in Austria with a psychologist called Professor Graham Milburn for intense one-on-one tutelage that cost him $15,000. It wasn't mind-reading, and it wasn't an infallible process, but even so, the equivalent of a three-year college degree crammed into such a short time gave him something of an edge when dealing with different personality types—be it cops, clients, or opponents.

Alfonse struck him as a benevolent narcissist. It wasn't necessarily a bad thing as long as those surrounding him delivered with the same quality that he demanded of himself. Narcissists weren't all delusional, but they all lived as if they were the center of the universe and acted accordingly. Here, as they wandered

Alfonse's pristine art-lined hallway, even Jules could not help but be pulled into the man's orbit.

"These people, this Institute," Alfonse said, swinging his arms around in the manner of an opera singer, "we know each other a long time. Toby the longest. A good man." He slapped Toby's back. "And Harpal." He lowered his voice as if confiding in Jules. "We didn't always get along."

Harpal plainly felt no need to adjust his volume. "Because I helped bust a ton of his operations before he went legit." He grinned at Alfonse.

"Hardly a 'ton.' Maybe a few kilograms." The Sicilian bristled but left the genial smile in place. "And I am forever making up for it."

Toby took up his mantle of human encyclopedia. "Alfonse used to run with a bad crowd. Drugs, prostitution, extortion."

Alfonse stopped and faced the group, smile fading. "Toby, Toby. I did not run *with* anyone. I *ran* the operations. Please, if you must sully me by bringing up the past, at least get it right."

"Mafia?" Jules said. "Seriously?"

Toby bowed his head before offering an awkward wave of one hand. "Alfonse's Italian... *family*, shall we call them? They set him loose from the *family* business when he made confession to Cardinal Valdez at the Vatican."

Alfonse laid a hand on his heart. "I came away with my penance. To do nothing but God's work for the rest of my days."

Toby turned to Alfonse. "And doing a wonderful job, I might add."

Alfonse guffed out a big laugh and reinstated his happy demeanor. "This way!"

As the three men followed Alfonse through a wide doorway, Jules walked slower next to Bridget. "Your sweet guy is a gangster?"

"*Ex*-gangster," Bridget said. "He really is a sweetheart now."

The next room was airy and bright, the French doors open to a pool, beyond which the vineyard stretched for just under two miles. Out on a patio, white sofas and chairs formed a loose circle. The table in the middle bore water, coffee, and wine. When they stepped through the doors, Jules spotted the first of Alfonse's armed guards.

The man wore a white shirt and tan slacks, equipped with a shoulder strap from which dangled an MP5 submachine gun. He wandered a hundred yards away, sunglasses facing out, making a deliberate sweep of the land as he patrolled.

There would be others.

Jules sat as invited, although he picked a chair that positioned his back to the building so he could scan the scene at a 180-degree angle.

Alfonse did not sit, instead adopting the pose of a manager about to embark on a presentation rather than the game-show host supposedly retired. "Thank you for coming. You were in Windsor, looking for the journal of Saint Thomas. The one stolen from Kerala in 1882, correct?"

A pregnant pause fell over them before Toby answered, "Yes. That's correct. We were hoping Colin might loan it to us—"

"Of course you were! A loan. What fun. Unfortunately, the manuscript was stolen last month. A great, massive embarrassment to our mutual friend Colin Waterston."

"Mutual friend?" Jules said.

"We met last year at a gala in Paris. One of my people used a device to clone his phone. I get to know so much about him, I feel we are *friends*."

"So you did steal the manuscript?" Toby asked.

"Sadly, no."

"But you *had* it stolen?" Dan said.

"No, no, no." Alfonse held up two defensive hands. "You forget, I am legitimate now. I only set my people to break earthly laws in the service of our Lord." He untucked a gold crucifix from the tangled gray hair inside his shirt and kissed it. "No, the world is a bad place. I made it worse during my time, and I am trying to fix it in my small way. Governments are corrupt. They lie. They cheat. They make policy to keep themselves in power, wage wars for profit. Gangsters such as my former colleagues lose their code of honor because their enemies grow more brutal. So I try. I hear of injustice concerning the church, and I help make it right. This is how I hear of the manuscript. A great wrong to take it from the Christians in India, of course, but it was safe with the curator at Windsor. Until it wasn't."

Jules managed to keep half an eye on the landscape, spotting another man patrolling between the vines, and the rest of his attention on the task of working out exactly why they'd been summoned here and why Toby and the others wouldn't speak about it on the plane over.

He said, "So who stole it?"

"No one knows. My inquiries turned up nothing except a dead investigator."

"Oh," Bridget said. "I'm sorry. Did you know him?"

Alfonse crossed himself, forehead to navel, shoulder to shoulder. "A subcontractor, but an innocent one. After that, I reached out to my... family." A quick nod to Toby. "They hear little, except one outfit who usually smuggle weapons and explosives, they are suddenly silent. This is odd. Stranger than this outfit making noise. Then we get a message that Mr. Waterston has heard from a certain Toby Smith. A certain Toby Smith who is in town and wishes to drop by at short notice, and so I ask myself, 'Why is he coming?'" Speaking directly to Jules now, he said, "You see, I know Toby. I know the Lost Origins Recovery Institute. They help me sometimes, and I make a contribution to them." To Dan, he said, "You are looking after my airplane, eh?"

"She's holding together." Dan sipped coffee. "Great stuff."

"Only the best here!" He spread his arms. "So I make connections between LORI and manuscript. Day before you book meeting with Colin Waterston, you look for a piece in Prague. But little rich boy Valerio Conchin steals it from under your nose. And guess what?"

Jules had guessed as soon as Alfonse mentioned the cloned

phone, but he'd held off voicing it until now. "Valerio paid for the manuscript theft but waited 'til he had my bangle to pick it up. Lets the heat die down. Now he has one bangle, he's hot on the other. The manuscript's gonna surface. Or it already has."

Alfonse had lost his smile. A cough from Toby prevented Jules from adding more.

"Sorry," Jules said. "Go on."

"An impressive insight." Alfonse picked up his previous rhythm. "Yes, it seems he had a specialist group obtain the document, and when Mr. Waterston realized it was gone, he moved the remaining contents elsewhere. Mr. Conchin is on his way to Rome to collect it."

"Rome? That's convenient." Jules clamped his mouth shut. He didn't want to offend the man, but that just slipped out, and now Alfonse was frowning again.

Bridget patted Jules's leg. "I imagine that convenience came about because of Alfonse's moves in the international markets. Am I right, Alfonse?"

Alfonse softened again. "You are correct, my dear Bridget. I doubled what Mr. Conchin was offering, and this has developed into something of an auction. As the person initiating the auction, I insisted it happen close to my home. I could not bring them all the way to Sicily, but Rome is a short flight."

Toby crossed his legs and leaned back. "What's in this for you, Alfonse? You want to donate the manuscript to the Vatican? I doubt the House of Windsor will take kindly to that."

"If possible, yes, but that is not all." Alfonse clasped his hands before him. "The bangle you lost in Prague is one of a pair. I strongly suspect the manuscript will lead to the other. And since my friend and confidante Cardinal Valdez knows of only one other such bangle lost to the ages, it is an educated guess that you also wish to obtain an item worn by the mother of Christ."

Toby nodded in understanding. "You want the Mary bangle."

Alfonse's hands spread open, feigning that he was the most innocent man in the world. "For the Church, my friend."

Toby looked at Dan, who shrugged. Harpal leaned in, and Toby inquired in his way, silently. Jules began to wonder whether they believed themselves to be telepathic.

Bridget said, "It won't be cheap."

Alfonse laughed. "It never is. But, my dear, I am willing to pay."

He swept a hand to the side to reveal a smart man in tan slacks, white polo shirt, and sunglasses stepping out of the house with three rucksacks—two red ones over his shoulders, a black one in his hand. He dropped the black bag on the tiled floor.

"This bag," Alfonse said, "contains the four hundred thousand euros the mercenaries are demanding for the manuscript, plus another hundred should the price rise. The next... *Carlo.*"

The newcomer responded by passing one of the red bags to Toby, who opened it to see it was full of cash. Harpal whistled, impressed. Dan settled for a single nod.

"Five hundred thousand for you, Toby," Alfonse announced. "Up front. You take your expenses from this. When you deliver the Mary bangle to me, you receive the other half of your fee."

On cue, Carlo held the final rucksack out in one hand but did not relinquish it. After a beat, he disappeared back inside.

"A million euros," Bridget said. "That would keep the institute going for some time."

Toby hadn't taken his eyes off the cash. "And accelerate a few other projects."

"Right," Harpal said. "This is great, but could we transfer it to something else? Maybe a more traditional briefcase or a big hand-bag? Folks get tetchy around backpacks these days. Especially if I'm in the vicinity."

Jules was more interested in the first bag. "This buy, why isn't your, uh, family buying the book for you?"

Alfonse gave him a faintly sad smile. "Alas, they will help with information where they can, but they will not partake. My mission is holy now. I cannot taint it with their bloody ways."

"And this manuscript, it definitely tells us where this other bangle is?"

Bridget reached over and closed the bag of money, drawing Toby back to the matter at hand. "There are no definites. It'll be written in Hebrew or Aramaic, possibly something more complex, so I'll need time to translate. Even then, Thomas may not have committed to a specific place. It certainly won't be latitude and longitudinal coordinates."

Jules snorted, a well of impatience bubbling again. "Look, I'm all for creeping around stealing old dusty books, but we know this Valerio Conchin has my mom's bangle. Why don't we just take it from him?"

"Because you cannot," Alfonse said. "This is a man who was small time until five years ago. Since then, he has used his wealth to seed a worldwide network, one searching for antiquities, out-of-place objects that he might use, and many construction and IT projects. Projects normally denied to such people. But he has accelerated them through bribes and blackmail. It is rumored he bought a whole village in the Ladoh region in northern India, where he imported skilled workers from across the continent to work on powerful computer research. Julian, my friend, he has murdered *dozens* in his search for the oldest antiquities of mankind."

The big man stepped closer, his shadow falling over Jules as if the sun had shifted in order to emphasize the point.

"He is obsessed, my good friends. Or at least this is what is whispered in the shadows. The older the artifact, no matter its value in jewels or gold, he wants it. And he buys the best. His bodyguard, for one example, is known only by the name 'Horse.' In my former family, we know many assassins. He was one of the most sought after. The most expensive. Now he works exclusively on retainer for the other party interested in the Thomas manuscript. Be careful."

Jules focused on the man's mouth, unsure why exactly. Partly, he thought, because it helped cut through his accent, but also because what he was saying was direct, actionable intel, something in short supply around here.

Specifics.

"Valerio Conchin is scheduled to land at one of Rome's smaller private airports," Alfonse said. "You must beat him to the salesman. Leave now. Complete the transaction today. Or you will never get hold of that manuscript."

CHAPTER
EIGHTEEN

ROME, ITALY

With Charlie online back in the UK and her husband smoothing over the landing permit at Ciampino Airport, the smaller of Rome's two internationals, LORI flew in on their jet donated by a former mafioso. With Alfonse's help, Dan collected two compact Glock 19 pistols from someone on the tarmac—one for him and one for Harpal. He'd offered Jules a third, but Jules had learned through bitter experience that when you carry a gun, your opponents obtain bigger guns to come after you. Plus, the trouble a person could get into with an unlicensed firearm was pretty severe, so nonlethal weaponry was just a practical requirement for him.

Although his clothes looked light and casual, the lining of his jacket hid six throwing knives (non-lethal unless he made a mistake), a telescopic baton inserted up one sleeve between the crook of his elbow and his wrist, a bungee cord and grappling hook up the other, and his belt held six mini flashbangs.

From Ciampino, they drove into the city where Jules had made an unclear number of enemies. He'd traveled under the name

Frederick Pickles today, which wasn't a perfect cover, but it was enough for crossing between EU countries thanks to the bloc's enthusiasm for free movement.

LORI used two vehicles, again arranged by Philip Locke—a small SUV for Dan, Harpal, and Toby, and a white Prius for Jules and Bridget. It was beginning to feel as if the men were avoiding him, leaving Bridget to babysit—first in London, now here.

Could it be that Jules wasn't making enough of an effort, and the men felt snubbed?

On the other hand, Bridget seemed genuinely interested in him. He just hoped it wasn't romantic interest.

Like the notion of conventional friends, he had little time for intimacy. He'd tried it. He'd tried it plenty. But ultimately, it was pointless. Every girl he met, even those who loved the adventure, aspired to "cure" him of what they always ended up calling his "obsession." The bangle became a problem to fix, not an achievement to aim for.

Bridget wanted to solve it the same way as Jules. They just had different reasons.

Bridget drove, claiming to "know the streets here" and Jules didn't dampen her spirit by revealing he had already mentally mapped every road within the ten square miles of Rome's center. Entering the city limits with Italian radio playing, though, he conceded that some of the layouts and architecture had changed in the two years since his last visit, so he wouldn't be confident racing around here the way he used to. He was a GPS unit in need of an update.

Nearing the central area, Bridget pointed out landmarks that he was already highly familiar with, taking a route that marked them as tourists. She beamed when, in the distance, the dome of Saint Paul's within Vatican City came into view; chattered nonstop as they whizzed by the fountain of the Piazza Navona; and like many out-of-towers, she slowed to a crawl past the Colosseum, drawing honks from irate locals as they maneuvered around what must be a mundane sight after living alongside it for so long.

Despite the circuitous route, they parked at their destination ahead of the men's car, which Bridget took great pride in. "Like I said, I know these roads. I did a six-month placement here."

Jules sensed she wanted to elaborate, but he did not encourage her in case her interest in him stepped over the line of the professional.

Ego? Yeah. But he wouldn't be crushed if it turned out she was just being friendly.

The bar they were supposed to meet in, L'Esploratore Bello (the Handsome Explorer), was situated atop the Vatican View Hotel on a wide side road off Via Giulia. They adjourned to a café across the street that had tables arranged on the sidewalk behind a rope barrier. Arching their necks to look around the foot traffic, through the ornate buildings lining the quaint avenue, they could just about see Vatican City, a quick hop over the River Tiber.

Jules ordered water, Bridget a Diet Coke. No food, which caused the waiter to bow slightly and say "Bellissimo" in a tone meaning, "Go to hell, cheapskates."

The Vatican View Hotel offered four stories of mid-budget accommodation, linked to the building on its left—a clothing store that claimed to produce "genuine-looking Armani, made to measure"—with a gap to its right and a sign that read "Car Park" in Italian, English, French, and German. According a travel website, the bar boasted a partial awning but could be fully covered depending on the weather, and because this was a street made up of buildings of the same height, L'Esploratore Bello afforded the best chance for the hotel to fulfill its name's promise.

The mining of public records revealed that L'Esploratore Bello was owned privately, the space rented out by the hotel to one Giovani Trussot, although his wife appeared on the books as the assistant manager. While their local tax affairs seemed to be without fault, Giovani himself owned three all-but impenetrable numbered accounts: one in Switzerland, one in the Caymans, and one in Russia, indicating he was likely a go-between for the gang who stole the manuscript and the buyer; a classic double-blind sale.

Dan and Harpal, now changed into suitable business attire, entered the Vatican View Hotel, Dan in possession of the briefcase full of cash.

Jules and Bridget left money for the drinks and a generous tip and followed. Again, they utilized the tiny Bluetooth bone-conducting earpieces linked through their cell phones. Toby held back in a parking spot by the river, monitoring police bands. From Greenwich, Charlie concentrated on footage from a high-end civilian-grade drone. As with the setup in Prague, a jerry-rigged cell phone served as both camera and secondary controller, cloned to Charlie's computer in London.

"Is it necessary?" Jules asked in the lobby. "The drone, I mean."

"Charlie can hack traffic cams and CCTVs, but only if they're connected to the internet," Bridget replied. "We don't always need this, but Toby's worried about others showing up."

"*Others*. Meaning the other buyers."

"But with Alfonse's influence, I doubt anyone would double-cross him."

Jules wasn't so sure, but he and Bridget took the elevator to the fifth floor, anyway.

They stepped out to the rooftop bar, where the Vatican was indeed visible, hazy in the middle distance. An awning stretched over the bar itself, a kind of long hut, and extended a quarter of the way over the rooftop seating area, the remainder exposed to the cool spring sunlight. There was a sign hung over the bar featuring a handsome explorer that was obviously supposed to be Indiana Jones, but was painted just badly enough to avoid copyright infringement. The only patrons consisted of an elderly couple sharing cocktails and a single young man sipping a beer and reading a book.

The bartender was a leathery-skinned man with a shock of

white hair, the top four buttons of his shirt open to reveal a crucifix amid his stringy chest hair. He matched the photo they had of Giovani Trussot.

Jules and Bridget perched on tall stools at the bar in the shade, where Jules again ordered water while Bridget chose an espresso. Giovani lingered longer than necessary after delivering their drinks. Jules held his eye.

The time was right, and they were strangers in a bar where he likely got to know regular guests. Plus, Bridget's stiff demeanor since emerging onto the rooftop would give her away to any experienced operator.

Over comms, Toby said, "Dan, are you ready?"

"Affirmative," came Dan's reply. "Charlie?"

"All good," Charlie answered.

Dan and Harpal sauntered out, sharing a silent joke. They'd checked in as guests under fake names, so they came across as any pair of businessmen on a trip. They leaned on the bar and ordered beers. Dan held the briefcase low.

Giovani served them and in a strong Italian accent said, "On the house." Then he stood, waiting.

Harpal looked around. Jules did too.

The elderly couple and the younger guy were well out of earshot, and none appeared interested in the group.

"Food?" Giovani offered. "I can have traditional pasta dishes brought up or American hamburger or proper pizza. The thin variety. Not your silly inch-thick base."

Jules frowned. "Is the depth of the base important in making decisions about pizza?"

"Of course!" The serious expression left Giovani; talk of food clearly excited him more than international antiquity theft. "The thinner base allows you to taste the sauce, the cheese, the toppings. It is about *flavor*. I hear American companies fill the crust with cheese, and even meat." He pulled a sour face. "Sacrilege."

Jules took note.

"We have the money," Dan said. "Let's see the package."

Giovani frowned. "But we were having such a fine conversation. Perhaps I should offer a sample, no?"

Harpal sipped his beer, adjusted his sitting position, tilting to one side. Casual, but Jules could tell Harpal was loosening his clothing, allowing him to more easily snatch the Glock that was still hidden from view.

Giovani continued, "A phone call, yes? The kitchen will send up their finest pizza—"

"We came here for business," Dan said.

Jules slipped off his stool and positioned himself behind Bridget. Giovani traced his movement, then his eyes darted back to Dan.

Jules took his drink and beckoned for Bridget to join him. She complied, and he threaded his arm around her waist, his back to Giovani. Color flushed into her cheeks, her gaze toward the floor.

Jules pointed with his drink hand to the Vatican. Out of Giovani's earshot, he said, "I got a quick assessment for everyone listening. Guy behind the bar is real experienced in selling artwork, but he wants to talk food more than money."

"He's Italian," Toby said.

"He also frowned when Dan brought up the subject of business. And he don't just *like* food chat. He *leaped* on the opportunity. But his conversation was designed to probe, draw an argument from patriotic Americans who prefer thicker-based pizzas."

Charlie butted in. "Deception indicators, Toby."

"Then he focused on me instead of the real threat, which is Harpal, who clearly has a gun. But he's relaxed on the surface. *Desperately* relaxed."

Jules glanced at Dan, who was now seated, sipping his beer alongside Harpal, both reading a one-page menu the size of a trade paperback.

Eyes on the menu, Dan replied low enough to avoid Giovani's ear. "Jules is right. I picked up the same."

"Agreed," Harpal murmured.

Jules said, "Charlie, you sure none of this Valerio dude's people're in town?"

"Nothing arrived in the past twenty-four hours," Charlie said. "No known aliases, nothing from his shell companies."

Bridget held Jules tighter. She asked, "What about leaving?"

"Leaving?" Toby said.

"We were in France for a whole day after Prague, then England for another. What if he was already here? Came in by road from Prague?"

Jules kept his tone even, despite the urge to abort. "He'll want a quick getaway." He located the drone, a dot too high to be audible, and you'd only see it if you knew what you were looking for. "Flight manifests leaving in the next twelve hours."

"On it." Charlie presumably engaged autopilot or handed control over to her husband because the drone did not move.

Jules and Bridget sashayed back to the barstool and offered smiles to Giovani. The barman replied with, "Beautiful, no?"

"Gorgeous," Bridget said. "Always breathtaking."

"I did not mean the Eternal City. I meant you two. Beautiful people. Beautiful babies, yes? And such a mix. The African and the... Irish? With that shining hair, you must have Irish somewhere."

"Scottish, actually." Again, Bridget was blushing. Pulling strands of copper hair over her face, she added, "I'm fifth generation, though, so the genes are pretty old."

"And very strong."

Charlie came back on the air. "You're right. Omni Fuel Corporation has a private jet scheduled to leave Pope Francis Airfield in two hours. No destination logged, but that isn't required with private airports. Omni Fuel is one of Valerio's legit operations. Renewable energy research."

Jules took it all in.

This deal was set up by mafia connections, and no one screws with them; the promised money was on the table; yet here was the bagman, stalling. Now Jules was more interested in what was missing.

He said, "Giovani, this is a great place. But where's your wife?"

The tan bartender's skin appeared loose on his face before it snapped back into that effusive, beaming vigor he'd almost maintained throughout. "My wife? It is... her day off."

"Did they take her?"

Harpal and Dan stood. Bridget sat up straighter.

Jules said, "There isn't much that'd make a man double cross the mafia here. It's okay, Giovani. You can tell us."

Giovani's mouth turned down, and his eyes glistened with tears. He must have been debating internally, coming up with excuses for his shock, but Jules had caught him off guard. Denials were pointless.

He said, "Two days ago. They took her two days ago."

"Uh-oh," Charlie said.

"What does that mean?" Dan asked.

"I had to keep you talking," Giovani said.

"Not you." Dan turned from the bar, focused on the drone. "Charlie, talk to us. What's 'uh-oh' mean?"

The drone started to descend.

Charlie said, "The cell phone coverage just died. I'm down to 3G, which is much slower, so—"

Dead air returned. Back in Windsor, Dan had explained their earpieces and throat mics fed through the mobile networks in their individual phones, which were conferenced in via a central satellite phone, so even when underground, they usually had some comms. The air never died. Not completely.

Bridget lunged at Giovani over the counter, stopping halfway across to touch his hand. "Do you still have the book?"

"Yes," Giovani answered. "They said they were sending someone, but other interested people might arrive first. I had to keep you talking until—"

"Get ready," Dan said. "This is gonna be tough."

And then a small explosion announced the presence of Valerio's people.

CHAPTER
NINETEEN

The drone, already dropping from the sky, took a shot to its body and careered to the floor of L'Esploratore Bello, shattering into shards of plastic and metal. Dan would have preferred more warning, but at least he'd had a chance to prepare mentally. That Jules worked out the setup just seconds before he'd processed the scene jabbed at him and made him dislike the kid slightly more, but he was also glad he wasn't the only one with decent situational awareness. With Jules covering Bridget, Dan could cut loose with what he did best.

He and Harpal drew the Glocks, unsure where the next attack would come from, but a glint of light three streets over provided the answer.

"Sniper, four o'clock."

Dan swept his open hand toward the best position of cover. Jules slammed Bridget aside, the second time this week Dan's miscalculations had endangered her. He'd have to trust Jules would keep her safe now.

As Dan chased after Harpal to share their wall, the first bullets fried the air. The glass around the wall's edge shattered. The elderly couple and lone traveler ducked under their tables, hands on their heads. Other tables pocked and splintered. Floor tiles cracked. Debris and dust plumed all around.

High-caliber rounds. Armor piercing, probably.

If he'd reacted half a second later, his head would have been vaporized.

Unless the assailants were particularly sadistic or random, the bystanders were far enough away to be safe from any cross fire, but LORI was pinned. The barrage came in from two angles and showed no sign of letting up.

"This is tactical," he said to the bunched group. "There'll be a second wave. They want what Giovani has."

Speaking of the bartender, he'd hit the floor as soon as the shooting started, but that hut-like bar was made of wood. It wasn't exactly a block of swiss cheese yet, but it had taken a few hits.

"It's behind the bar," Jules said. "If they couldn't collect before now, it'll be close."

"Don't even think about it," Dan said.

"What?" Bridget snapped her head back and forth between the bar and Jules. She constantly harangued the team to give her more fieldwork, but she'd never come under fire like to this. Even someone as experienced as Dan struggled to keep his head. "What shouldn't he be thinking about?"

"He's going for the book," Harpal said.

"Gimme some covering fire." Jules pried Bridget from him, but she clawed at his back as he rose half a foot into a sprinter's stance, head still below the outer wall, hidden from the snipers. "You saw one shooter already. Located the other yet?"

Dan had pinpointed the approximate position from the angle: the second shooter was forty-five degrees north from the first, which was less favorable since it had to come from the side of Giovani's serving hut. "Yeah, I got it. But Glocks are short-range weapons. Densely populated area. Even if the gunners are in range, no one's that good."

"I only need three seconds. Just point your barrels that way."

Dan popped his head up, timed half a second, then ducked back down as a grouping of three slugs skimmed off the wall. "They're good."

"Human instinct. Gun pointed at 'em, even through a scope, they'll hesitate or even move." Jules placed one hand on Dan's gun, another on Harpal's. "Aim high. Fire. Count one second. Fire. Fall back. Okay?"

"One second?" Bridget said frantically. "You said three. You need *three* seconds, not one."

"First second to set off. They'll need that to draw a bead. Dan and Harpal distract 'em—that's another second while they hesitate. They'll take a third to reset and a fourth to loose off another round. That's like twenty-five percent more time than I need."

Bridget was trembling. The only one of the four who had never experienced this. Jules clearly had.

"On three," Dan said. "One."

Harpal nodded.

"Two." Dan readied his crouch, waiting for Harpal to do the same. When Jules nodded, Dan said, "Three."

Jules launched himself forward. Legs pumping. Head down.

Dan and Harpal popped up, shoulder to shoulder, aiming in the approximate directions of the snipers. Both fired way over the snipers' nests to avoid collateral damage.

But then, at the end of second number two, the doors leading from the hotel burst open.

Dan and Harpal dropped back behind cover, and Jules leaped from the damaged tiles. Bridget screamed, "Look out!" but the eight-strong team, with Horse taking the lead, streamed into the scene. All armed. Spreading out.

Dan didn't hesitate, firing on the one who looked the most ready, which dropped him with a head shot. Then he squeezed the trigger twice more, the slugs impacting a lanky gunman raising an AK-47. Harpal killed a third guy, leaving four plus Horse and two snipers.

After that burst of frenetic gunfire, Dan and Harpal dashed

sideways, Bridget in tow. Dan guessed she'd be angry with herself for playing the damsel in distress, but it was nothing to do with her gender; she was a civilian with zero experience in gunfights. And gunfights are scary.

Understatement.

The three made it behind the end of Giovani's bar just as the remaining attackers got their acts together, and their coordinated fire battered the thick wooden structure and the wall beyond.

Dan worried about ricochets, but once the tiles were penetrated, the sandstone beyond absorbed the bullets' energy. At least their angle from the snipers was safer.

Quit the ballistics analysis and fight.

During a lull, Dan whipped his head out and pinpointed the attackers: two left, two right. Their barrage resumed as soon as he showed himself. But one thing bothered him.

"Horse is missing," he said to Harpal. "Watch our six."

"Okay," Bridget replied. "I'll try."

"Not you." Dan hadn't realized when he spoke, but Harpal was gone.

Dan skittered to the back of the bar hut. It stood flush to the wall. No way through.

He returned to the edge and held his gun around the side. Fired once. Checked visually, then fired again. Another head shot.

Back behind his post, Dan said, "He went upward?"

Bridget nodded.

Where is Horse?

A succession of reports from up above boomed. Dan counted five or six.

Harpal wasn't as good as he thought he was. He'd undergone *some* training in his previous occupation, which they all assumed was MI5 or MI6, but he'd never confirmed. He thought squeezing off several quick shots at once kept an enemy pinned better, but really, it just gave away your position. One well-placed bullet was enough to make them think twice, to make them nervous. They'd had this discussion so many times Dan was bored with it.

But Horse was tricky as well as big. And when Dan jumped to the lip of the bar hut's awning and pulled himself up, sure enough, Harpal was hunkered behind a fake chimney that didn't look especially bulletproof. And although they couldn't necessarily see either Harpal or Dan at this angle, the snipers were still out there.

Horse popped up, likely the reason the long-range shooters hadn't engaged yet. On his belly, legs dangling, Dan fired on Valerio's main man. Horse ducked away again.

Hidden from the snipers, Harpal belly crawled along the peak while Dan switched his view to the front section.

Still no sign of Jules.

One of the remaining gunmen dashed across Dan's peripheral vision. Against his better judgment, Dan switched his aim and fired once into the man's torso. The impact proved he was wearing body armor, so Dan fired a second into his head. The distraction gave Horse his opening.

The big Aussie zipped around from the far corner, barely a flash of head and shoulders at the end, ducking under the bar's awning.

Harpal reached that end, but he only ended up exposing himself to the last three gunmen.

Dan fired three times down into the awning in the hope of a lucky shot, then rolled away as the expected reply blasted his first position. The torrent followed, and he had no choice but to drop back, rejoining Bridget on the floor.

Eyes wide, mouth small, she asked, "Harpal?"

"He's okay," Dan said, prepping a second magazine. Although not out yet, he'd lost count of his rounds. "But Jules is stuck."

A grunt of pain sounded.

Dan leaned around the post to view Horse's position, which was behind the bar with one of Jules's throwing knives embedded in the meaty part of his forearm—the same forearm Jules had stabbed back in Prague. Only this time, Horse hadn't dropped the gun, instead holding it at Giovani's head.

Dan could guess what had happened: a brief skirmish in which Jules defended himself with a blade, but it didn't have the usual effect of disabling his target. A shot of morphine to ease the earlier wound?

From the side, two shots from Harpal's Glock took down one of the dumber raiders, and the final two hunkered behind potted plants the size of small cars.

Behind the bar, Horse spied Dan drawing down on him.

Craning, Dan found Jules on the opposite side of the bar from Horse and Giovani. The kid held a package with dimensions somewhat larger than a legal pad, albeit four times thicker, bound with brown paper. Saint Thomas's manuscript, no doubt snatched during the firefight.

It looked wet, and Jules swayed a lit Zippo beneath it.

"You won't burn it," Horse said.

His voice was deep, but whenever Dan crossed Horse, he was always surprised at how well spoken the larger man was.

Not just a big guy.

Jules backed away a step. "All I care about is one item. The one you got. I don't need this relic to find it. Just gotta find *you*. And guess what? I found you."

"Back off, Jules." Dan drew his bead tighter. "I got this."

Bridget pawed at Dan's shoulder. "Don't let him burn it. Please. It's almost two thousand years old!"

"And he has a hostage." Dan tried to line up Horse's face in his sights, but the killer was too experienced for that. "Let's not forget the hostage."

"Lowlife." Jules sounded tough, adopting a stereotypical gangsta tone. "Sells to the highest bidder. Why'd I care about that asshole? Now, I'm walkin' outa here. And you ain't stoppin' me. Clear?"

Horse continued shifting Giovani around to prevent Dan's angle from winning out. The blade in his arm oozed red, but didn't hinder his movement. "What's clear, mate, is you got skills. But you don't carry a gun. We watched the footage from Prague, so we know you can handle firearms. Which gets me thinking you got some kind of hippie-hippie respect for human life."

Jules held firm, but if Dan detected the minute shift in his lips, Horse surely did too.

"Maybe I'll demonstrate." Horse glanced out to the patio area where the elderly couple huddled in a corner behind a scattering of upturned chairs and stools and what Dan took to be a student, who remained curled in a ball under one of the few tables yet to be hit. "The young one, Stephen. Just the leg."

Jules swung the Zippo away from the package. "No, wait!"

"Too late."

One of the snipers was plainly named Stephen, as a single muffled gunshot rang out, and the young guy under his table yelped in agony as a cloud of blood burst from his thigh.

Although Dan couldn't see his whole face, Horse's eyes creased in a smile.

"The manuscript," Horse said. "The next one goes in the old lady. Think she'll survive a flesh wound like that?"

Dan felt the gun's handle slick in his palm. "Jules. We can handle this."

Horse shifted forward. "Hand it to Giovani."

"Let the others go first," Jules said.

"I don't think so."

"It's a good deal. Take it. You ain't got time to argue. Listen."

A pause. The high-pitched whine of the *polizia* sirens echoed through the canyons of streets. It was impossible to tell whether they were one block away or five.

Dan could see the gears turning in Horse's mind.

Jules said, "These guys don't matter to your prime objective, do they? They're just in the way."

He shifted the lighter closer again, the bluff about 90 percent nullified now, but with just 10 percent, it was still a chance. Slim, but—

"Go," Horse said to Dan. "*Now*, before I call him on it."

"Get Bridget safe," Jules said. "You got one minute."

If Dan didn't comply, Horse had the advantage and could kill them all. The manuscript was plainly too valuable to him, though. Dan had to choose before Horse calculated the odds were massively in his favor.

Dan held out his free hand and took Bridget's, pulling her gently behind him, acting as her human shield as she sidestepped from cover. He was aware that this exposed her to the snipers, but he doubted they'd fire with Horse positioned on the other side; even a tenth-of-an-inch mistake on their end could result in a two-inch miss on the ground—and a serious risk of hitting their boss.

Once clear of the bar, Dan moved Bridget to march in front of him, sweeping his gun arm between the two potted plants concealing the remaining gunmen. With a final glance back, he escorted Bridget into the hotel with just one thought lingering.

Where did Harpal get to?

CHAPTER
TWENTY

Harpal had found a storeroom around the back of the bar hut. While the gunmen were occupied with Dan's standoff, he'd slipped inside. The setup had a door to the rear, a lift-up flap to access the customers' area, and this large closet packed with beer bottles, juice, and spare glasses. Harpal cracked the door open.

He heard everything, saw a little of it: Horse with Giovani behind the bar, Jules on the customer side with the book, and Dan shielding Bridget as he escorted her away. Once the pair were clear, he steeled himself to screw up Jules's plan.

"Hand it to Giovani," Horse ordered. "Giovani, you hold on to that, do as you're told, and maybe you and Mrs. Giovani live to see your next sale. 'Kay?"

Giovani nodded.

Jules flicked the Zippo shut, extending the vodka-rinsed package nervously in one hand over the bar between them. Giovani grasped the book and stepped back, then dropped it into a satchel dangling from Horse's hand.

Harpal eased the door open minutely farther and firmed his grip on the gun. Two-handed. Mouth dry. Unsure where to plant his feet. Two meters from Horse.

The big Australian shoved Giovani aside and pointed his gun

at Jules, injured arm dripping red. "You know I've got to kill you now."

"Guessed as much," Jules said.

Harpal opened the door fully. "Freeze!"

Horse snapped that way. Jules flicked something, and the air crackled around Horse's head. Horse flinched, and Jules dived toward Giovani—and the book.

Harpal fired three times into Horse's chest, but he was wearing what must have been incredible body armor. He merely staggered with a grunt and rolled across the counter, halting Jules with a raised weapon, meeting him halfway.

Jules was too quick. He slapped the gun and scrambled out of sight. Then Horse dragged Giovani over with one hand while loosing off four rounds at Harpal, forcing him back in his hole.

A second later, Harpal dared to poke his hand around and fired twice at Horse's last location. When no shots returned, he risked an eyeball between frame and door. Seeing no one present, he crawled out fully. Not even Jules was there.

What the hell...?

Jules sprinted out from the bar's blind side. "They got the manuscript. Come on."

Harpal followed, covering the corners that Jules appeared to ignore. There was no one left. No more sniper fire. Still no mobile reception.

Jules passed the terrified civilians without checking on them and peered over the edge, out into the street. When Harpal reached him, Jules said, "They'll be going a different way. Won't risk Dan ambushing 'em. Which is the obvious route?"

"Front exit."

"Second?"

"Back way, through the kitchens."

"Meaning..."

"I don't know," Harpal said.

"I wasn't really talking to you. I was thinking. Figured it'd be polite to include you."

"I'm glad you were polite about it."

"The building next to this." Jules dashed to the other side of the patio. "There's a gap one way, but they're connected. A back way on the balconies'll give 'em access. Plus, y'know, cops."

Jules leaped up the wall and ran along a ledge, all of four inches wide, and disappeared down the uneven drop to the next building—a knockoff fashion store. Harpal could only watch as Jules sprang up onto an AC unit and somersaulted off the other side, disappearing from view.

Harpal had skydived, snowboarded, even used a wing suit for fun, but this was hard-core. So screw that.

He made for the conventional exit, back into the hotel, pausing to shout at the hurt student, "Help's coming."

The *wah-wah* sirens of the *polizia* whined, echoing up from the street.

Inside, Harpal descended one floor and sprinted along a corridor, picked a room facing the back of the building at random, and hammered on the door.

No answer.

Harpal shot the lock off, the gun clicking empty. He kicked the door in and replaced the mag as he hustled through to the French doors. A second lock to shoot.

Ears ringing after the two reports in a confined space, he stepped out onto the balcony.

It wasn't much of a view, just an extension of the hotel's parking lot and a few spires and the top of a dome over the modern buildings. He looked both ways, locating Jules atop the clothing shop.

Sure enough, someone had formed a makeshift bridge using a bed frame to reach the shop's third floor from two windows away.

Then, up above, Jules fell away from the roof and descended into open space.

What the...?

It took Harpal a second to spot that the line was secured on a railing, and as Jules plummeted, his speed reduced rather than increased.

That elastic thing again.

Show-off.

Harpal holstered his Glock, swung a leg over the balcony barrier, and used a drainpipe to descend as fast as he dared, in the manner of a sticky fireman's pole. As soon as he hit the parking lot, he dashed toward where he guessed Jules would land.

Up a narrow backstreet, not wide enough for a car, he emerged onto a busy, sunlit thoroughfare where a gaggle of pedestrians scattered away from something that had spooked them.

Harpal put his head down and sprinted, glimpsing Jules as he crossed a road chock-a-block with small cars whizzing in and out of gaps. Horns *parped* and brakes squealed. Men and women leaned out of the vehicles to swear and make lewd gestures. And when the traffic all but ground to a standstill, Jules continued in a straight line, vaulting over the vehicles.

Harpal darted between the cars and mopeds, assuming Jules had a bead on Horse, although why they didn't have a getaway vehicle waiting, Harpal couldn't say.

Then he saw why.

The four people they chased were heading for a piazza, a wide-open stretch with a fountain at the center, lorded over by a huge slab of a building, four stories high and a dozen windows wide.

Motorbikes waited. Six of them. Big beefy Ducatis. Each a Monster 1200 R with an L2 Testastretta 11 Dual Spark R motor—ninety-seven pounds per feet of torque, 160 horsepower. Harpal knew his bikes, and these were works of art to be used as getaway vehicles.

They'd expected to kill everyone and walk calmly away to this staging point.

Jules flipped himself off a car's hood, then somersaulted over a speeding moped with two women astride it, causing them to veer crazily to a stop. They yelled obscenities in Italian.

As Harpal hurtled past them, he said, "*Scuzi.*"

Horse and his men reached the bikes. Horse had a satchel crossed tightly over his body. He looked back and shouted something that Harpal didn't catch, and the two gunmen peeled away on foot.

A hundred yards ahead of Harpal, Jules spoke to him via the earbud. "Cover me. I'm going for the manuscript."

Harpal knew Dan would chew him out if he opened fire near civilians, but the pedestrians had already spotted the submachine guns on Horse's goons and were clearing the piazza in a panicked stream.

"Now, please," Jules said.

Harpal drew the Glock and aimed. Waited for a long gap in the to and fro. He fired at one guy, taking him in the leg, which dropped him flat to the ground.

Horse made it to a bike and kicked off the stand. Jules snapped his arm forward, and Horse looked down angrily. The tire was flat.

Another knife, courtesy of Jules.

Horse pulled his own gun, firing over and over, forcing Jules sideways behind the low fountain wall.

Harpal used a trash can for cover.

Screams filled the air, the evacuation now a stampede, bodies fleeing in both directions.

And then Horse was away. On another bike, he sped across the piazza in a cloud of tire smoke.

"Shoot him," Jules demanded. "But don't kill him."

Harpal moved sideways, but he was pinned by the final merc. "I'm kind of stuck."

Jules unraveled something else from his jacket and tossed a series of small cylinders at the gunman's hiding spot on the other side of the fountain. The flashbangs detonated in quick succession, causing the guy to stagger.

Harpal popped out and shot him in the head.

"You killed him," Jules said angrily.

Horse was right: *a hippie-dippie respect for human life.*

Both Harpal and Jules dashed forward for the only bike left standing, where Giovani cowered nearby. Alive. Uninjured.

Harpal lifted his leg over to sit astride the beast and fired her up. The engine growled through him, and he was almost looking forward to pursuing a professional killer on it. Jules got on behind. No arguing about who was driving. Harpal engaged the clutch, hit first gear, and ramped up the accelerator. They shot off, hitting sixty in less than three seconds.

Jules clung around Harpal's waist, leaning into the bends with him to keep the balance even. They roared between cars along the main road, the shops and monuments flying by, yet the deaths of the men back at the hotel gnawed at Jules.

In some situations, he treated killing the same way vegetarians occasionally treat meat eaters: *you go ahead, but it's not for me.* But in this case, Jules was a part of it.

Was I complicit?

A vegan working the conveyor belt in an abattoir?

Within a minute, as Harpal accelerated up Lungotevere dei Sangallo alongside the River Tiber, Jules forced the existential questions to the back of his mind and concentrated on the fleeing motorcycle that was shimmering into view through the haze of exhaust smoke. The San Giovanni dei Fiorentini loomed, the small basilica resplendent in the afternoon sun, a long bend in the road approaching at a crossroads—one artery to the left toward Vatican City, the other to the right, heading deeper into the Roman center. Jules guessed Horse would push straight on north, toward the airport.

Ten yards from the junction, their target glanced back at them. And leaned right, taking the less intelligent option.

Denser traffic.

More cops.

Was he rendezvousing with someone?

Leading them into a trap?

Harpal didn't seem to share Jules's concern as he dropped a gear and sped up, cutting between columns of vehicles with the sort of abandon Jules used to employ. But the adrenaline-soaked thrill of the chase was just training wheels. Now Jules had a target.

And it was getting away.

Because Horse was smart. Way smarter than anyone of his appearance ought to be. Like calling Jules on his bluff that he didn't care about the bystanders getting hurt, then using the adjoining building because, undoubtedly, Dan would have set up an ambush once Bridget was safe. And the backup escape option.

It was all planned.

Yet, the street he turned onto was not a prime escape route. Nor a great place for a trap.

Decelerating to take the same corner as Horse, Jules tapped Harpal on the shoulder and yelled, "Stop!"

"What?"

They could barely hear one another over the engine and the whoosh of wind, but the tech allowed Harpal's voice to crackle in Jules's ear. They were out of jamming range.

"The manuscript," Jules replied at his normal volume, assuming the throat mic would pick it up. "He don't have it. It's back at the Palazzo Farnese."

"Where?"

"The place we got the bike, the Palazzo... forget it. Just go back to the fountain."

"Guys?" came Charlie's voice. "You okay? What's that noise?"

Jules loosened his grip, straining to keep the annoyance from his tone. "The noise of the manuscript getting away. Harpal, *stop the damn bike.*"

They took the corner, but without any sign of slowing. He wasn't going to listen.

Jules let go of Harpal. Pushed back minutely, enough to dismount. The soles of his feet hit the tarmac, but he was already running. He tucked, rolled, scraped his shoulder blade, and sprang up. With a midair flip, he righted himself.

As the Ducati tore away, he took his telescopic baton and unscrewed one end as he trotted to the sidewalk where a line of mopeds was parked. People gawked, having just seen him stroll casually away after falling from a motorcycle.

"Jules?" Harpal said. "What the hell did you just do?"

"He don't have the book." Jules shook his stick, and a multi-tool landed in his palm—a grittier take on a Swiss Army knife designed for handymen. "He went the wrong way. He's just keeping us busy. Charlie, you there?"

"Still here. Where's Dan? Bridget?"

"They got away but probably hanging 'round the jamming zone. Cops're all over it." Jules nudged the handlebars of one motor scooter after another, each so far having locked its steering correctly. "They run, they'll look suspicious. Right now, you gotta get eyes on the Palazzo Farnese." One moped's handlebars swung from side to side. He crouched beside it and levered the ignition housing open with the screwdriver on his multi-tool. "Eyes on the piazza?"

"Got it," Charlie said. "Cops've cordoned it off. What do you need?"

Jules stripped two wires and sparked them together, starting the motor. "Giovani Trussot. The cops got him?"

"Not that I can see. Toby?"

"Here." Toby sounded distracted. "They're engaged in counterterrorism measures. Securing the public, establishing a perimeter. No mention on the radio of anyone that sounds like Giovani."

"Running a search."

Jules didn't wait for the results. He took off on the moped using a cycle lane against traffic and turned correctly onto the main road that would take him to the airport.

CHAPTER
TWENTY-ONE

Jules ignored Toby's and Charlie's demands to turn around and regroup. The manuscript was leaving the country. With Toby, Dan, and Bridget stuck inside the security cordon and Harpal still circling in search of Horse, Jules couldn't even use the powerful bike to speed out to the private airport. He considered stopping to pick up another, but high-end bikes were usually fitted with alarms and LoJack, which could be activated remotely, and a car might get stuck in traffic, so he continued with what he had.

When he was forced to refuel, he bought a crash helmet, partly to blend in, but also because he had no idea whether his image had been captured on cameras that the *polizia* might access. Back on the road, when it became clear he was not going to turn around, the LORI guys begrudgingly cooperated.

Charlie said, "That piazza with the fountain, your whole episode was caught on camera, but it's all automated, so no clear view of you guys. Or Horse for that matter. I'll wipe it and do a video-site and social media sweep soon, make sure no camera phones got you."

"Not helpful right now," Jules said. "Tell me something that matters."

Charlie made a noise like the audible bristling of fur. "Back when you boys took off, I got Giovani leaving the scene. He's carrying something up his shirt. Can't see it perfectly, but it's the right size you described. He's out of frame now." Typing. Clicks. "Okay, there we go. Police car pulls up on the edge of the piazza... I'm running the plates while I watch... he hands the package over... car's gone. Okay, get this. It's not a police car. Written off by a scrapyard two months ago. Must've been repurposed."

"Right," Jules said. "They knew we'd follow Horse, so they had Giovani pass on the manuscript. We gotta assume they'll want it outa the country ASAP. Anyone wanna back me up at the airport?"

"Negative." Dan's voice now joined them. "We regroup. We don't rush headlong into this."

"Negative? *Negative* right back at ya. We know he's at a private airfield twenty miles from Rome International cause that's where the shell company's flight is scheduled to leave. Once they're gone, they're *gone*. We can't track him on a private plane. This is our only chance to get what we need."

No one spoke. Jules wasn't about to break the silence. He'd made his point.

"I'll go," Harpal said. "I'm mobile already."

"I said *negative*," Dan hissed. "We regroup. We do the intel. No full-frontal assaults on an airport when the whole of Rome thinks a terrorist incident just hit."

Another pause before Charlie came back on the comms. "Giovani went home."

"Home?" Dan sounded confused. "Where's home?"

"The hotel. Tracing his last movements on the street cams, he was headed back in that direction."

"Then that's where we should be," Toby said. "But let's see if we can avoid the police. Jules, may I make one final plea for you to stop what you are doing? It's reckless, and may end up costing us more than we gain. Valerio is not a person to underestimate."

"Nor am I." Jules slipped the phone from his pocket and tapped the command to kill the earbud and shut out further chatter, then focused on the road, hammering the scooter at full speed —a little below fifty miles per hour.

He was on his own for now.

———

Off-air, in the café opposite the Vatican View Hotel, Toby asked Dan to take it easy on Harpal after he'd lost first Jules, then Horse. They needed clues as to where Saint Thomas's manuscript might be headed, and Toby's only remaining play was an unlikely one: Giovani Trussot himself. They moved from the café to a stakeout from the SUV up the street, where it didn't take them long to spot him.

Yes, Giovani returned to the hotel, to his bar. Dan posited that the instruction must have come from Horse and that, once the package was secure, Giovani would hear from his wife's kidnappers. However, the *polizia* had arrived and swarmed the place, not to mention the paramedics and the Rome coroner, so Giovani retreated out the back—watched by Harpal in the buzzing lobby —and soon pulled out in a Fiat Punto.

Dan had said little since rendezvousing with Toby, a faraway stare telling Toby not to speak to him unless absolutely necessary. The man took failure personally, and there was little anyone could say or do until he, in his own mind, made amends. So, with Toby and Bridget as silent passengers, Dan pulled out after the little Fiat.

Through thick traffic, exacerbated by the shut-off streets, they tailed Giovani's car from six vehicles back. When Dan finally spoke, it was to voice a concern. "We're too visible. Harpal, you still got that bike?"

"Already on it," Harpal's voice replied. "I'm ten behind you."

Toby tried to spot him in the passenger mirror.

Dan said, "And who ordered you to do that?"

"I used my initiative," Harpal said.

"And what I needed you to—"

"Can you two cut it out?" Bridget interrupted. "You need Harpal to swap with you in case Giovani makes us. Let him get on with it."

She'd been quiet since the shootout. Hugging her knees to her chest in the car, her hand over her mouth one minute, clasped in the other the next, and a frown bearing the lion's share of expressions. She might well have been in shock. Yet she *said* she was fine, so Toby had to trust in that.

Harpal trundled past them and pushed on. They'd know where Giovani was headed soon enough.

Security wasn't great at the airfield. Not *nonexistent*, but definitely not strong. As the sun dipped away, Jules stripped to his midnight bodysuit and gained access by circling to the north and running cross-country for a half mile into a densely populated wood. It was chilly. The grass between the tree line and the fence was untended and allowed him to crawl right up to the barrier. Using his multi-tool, he snipped two vertical lines three feet apart in the wire mesh, peeled it up, and slithered under. When the flap dropped behind him, a person would only notice if they were looking for it specifically. Which no one appeared to be doing.

Four hangars large enough for medium-size passenger planes.

Six smaller ones dotted around.

High-end private jets parked in the distance, reminding Jules of the mopeds by the side of the road.

Floodlights illuminated pretty much the whole airport.

A single runway.

The majority of security congregated at the gate with cameras pointing out on the surrounding fence, all of which he'd avoided. But this was a working airport, so there were around a dozen more cameras spread between the runway, what Jules assumed to be an office, and the various hangars. Not blanket coverage.

Safe in the darkness of the outer shadows, Jules watched for another ten minutes, wishing he'd brought binoculars, then glided along the perimeter until he came level with one of the smaller hangars. This was the only one with no label, but two people circled it, dressed in overalls and orange high-visibility vests.

From the way they carried themselves, Jules could tell they were armed. When he sneaked nearer, he concluded they had holsters at both shoulder and ankle. They stayed separate, though, not a pair.

Five hundred meters of tarmac stood between him and the hangar's side door.

The men replicated their route every three minutes. But not every time. Sometimes it took a touch longer or a touch less.

That meant the side door was unattended for a *maximum* of ninety seconds at a time, and a *minimum* of eighty.

One minute, twenty seconds.

The world record for a two-hundred-meter sprint is 19.19 seconds, and Jules was some way behind that at twenty-four seconds, but that was under optimal conditions. Five hundred meters is two hundred multiplied by 2.5, so 2.5 times twenty-four is an even sixty.

One minute.

Add on ten seconds for muscle fatigue, lack of energy thanks to not eating for the past six hours, and to cater for the untested running surface.

A ten-to-twenty-second margin of error over five hundred meters was acceptable.

One more test to be sure.

The first man passed the target area. As soon as he left that side of the hangar, Jules started counting. The second one strolled by, a clipboard in hand for the sake of the casual observer. Eighty-six seconds after his colleague left.

One more.

The second man feigned observing something and headed the same way as his fellow guard. Ninety-one seconds until the first guy showed again.

Okay. This is it.

The first guard was less subtle. He smoked as he moved, bobbing his head as if listening to music as he rounded the corner out of sight.

Jules launched.

It wasn't his best time out of the blocks, but over this distance, it shouldn't matter. His feet pounded, thighs and ankles in sync, torso high, arms pumping. He was now exposed should any random employee or passenger happen to look that way. His shadow splayed in several directions at once because of the various floodlights.

He made the door in sixty-six seconds, a pleasing time given his poor start.

His hand wrapped around the knob. Turned. It was locked.

In less than thirty seconds, a guard would reappear.

Giovani's apartment building proved difficult to break into. Dan scouted it and found ten stories of luxury and alarms, so he suspected the Fiat that Giovani had driven here was part of his cover: a guy who ran a bar, not an international fence for smuggled antiquities. That he parked a block away rather than behind his building's gates added to that theory. Whatever, Dan was going to make someone pay for what happened today. He didn't care who.

Harpal had gone rogue; Bridget was inexperienced; as for Jules, if Dan ever saw that guy again, he'd slap him so hard his head would fly back in time.

What really drilled into the meat of Dan's throat, though, were his own errors. At least when he served in the Rangers, mistakes leading to casualties were usually due to poor intelligence received, not his own judgment. Not falling for a clear stalling tactic; the Italian bartender-come-middleman had put on a genial show until Horse and Valerio's other people were in position.

Now Bridget had come up with an idea. Dan didn't like it, but he was fresh out.

She'd stripped to her underwear in the SUV and changed into Dan's shirt. He watched as she mussed up her hair and trotted over the road to the street entrance. She hit each buzzer in turn until she found someone who spoke a smattering of English, then presented herself to the camera so they could see her in full: a beautiful young American redhead in a man's shirt and—it seemed from her appearance—nothing else.

"I'm with Gio," she drawled. "On the top floor? I came down for a smoke, and he's in the shower. Please let me in. I swear I won't say anything."

She put her hands together in prayer, and the English-speaker released the door.

Jules wouldn't make it back to the perimeter, and he'd left his lock pick with his luggage on LORI's jet.

Ten seconds max, maybe five until the first guard sauntered around that corner.

Jules looked up: corrugated steel outer, sheer face, nowhere to go.

So he followed the same route as the guards took, gambling that the second man's slightly quicker pace would mean he was alone. He reached the end in three seconds, nipped around the corner, and froze.

The man patrolling the building was about to turn the next corner, but hadn't made it yet.

Jules resisted the urge to pin himself flat to the wall. Sudden movement was worse. All he shifted were his eyes, calculating his escape, his run to the fence, his dash through the woods...

The man continued out of sight, and Jules breathed.

But he only had a few seconds' grace. He didn't think following the guy again was a good idea, a sort of farcical sneaky approach with too many variables.

Up again?

Yes!

There was a window ten feet up. Jules was almost six feet and could easily jump four feet off the ground. All he needed to add a couple of inches was a running start.

He took a throwing knife from his belt, bit it between his teeth, backed away far enough, and then ran forward. He pushed off, swung his arms up for maximum height, landed his rubber soles silently on the wall, and pushed himself up the final inches to catch the ledge one-handed.

The window measured a couple of feet, and as expected, it just required him to stab his blade into one side to flick it open. He pulled himself up. But he did so too quickly.

Desperate to swing his legs inside, he didn't concentrate on his hands and caught the throwing knife on the frame, fumbling it so it dropped from his grasp.

Metal landing on the hard walkway would give him away for sure.

He snatched at the air. The blade tumbled end over end until it was away from him. Falling. He moved to catch it with one foot, but that was useless as it might stab him, so he angled his toes inward and kicked.

The knife flew out over the tarmac, just far enough to land noiselessly on the grass beyond.

It took a lot to raise Jules's heart rate, but that had done it.

He wriggled inside, focusing on a calm center, and once his pulse steadied, he found himself in a bare office lit only by the ambient glow from outside.

Prowling over to the door, he cracked it open, finding a dark mezzanine with a thin carpet over the metal shell and a handrail overlooking a Gulfstream jet. The hangar floor was almost devoid of the usual business of setting up for flight, meaning it was already prepped.

A suited man with a shock of blond hair and a yellow complexion paced beside a metal-topped table where a woman of approximately fifty turned an object over in her hands. She laid it on a wad of crinkled brown paper. It was the package from Giovani, unwrapped, the book lying right there. The woman wore white cotton gloves and a jeweler's loupe wedged to her eye.

She said, "It is real." Her Italian-accented voice echoed up into the metal building. "The age is correct, and I believe it is the item you want."

"And you can translate it?" Valerio Conchin asked, still pacing.

"I think so. Most. But you must free my husband. I am doing nothing until then."

Valerio appeared satisfied, but it was hard to discern a smile or annoyance from Jules's distance. Valerio pulled out a phone and dialed. Held it to his ear. "Horse, you may inform Mr. Trussot that his wife is cooperating. Disarm the bomb, but—" Valerio exhaled through his nose as he listened. Turned his body to the woman. "Disappointing." He shrugged. "Is the new kid with them?" Pause to listen. "He intrigues me. I wonder if he might be important." Another pause. "Yes, that glowing thing… it might be nothing, but…" Valerio paused again, this time in thought. "You mentioned the Trussots have grown-up children living nearby?"

The woman stood, hands waving no before her chest, her face strained.

"Okay, do it," Valerio said. "Then leave some men with the daughter and get back here. Tina will translate for us in the air." He hung up and gestured for Tina Trussot to sit. When she shakily sat back in her chair, he said, "I'm sorry, but we won't be disarming the bomb in your apartment after all. Your husband is consorting with a *really* annoying bunch of people, so…" He slapped his hands together. "*Boom.* You're a widow."

Tina made a noise like a dog being kicked. "No. Please…"

"But the good news is… new hostage! So it's like this now: we won't kill your daughter *if* you cooperate. Okay?"

Before he could observe the woman's reaction, Jules ducked

back into the office. Who else could be with Giovani Trussot right now? The people who stole the manuscript from Windsor?

Or, more likely...

Jules reactivated his earbud, hoping the cell phone network connected out here. It did. Just took a second. "Anyone hear me?"

No answer.

"Anyone?"

A rattle sounded. Charlie's voice: "I can. Is that you, Jules?"

"Yeah. I gotta ask, are the others meeting with Giovani Trussot? At his apartment?"

"Yes. Dan and Toby agreed they couldn't get into the airfield—"

"Well *I* did. I been listening. Giovani's being watched. There's a bomb in his place, and it's about to go off."

"What?"

"Betcha they're jamming the cell signal again. Ask 'em."

Movement on the other end. Then, "They can't hear me. I can't warn them."

CHAPTER
TWENTY-TWO

The penthouse elevator required a keycard, which was less of a problem than the front gate. Picking that would have taken far too long, even for Harpal, but Charlie had engineered eleven cards of differing sizes for such electronic measures. Each was chipped with administrator privileges for the eight biggest manufacturers and software providers of elevators in Europe and the US, meaning Harpal simply had to find the correct one to override security.

Sure enough, Giovani's building owners had opted for a top-five specialist.

The elevator hummed to a stop on ten. Dan's and Harpal's Glocks were already drawn. The doors parted.

They stepped out into a thickly carpeted hallway. As expected, the elevator split open into the apartment, a pair of double doors directly ahead. Not the type to be dead bolted or armored.

Bridget and Toby held back, while Harpal followed Dan's silent orders.

Dan kneeled by the handles that met in the middle. Nodded. Harpal took that to mean there was no need to pick them. Dan rose and, yes, drew back his leg and kicked forward. The door burst inward.

Harpal trailed in Dan's wake, splitting off exactly as the ex–military man rehearsed with him many, many times. While Dan arrowed right into the open-plan living area, Harpal pealed left into a spacious kitchen with a massive stove and long, stone-topped counters. Very clean. Bright.

"Clear."

Harpal turned and followed his gun out into the next corridor, delving into the dark and throwing open the first door. A bedroom. He checked under the silk-adorned bed and in the walk-in closet. No one.

"Clear."

Back out and down to the next room. Another bedroom, a spare by the looks of it, draped in netting and fine cotton linen. He performed the usual sweep.

"Clear."

Then it was the corridor again, which circled around to the living area that Dan was taking on. When Harpal poked his gun and head around the corner, he found a sunken section with couches and chairs, an open fireplace in the middle with no flames, and the upper level was dotted the latest technology—curved TVs, a digital stereo, two impressive computers at desks with state-of-the-art monitors. What was missing, however, was any artwork.

The owner was seated on one of the cream leather sofas with his hands linked atop his head, Dan perched on the end, holding the man at gunpoint. "You just ignoring me again?"

"I didn't hear you," Harpal said.

"Updates, Harpal. Key here is communication."

"I called 'clear' in every room."

Dan held still. Flicked his eyes to Giovani. "You got a cell jammer in here?"

Giovani shook his head.

From the elevator, Toby and Bridget approached tentatively.

"It's okay." Harpal beckoned them. "Just him."

"We couldn't hear you, and you can't hear us." Toby indicated his ear.

"They're coming," Bridget said, "aren't they?"

Dan gripped his gun. A half smile. Like he was dying for the opportunity to prove something. "Yeah. They're coming."

Jules skirted the edge of the aircraft hanger's mezzanine, trying not to think about the fate of Bridget and her gang.

For the first time in his life, Jules felt bad about going his own way. He should have waited, brought them, *showed* them he was right instead of shutting them down and taking off. Nothing he could do about it, though, so he had to press ahead with his own business, hoping Charlie found a way to get in touch with them.

One ex-girlfriend called him a sociopath, but that wasn't true; he felt sadness. He wanted to explore the notion of friendship, especially since he was so close to his goal, and Bridget was a smart one. Toby was dull but smart, someone Jules could probably hold a conversation with once he trained the old man to temper his unnecessary filler chat. Harpal was interesting enough, and Charlie knew her own mind, which was always a plus, while Dan was a closed-off alpha who would likely never really warm to Jules, no matter what. Four out of five wasn't bad.

On the mezzanine, no one had turned on the lights, but he wasn't invisible. He stuck to the walls, making slow progress. The stairs were out because he would simply emerge into the lit section. Neither could he leap out onto the jet itself for fear of the noise and the sudden shift in weight.

So—inventory.

Three throwing knives.

His multi-tool with—among other things—snips, screwdrivers, Allen wrenches, and pliers.

Cell phone routed through a satellite comms system.

He'd used all his flashbangs, and his bungee cord was dangling from a low-end clothing boutique above Rome.

Which left an option he didn't like: jump down, beat up Valerio, steal the manuscript.

The possibility of silence while doing that was slim, but not impossible. If Valerio raised the alarm, Jules would be facing two armed mercs of indeterminate skill; they might be local knuckle-draggers hired at the last minute, or they could be former Navy SEALs.

Big risk.

Valerio stood over the woman, Tina, who examined the first pages.

"I will be some time," the woman said glumly. "Coffee would help."

Valerio rocked on his heels and glanced around as if expecting a servant to pop up with a tray. When no one emerged, he shrugged, gave a mild chuckle, and turned with his hands in his pockets. Jules lost sight of him as he wandered beneath the mezzanine to a presumed kitchen.

A kettle started to boil.

The woman turned a page. Read for several moments. Made notes.

Jules hated guesswork, yet he couldn't help hypothesizing.

If Toby and Bridget were correct, Thomas commenced his ministering with this document already in place—his transcription of Herodias's stolen book concerning the bangle that her brother had gifted her. He then added to it as he learned more about the bangles that Philip had held on to for safekeeping. When Thomas discovered where it led him, he sent for the bangles. Then—because Philip was murdered in the meantime—he split them up.

The reasons were irrelevant. What mattered was that Thomas authored a document concerning his travels while in possession of the bangles. A document that was already partially written before he departed for Syria. Meaning the bulk of the earlier pages were nothing to do with Thomas's travels.

Conclusion?

The juicy business was at the back, perhaps even the location of the Mary bangle.

Either the prisoner did not know, or she was stalling intentionally.

The kettle clicked to a finish, and Jules listened to Valerio stirring a cup. Assuming Valerio would return at roughly the same angle he exited, Jules made a decision: he was going to drop the eight feet to the hangar's floor, render Valerio unconscious before he could raise the alarm, then swipe the book, and work out an exact escape route afterward.

That all rode on the notion that the Aradia bangle—the one belonging to Jules—was not present. If it were here, Jules would take it and Valerio could keep the damn book. Mission over.

Footsteps.

Jules crouched, hands on the rail. Waiting for that mop of blond to pass beneath him. He again ran through how fast he'd hit the floor, how he'd need to cushion it through bent knees, and the biology of how much pressure to exert on Valerio's carotids while applying a sleeper hold.

An engine's low growl accompanied the crunch of tires on loose stone, and a headlight swept into the hangar. Jules didn't need to see who was here; he recognized the noise. Horse killed the engine of the Ducati Monster 1200 and strode toward Valerio, who emerged carrying a steaming coffee cup. Horse now had a bandage poking out of his cuff, courtesy of Jules's blade, adding to the injury sustained in Prague.

"Is it done?" Valerio asked.

"Just waiting for confirmation," Horse replied. "Soon as we got the woman's kids in sight, we'll light the others up."

"I am cooperating," Tina Trussot said. "Please do not do this."

The two men looked at her. Horse deferred to Valerio, an air of sympathy about him.

Valerio shook his head. "Do it. Do it now."

Horse keyed his cell phone, held it to his ear, and stepped away toward the bike to speak.

Valerio leaned over the table and put the coffee down. He lowered his face to the same level as Tina's. His hand pressed down over the book, closing it. "We have to leave now. You're coming with us."

"But—"

"No, no." Valerio wagged his finger at her. "No buts. Just take this..." He slid the manuscript toward her. "Continue on the plane."

Jules couldn't simply drop in now, not with Horse there. And as Tina boarded Valerio's jet with the document, swiping it and running like the wind was suddenly so much harder.

Jules took in the space again just to be sure. On his second sweep, in the very top corner, he spotted a possibility. He slowly, silently retreated into the office and tapped his earpiece back on.

"Charlie? You there? I got an idea."

"You'll have to hold," Charlie replied. "I'm busy."

In her Greenwich home, Charlie Locke spun between three PCs. Phil was bathing Joan, the youngest of their three kids, while Alexander read a story to his older sister, Boadie. The den was part of their double garage, converted for just this purpose. She had paired the setup with the Demon Server in Brittany, but the original plan had been to program her bespoke IT project with algorithms that were supposed to perform most of her job for LORI without her physically being around.

It was no longer her world. Not after the scramble for historical artifacts and straight-up treasure hunting had intensified into a fight for people's lives. At one point, she found Toby planning an almost paramilitary operation, seeking to recruit the sorts of mercenaries contracted to Valerio Conchin's payroll and maybe even Colin Waterston's. That was the first time she quit the institute.

The second was when her lover—now her husband—almost died.

There had been other resignations and other one-last-jobs, but it wasn't until Bridget came on board and softened Toby's ambitions somewhat—or at least his outlook—that Charlie recommitted her skills, albeit part time. The Demon Server was one of only two demands.

First, allow her to develop algorithms for code breaking, facial recognition software to scrub LORI's images from the net, and the rendering of geographical imagery.

And second, to avoid the type of situation they'd been sucked into tonight—work that endangered her friends.

Once Jules hit her up with the fact a bomb was about to kill four of the best people she'd ever known, she performed some of her most intense work, hoping the kids' baths would stall Phil long enough for her to escape explaining why she was breaking her promise to him again.

It should all be behind her, yet she had to do this, contacting authorities via blind comms links, tracing the source of the jamming beacon, and tapping into someone's security feed in their home across the street to observe. The Internet of Things was wonderful for people like her; she could hack a toaster or a washing machine if she chose.

After calling the Italian emergency services and failing to find an English speaker, all she could do with regard to the police was issue an alert that terrorists were making bombs in the penthouse apartment where Giovani lived. She manufactured intelligence that appeared to be from Europol that an attack was imminent. Still, no squad of armed *polizia* had swarmed forth. So she tried something else.

Something that she didn't think could work, but it was her final shot.

Three minutes later, her screen filled with white light. The bomb had gone off.

CHAPTER
TWENTY-THREE

"Still nothing." Dan stepped away from the window, tension squirming through every limb.

Harpal kept his gun aimed down the elevator corridor. "Think they're waiting for us to come out?"

Toby had been watching the rear windows from the safety of the kitchen island in case the glass exploded inward. He called to them, "Nothing here either."

Dan had stashed Bridget and Giovani in the walk-in closet, the back of which opened into a panic room. All Giovani's camera feeds entered there although only the hard-wired signals remained. One of those was the roof, which looked empty. Bridget ran in every five minutes to tell Dan this, despite asking her to alert him only if contact was imminent, not that everything was fine.

He massaged his brow, the stiffness in his skin suggesting he'd been frowning for some time. "They're waiting for us to come out. We got the high ground, we got a swanky neighborhood. One gunshot, one phone call, the cops'll be here in minutes."

Bridget wandered in. A vacant expression this time, not the whirlwind of information as she had been the past three times.

"What?" Dan said.

"Come look at this." She twisted her head behind her and back again. "It's weird."

Reluctant to leave his post, he figured following her was quicker than getting her to talk. In the panic room, Dan found Giovani staring at the monitor, a cathode ray model that likely came with the room when it was installed circa 1985.

"So instead of the wide angle I instructed," Dan said, "you've zoomed in, narrowing the field of view and leaving us vulnerable. Nice."

It was one of the things he never got used to outside the army. When an officer or team leader says something, you do it. When tracing an ancient Hebrew map through a cave system, Bridget and Toby had an edge, but when defending a position against superior odds, Dan was king.

"No, look." Bridget tapped her fingertip on one of the apartments across the street. The camera didn't zoom particularly well, but it was clear what she meant. "Is this intentional?"

A light in the apartment turned on and off at semiregular intervals.

"Can't be," Dan said.

"What is it?" Giovani asked. "Is the power going to go out? I have a backup, I think, but—"

Dan held up a hand to cut him off, concentrating on the Morse code flashing. "o-m-b-o."

"Ombo?" Bridget said. "What's 'obmo' mean?"

"It's Charlie." Dan hustled Giovani from his seat and pushed them toward the exit. "o-m-b-o-o-m-b-o. Or b-o-o-m."

Bridget rushed out ahead. "Boom?"

Dan guided them harder, faster. "She probably means 'bomb.' Charlie sucks at Morse code." Back in the living space, he didn't stop. "*Out*. Now. *Evac*."

Neither Harpal nor Toby questioned him, just trailed behind quickly, Harpal bringing up the rear with his Glock pointed to the floor.

Dan pulled the fire alarm, which set off a wailing siren. Red bulbs flashed nearby. Then he hit the crash bar to the emergency stairs and took point as they dropped one flight after another. He urged them to remain one floor behind him in case Horse planned an ambush.

On the ground floor, Dan slipped into the lobby, other residents joining them, some milling around in their comfortable eveningwear, some in pajamas, a couple in suits looking incredibly annoyed. Not upscale enough for a doorman, it nonetheless boasted impressive faux-marble fittings and a solid bank of mailboxes. Dan was about to take charge, using Giovani as a translator, when a thunderous roar shook the building.

Lights flashed, the floor trembled. People fell. Others ran out the front but quickly ducked back inside as debris rained down.

Smoke and dust billowed as everyone froze, awaiting a signal that they were safe.

When the shower outside ceased, residents ventured out a handful at a time. Dan took the others with him, keeping low, using the crowd as cover. After a moment of quiet, he led them farther into the street, virtually dragging Giovani as he wafted at the remnants of the gray dust cloud hanging in the air.

He could just about make out that the top floor was gone. There weren't many flames, but a couple licked the night air. The floor below the penthouse was toast too, and Dan hoped they'd acted quickly enough to get everyone clear.

The racket of emergency vehicles closed in.

Dan led the group back to their car, a block away, eyes peeled for tails or loitering individuals. He saw no one. After a swift but thorough check under the SUV, Dan unlocked it, and everyone scrambled inside.

"What now?" Bridget asked.

"My wife," Giovani said.

"The airplane." Toby wiped his face with a handkerchief, shaking. "Let's get out of here before our faces appear on a wanted poster."

· · ·

With Charlie on radio silence, Jules had little choice. Not this close to recovering the bangle. He would jump down on the plane, go for Valerio with a blow to the head rather than a sleeper hold, then take his chances against Horse. A couple of knives should even the odds somewhat.

Charlie's sudden transmission paused his plan. "Jules, you still there?"

"Yes," he said, "I'm here."

"The team got out okay. They're heading to the Lear. They need to get out of the country. Or at least back to Sicily."

"I'm glad." He meant it, but pushed away any positive feelings in exchange for direct action. "You know the airfield I'm at? Where Valerio landed?"

"Yes?"

"Can you access its emergency systems? I need a distraction."

Typing accompanied her reply. "You and Dan should hang out sometime. Compare notes."

"Is that how Welsh people say yes?"

A brief laugh from Charlie preceded the speaker up in the top corner bursting with a static-filled *aaooooooga* alarm. It was what Jules had spotted before getting in touch with her, a chance to clear the hangar no matter how briefly. The same noise blasted across the other hangars, too.

Valerio, as hoped, rushed to the open doors, Horse with his gun drawn, as they both searched for the source of the problem.

As soon as their backs were turned, Jules hopped over the handrail, landed with no more than a scuff, then ran, ducked under the wing, and darted up the three steps into the Gulfstream's cabin.

Tina Trussot sat up in shock. "Who are you?"

"One of the good guys." Jules spotted the manuscript on her lap. "Your husband's safe. Cops'll be heading to your daughter's house."

"You will free me?"

"Just need that book."

"No." She clung to it. "Get me out of here."

He could take it from her easily, but that might be the wrong thing to do. Morally. If she put up a fight, he'd have to hurt her, and he couldn't do that to an innocent person.

He peered out the window, the angle favoring him so he could see Valerio and Horse discussing the situation with one of the men who had been circling the hangar.

Jules said, "To get you outa here, I'd have to sneak you past three trained killers and a guy who's probably less well trained but armed all the same."

"Then you can't have it." She hugged the book tighter, making the white cotton gloves pointless.

"Okay." Jules stepped forward, eyes on the window. Suddenly, he whipped his hand out and snatched the journal. "Sorry." He moved for the door.

Tina gawked down at her hands and then stood. "I will scream."

Jules halted. Sometimes, he hated being right.

He returned to face her, taking in the cabin. "Keep watch."

The alarm still blasted, and no one from Valerio's crew had so far returned. The perimeter was secure, so why would they?

"What you do?" Tina asked.

Jules set the book on a miniature mahogany desk attached to one wall beside a private cabin. He opened the book to the back pages, feeling their brittle edges, fearful of damaging them. The material still bent, though, and a remarkable sense of responsibility flowed through him, the rush of history physically gripping his chest.

Was this what Bridget felt about all those lost words?

Jules brushed it off, took out his phone, and opened the WhatsApp feature.

Tina joined him. "I ask you a question, tough guy."

"I'm getting the intel to people who can use it. Then I'll help you. Fair?"

"I watch for men."

He snapped a picture of the last page, a language he didn't understand. Hebrew, he could just about get the meaning of if not the nuances, Greek was easier, and Latin was a breeze. But he suspected this may be a form of Aramaic or Sanskrit, which he'd struggled with, but was currently studying. Languages were always useful.

Good job Bridget was a "human Rosetta Stone."

He checked that his photo showed the etchings clearly and transmitted it to Charlie since she'd have the best tools to sharpen the image. The next two pages had only words, which he sent off too, but the following ones showed diagrams that appeared to be basic representations of the two bangles. He snapped photos and turned the page. Then again. And dozens more, until the alarm died.

Then he turned the ancient pages faster. More writing. More photos. Another sketch. More digital signals into the ether.

"Men are coming," Tina said.

Jules crouched, shifted to a better angle, and peeked up.

Yes, all four men were returning: Valerio, Horse, and both guards.

Jules returned to the desk and closed the manuscript. "I really need this book."

Tina rushed to block his exit. "I tell you, I scream. Your friends have writing from back of the book. That is what you need, yes?"

"I don't know if I got all of it."

Jules detected voices now. The men were even closer.

Tina said, "You get me out. Free me."

Jules placed the manuscript down.

Judging by the casual nature with which Valerio and Horse were willing to bomb an apartment building, they would definitely murder this woman once she was no longer useful.

"I can't get either of us out now. Wait till we land. Then we run."

"Wait, you come with us?"

Jules opened the rear door to a galley kitchen with a second door that led to a unit resembling a studio apartment: a bed, a couch aimed at the TV, and an en suite bathroom. "Don't pretend. Don't stall too much. Work it chronologically. They don't know what they got here, not exactly. Do as you're told. When they get what they're looking for, they'll need you again. Tell 'em that. Stay alive, and I'll get you clear, soon as I can. Okay?"

"Why should I believe you?"

"Because in the time it took me to say all that I coulda knocked you unconscious and been outa here with the manuscript."

She held one hand in the other. Thinking. "Fine. But where will you hide?"

"I'll think of something. Now I gotta go. I need to make a couple of phone calls before we're outa range."

Jules entered the bedroom, its square footage taking up half the plane, and searched for somewhere to conceal himself. Under the bed was the obvious place, but no telling if he'd be spotted or if Valerio used it for other activities aside from sleeping. The bathroom might get used. All the furniture was bolted down, including the couch that stood a foot away from the wall.

It was tight, but Jules managed to squeeze himself into the gap between sofa and wall just before voices resonated outside the door. He wriggled farther down to where the back of the couch angled out a few more inches, allowing himself a tad more breathing space.

For this ridiculous situation to succeed, he needed to ensure Charlie received the photos, that the LORI brain trust could interpret them, and that this next bangle could be obtained without Valerio getting there first. That required brief conversations conducted in a low voice through the bone-conducting earpiece.

Once satisfied, he turned his cell phone off and, lying on his back behind the opulent leather sofa, he had little choice but to meditate until the chance to escape presented itself.

PART FOUR

We didn't go to the moon to explore or because it was in our DNA or because we're Americans. We went because we were at war and we felt a threat.

—Neil deGrasse Tyson

I know where I'm going and I know the truth, and I don't have to be what you want me to be. I'm free to be what I want.

—Muhammad Ali

CHAPTER
TWENTY-FOUR

SICILY

After four hours with the twenty-six pages Jules fired off to Charlie, printouts of Saint Thomas's journal spread over the shiny dark wood table, Bridget should have been in heaven. An unknown pre-Christian language mixed with Aramaic? *Yes, please.* Bridget would literally have paid for the privilege of solving this.

However, as soon as Jules called everyone he needed to, he went dark. All he said about his location was that he'd be on Valerio's tail, wherever that led.

Still paranoid about using the tracker, she guessed.

After ditching Giovani to deal with the cops himself and advising him to be honest about his wife's whereabouts, Bridget and the others had flown to Sicily, where Alfonse granted them the use of his villa. He was out and about on business, and since Alfonse's main acquisition was to be the Mary bangle, they agreed there was no need to inform their paymaster of their failure yet. The manuscript was just a means to an end.

These days, most cell phone cameras rated alongside document scanners, so in almost every snapshot, the words and markings were legible. In some of the later ones, Jules was plainly rushing to ping as many clues to LORI as possible, so half an inch or so got cut off at the edge.

Oh, why aren't I holding the real thing right now?

The photos also printed the timestamp, so she reversed them to make the pile chronological. She read the words she already knew, jotting those down, and left spaces for those she didn't, like a massive, multi-page sudoku puzzle. Then the team began talking.

"You sure he'd have done it that way?" Dan asked.

"I can't be sure at all," Bridget replied. "But it's a logical assumption."

"Even in someone as reckless as Jules?"

Bridget looked up from the first photo. "He got us this."

"He's dangerous," Charlie said on the screen, conferenced in using a laptop webcam stationed in Alfonse's dining room. "So calm when you were in danger. Reminded me of someone waiting for the result of a TV poll to come in."

"Calm under fire." Toby eyed Dan across the room from where he prepped a coffee pot. "Not the worst trait I've come across."

"He's a control freak," Harpal said. "Remember when *I* first came on board? I know Dan and Charlie were fine with jumping out of planes and what have you, but we've entered hard-to-reach places using *wing suits*. I persuaded you all to race those sports cars in Germany after selling that necklace to the duke or whatever he was. You all loved it. Started to see why I go for the extreme sports instead of football. I think Jules is like that. Maybe he needs it."

"That makes him controlled?" Dan asked.

"That's what extreme sports are all about. He drops off buildings with a homemade bungee rope. He's leaping over vehicles, walls, all at full pelt. Apart from the speed of his mental calculations, it's all the same as the folks I hang around with when I'm not here."

"Wait," Charlie said. "You do other stuff?"

"Of course. Me and the girlfriend."

"You have a girlfriend?" Dan said.

Toby started pouring mugs of coffee. "We're getting away from the point. You're *all* correct. He's an oxymoron of the most intriguing kind." He poured the last of the coffee, picked up the tray, and made for the table. "A reckless control freak." He placed the tray at the end opposite the laptop.

Harpal selected a cup. "A useful asset or a disaster waiting to happen."

"So we win big or lose big," Dan said. "Great."

Bridget jumped to her feet. "Would you all *please* stop talking about him?"

Everyone stared.

Bridget said, "Right now, he's got Valerio Conchin in sight, and we don't have the first clue where he is or how much danger he's in. But he's in that danger to get us these photos, and I've nearly got a decent start. So please, if we can stop speculating, I might dig up some answers."

Silence.

Until Charlie said, "He only got us the photos so we'll help him get the bangle."

Bridget resumed her seat and found her place. "We don't know that. He might not be the awful person you all assume. Now, *please* give me some quiet."

VALERIO'S GULFSTREAM, AIRBORNE

Valerio Conchin was never a sickly child. Athletic and intelligent, he had straddled high school's social divide and thrived because of it. Without that combination of brains and brawn, he'd never have developed his first app or made his first million.

Weight loss and exercise were a fledgling fad when he launched Fit Freak, but the fad grew into a multibillion-dollar industry. Because Valerio was building from a solid base, his additions were a big splash in a big pond.

As an adult, though, he'd developed a rare liver condition

which might kill him at any second. On the other hand, he could live for another five or even ten years. It was not something he liked to think about, but on long, aimless flights, he couldn't help it.

He and Horse were sitting opposite one another in swivel chairs while the antique smuggler's wife pored over the manuscript stolen from Windsor. Valerio stared out into the night without seeing anything. "How much longer?"

Horse twisted toward the Trussot woman. When he came back, he said, "Hard to tell, boss."

"Not good enough."

Very rude of that amateur outfit trying to double deal them like that, but they'd paid the price. Shame, really; they were a gutsy bunch with plenty of big brains among them. At least that left the way open for Valerio to track down the kid who made the bangle glow.

Horse sat forward, elbows on his knees, and adopted a kinder tone. "Boss, you know I'm with you all the way on this, don't you?"

Horse picked his own terminology. He insisted on the name "Horse" rather than his given one, which Valerio had forgotten a while ago, and started calling Valerio "boss" about a year into his employ as a personal bodyguard. As he heard more and more private business, Horse interjected with ideas, and it soon became apparent that his military experience carried transferable skills to seeking out objects of potentially arcane origin. At some point, he also began acting as a counselor, and at an even more blurred moment in time, he graduated to friend. Without losing the paycheck, of course.

You know I'm with you all the way on this.

Valerio said, "I guess."

"So you gotta have faith here. What do we need?"

"The location of that second bangle."

"Right. I found you the intel on the Queen's manuscript.

Might be helpful, might not. We'll know soon. But you should rest."

Valerio nodded, his impatience softening somewhat. "Where are we headed?"

"The pilot's plotted a course back to Strionia near the Russian border and filed a flight plan. It was the least suspicious option, but we can divert mid-flight. If we don't have a location before we land, we'll refuel and take off as soon as we get a destination."

Valerio yawned. He'd been fighting fatigue for hours. It was a stressful business, and he didn't particularly enjoy kidnapping and murder. They were tools, like this Gulfstream or a trowel or a car or a gun. But if Giovani had obeyed instructions, he would still be alive.

Because men such as Valerio didn't become rich, powerful, and benevolent overnight. The riches were a result of his brilliance, the power had come from his riches spent well, and benevolence started as part of his cover. He grew to genuinely like and value charities and other good causes, ones that furthered humankind; they helped him prove to himself he was not a bad person. Not really. He only killed those who went against him, and it wasn't fun.

Fun was visiting an African village, meeting kids who'd benefited from his investment in a new pump system for their well.

Valerio smiled.

Yes, his acts of goodwill far outstripped those some might deem irresponsible or selfish; for instance, blowing up six people in an apartment building without considering the potential for collateral damage. Was it six? Of five? Or seven?

Didn't matter.

What did matter was that he continue his work for the good of the human race.

"I'm going to bed for a while," he announced, standing.

Horse nodded and shifted his legs aside.

Valerio made his way to the back of the plane, pausing by

Tina. He opened the door to the kitchen. "Can I get you anything? Coffee? A bite to eat?"

Tina froze in whatever she was writing. "Coffee. Strong."

Valerio waved a hand at Horse, who rose and acknowledged the request. Then Valerio went through the kitchen and into his bedroom, where he closed the door and flopped on his bed. He didn't bother to undress.

By the time he awoke, he might know the answer at long last.

SICILY

"Thomas left India," Bridget said, almost breathless as she triple-checked her work and came to the same conclusion. "Northwest, to be precise."

"What do we have?" Toby asked.

Since Bridget demanded peace and quiet to work the language, Charlie had muted her connection while Dan ditched his coffee and went to lie down. Harpal played a video game in another room, and Toby refreshed his already-impressive knowledge of Saint Thomas by accessing as many resources as he could. Not easy when only using the internet. Too much misinformation, not like the source texts.

Still, Bridget supposed it was better than nothing.

"I'm not entirely sure," she said to the team, who had now gathered again. Charlie was back online. "It's partly Aramaic, partly what might be Hindi, but must be a precursor to that. Harpal?"

Harpal looked at the page in her hand—number twenty-one. "Yes, it looks kind of like Hindi."

"You recognize anything?"

"No, I only speak a bit because of family. Read and write enough to keep them happy. These make no sense to me. At all."

"Really? You're not curious enough about your heritage to become fluent?"

Harpal stepped back. "Nah, I leave that to my parents. Arabic,

I'm fine with, pretty good with the Chinese dialects, and Russian of course. I'm all about the future."

Toby shook his head. "What an odd career choice, then." He looked at one of the three pages featuring illustrations, the first showing an arched door. The notations were in the unknown language. "Will you be able to decipher it?"

"There's all sorts here." Her finger ran over the words written by a true historic figure, the real Saint Thomas. "Some of it is almost a stream of consciousness. No real narrative, just his feelings on aspects, like... like he wasn't making sense to himself. He mentions forging history, receiving power, ultimate knowledge."

"Common themes in those days. A major religion was being birthed after all."

"I've also got this symbol repeating, and this one." She pointed to one glyph, a circle with a short break at the bottom like a tight letter C facing down that showed a dot in the middle, then another character of nearly identical shape, this one with the break in the C facing up. "It stands out because the rest appears to be a written language, whereas this symbol is more like a hieroglyph."

Toby frowned. "Indus."

"Pardon me?" Dan said.

"Indus," Bridget answered. "Exactly what I was thinking. They had spoken language back then, but not much in the way of writing. At least not letters and words and sentences like we use."

"More like Egyptians?" Harpal asked.

"Kind of. The Egyptians were more literal in their writing. It didn't always translate to the spoken word. Indus did. The spoken language was translated around 3,000 BC."

Toby held up a finger in his point-of-order way. "That's the earliest *discovery* of the language being used. In its *complete* form. It may have been developed earlier."

"Yes, thank you, Toby. My point is... this was *copied*. Translated from something else, then transcribed. The only reason to use an out-of-place symbol in the middle of a sentence is if there's no direct translation or it needs to be incredibly specific."

"Like a name?" Charlie suggested.

"Or a unique object. Judging by the shapes, they mean one bangle or the other."

"They couldn't just write 'bangle' or 'bracelet'?" Dan said.

"The only reason they wouldn't is if... if they knew they were special." Bridget wasn't sure how long her brow had been furrowed, but it was starting to ache. She relaxed her skin and rubbed it. "Other than that, I've only got guesswork to offer."

Toby patted her on the back. "Your educated guesses, my dear, are better than most peer-reviewed theories. Let's hear it."

"Most of the additional pages are Aramaic, which is Thomas's... travel journal for want of a better phrase. He's talking about places and people, and I should be able to translate quickly. But this Hindi script... it was written by someone who spoke a two-thousand-year-old version of whatever came before Hindi. I *think*, and this is the guessing part, that the author was *translating* Indus."

"Could the author have been Thomas himself?"

Bridget focused on the words and the vastly differing languages and forms. "They're too dissimilar. It's like comparing your handwriting to a drawing of a car."

"But you can crack it, right?" Harpal said.

"Bearing in mind that Hindi only dates back a thousand years, we either need a Hindi entomology expert, or... I'll need more coffee."

VALERIO'S GULFSTREAM, AIRBORNE

Tina Trussot had been obedient, which was good. Valerio was still going to kill her, but it would be painless. A shot to the head. The back of the head so she wouldn't see it coming. Yes, that's kinder. Fear is a form or torture when it's drawn out by, say, staring down the barrel of a gun.

He woke an hour ago feeling exhausted. His arms barely moved, and his leg muscles were tight. His head throbbed. He called these periods of downtime "episodes" but his doctor explained how his body would fight against the disorder while he rested. It was the best time, after all. The injections kept the cancer-like condition under control, and pills alleviated the symptoms, but most of his days were spent as any other. Albeit with yellow skin.

That was what irked Valerio the most. Not the fatal nature of Fybert's syndrome, but that it first manifested in his liver. While they had halted its progress, the initial damage was now irreversible without a complete transplant, and because Valerio was special in many ways, including his blood type, a donor was unlikely to appear soon.

He had, of course, explored the possibility of simply *taking* a liver from someone less beneficial to the world, but it had proved more difficult to locate both a viable donor and a surgeon willing to work under such conditions. Again, kidnapping a family member and forcing someone to perform the operation was a possibility, but when he calculated the risk of a surgeon working out of sheer fear, it became too much. Especially since the yellow skin was mostly cosmetic.

Besides, a transplant would not save Valerio's life; Fybert's could only be slowed, not cured.

As he lay there deciding whether to move his aching body, he considered his dedication to what his father called "these eccentric quests." Clues to medicine that the modern world had long forgotten or written off. After eight failed attempts at tapping into ancient knowledge, perhaps it was time to consider the horrible procedures that would extend his life. Maybe they'd be worth it for a handful of extra years.

"No." Valerio sat up, his hips creaking with the effort, shoulders tight and painful.

He had seen enough to believe an alternative answer existed. Only three months ago, he had touched a staff they tracked down in South America, fixed into an altar located within an unremark-able temple beneath the jungle canopy. It had seemed a nothing location at first, grave robbers having stripped it bare centuries ago. All except the staff. Made of gold, it stood eight feet tall, embedded in a stone slab covered in slashes that indicated hundreds of years of sacrifices.

Valerio wondered immediately why it had not been looted along with everything else, an object referenced in not one but *four* conquistador texts as imbuing the priest with mystical powers, not least of which included healing. When Valerio touched it, his hand vibrated. He held it tight, and his whole arm and soon his body did too.

A cursed relic that would have kept superstitious grave robbers at bay.

He'd hollered and laughed and whooped with joy, but when his men dislodged it, the vibrations died. They inserted it back into its original housing, but nothing happened. Not even a tremble.

That triggered something of a tantrum, which Valerio was still embarrassed to recall.

Now, though, the painkillers on his bedside table relieved the aches while the jelly bean–size pills flushed his body of its attempt to combat Fybert's syndrome toe to toe and rolled him back to his pre-nap state. He dressed in a fresh shirt and splashed water on his face, then made his way out to the cabin.

Horse drank coffee while reading the Trussot woman's note-book. She slept in a flat chair with a woolen blanket over her.

The big man looked up and stood. "Boss, we have something."

Valerio waved Horse to sit and poured his own coffee. "A location?"

"I got guys making calls to confirm it. But turns out the language was known to one of Mrs. Trussot's colleagues. We set up a satellite link, and the initial translations are promising. Don't worry, I made sure she didn't get him a message or anything. To be honest..." He glanced at the woman's sleeping form. "I think she's as curious to solve it as we are."

"Academics." Valerio smiled as the coffee warmed him. "So, where are we headed?"

SICILY

"So," Bridget said, going over her notes one more time. "We don't have his exact starting location, but Thomas is traveling north from India, intending to split up the bangles. He relinquishes the Aradia bangle to a courier who will transport it to Carthage into the hands of Peter. But he also needs to find someone to send Mary's away too. He chose John. This second courier didn't show, though, so John never received the one meant for him."

"John?" Dan said.

"John the apostle, not John the Baptist."

"I knew that. Saint guy. Is Tommy sure about the other John's address?"

"Fascinating," Toby said. "John and Thomas were in conflict about many things, and there are strong hints that John actively tried to discredit Thomas. It is only mentioned in *John's* gospel that Thomas doubted the divinity of the risen Christ, not in any of the others. Interesting that he would choose John as the recipient."

"A bluff?" Harpal said. "Maybe they were buds, but didn't want anyone to know?"

Charlie answered before Bridget could. "And they just, what, lied in the Bible? I doubt that."

"More likely a prearranged drop-off," Toby said. "Or John was the only apostle whose location he knew. Or John's account was accurate, but the others didn't mention Thomas's doubt. Or the others were edited by the Roman Catholic Church, or John's was, or blah blah blah. Sorry. We could speculate all night, but let's concentrate on what we do know. Bridget."

"He preached," she continued. "As he had around Kerala and

beyond. They'd built their churches, so off he went on another pilgrimage. North then west. Across the steppes."

"Steppes?" Harpal said. "As in Genghis Khan country?"

"As in the steppe region, Genghis Khan's birthplace. Hundreds of years after Thomas visited, though. They never met, if that's what you're thinking. But speaking of Genghis Khan and his birthplace..." Bridget held up one of the sheets with a drawing on it. "This isn't a diagram. It's a map. Thomas's last destination before heading back to India... was Mongolia."

"Huh," Dan said. "I never been to Mongolia. Sounds like this'll be a treat."

CHAPTER
TWENTY-FIVE

VALERIO'S GULFSTREAM, AIRBORNE

"Mongolia? Is she sure?" Valerio asked once Horse relayed what Tina Trussot had translated so far.

"Sure as she can be." Horse dropped her notes on the desk next to the two-thousand-year-old manuscript. "Can't map the exact location, but—"

"Wake her up. Let's get her back to work."

"But, boss, I think she—"

"I don't pay you to think, I—"

"Actually, you *do* pay me to think. Good thing too, cause I'm the one who pinpointed Mongolia from the translation."

Valerio's head thickened inside; pressure built behind his eyes. He waved his hands, frustrated. "Fine, fine. Whatever. Just wake her up. I have follow-up questions."

The large Australian obeyed, and Valerio furnished Tina with coffee and a donut. Once she appeared to have rebooted, Valerio asked for more input, more details about the supposed trail.

"There were temples in the places Thomas visited," Tina said. "Buddhism was only five or six hundred years old. The temples were crude—in line with the Buddha's teachings.

Thomas befriended many priests and monks from other religions, not just Buddhism, but this appears to be his main target—"

"Shut up," Valerio said. "Do you have an exact location?"

"We narrowed it down to a hundred square miles." She glanced at Horse. "Once he found the map, and we worked out which area was which, and by looking at Thomas's route out of Nepal... it is somewhere around one of the former trading posts of Mount Bogd Khan Uul."

"Why didn't you just say so? How narrow is your information? How close can we get?"

"Guesswork only. A temple. Possibly one reference that is obscure. I have no idea where the phrase fits in Mongolia or what it refers to."

"And what is it?"

"A tomb. The author sometimes calls it 'the tomb of Aradia' and sometimes 'the tomb of the first priest.'"

SICILY

"At least I think that's what it's called," Bridget said, still unsure whether she'd translated correctly. It was an inexact science at the best of times, doubly so when rushing the process and under pressure. And tired. So very tired. She yawned. "Mount Bogd Khan Uul overlooks the land north of Ulaanbaatar, today's Mongolian capital. All over that region, you get these amazing royal tombs up to two thousand years old. The Tuul River attracted settlements dating back to the Upper Paleolithic period. There are tools that date even farther—"

Dan dropped his head onto Harpal's shoulder, eyes closed, and Harpal leaned his own head on Dan's. Both snored.

"Fine, fine." Bridget rearranged her notes and workings-out. "When Thomas arrived in this region, there was a temple of mud and brick. He befriended the Buddhists, and he states he is worried that the second courier, the one due to collect the Mary bangle, was intercepted. By bandits or by people who wanted these bangles."

The two men "awoke" and Harpal asked, "Why'd he make friends? Thought he was trying to convert them."

Bridget paused, hating to voice something she'd long accepted as a possibility, her Christian upbringing conflicting with the notion of critical thinking. As a family of faith, they accepted certain things as truth, but the scientist in her did not.

"Christianity and Buddhism are really similar," she replied. "Some people think they're even the same thing. Some say they're not *the same*, but that the basis of Christianity was *inspired* by Buddhism."

"I'm no Christian," Dan said, "but even I know one is heaven and the other is reincarnation."

Toby made that "ah" sound and gave a smile that suggested he was going to lecture them again, regardless of their objections. "There were six hundred years between Buddhism and Christianity springing up, and six hundred years is a long time. Only two hundred-and-thirty years ago, the United States was fighting to become a country rather than a colony, and think of all that's happened during that short time span. Six hundred years of trade and communication between the Far East and the Middle East..."

A raised eyebrow elicited no response.

"The two religions have much in common. Heaven, an afterlife, exists in both. Buddha and Jesus both conceived in a miraculous manner—for Jesus, God planted his seed inside a virgin; Buddha's mother dreamed a white elephant entered her womb, and the child was birthed painlessly. Both fasted for a long period while traveling alone. Both were tempted by the devil but resisted him. Both cured blindness and walked on water, rejected riches, and demanded the same of their followers. Buddhism and Christianity teach the same things too: do unto others, love one another, even your enemies, or they will never be friends, do not judge other people, no killing... among others."

Harpal faked a yawn. "Anyone else getting drowsy again?"

Dan pointed at his face. "I'm thinking about painting eyes on my lids. Will you nod my head for me occasionally?"

"Okay, okay," Toby said. "But here's a far-out idea. Scholars inside and outside the church have long wondered what happened to Jesus between his infancy and the Sermon on the Mount period. It's a gap of almost thirty years. There is evidence, locked away in the Vatican, that Jesus traveled, learning about the world. That he got as far as... guess where?"

"I'm on tender hooks," Dan said.

"First of all, it's *tenter*hooks not *tender* hooks. Secondly, the answer is..."

Harpal held up two fists. "Are you waiting for a drumroll? Because I can give you a drumroll."

"India," Bridget chimed in. "Nepal, all around that region."

Toby nodded with a satisfied smile. He really couldn't shake that university lecturer's style of teaching. "Where Buddhism was a fledgling religion."

"So Buddhism informed Christianity?" Charlie said.

"It's a theory that held for many years but was suppressed in the fifteenth century. With the rise of Islam and the costly Crusades, the church needed to shore up Christ's divinity. Even now, the writings of those early scholars are only accessible by the highest-ranking cardinals. Bridget, my apologies, I interrupted."

Bridget resumed seamlessly. "Thomas writes about his friendship with an unnamed Buddhist priest. A temple he stayed in to recuperate when he contracted an illness. He believed his life to be at an end, so he entrusted the Mary bangle, which he calls 'the second jewel,' by the way, to his friend. After his recovery, he concluded he must return to the original tomb where he would 'forge history' and, quote, 'rest for all time in the light beneath the midnight gaze of Zephon,' end quote. The tomb of the first priest."

"Or Aradia," Harpal pointed out.

"Or Aradia. Take your pick. And 'the light' might mean fire. Or maybe burning."

"And Zephon?" Dan asked.

"There's a star called Zephon," Charlie said.

"It's also the angel that Gabriel sent down to hunt Satan," Toby said.

Dan snapped his fingers. "Oh, he probably means *that* Zephon."

"So the bangle isn't in the first priest's tomb?" Charlie said.

"Seems that way," Bridget answered.

"Who is the first priest?" Dan asked.

"Doesn't say. Unless it's in the earlier pages Jules didn't get to."

"Could 'the first priest' be Jesus?" Harpal suggested.

Toby laughed. "No, no, if there is a tomb of the Christ it's in the Middle East. From everything Bridget has found, this first priest is entombed in the steppe region. Or perhaps India."

"Or the first priest is Thomas himself," Bridget said.

No laughter. Some frowning but no laughter.

She added, "Back then, important figures gave specifications about their own burial arrangements. Thomas founded the Kerala Christians. It's one of the strongest achievements of the known apostles. Couldn't it be possible this illness took a lot out of him and he wanted to be sure his burial would be honored?"

"Maybe supplanting the Aradia tomb?" Charlie said. "Naming it after Thomas?"

A lot of pouting, thinking, and nodding followed.

"Possibly," Toby finally replied. "But the term 'Aradia' stems from Herodias."

"Or the ancient term Aradia was applied to Herodias retrospectively," Bridget said.

Toby nodded. "It's certainly possible. Could be, he intended to be buried there, but ended up being killed in Mylapore and his bones interred in Chennai after all."

"Or he didn't make it back to Mylapore, and those bones are someone else's. Records like that are never straightforward, and there are no dates in the journal."

"Quite. We have no way of knowing. Let's keep an open mind for now and return if it's important."

"Agreed." Bridget pressed a finger to her notebook. "I guess you want to know the location of this temple now?"

"Wait, you had it all along?" Dan said. "It's way past my bedtime, and we're talking Jesus versus Buddha. Out with it, and I'll get the jet fueled up."

VALERIO'S GULFSTREAM, AIRBORNE

Tina appeared animated, almost happy, as she spoke, as though she'd forgotten her scumbag smuggler of a husband was dead. Perhaps she had allied with this game out of passion, and it had turned to greed over time. Valerio didn't judge, though. He committed to it for the reverse of that: first for selfish reasons, and now because it fascinated him.

She said, "Churches are built on top of older sites. On castles, temples, yes? Just like Gandantegchinlen Monastery."

Valerio tried pronouncing it but failed. "Bit of a mouthful."

"Even the locals use 'Gandan' for ease. Restored in 1990. There are one-hundred-and-fifty monks living there. The Tibetan name translates to the 'Great Place of Complete Joy.' It came under state protection in 1994."

Valerio turned to Horse. "Strategy?"

Horse had already brought up the monastery on his tablet's Google Earth app, as well as a number of pages describing it. "We can assemble a team, twelve should be plenty, deliver some shock and awe, round 'em up in the main courtyard and execute a couple. Make 'em tell us where it is."

"It is unlikely they would know," Tina said. "Even if it is still there."

"It's not there?"

"No. Before the restoration, they brought in ground-penetrating radar to check they were not destroying anything beneath the original construction."

"They discovered something," Valerio said.

"Yes."

"Bottom line." Valerio now paced. "Do you know what they found, and do you know where it went?"

Tina nodded, glancing at the kitchen. "I do."

She was probably hungry. Valerio would make sure her final meal was a good one. Once they confirmed the location of the Mary bangle.

SICILY

"Gandan was built to honor Avalokiteśvara," Bridget said, after explaining that several artifacts were found within a vault beneath the site and taken to the Mongolian Natural History Museum in Ulaanbaatar. "It features a twenty-six-meter statue of the deity, also known as the 'lord who looks down.'"

"Sound familiar?" Toby said. "Neither male nor female. At least no cultures can get together to conclude which. The Mahayana account says the sun and moon were formed from Avalokiteśvara's eyes, the god Shiva from its brow, Brahma from its shoulders, Narayana from its heart, Sarasvati from its teeth. The wind was born from this major god's mouth, the earth from its feet, the sky out of its stomach—"

Dan pulled an *eww* face. "This god *vomited* the sky into existence?"

"In other words," Toby said as if he were never interrupted, "this god looks down from his or her dwelling place, created everything from him or herself. Again, does anything sound familiar?"

"Creation myth," Charlie said from Alfonse's tabletop. "Fairly standard, and all religions have them. Where does it leave the bangle?"

"With this." Toby unlocked his phone and scrolled through his contacts, resting on one, which he dialed. When the person on the other end answered, he said, "Arthur! Yes, yes, rather well. I'm sorry to contact you out of the blue, but I believe you did a couple of years in Mongolia. Yes, yes, the salt pyramids. Wonderful paper, might I say... listen, I hate to call after all this time asking for a favor, but might you have a contact in that part of the world? I'm thinking near the capital. Where would a pre-Buddhism artifact end up?" A pause. "Of course, of course. I should be in Berkshire in a matter of weeks, actually. It'll be lovely to catch up. Indeed. Goodbye, Arthur, and thank you."

"Old archeology contact?" Bridget said.

"Archeology, yes," Toby answered, but without conviction.

Toby's past was pretty much a sealed book, and although his passion was clearly art and antiquities, the number of contacts he could drum up for information in virtually any area of the world suggested to Bridget that he'd been involved in more than curating the royal family's treasures.

When his phone bonged with a text, he smiled and said, "Thank you, Arthur," then turned to the group. "Arthur will make an introduction for us. Amir Fong is the curator at the Mongolian Natural History Museum. If anyone were to know what became of the items recovered from Gandan Monastery, it will be him."

"Can we really just call and ask him?" Harpal said.

"Unless you would rather drive an excavator through the front door and pull the place apart."

"So we go there in person?" Bridget asked.

"We don't all need to go. Charlie is in London, you're fine here. I'll use my diplomatic clout to get a meeting, and—"

"Dan," Bridget said. "How hard is it to fly a Learjet into Mongolia? *Four* passengers?"

"Toby's right," Dan replied. "You nearly died back in Rome, and... I can't be watching out for you in a foreign country, especially one like Mongolia. We don't know the language, the customs, the laws. I'm sorry, I—"

"Oh, come on. I may not be able to fight like you guys, but I'm still useful. I *will* be needed if there are more clues out there. Toby, think for a second."

Toby shook his head. "We can't lose you."

Charlie said, "Listen to them, hon. We got the documents at the same time as Valerio. We had the same amount of time to work it out, so he may have, too."

"He's probably on his way," Dan said.

Silence. Bridget had a knack for getting her own way, but she sensed there would be no budging them. "I don't have to come to the museum itself. Just think about it. If you pull it off and find the bangle, there's a possibility there'll be other things too. I mean, even after we get it to Alfonse and Jules gets his mom's, we're not just sitting on this, are we? That place Thomas mentions, the tomb. It could be Saint Thomas himself!"

She let her words settle, recognizing Toby's facial tick.

"Imagine the literature, the burial possessions... heck, just finding *him*. I mean, if he's there instead of Chennai, I know it'll annoy folks in the cathedral, but... can you believe what that will mean?"

Toby stood and straightened his belt, looking at Dan. "She stays out of the field. But she might be of use."

"Okay," Dan said. "Looks like we're definitely going to Mongolia. Let the treat begin."

CHAPTER
TWENTY-SIX

NORTH OF ULAANBAATAR - MONGOLIA

The first part of Jules's escape from the Gulfstream—after Valerio, Horse, and the two pilots departed—was freeing himself from behind the couch. He was able to flex and shift his limbs in small ways, meaning he hadn't seized up completely, but remaining in that position for over twenty hours was going to take a toll.

At one point, when Valerio had risen from his sleep and vacated the room, Jules risked a stretch then too, but hadn't progressed to listening at the door. All it would take was Valerio returning for another nap without announcing it, and he was done for.

They landed to refuel six hours after taking off from Rome, where none of the three disembarked, despite most countries requiring passengers to do so. It was the only time Jules had ventured out to eavesdrop—a swift five minutes—and listened through the door to Horse calling people and speaking Russian. He made four phone calls, and all he said to Valerio when he ended the fourth was, "We're on. They'll meet us there."

The next leg of the journey lasted nine hours. To say Jules was stiff was understating the word. And starving wasn't far behind in his list of most pressing sensations.

Now, having landed once more, the impatient Valerio demanded they disembark ASAP, and Jules took the chance to use the head, having held on desperately for the better part of a day, and to perform fifteen minutes of yoga to loosen himself up.

Then he set about figuring what to do next.

It was dawn outside, so they'd traveled east. But since he had no idea of their starting point, that fact didn't help. All he could do was switch his cell phone back on. When he found no internet —not even 3G—he closed the mapping app and call Charlie.

"Jules?" she said. "Where are you?"

"Hoping you can tell me. And quickly. I'm almost outa power. Ten percent."

"Activate your tracker. I'll tell you right now."

"Don't give me that line. You can find out where Valerio's jet landed."

"Do you know if they translated the manuscript?"

"They kept that smuggler's wife alive. She's some kind of expert."

"Then I don't need to track you. You're in Mongolia. Probably close to the capital."

"Jeez, that's great news." He looked himself over, still in his bodysuit. "Anywhere I can take a shower and get some clothes that don't make me look like a cat burglar?"

She muted him for thirty seconds, then came back on and said, "There's a guesthouse with a western name. Oswald Backpacker Hostel. If you make it there, Toby'll have a change of clothes and probably a cloth to freshen up with."

Jules thanked her and hung up, unsure of what he was feeling.

Basically, he'd gambled on a bunch of other people, competitors in many ways, and for once, it hadn't resulted in a pit of regret and self-recrimination. The strangers had understood what he sent them, acted accordingly, and now they'd supplied a way out of a problematic situation.

After hearing nothing in the cabin, Jules palmed one of his final throwing knives, opened the door, and stalked out into the plush space. Empty, except for a sleeping woman, gagged, her hands bound and secured to a floor-to-ceiling handrail. He kneeled beside Tina and tried to shake her awake.

Nothing.

She'd been drugged and left while Valerio sought out the bangle.

A quick recon out of each window revealed they were on open land, with no guards in the vicinity. Why would there be? He was in a country thousands of miles from Rome, and Valerio plainly believed LORI had been eliminated.

Jules levered the emergency release to open the door, the hinge on the bottom smooth and air cushioned.

He found himself on the edge of another private airfield, even smaller than the one in Rome, and bitterly cold. The property seemed to belong to just one company; banners appeared on each of the four hangars with "Huang Jay" emblazoned in black letters on a yellow background in both western and Mongol script, and a matching logo adorned the sides of three small propeller airplanes. Men—mostly men—lugged parcels and sacks in a variety of shapes and sizes.

Jules guessed it was a delivery service similar to UPS or DHL and that Valerio had rented this strip at short notice.

Appears to be a legit operation.

Running would draw attention.

A man such as Valerio would also demand privacy.

Jules concluded the best course of action was to appear part as of Valerio's entourage, so he ducked back in the plane to untie Tina. Next, he donned a jacket from Valerio's closet that was slightly too small and found the trousers were too tight, but he didn't bother searching out Horse's garments as their size would make him look like a clown. The jacket would have to suffice for now.

Having dressed as well as he could, Jules threw himself out the door to dash across the runway. Yes, drawing much attention.

Running, appearing scared, he escalated as he neared and adopted a face of panic as he arrowed straight for one of the larger groups.

"Hey!"

They all stared at him as he arrived, faking a panting fit, like most people would suffer after a burst of energy like that.

"Anyone speak English?" He doubted Latin, Hebrew, or Arabic would come in handy here.

One woman at the back nervously raised a hand. "Little English. Speak slow."

Jules feigned relief. "My friend. In plane." He pointed, annoyed at himself for dipping into pidgin English. "She's sick. Won't wake up. Ambulance."

"Oh." The woman stared at the plane, then back at Jules.

"You were told... 'do not approach the plane.' Right?"

"Plane isn't here." She shook her head. "We just work."

"My boss's wife. He will be angry if she dies. That means *your* boss will be angry. Understand?"

"Yes." She nodded. "Ambulance." She spoke rapid-fire to her colleagues, and three of them rushed away. To Jules she said, "Ambulance come."

"Thank you." He gave a shallow bow in response, hoping it was the correct cultural norm. It drew an audible rumble from his empty stomach. "Now, since I'm obviously a very important guest, I need to borrow a car. Something with satellite navigation, and I want to get to Ulaanbaatar. So which way?"

Blank looks all round.

Okay, take it slowly.

"Car." He mimed driving and pointed at himself. "For me."

This might take a while.

ULAANBAATAR

Toby rarely went against his better judgment, and he knew when he agreed to let Bridget come along that she'd wheedle her way out of staying on the plane. Bridget pointed out that she'd be spending several hours alone in the Lear, parked on a runway in a strange country where they had no official status—other than the temporary visas arranged by Harpal through channels into which nobody inquired too hard.

As far as the authorities were concerned, they were academics seeking to make a financial contribution to the government-run museum.

Money. The only way to get an audience with the top man.

To remain low key, after their trip in an old Land Rover with no heating, they'd checked into Oswald Backpackers Hostel in the manner of any group of travelers exploring this part of the world. They arrived late last night and slept a couple of extra hours in a six-berth room, having bought all six beds under the pretext that others would join them later.

Their appointment with Amir Fong at the museum was for ten a.m., but at eight, the call from Charlie interrupted their breakfast of fried buns, far-too-milky tea, and a helping of bread that tasted like yogurt. That Jules was en route almost certainly meant Valerio was indeed going to be a pain at some point. Time would tell. And time was now at a premium.

At 09:15, Jules pulled up outside in a yellow van, made his way to the hostel's dining room, took in the deeply basic decor and furniture, and headed for Toby and Bridget. He sat and stuffed a fried bread roll into his mouth. Chewed.

Bridget immediately hooked her hair behind an ear and looked at him side-on. "Now, ain't that a tad unhealthy for a man of your disposition?"

"I haven't eaten in a day," he said between bites. "I'm carb cramming. Valerio's here with Horse and a team of guys arranged at the last minute. No idea on numbers. I don't speak much Russian."

He outlined his experiences in a succinct way, emphasizing he heard very little while sequestered in the bedroom, but enough to learn that Valerio was well equipped and willing to take the violent option if required. With some time to kill, Bridget summarized what they had learned so far, from Saint Thomas's wanderings, to the odd reference to Zephon; an angel and, perhaps, a star.

Between mouthfuls, Jules floated the possibility of using the constellations to track the approximate location, but the reference was too vague. Charlie had mapped it to an area visible in the southern hemisphere. To rest beneath a single star at midnight would have felt accurate in ancient times, but today, knowing the earth moves through space and rotates, it could be anywhere. Unless they had a starting point, evidence to cross-check. And they lacked more information, so it was filed away for later.

Once they were all fed, Toby didn't even try to dissuade Bridget from accompanying them. Short of treating her the way Valerio had Tina Trussot, she would find a way to participate. It did make him wonder what she was trying to prove.

A call came in from Dan, scouting the lay of the land around the museum. "All clear. Best as we can see, there's no surveillance."

"Doesn't mean it ain't there, though," Jules said.

"No," Toby agreed. "We will tread very carefully. If we're all ready, let's get moving."

CHAPTER
TWENTY-SEVEN

Ulaanbaatar was a working city, not your typical tourist destination, but people who travel for the sake of traveling are drawn to such places. From what Jules understood, it was mostly used as a port to access the steppes, where the largest industry—aside from cheap and plentiful Genghis Khan memorabilia—had sprung up around the late 1990s in the desert regions where folks could camp in yurts or take up with genuine goat herders for a couple of weeks.

There was some effort on the streets to cater to the tourist dollar, but it wasn't comparable to London or New York or Paris. There were bead salesmen in colorful hats and others hocking lucky charms, fake jade ornaments, and sculptures too large for the average backpack. The cars were old, as was public transport, and clothing appeared to be applied in layers rather than in bulkier items.

And it was colder than he'd expected.

His fresh clothes came from Harpal, which meant they were a little short, but he pulled them off, and Toby bought him a dark-brown leather jacket on the walk over from the hostel. It fit nicely. Certainly suitable for a brisk stroll across to their destination. The only downside was that his cell phone had died. Toby said it didn't matter; they would only break radio silence if something looked hinky.

Jules had been in hundreds of museums since leaving his final foster home. The Mongolian Natural History Museum wasn't one of the most opulent, but it was far from the worst. Certainly not hinky. Some were little more than cabins or pop-up shops with a few bits of rock and the occasional sculpture. This was a proper museum, like a smaller take on the Smithsonian. Olde World–style architecture opened into a wide, breezy reception where Toby informed a woman at the desk that they were here to see Amir Fong.

She made a call.

They waited.

Behind the reception desk, the first airy presentation area spread before them, an effigy of Genghis Khan on horseback to greet them, his bow and arrow aimed at the heavens. A skylight bathed the scene in natural light. He was still revered even more than the way Americans remembered Washington and Lincoln; the British, Churchill; and South Africans, Mandela. Genghis had endured for centuries since the fall of the Roman Empire. This man's influence was in everything here. No wonder he featured in the Natural History Museum *and* his own dedicated monuments; his legacy shaped this country and bestowed a sense of identity.

The sprinkling of tourists was foreign to the region. Chinese mainly. There was a handful of Caucasians, likely British or German, farther inside.

"Mr. Smith!" A Mongol man in an open-neck shirt and pinstripe trousers approached. When Toby accepted a handshake, the man said, "I am Amir Fong. Welcome to our proud museum. So honored to welcome our colleagues from Britain's Natural History Museum. We are smaller, but yes, we have worked hard with others from your country. You know Arthur Jenkins? He said I should give you all the time."

Toby introduced Bridget as Dr. Carson and Jules as Mr. Sibeko, and Amir gave Jules a somewhat startled look that morphed into a forced smile. Amir led the way with Toby up front.

Following, Bridget asked Jules, "What's his problem?"

"Black folks ain't exactly common 'round these parts," Jules said. "Fong don't look like he hates me, but a lotta attitudes in the region ain't exactly progressive. Like the States in the sixties and seventies. It's worse in Korea, but—"

"Keep up, keep up," Toby urged them. When they did, it seemed Toby had suddenly learned to be brief in his chats. "I've explained to Dr. Fong what we are interested in and he—"

"Dr. Fong? Who is this?" Amir said, opening his arms. "Please. Amir. We are all friends, no?"

"Indeed." Toby tilted his head as if about to doff a hat. "Amir thinks he may know what we are seeking to borrow."

"Borrow?" Jules said.

Bridget squeezed his arm, firing Amir a big smile. As they turned, she whispered, "We ask for a loan first. Test the water. Then maybe we will buy it. The less conflict, the better."

Rooms branched off this initial approach, some with art, others with ancient tools, some simply with information about the Mongols under Genghis.

"Hey," Jules said. "Nice place you got here."

"Thank you," Amir said.

"What's that?" He pointed to a five-foot sculpture of a warrior bearing a shield and spear.

"One of our lesser pieces, but interesting. From the sixteenth century, it is carved from flint. Not much flint is found here, and it is a very hard stone. It would take someone of great skill to produce this."

They proceeded through the grand halls, each dedicated to a different period in Mongol history. Amir talked them through the reconstructed bones of a saber-toothed cat, a rhinoceros, and finally a woolly mammoth, indicating that his countrymen were working with the Russians on gene splicing in an attempt to re-create this creature with a helping hand from the African elephant.

"Resurrecting extinct creatures," Toby said. "It's something we'd all like to see, I'm sure."

They entered the human history section, a smaller space with lower ceilings. Glass cases displayed models of men that had been discovered in mummified conditions amid the dry expanse of the steppes. Structures uncovered from beneath the sands followed, demonstrating that people here enacted burial ceremonies three thousand years before Thomas departed Jerusalem.

"We found many, many items under Gandan monastery," Amir espoused. "Beautiful jewelry and vases predating the Ming dynasty. Not as well crafted, but functional. This, for example." Behind another glass pane, recessed into the wall, a two-foot tulip-shaped vase rotated slowly on a plinth like a potter's wheel, a linear pictorial story playing out in a brown spiral over its cream surface, boats swamped by giant waves as people herded animals and carts onto larger ships. "We have other items from the same era. A painting on a slate tablet shows a king facing the waters, but it is too faint to see under normal light."

"Every civilization has its flood myths," Toby said.

"Like Noah," Jules added, preempting another story. "Atlantis, Ozymandias, yeah, every place that gets flooded thinks the whole world's underwater."

"And this," Amir said, halting at a window into another recess, "is the item you asked me about. The Ruby Rock bangle."

Perhaps it was his poor personal health over the past day or so —erratic eating, little water, cramped quarters—but Jules didn't take in what the man said right away. It was a dreamlike moment, something he was certain happened but evaporated in a mist of words. It wasn't until he noticed Toby and Bridget transfixed by the exhibit that he snapped out of it.

"Are you serious?" he said. "It's just on display? Here?"

Amir nodded several times, pointing. "Yes, yes. What else would we do with it?"

Jules stood behind Toby and Bridget. "Ain't in a vault or safe or...?"

The shelf built into the wall laid out an eclectic mix of wearable items: buttons, bronze bracelets, a jeweled brooch. Each bore a small plaque stating its origin and provenance, labeled in Mongolian and English.

The C-shaped stone bangle lay on its side, its plaque declaring it an early example of Mongol ingenuity, chipped and dull but plainly crafted by the hands of man. It was smaller than Jules's item, but not by much, and held a deep-reddish color rather than his mother's green one. As he swayed side to side, light caught the flecks, giving the impression that it sparkled. Again, dark-red instead of green.

"How come it's just out in the open like this?" Bridget asked.

Amir drew a crafty smile from his lips, reflected in the spark of interest in his eyes. "You know it is different, don't you? This is why you want it."

Toby faced him. "We would very much like to borrow this. For further examination. Any discoveries we make, we will share credit with you, fifty-fifty."

Amir shook his head.

Jules paced slowly.

This was their usual approach, it seemed. Ask for a loan, get turned down, start bribing, then offer to buy it for a ridiculous sum. Half a million dollars was a lot to a museum such as this.

On the off chance they didn't succeed, Jules noted the windows high up by the ceiling were large enough to crawl through, and on the way through the other rooms, he'd spotted several motion sensors. Sure enough, this room possessed them, too. The cabinets and glass panes appeared to be double thick, each with a fixed contact pad on one corner. The display with the Mary bangle was protected by *four* contact pads, one on *every* corner.

With just a single contact, a laser cutter allowed a thief to open a hole at the opposite end without the sensors picking up vibrations. Assuming he could access the building and take the corridor's motion detectors offline, even the steadiest laser wouldn't breach the glass without alerting security.

Back to the trio discussing the bangle, Jules heard another refusal. "I am sorry, Mr. Smith, but even for a hundred thousand dollars... What is so important about this? Why must you have it?"

They'd played their hand too soon. Time was ticking by, Valerio on his way.

"He ain't biting," Jules said.

Amir glanced at him, mouth closed tight. "Correct. Perhaps we can arrange for some other items—"

"Why?"

"Why? Because it is precious and you are insulting us with your money."

"I'm sorry, Amir," Toby said. "We do not intend any disrespect, but we have reason to believe this bangle may be connected to a civilization in the Middle East, something that—if we can prove it—will give you even more prestige."

Once more, Amir shook his head, hands clasped before him. "May I invite you to my office for some tea?"

Jules focused on the bangle, his fingers splayed on the glass.

"Please do not touch that," Amir said.

"Why is this display alarmed better than the others?" A glance at Amir revealed the curator was taken aback by the question. "You won't let it go for a hundred grand, probably not the full five hundred we're willing to go to, right?"

Amir stared at the floor, his hands still clasped. "The item was gifted by the monks under the condition that it must always remain."

"Oh, that's it!" Jules spun, a light flaring inside himself. "You've seen it, haven't you? You've seen what it can do."

Toby stepped back, wetting his lips. Bridget's eyes flicked between the men. Amir swallowed.

It was a moment of calm, where tension flowed out of Jules, and he sensed the same in the group, where all subterfuge suddenly ebbed away.

"Fine, follow me," Amir said.

CHAPTER
TWENTY-EIGHT

Bridget rarely gloated. She thought it unbecoming of a lady, especially one raised with southern manners and a conscience that dictated respect for others' feelings. However, being right about Jules was something she wouldn't easily let drop. He wasn't simply a free-running, arrogant, self-obsessed weirdo; he really was able to relate to people. He had read Amir and bonded with him through honesty and openness, unlike herself and Toby.

Amir led them through a series of halls and corridors, ignoring the displays now. "We restored Gandan monastery in 1990, but the work started in 1987, checking foundations, make sure we do not destroy anything important or desecrate ground. I was part of the first team."

Amir unlocked a door marked in both Mongolian and English with "Staff Only Please." Bridget followed him through, Toby and Jules at the rear.

"A monk presented us many items, but this batch of treasure, it was recovered from a section the head priest swore they did not know existed. It was only because our team checked the old foundations. But this one item, the bangle you want to take, it was *glowing*." His speech patterns had sped up, which he must have sensed as he now slowed again. "Only one monk could make it light up, though. A young man, recently accepted into the order. When anyone else holds it, nothing. Just a rock."

Bridget searched for anything in Jules's expression, but nothing changed.

"Something in the oils?" Toby suggested. "The hands secrete differently depending on the circumstances."

Amir took them down a tiled corridor, voices echoing. "We could never replicate it. Only that one boy. We even cut a tiny slice away with a laser to test. We aged the bangle to between 50,000 and 30,000 BCE."

"No," Jules said. "You mean 5000 and 3000 BC. You added a zero. And an *E*."

"No," the curator answered firmly. "I did not add a zero."

"Or an *E*," Toby said. "'BCE' is the non-Christian abbreviation. 'Before Common Era.' Not 'Before Christ.'"

Bridget calculated the math in her head. "The oldest jewelry like this is seven thousand years old... 5000 BC Mesopotamia."

"What's the big deal?" Jules asked. "The rock alone is real old. Don't mean the actual jewelry is the same age, does it?"

"Actually, no," Amir said. "The jewels you see inside the stone, the minerals it is made of... all the same age. A compound. Man-made. Not occurs in nature. Wide margin of error because we could not fund more research, but much older than it should be."

"Impossible," Toby said. "These cod-scientific theories have been debunked multiple times."

"What theories?" Jules asked.

"Do you really want to know?"

"Will it take long? Cause, we're on a clock, but we don't know exactly what time we need to be outa here, if you get my drift."

"Okay, the abbreviated version is the CliffsNotes history of humankind. Like Bridget said, the first civilization as we know it —towns, social structure, jewelry, trade—emerges from the Sumerians in Mesopotamia around 4000 BC, or 6000 YA."

"'YA' meaning 'years ago,'" Bridget explained. "We use that instead of BC and BCE for really deep in the past."

"Thank you, yes, 6000 years ago. At 10,000 YA, agriculture develops. At 12,000 YA, European and African man makes it to what we call the Americas. At 30,000 or maybe 35,000 is cave art. At 70,000 YA was the Toba catastrophe—"

"I read about Toba," Jules said. "Everyone nearly wiped out by a supervolcano."

"We think the population dwindled to as few as ten thousand human beings. *Early humans*, not as we see ourselves now. And the only way they could have survived is to evolve, either through interbreeding or working things out where necessary. For hundreds of years. *Thousands*, actually. By 50,000 YA, we suddenly start making clothes from animal hide, burying the dead with ritual, and hunting with weapons designed specifically for that purpose."

"It's a period of time called 'the Great Leap Forward,'" Bridget added.

"The fastest increase in brain size, breeding, and societal advancement ever seen in a creature," Toby said. "In evolutionary terms, it's the equivalent of someone physically transplanting the brains of monkeys with the brains of slightly dim modern humans. The crackpot theory is that there were highly advanced civilizations pre-Toba. With electricity, massive ships, sprawling cities, but Toba forced them to breed with the dumb ape descendants in order to survive. Nonsense."

"But Toby," Bridget said, "we've found things older than six thousand years."

"Not this complex. Tools that suggest an older sophistication, in isolation, microliths, weapons, not... jewelry."

"Whatever the conventional history," the curator said, "it is the result that came back to us. I offer no theory on Atlantean or Annunaki or whatever conspiracies are fashionable on YouTube. All we know is this item is very old and possesses properties only one man so far has been able to activate."

"Yet it's on display," Toby said.

"To hide it would draw attention. More tests. The government will come, ask questions. Soon, they find out about the monk who made it glow."

"Who is he?" Jules asked. "Can we meet him?"

"Sadly not." Amir halted at a thick steel door with a keypad, out of place in this old building. "He died four years ago. Cancer. Very sad." Amir took a moment, then clunked the handle down and opened the door. "But he has family—brother, sister, nephews, nieces. We will not expose family."

A back room greeted them, plain, narrow, seemingly a stud partition, with only a cart on wheels equipped with precision tools and white cotton gloves. Amir produced a key ring with three small keys, disarmed the security via a fingerprint, and unlocked a thick panel in the wall.

He donned a pair of gloves. "Which one of you is the special one?"

Toby turned away from Jules. Bridget cast a quick glance his way.

Jules said, "I don't know about special, but I made a rock do hinky stuff before."

Amir peered out through the display case before reaching in and lifting the stone artifact. He held it at chest height. "Tell me, if I release this to you, what will you do with it?"

"Make it safe," Bridget replied. "Make sure the wrong people don't get ahold of it."

To Jules, Amir said, "Show me."

Jules reached out. Fingers extended. An inch away, a static charge shot out into his palm, and he snatched his hand back. "Ow."

"I feel it." Amir beamed, eyes wide. "It trembles."

Jules made contact again, the red sparks flashing between rock and skin, a more active reaction than the Aradia bangle, which had simply lit up. Jules pressed on, grasped the item, and it calmed, the deep-red flecks emanating a muted glow. In daylight, he would struggle to see it.

Everyone concentrated on the sight before them. The vibration was obvious and grew more intense the more Jules wrapped his hand around it. He ran his finger along the inside, smooth like his mom's, and the vibration eased. That inner section showed no flecks.

"It's the metallic flakes that react to my touch," Jules said.

"Not only your touch. When the boy monk tested it with us, we found it reacts badly to liquids. Mostly water. But especially to *salted* water. The less pure, the more the bangle repels it." Amir delicately moved it away from Jules. "You see how special this is."

"We are willing to compensate you," Toby said. "Our euros convert to a half a million US dollars."

"This item holds more value than simple cost. I am sorry, Mr. Smith, Dr. Carson, Mr... I am sorry. I do not think I got your name."

"Sibeko." Jules watched the bangle as Amir replaced it in the cabinet, locked the door, and rearmed it.

Jules was already mapping out his plan to return later. He knew his access point, and he knew how to get into this room. The panel would require either a lot of technical work or a directional charge and a clear escape route that would lend more to speed than stealth.

One way or another, Jules was getting that bangle.

But right now, Toby played the diplomat. Shaking hands, rueful smiles, outwardly friendly. No one spoke as Amir escorted them out of the room and into the back corridor. In the main hall, they passed the display cabinet, slowing to observe it a short while longer before moving on to the woolly mammoth section.

Then, out toward the exit, Amir spun on his heels, finger in the air. All he was missing was a light bulb over his head. "A proposal."

"Yes?" Toby sounded excited.

"You stay here. As our guests. Research this with us. Instead of buying the Ruby Rock from us, let us explore it together."

Two security guards stood close by, as if they had been summoned by a silent signal to accompany them out. Probably in case they caused trouble after Amir declined their offer.

"What do you think?" Amir asked hopefully. "Please say yes. Is win for you and for me. For Mongolia."

"We will have to think about it, sir." Toby held out his hand again.

Amir shook it. "Excellent. I hope you will make the wise choice."

The handshake ended, and Amir moved on to offer Bridget the same when a massive crack echoed through the reception hall. One of the guards flopped to the ground, blood streaming from a bullet's exit wound in his chest. Another loud report. The second guard dropped.

Jules pulled Bridget behind him, and Toby spun around, eyeing the exits. Amir simply cringed.

Four masked men with submachine guns flowed in through the main doors while a team of two cut off the passage behind the reception desk. Another set of footsteps and shouting heralded a unit farther within the museum.

Then they opened fire, and more people began to die.

CHAPTER
TWENTY-NINE

Dan abandoned his surveillance within seconds, ordering Harpal to meet him at the prearranged spot by the statue of a horse one street away.

Damn it, they'd swept everything. No one watching the place, no one suspicious. Now this. In Dan's defense, there was no way he could have predicted that an assault would be led by helicopter. If Valerio could engineer the theft of Saint Thomas's manuscript from beneath Windsor Castle, surely he could manage a subtler approach here?

Once again, comms were jammed, but as he tried to contact those inside, he heard static and squeaks and squawks, meaning it wasn't a total blackout. Frequency modulation rather than an outright cutoff.

Old tech.

This reminded Dan of the kinds of raids he saw when on active duty, predominantly Islamist terror groups storming hotels, bars, beaches. Gunfire from within the Mongolian Natural History Museum also suggested a kind of slaughter Valerio had never enacted before.

That we know of.

The two Russian military choppers had touched down in

wide-open spaces near the building, scattering local traders and civilians, engines muffled, so it would be unlikely those inside the thick-walled museum would hear more than a harsh wind beating. Then two columns of masked gunmen hit the place with speed, one winding around the side. Once they got in, the shooting commenced.

Harpal was already waiting, his jacket pulled tight against the cold, concealing the black market Ruger pistol they'd managed to arrange—well-oiled, with three extra magazines apiece. They'd coped with worse.

Dan relayed what he'd seen.

"Mercs again?" Harpal said.

"Seems to be Valerio's MO. If this is him, he's escalating."

"Isn't that always the way?"

Dan checked his weapon, and Harpal copied him. "We should've got suppressors. I'm not sure how to do this once we're in."

"We're going in?"

"Yeah. Those guys aren't messing around, and we can't rely on Jules to go all *Die Hard* on 'em."

The term "aikido" means "the way of harmony of ki," which translates further to "the way of unifying with life energy," or even "the way of harmonious spirit." The master Jules studied under between the ages of seventeen and twenty-one spoke of its similarity to a doctor's Hippocratic oath of "do no harm." That's why many of the techniques involve using an opponent's strength and momentum against them, *unifying* the victim's life energy and syncing it with the aggressor's.

When Jules was in full flow, he morphed into a magician, or so people had told him, seemingly levitating opponents and twisting them around as if they weighed nothing. What appeared to be little more than a gentle slap could floor a man twice his size. It was a martial art which, unlike many skills when committed to his computerlike brain, he needed to practice for several years.

Yes, he'd accepted and even embraced the fact that everything he concentrated on, practiced, and committed to, he absorbed and retained, like the physics and trivia around firearms and gravity that was pretty much a constant, but aikido... Of all the philosophies he'd studied, from Christianity to Taoism, aikido was what brought him the most peace, the highest sense of accomplishment.

Today, though, as he ran ten scenarios through his mind in less than five seconds, he could not see a way to survive without breaking his key tenet of "do no harm."

So—engaging the surgically logical side of his decision-making—he amended it to "do no *lasting* harm... unless it couldn't be helped."

Having ushered Bridget, Toby, and Amir behind a free-standing display case as soon as the shooting started, he tuned out the ear-splitting clatter and stepped from the path leading into the museum's main body. The rendering of Genghis Khan partially hid him from those who shot the two security guards and now fired upon the receptionists, killing them instantly.

So much death.

So much *pointless* death.

Jules darted out and yelled, "Hey," then sprinted back through the open area, toward the other shots blasting from within.

He hurried into one of the side rooms containing artwork as the semi-autos roared his way. As hoped, his escape had prompted a pursuit.

The room had no exit except for a window high up near the ceiling, but that didn't bother him. The gabled doorframe would suffice.

He leaped onto a radiator, then pushed from there onto the doorframe, which gave him two inches of purchase, his hands braced against the roof.

The two gunmen entered, weapons at their shoulders, each

taking a direction to cover two corners apiece. Standard counterinsurgency tactics.

Jules dropped between them, too close for either to swing and draw down on him. He grabbed one gun on the top, away from the bullet case ejection port, but the second guy stepped away for more room. Jules levered the submachine gun down, jumped past the man's shoulder, wrapping the strap around his neck, and kicked his feet out, which threw the man forward. The tangled gunman hit his buddy, which made him fire a burst of three into the floor.

Using the first guy as a ramp, Jules slammed his knee into the second one's temple. The gunman's eyes died behind the mask and rolled back, and by the time his unconscious body keeled to the ground, Jules had wrapped his legs around the other's neck and pulled him down where he held him in place, knees and ankles locked. There, Jules choked him until he, too, passed out—more Krav Maga than aikido, a fighting art designed to do as much harm as quickly as possible.

Less than half a minute had passed since he left the reception area.

Jules then risked another fifteen seconds to break down the semi-autos and toss the firing pins into a trash can, one of their sidearms in another. He kept a Beretta and two magazines plus their knives, which he strapped around his waist, and pocketed a radio. Then he shot them both twice, once in each thigh. They groaned but did not wake.

No *lasting* damage.

Bridget wondered whether people ever got used to this. While she was determined to pull her weight outside the lab and the office, she could barely move when gunfire commenced. Her fight-or-flight response was most definitely geared toward flight, but that wasn't in the cards right now; *hide* was the only action her body would allow. Or more closely aligned to a third option: *freeze*.

Toby and Amir, on the other hand, appeared frightened but calm.

Either she needed more experience or she should give up this notion.

From what she'd seen, the gunmen shot a total of four security personnel, the two receptionists, and three tour guides, along with two visitors. This was less a robbery, more a mass murder.

She literally wanted to vomit.

No one had seen Toby and Amir nip behind the wide display case, though. Originally focused on the runner—Jules—they were now systematically roaming amid the exhibits. This cabinet would only hide them for so long.

"Bridget," Toby hissed. "That door."

He indicated another "Staff Only" room.

"Sometimes is locked," Amir said. "Sometimes not."

Bridget tried to ask a question, but her throat was too tight. If she uttered a sound, she would burst into tears.

Toby said, "What are the odds?"

"No odds," Amir said. "Is locked or is not locked."

"So fifty-fifty." Toby held both of Bridget's shoulders. "I'm sorry. I should have been stronger. Made you stay behind."

Bridget shook her head and unclenched her jaw. Still trembling, she said, "Let's try."

The two men silently agreed and readied themselves for a dash.

Bridget forced herself to look through the glass display, located the men searching for stragglers. When they explored a section shielded from them, she pointed—*go!*

The three ran, crouched. At the door, Amir turned the knob.

Locked.

"Oh-ho!" The voice came from a hundred yards across the other side of the museum floor. One of the invaders raced toward them, raising his submachine gun.

· · ·

Some days, Harpal wished he didn't get such a rush from this job. He long ago stopped caring about taking the lives of professional mercenaries when they obviously knew their actions were wrong, so he concentrated on keeping himself alive. And although this was crazy, he'd have gone for it even if his friends were not in danger.

Opposite him, Dan snapped off the other latch on the skylight high above the museum's hall and flipped it open. Harpal opened his own.

"Dan?" he said.

"Yeah."

"You were right to bring the ropes."

"I know."

Dan went first, dropping his line in and pitching himself through after it. Harpal did likewise.

His acceleration was faster than it should have been, but they only had the Rugers up against H&K MP7s and AK-74s—the modern equivalent of the famous AK-47—so speed was essential.

In motion, Harpal squeezed off two shots at a running gunman, dropping him and smearing the floor. Another man cornered Bridget, Toby, and what Harpal assumed was a museum employee, probably Amir Fong. Harpal tightened the clasp on his line so he ceased falling, drew down, and as the guy was about to fire, Harpal took him in the head.

That left two bad guys to shoot at them as they dropped. And they were completely exposed.

Jules had seen the shadows up above and was 90 percent certain they belonged to Dan and Harpal. He was about to fire a bullet into the leg of the man approaching the trio, fleeing for the back door, but as soon as the two above commenced their breach, he figured they had the situation under control. Dan killed the backup, while Harpal blew away a section of the main threat's skull.

It's not for me, but you go ahead—such a lame thing to feel about the lives of fellow humans.

Jules wished he could do more, but this was no time for evangelizing. What they were doing was faster, safer, more efficient than if Jules were doing the work.

But the two macho men dwelled on their victory for a split second too long, and the last of the raiders had them cold. Jules saw no other choice.

He sprang out and aimed carefully, squeezing off two shots—one in a shoulder of each gunman. He still refused to kill, but it gave Dan and Harpal time to land and find a better position.

With LORI almost back in control, Jules ran away from the entrance hall, through the prehistoric mammal section, aware of every sound in the vicinity, watchful for the last of the killers.

While the gun battle fizzled out in the other room, Jules located the Mary bangle. No one had attempted to gain access, which meant the raiders did not know its exact location.

Jules raised the Beretta and fired at the case. The bullet ricocheted across the room, the glass barely scorched. Other than the gunshot, the loudest noise was now the alarm triggering, a warbling jangle of bells repeating like a giant, panicking animal.

The case wasn't just glass.

Bulletproof polymer.

There was no such thing as completely bulletproof. Not really. Anything will give if enough force is applied. This particular glass, though, would stand up under three mags of 9 mm slugs. He'd need a series of .50-caliber shots to make so much as a crack in it.

And he still had no idea where the final gunmen were.

Shifting his attention away from the glass itself, he fired into the wall at one corner. Plaster spat from the brickwork, but the pane extended farther into the facade. He shot away another section and found the edge two inches into the wall. Careful to angle the bullet in case of another ricochet, he shot several times to create a deep groove, then swapped out the mag and blasted fifteen more. It left him with a whole side exposed and a slot thick enough for his fingers.

He pulled at the edge, but it wouldn't budge. He just wasn't strong enough.

He strained to listen for threats. The firefight in the entrance hall continued, although it was hard to keep up with over the alarm's din.

He risked another ten rounds from the final magazine, chipping away more plaster to hopefully give him less resistance.

No. Didn't work.

He *had* to get this bangle. Ransoming it for his mom's was starting to look like his best hope of resuming his life. Of *starting* his life.

Was it even worth it?

Of course it was. He wasn't about to waste all that training, all that effort, just to give up now.

He placed the gun down and moved to the five-foot-tall flint warrior they saw on the way in. It weighed a ton, but by tipping the mass into both arms and carrying it as he would a baby, he could transport it to the display case.

"Hard stone, really tough," Jules said, and swung it into the side of the exposed pane.

The whole sheet of glass shunted half an inch.

"Nice."

No more gunfire emanated from the other direction. They'd be coming. Who "they" were was debatable. If Dan was as good as he thought he was, it *should* be LORI.

Jules swung the five-hundred-year-old statue again, trying not to feel too bad as both the statue and the wall lost fragments to his assault. Still, the glass held. The gap between the pane and the brickwork was wider, though. He jammed the statue in the gap and used it as a jimmy, levering his way in.

The jangling alarm sounded more like a countdown clock than ever.

Sweating, straining, pushing, the cement rectangle cracked

and split, and the polymer sheet crashed out, exposing the display.

Jules breathed deeply three times, wiped his face, and reached for the bangle. Again, it crackled and spat until he held it firmly, then he slipped it on his wrist to wear like an accessory. With the outer stone out of contact with his skin, the lights faded, and he paused to make a choice: proceed to the only escape route he dared use or delve back into the museum to check on LORI.

Overhead, a helicopter hovered low, not even trying to hide, and as soon as Jules jogged in the direction of the people he, logically, should not be risking his life over, an explosion shook the building and silenced the alarm.

More gunmen infiltrated the hall, this time five of them rappelling through the hole in the roof that used to be a skylight. One of them was far larger than the others because he was wearing a flak jacket. It wasn't something Bridget usually noticed, so maybe she was getting better at this.

Was there no end to these people? They were like cockroaches.

When Dan and Harpal saved them, she'd made a dash for the next sturdy-looking display table and cowered there while the bullets flew. She thought she saw Jules joining in, but then he was gone.

In what could only have been fantastic timing, two other gunmen ushered a team of what were clearly staff into the hall, four in lab coats, six in the uniforms of guides, and the new armed men sought to suppress LORI, not kill. They fired over Dan's and Harpal's heads, corralling them into a nook so they were trapped, but didn't pursue them.

Once the pair were subdued, two men with Russian accents rounded the case full of trinkets and arrowheads, behind which Toby and Amir had joined Bridget.

The trio lowered themselves to their knees, hands on their heads.

This situation was different from before. They were controlling the scene with precision, not slaughtering en mass.

Predictably, the huge beast of a masked gunman stalked toward them, removing his balaclava to reveal that he was indeed Horse. "Damn. I hate being right. You're not dead."

Somewhat less predictably, Valerio Conchin himself strutted through the front doors and skipped on past reception and the dead bodies of his men and their victims. No mask, no disguise. Simply a light suit, a blue oxford shirt, and the smile of an inmate just released from prison.

He clocked Amir, Toby, and Bridget. "My, oh my, what have we here? You look surprised. Now, let's talk about that little rock." He turned a full circle as a dancer might, pointing and winking at the now-captured Dan and Harpal. "Oh, full house! No matter. Mr. Fong, please stand."

Amir did so, his chin high, eyes darting, and lowered his hands slowly as directed.

Getting up in Amir's face, Valerio's expression was fixed in a rictus grin. "Take me to what I want. Now. Or everyone here dies."

CHAPTER
THIRTY

Dan froze fifty yards from the hostages, one gun leveled on him, another on Harpal. They were caught, and Dan saw no way out. He wasn't sure what stung the most: that he was about to die, or that he'd miscalculated the force of their enemy.

A total of four gunmen joined those already in the museum, rounding up staff. Plus Valerio and Horse. Bad odds. At least they'd ceased murdering people at random, a ruse Dan suspected they planned to blame on a terrorist attack—either Islamic jihadis or whatever local groups made their political points by killing innocents.

The staff were gathered in one group, with Bridget and Toby hunkered among them, the remaining tourists in another.

Valerio's attention rested on Amir. An arm around the curator's shoulder, he pointed at the tour guides and back office personnel sitting cross-legged on the floor, hands on their heads.

Valerio said, "Pick one."

"One?" Amir looked puzzled.

"Who will die first?"

"I... I cannot pick someone to die."

"Oh." Valerio bowed his head. "Disappointed! Horse? Would you be so kind?"

Valerio's bodyguard pointed a handgun at a lab-coated man and fired. The man's chest bloodied, and the report echoed throughout the space, its noise still ringing after the victim ceased writhing in pain and lay flat on the floor, unmoving.

Dan flinched internally but remained stone on the outside.

"*Hwang,*" Amir said, about to run to the dead man.

Valerio grabbed him by the shoulder and twisted him around. "Now choose a different person."

Amir alternated his view between his colleagues—many now weeping openly—and Valerio himself. "You want something. To stop killing my people."

"Ten points to the Mongol!" Valerio slapped him on the back. "Yes, I want something, and the presence of *these* people..." He pointed at the LORI contingent. "Them being here means you know *exactly* what that is."

Amir nodded so hard it was a wonder his neck didn't snap.

"Then let's go." Valerio beckoned, and Horse shoved Amir away from his boss. Following, Valerio clicked his fingers and added, "Have them kill the tourists and the competition before we get back."

Horse barked in Russian, calling one of the men "*Capitan,*" presumably the independent group's leader. The captain replied, "*Da.*" Meaning "yes."

Dan's Russian wasn't fluent, but he could get by with a few words.

As soon as they were on their way, the captain ordered his men to spread out. Two aimed their submachine guns at the grouped tourists—thirteen of them—while the captain separated Bridget and Toby from the staff, all trying to stay out of the dead scientist's blood.

"It is important." Amir stopped in his tracks.

Dan's chest sank, his stomach fluttering with anticipation. Going by Amir's sagging body language and resigned expression, he sensed something bad was about to happen.

At Valerio's confused frown, Amir fixed his gaze on Toby. "Do not let them discover the Ruby Rock bangle's secrets."

Sometimes, Dan hated being right.

Amir swung an elbow at Valerio's gut, winding him. Horse brought his gun up and popped a shot into the man's head. Amir slapped to the floor, and Dan wondered whether the smile on his face was satisfaction or just a motor response as he died.

More shots sounded from the north corridor. Single cracks, forcing the bad guys to take cover without hitting any of them.

Jules.

Those guarding Dan and Harpal flicked their attention to their employer, and Dan deflected the nearest guy's gun and planted a flat hand through his windpipe.

Harpal reacted too, a combination of punches to his guy's gut, a jab to the eyes, then a heel through his temple.

Easier than with some urban jihadi fighter in a similar situation. Those guys could explode at any moment. The museum attackers had no such commitment to the afterlife. But that didn't mean Dan wouldn't send them there.

Dan and Harpal secured the downed men's weapons and immediately spread out, spraying bursts of three at judicious points. They missed, but it scattered the killers, allowing Toby and Bridget to run their way.

"Is Charlie back online?" Toby said over the racket.

"Yeah, got her before we dropped in," Dan said. "She's getting the lay of the land, but it isn't easy here. Stay close, we'll get out of here. *Harpal*, three o'clock."

Harpal laid down covering fire at a right angle to Dan, pressing Horse into a retreat, unable to fight *and* maneuver his injured boss out of harm's way.

"The bangle." Toby pointed in the direction from which Jules had fired and then quickly disappeared.

Without spare ammo, Dan switched to single rounds, picking off one overly ambitious scumbag who tried to flank them. The last three grunts were too close to the hostages for Dan to attack directly.

They made it out of the entrance hall and into the section featuring bones and furry beasts. After there, they reached an exhibit full of knickknacks, mostly behind glass. One display was utterly destroyed.

The one Toby was gawking at. "It's gone!"

"Right here." Jules's voice came to them from higher up.

He was standing on a cabinet eight feet off the floor where he'd propped the small window open with a statue. "This way." He rolled up his sleeve to flash the rock bracelet. "Hurry, I can get us out."

Jules thought they'd have been elated, but Dan and Harpal took cover and aimed back the way they'd come, utilizing the bottleneck to their advantage. He told them his phone was dead and so he hadn't been able to communicate his plan. They seemed reluctantly satisfied.

Toby shook his head. "I can't get up there."

Jules crouched and lowered his hand. "I'll pull you up. Dan can shove below. You're a bit wide, but we can squish your gut through."

Even on the run for his life, Toby placed both hands on his stomach and sighed.

"Now would be good," Jules said. "This drops to an evac point they ain't guarding, and—"

The PA system screeched with feedback, then crackled, and Valerio's voice reverberated around the building. "Hello? Can you hear me?"

"Valerio," Toby said.

"You got away," Valerio continued. "Well done. No doubt you have the bangle already. With the approach to your hidey-hole being so gosh-darned narrow, you'll pick our guys off. Or escape the building before we can send a couple of rockets your way. But let's not forget about the hostages."

"I'm outa here." Jules ducked toward the window. "I'll meet you back at the hostel—"

"Where are you *going*?" Bridget demanded.

"You see, *I* get to decide their fate," Valerio's voice boomed, its echo all around. "Kill them probably. But let's try negotiating first."

"I got what he wants," Jules answered. "I'll draw them away. Hole myself up, ransom the Ruby Rock bangle for my mom's, and—"

"In exchange for the bangle," Valerio went on, "I will give you *half* the hostages. When I am safely away, I will order the release of the remaining ones. That sounds fair, doesn't it? Yes, I'm certain it does."

Jules groaned. "Those people're dead, anyway. We could follow every instruction, every command, but Valerio can't leave witnesses. It's a trick to draw us out."

"Are you absolutely sure about that?" Toby said. "Or are you just blinded by your crusade?"

Jules took out the radio he snagged earlier and flicked it on. Thumbed the button. "You hear me?"

"Yes," Valerio replied over the PA system. "I hear you. Don't mind if I continue using this, do you? I kind of like it. Makes me feel all... godlike. I know, I know, a psychologist would have a field day with that one, but it's fitting, don't you think?"

"Sure." Jules perched on the edge, then dropped to the floor. He was eye level with Toby for a moment as he rose from a crouched landing, his thumb on the button. "Narcissism and god complex go hand in hand."

He was now resigned to doing things Toby's way. He could live with someone else killing those people; Jules didn't ask Valerio to be a murderous sociopath, and he doubted there'd be anything he could do to save the billionaire's victims. But this group seemed to squeak out of tight spots by sticking together.

He said, "I'm coming out. Hold your fire. I ain't armed."

As he lowered the radio, Bridget said, "Don't just give yourself up."

"Yeah, that's dumb," Harpal added.

"Make your minds up," Jules said. "Either I go out or I don't."

"Stop being an asshole and listen," Dan said. "They didn't cut comms entirely. Isn't as easy in a place where there's less access over the web. So we got Charlie on the line, and she's mapping out an escape. Just gotta hold tight."

Jules stepped toward the exit. "Trust me, I can do this."

Toby placed a hand on Jules's arm. "We've been in more than one bad situation. How about *you* trust *us* for once?"

Up by the window, Jules had persuaded himself to do it their way. It went against every fiber of his being, but... *fine*. He relaxed his stance, fell in beside Bridget, and waited to see what they came up with.

If Valerio hadn't been so furious, he would have been impressed. Horse had never failed him before, and the non-demise of this Lost Origins group had triggered Valerio's decision to turn up here in person despite the obvious risk of revealing his identity to the world. Not that it would matter pretty soon, anyway.

The original plan fell flat, presumably in part because of *them*. With a jihadi-style terror strike on heathen relics and people who worshipped those relics, no one would be any the wiser. And since he'd tipped off the National Police Agency regarding an active cell of Mongol Nationalists several miles from here, he didn't expect to be bothered for at least ten minutes. Another reason he couldn't afford a protracted firefight.

One thing was for certain, though: he was genuinely enjoying lying on the reception desk and speaking into the mic that projected his words throughout the building.

"Narcissists are interesting creatures," he said, regaling the whole building. "Even self-aware ones don't really care what label you give them because they don't care about your world. Or your labels. It's *their* world. You just live in it. If they think the world revolves around them, that's because it does. It's the nature of the affliction. I believe myself to be godlike, therefore I am godlike. The difference between me and the kind of narcissist who denies he has any sort of mental condition is that I don't believe in my greatness *just yet*. I believe I *will be* great once I've proven myself.

"Even Mongolia's favorite son, Genghis Khan, knew he could not simply demand people worship him. He had to do more than rampage and pillage and threaten. He absorbed the tribes he conquered, inspired them to follow him, not out of fear but out of a promise of a better future. And he gave them that.

"And look at Alexander, literally, the *Great*. He only lived to thirty-two, but he dominated half the known world. Again, he did not achieve that through force alone. He provided for the people whose lands he took. Better than his predecessors.

"And then we have the first priest. A man who assimilated, who also provided for those he ruled over. Gave counsel, gave hope. But who was he? Have you even got that far yet?"

"Saint Thomas," came the reply from the radio on Horse's belt, the American who liked rooftops and knew how to move. "He learned what we wanna learn and scattered the knowledge. Hopin' his pals from the Jesus fan club would find their way back. But it ain't them."

An intruder drew all guns toward the center of the entrance hall. The young black man strode in, hands out to the side.

"The Saint Thomas Christians from Kerala," the intruder said. "They see him as the first priest, and you're lookin' for his tomb."

CHAPTER
THIRTY-ONE

Although Toby didn't have time to map it out in full, Jules appeared to take little convincing to go along with them. For once. But then, Jules's cooperation lasted for approximately a minute and a half.

Jules said Valerio was starting to sound manic, like he was building to something. It was the same as a guy he once encountered in Puerto Rico, a drug runner who'd turned his hand to acting as a middleman for the blood diamond industry. That guy, Jules told them, was on meth a lot of the time, and although he'd not witnessed Valerio snorting or injecting, he was definitely on a number of drugs. Prescription, maybe, but they could have side effects that exacerbated certain triggers.

Like killing innocents.

As soon as Jules took off against their wishes, Toby contacted Charlie again, who wanted to alert the authorities. But with Amir dead, Toby might well be implicated in the proceedings. More importantly, they would lose both bangles. And possibly Jules too.

"Dan, Harpal, go," Toby said, meaning the window Jules had opened. "Be subtle, though. We can still save the artifacts, too."

"What about us?" Bridget asked.

"We may be needed here. But we won't be out in the open long."

"Jules," Valerio said after the guy answered the question of his name. "Right, right, I have heard of you here and there. You were in jolly old England recently. Trying to grab my manuscript. And you were in Rome, of course. Do you even know what you're chasing?"

"Some piece a' jewelry." It was the usual line when someone asked about his motives. "I got a guy wants to pay for it."

"Money, hmm?" The yellow businessman-come-gangster-come-terrorist paced, tapping his chin with undisguised amusement. "So, you're all about the money?"

"It's how I make a living.

"In that case… if I were to offer you a million bucks right now, you'd hand over the bangle Mr. Fong gave his life for and go away?"

"Got it on you?" Jules asked.

"Yes. Well, it's in a helicopter not far from here. Do we have a deal?"

"You've interpreted the whole manuscript." Jules observed the two guns pointed at him and Horse holding his weapon low, working out the speed it would take to reach Valerio and whether it would be out of the question to simply leave via the front door. "You know the location of the tomb. The priest's resting place."

Valerio's eyes narrowed, his amusement now mingling with suspicion. "And...?"

"And there's more there. More than a random tomb. There's information. But not just that. Something more than what we've been lookin' for."

"What, though?"

"Christians believed that parts of saints' bodies had power. That's why they got bits of 'em in their altars and churches. You think Thomas's body is in that tomb, not the cathedral in India, and it can cure..." Jules waved his hand up and down, indicating Valerio's form. "You think it'll cure whatever the hell is wrong with you. You really believe the Aradia bangle and the Ruby Rock bangle do some hokey supernatural whizz-bang-bang, and boom —you're all pasty pink again."

Valerio grinned widely and gave a slight hop. "Ooh, I spy with my little eye the newest member of my team! You worked all that out from the information at hand? Gosh, that's clever. Yes, yes, we always knew the approximate location, and now it's much more specific. Used to be thousands of square miles, which we can't even cover with LiDAR, but now we've whittled it down to *hundreds* of square miles. And you know what? I could do with a hand over that final hurdle. Someone with a brain as fast as yours. I'll share the credit as well as the money. Not quite fifty-fifty, you understand. I do have overhead. Come on board, my boy, and—"

"Boy?" Jules said.

"I mean that in the generic sense." Valerio's wide mouth, his "smile," Jules supposed he called it, wavered. Then died. "I'm sorry, did 'boy' sound racist? Maybe it did. Like some southern cop on TV." He pressed his hands together. "Sincerely, Jules, I apologize. I was referring to your youth, not your race. Please forgive me."

"You for real, dude?"

"Yes. And note it was a proper apology. Not one of those fake 'sorry for any offense you took' apologies. I should have chosen my phrasing more carefully. I would hate for you to think I'm one of those racists who falsely believe words have no power. Now..."

He ran his hands over his lustrous hair, pinning it to his scalp before letting it go so it sprang back into position. As he did this, his sleeve rode up, revealing the stone bangle on his wrist.

He said, "Hand over the Ruby Rock bangle, or I'll kill everyone in this building. Including you."

· · ·

It wasn't the greatest hiding place, but Bridget was thankful she could stop pretending to be brave. A broom closet sounded like somewhere one of those cannon fodder teens in a slasher movie would meet their end, but she could not risk exploring too far. Dan insisted that Valerio would have dispatched people to look for them, so when he and Harpal escaped using Jules's plan, Toby found this hidey-hole. It might have only delayed their discovery, but if Charlie's intention to turn the cops from their current distraction worked, they would need spotters. Dan and Harpal could provide that. They just needed to retrieve a couple of items first.

They'd now also reestablished full comms with Charlie. According to her explanation, she identified which frequencies were inaccessible and circumvented the wave, returning them to full capacity.

Whatever all that meant.

"Ten minutes at least," came Harpal's voice.

"Yeah," Dan added. "They got beat cops all over the place. They know something's wrong at the museum, but the commanders seem to be holding 'em back."

"No way to tell if it's intentional, though."

Bridget adjusted her position, already cramping up in the dark. "Why would it be intentional?"

"Bribery, maybe?" Toby suggested.

"Like I said," Charlie replied. "Can't tell. Wait..." The comms went silent for five seconds. "Something's wrong here. That can't be right."

"What is it?" Toby asked in a whisper.

Then a more familiar voice arrived on the comms. *Jules.* Using the phone, Toby slipped him upon his exit.

"It's impossible," Jules said.

Valerio slipped the stone artifact off his wrist, far thinner than Dan's. He was actually *carrying* the Aradia bangle. The one stolen from Jules's mom. From her *corpse*. Pawned for five bucks before an antiques speculator picked it up for twenty whole dollars. For nine months, that was the only clue the cops revealed to Jules, and eventually admitted they'd never followed it up. The people who committed the murder were behind bars, and the city could no longer spare the resources to track property like that. For now, while not officially dead, the case was definitely—*sorry, kid* —comatose.

Even though it was just a rock, an ugly piece of jewelry that his mom refused to let him so much as touch while she was alive, he could not allow its theft to go unanswered. He had assumed whoever ended up with the bangle would protect it as if caring for an infant, but now Valerio held it before him.

It had been on the airplane he was hiding in. A safe in the bedroom? Jules didn't even entertain the notion.

Now he realized Valerio wanted it nearby so he could move quickly as soon as he reunited it with the Mary bangle. The *Ruby Rock bangle* on Jules's wrist.

I could've just taken it.

"This is the Ruby Rock bangle's twin," Valerio announced. "Not quite identical, but still special."

The mercenaries had spread out, two missing and two sighting down on Jules, so they had him in an angled cross fire. He'd have to be fast to clear himself from their range. There was also the small matter of Horse, his gun ready by his side.

"No such thing as special," Jules said. "Unusual, sure."

"If it's not special, why do you want it so badly? And don't give me that line about a cash reward. It has no monetary value. And I *saw* it glow."

Jules found no reason to lie. Not now. Either Toby's plan would work, or it wouldn't. "It was my mom's. I just want it back."

"Oh, come *on*! That's worse than the lie about the reward. Fine, you don't want to share. Maybe you can tell me why they aren't twins."

"The red one's slightly smaller." Jules stepped forward again, tracked by the guns. The hostages all eyed him, hope spilling from each of them. Jules didn't want to disappoint. He needed to stall. "Why don't you just kill me? You could take it."

"Because I like you. I mean, don't get me wrong, I totally planned to do that, but our nice conversation gives me hope you might be smart. Almost as smart as me."

"So, what makes them special?"

"Thought you didn't believe in special?"

No cops, no signal from Dan or Harpal.

"He's stalling, boss," Horse said.

"Is that right?" Valerio asked. "Are you stalling?"

Horse turned away, a hand to one ear. "Yeah. We need to be out of here in three minutes."

"In that case, this is your final chance... young man. Come with us, be a part of this. Or die. Right now."

"I ain't joining you," Jules said.

"Horse, kill him."

Horse raised his gun, but Jules said, "Wait."

Valerio waved a hand to stop Horse's shot. "Why wait? Why should I?"

Jules's shoulders sagged involuntarily. He pulled up his sleeve with one hand, met Valerio's gaze, and pressed his finger to the stone bangle. The red flecks sparkled, dull in the bright daylight streaming through the roof.

Valerio opened his arms. "Oh yes! Yes, yes, yes! Jules, my friend, now there's no doubt at all. I guessed there were more like you out there, but I didn't think you'd just walk into my arms."

Jules wasn't too shocked, but he was suddenly aware that this had been a mistake.

"You are a part of this whether you want to be or not." Valerio clicked his fingers, and the two mercs advanced, one holding a set of cuffs.

"Look." Valerio presented the Aradia bangle less than five feet from Jules, end on so he looked down it like a telescope. "The angle of this cut, where it almost meets." The ends of the C shape were angled in at forty-five degrees. "But look at yours."

Jules turned his wrist to his face. The smaller piece on his arm was cut at the exact same angle, but mirroring the Aradia bangle. A tiny groove now showed too.

"That's right," Valerio said. "Imagine. Bringing these items together. How do you think this might work?"

The two men who had approached awaited the final word from their boss.

Unable to move too quickly, Jules faked an emotion—confusion leading to devastation—and placed both hands to his ears, activating the earpiece to dial in Toby and the others. He hadn't wanted them to listen in before.

"It's okay." Valerio sounded strangely kind. "Hand over the bangle, come with me, and we can solve this problem together."

"It's impossible," Jules said.

"No. We will work together. You bring your special touch. I'll provide the muscle. The money. The resources."

"I had an offer like that before."

"And you wisely turned it down, Jules. But you see it, don't you? You see the connection?" His eyes were wide. That maniacal tone rising. "They *are* twins. Complimentary, but not identical."

Jules looked again at the Aradia bangle, his mom's jewelry, now literally within reach. He felt the Ruby Rock bangle on his arm. He'd worn them both and should have realized as soon as he slipped this one on. It was so obvious now.

He blamed the jet lag for his sluggish realization.

"The bangles aren't jewelry at all," Jules said. "They're magnetic. They slot together. Like the symbol for infinity." He swallowed, waiting to say it clearly, as much to counter his own disbelief as for Toby and Bridget to hear. "They're not jewelry... they're a key."

CHAPTER
THIRTY-TWO

As much as Toby valued Charlie, he worried sometimes at how cold she could be. She called it calmness, but Toby saw more similarities between Charlie and Jules than she would ever admit. As soon as Jules revealed that the two bangles formed a kind of key, Charlie told Dan and Harpal to hold off on the rescue.

"Why?" Toby asked. "Now is perfect. The police can surround this place and—"

"Your pal screwed us," Charlie said.

"What do you mean?" Toby's voice carried loudly in the closet, drawing a "shhh" from Bridget. He regulated his volume and said, "In what way has he 'screwed us'?"

Before Charlie could answer, the door opened, and light flooded Toby's eyes. His automatic reaction was to shield them with an arm. When he lowered it, two gunmen aimed MP7s at him and Bridget.

"Oh dear," he said.

"They are the key to so much more than a door," Valerio said. His fingers trembled, feet tapped. He hadn't blinked for two minutes. "A key to the tomb of the first priest. And more importantly, the priest's *gospel*. Secrets to awarding the finder untold power. The knowledge of the world."

"Even if that's true about the key," Jules said, his arms still free, the cuffs on standby, "the gospel's just another book. Intended for the other apostles to find. Not you, not me. But other writers from the Bronze Age."

"Jules, do you *see* what happens when you touch these trinkets? *Magic exists in this world*. Let me show you. Let me *teach* you. I'll prove it, Jules. I promise."

For the first time since holding a knife to the throat of the original antique dealer to whom he tracked that bangle in New York City, Jules wondered exactly why his mom had protected that thing so passionately. He'd long assumed it was sentiment. He even acknowledged a blind transference to him of its heritage, an acceptance of its importance to them as a family—a family that no longer existed.

Sentiment.

That was one thing he'd purged from his soul in his pursuit of it. He didn't need *sentiment* fogging his thoughts. It had killed his parents, after all.

Only now, if Valerio's story were true, *sentiment* had nothing to do with their deaths.

Did she know? Did they both? Were they somehow protecting more than just a memory? More than a five-thousand-year-old artifact...? Or even thirty thousand if Amir Fong examined it accurately.

"All I want is my mom's bangle," Jules said.

Valerio laughed. A head-back belly-out laugh. A laugh that required him to breathe quickly, to take time to calm himself. When he did, he shook his head. "Either you are dumber than I thought, sticking to your story like that, or—if what you're telling me is true—then you have a worse mental condition than my narcissism. You're an *obsessive*. And I know from experience where all-consuming obsession can lead. You'll never stop. Never give in. It'll kill you, or you'll win. Either way, whatever happens to you, *I* lose." Now fully calm, he straightened his suit jacket and pulled his shoulders back. "Here's my offer: come with me. Solve the mystery of the first priest. Let me meet him. Explore him. Figure him out. You do this one thing *with me*, and your obsession will be at an end. As soon as we open that door, when the first priest is before me... the Aradia bangle is yours."

Jules could not envisage a scenario where Valerio would honor that. And they were down to one minute.

"The hostages," Jules said. "Send 'em out, and you got a deal."

A pause, then Valerio flicked his hand and said, "Do we need them?"

Horse shook his head. "Too late. Ruse is up. We've stuck around too long. They'll know this isn't a terrorist attack."

"Then do as he says."

"Boss?"

"He'll comply. All he wants is this." Valerio waved the Aradia bangle again.

Horse ordered the surviving staff and visitors to make their way to the rear instead of the front, where a fire exit would grant them freedom. "Keeps our own escape route free," he explained.

Valerio extended one hand. "The Ruby Rock bangle. Pretty please."

The two mercs aimed their guns.

Horse supervised the hostage evac.

Jules could surprise them:

Duck and spring forward at the same time.

Take Valerio hostage using the knife.

Move outside.

Relieve him of the Aradia bangle.

Disappear.

That would work. He was fast enough.

Why was he hesitating?

Before he could answer his own question, the other two gunmen returned to the scene, only now they were not alone.

Hustled before them, Bridget and Toby emerged, hands on heads, providing Valerio with more leverage.

His last chance to get away clean was finished.

Something was very wrong, and it wasn't just that Toby and Bridget had been discovered. Charlie could no longer "see" the Mongolian cops that had been holding back from the museum since the first emergency calls came in, and that flash, that person she thought she caught a digital glimpse of... she couldn't find him again. Ulaanbaatar wasn't like London or New York or Paris; CCTV was rare, and CCTV connected to the internet was virtually nonexistent. With the bulk of Ulaanbaatar's National Police Agency personnel five miles away, hurtling back toward the city, there was no way the cavalry would make it in time. They were relying on locals, but the man she spotted, or thought she did, was not a local.

And the scant police presence here had started acting strangely. As if their early tactic to observe and contain had been overridden.

Dan agreed. He saw it too, now that he was outside.

So, although there was no need for Charlie to vocalize it, she did anyway. "Sorry, boys. This is a scorched-earth evac."

"Damn it," Harpal said. "I hate scorched-earth evacs."

"Me too," Dan answered. "But there isn't much choice right now."

With her chest hammering and fingers riding hard on the keyboard and mouse, Charlie used the infinitesimal number of web-enabled cameras around the city to guide Dan and Harpal to where they needed to be. A lot of it was guesswork.

Jules regarded Toby and Bridget as they shuffled in behind Valerio, unable to refrain from glowering at their stupidity. "Should've gotten out while you could."

"We couldn't leave you," Bridget said. "We thought it was under control."

A shadow flickered outside the main doors, too far away to be a threat, but it was the first time Jules picked up on it. Too big to be a bird. Too small for an aircraft or ground vehicle. Dan wasn't about to burst in at the helm of a tank.

"I don't even care about this thing." Jules slipped his hand out of the Ruby Rock bangle, which was tighter than his mom's. It lit up for a moment, but he spread his fingers inside to keep it from dropping. The lights went out. "I only want my own back. I even risked losing it all so I could get those other people outa here, but you gotta come back in and mess everything up."

More movement. Something outside was shifting. Overhead, too, a pressure change rippled on Jules's skin.

Horse noted it too. "Boss. We're out of time. Do it now."

"Jules?" Valerio still had his hand out.

Jules cast another glance at Bridget and Toby. "It would've worked too. If you'd just stayed out of things. Left me to do what I had to." He placed the bangle in Valerio's palm.

The man's bloodless yellow face darkened slightly, a reddish tinge to his cheeks as the smile spread to the corners of his eyes.

"Boss." Horse rushed past, grabbing Valerio by the arm, and the two mercs retreated toward the entrance hall. "Execute 'em?"

"They live," Valerio said. "As long as Jules comes with us."

"You heard the man. Come this way, or everyone dies." Horse pointed his gun at Jules. "Five seconds, retard."

"Thanks," Jules said. "But I only need three."

A metallic canister sailed in through the front doors and clattered to the floor, immediately joined by two more.

Horse cried, "Flashbangs!"

The mercs ran, Horse shielding his boss.

Jules dived for Bridget and Toby. He landed over their faces just as the canisters flared impossibly bright and pulsed explosions that clanged inside his head. Although he was prepared for it, had even subjected himself to the effects in an attempt to desensitize himself, he was still left dizzy, his vision fogged and blurry. He rolled off the pair, all three groaning.

Boots stomped.

Foreign voices yelled.

He made out SWAT-style paramilitary figures, cops maybe, breaching and spreading out.

"I could have done it," Jules said, suppressing the tears that were trying to break through thanks to the flashbang. "I arranged it all. I could have done it. You just had to get out of my way!"

"Arranged what?" Toby asked, struggling to sit upright and check on Bridget at the same time.

She was blinking rapidly, trying to prop herself up. "What's happening, Jules? What did you do?"

"What I had to," Jules said. "My backup plan."

Through the smoke, beyond the law enforcement figures stalking in, a tall, skinny man followed. Almost casually. Although he wore a flak jacket over it, his suit was plainly expensive, as was the watch peeking out from the cuff of his right hand. As he neared, his sallow face and birdlike nose grew clear.

Colin Waterston had arrived. "Thank you so much for the tip-off, Mr. Sibeko. We never would have thought to look here."

CHAPTER
THIRTY-THREE

Even without the stinging brought on by the smoke grenades, Jules couldn't have met Toby's stare. Or Bridget's.

Three medics checked them over, perched under the life-size Genghis model, where they rinsed the westerners' eyes with saline and tested for concussions. They didn't seem to speak English. The cops were a mix of the locals Charlie spotted and Interpol agents who had permission from the Mongolian government to execute an operation in conjunction with minimal backup. Unfortunately, Colin hadn't known the target until Jules got in touch. They were expecting a remote location, not slap-bang in the middle of the capital.

"I followed your progress after Mr. Sibeko messaged me from Rome," Colin explained, arms folded, head held high. His manner retained that rich-asshole poise of literally looking down his nose as he spoke. "We tracked Valerio's plane too, and Interpol got us ready. I just needed to have faith that your high-functioning savant would come good. And he did."

"I called 'em after I left you to bring the bracelet here," Jules confessed.

Toby blinked the solution from his eyes. "How could you?"

"Your way wasn't working. Just cause you accept mission creep, it don't mean I have to."

"Mission creep?" Bridget said.

"I came to Prague to find my mom's bracelet. Then we're in Windsor, then a gunfight in Rome. Now Mongolia. A manuscript, a second bangle. Only they're not jewelry, they're a *key*, and suddenly I'm needed to help some psycho find a tomb. Mission creep."

"Key?" Colin said. "Tomb?

"Quiet," Toby hissed.

"Come, my boy." Colin attempted a smile, but it came out as a grimace. "We simply must chat more."

"Boy?" Jules said.

"I need your memory of what you saw on that plane, the photos you said you sent to this Lost Origins Institute, and any other background that might come to you."

"Don't call me 'boy,' or we're gonna have a problem."

Colin exhaled hard through his nose. "Have it your way. But your friends are in the middle of something very unsavory." He gestured toward one of eight body bags arranged by the Mongolian National Police Agency. Cops had broken down in tears at the sight, unused to this level of violence outside the gangs and drugs smugglers on their society's outskirts. "Tell me... what were you here to steal?"

"We were here on legitimate business." Toby wafted a hand at the medic. "Thank you, but I'm perfectly fine."

The medic waited on Colin, who nodded to all three, and they departed to help with the removal of Valerio's victims.

"Legitimate business?" Colin's eyebrow popped up. "With whom?"

"I already made my statement. Our contact was killed in the raid."

"Right, right. A raid orchestrated by someone working with Valerio Conchin, no doubt. Valerio Conchin, who, I expect, will prove very difficult to pin down to this country. But there is one young man who flew in on his plane and sent some postal workers to free a drugged woman. I don't think it will take much to pin that on a member of your group."

"Valerio isn't a member of the institute." Toby stared at Jules for a beat before returning to Colin.

"Your boy here is directly connected to Valerio *and* to you. It's enough to hold you."

"Amir Fong was going to loan us a piece that might have profound bearing on our understanding of a short passage of time represented by gaps in the Bible. Nothing blasphemous, but a curiosity all the same."

"And he was just going to lend you this? Like you expected me to lend you the Kerala manuscript?"

"I asked nicely. And Mr. Fong wasn't quite the cad you are."

Jules had never heard the word "cad" used without irony before. He stood, stretched his arms. "What actually happens now?"

"Depends on you, my boy." Colin rocked to-and-fro on his heels, hands behind his back. "Do I arrest your friends and keep them locked up in Mongolia until we conclude matters? *Legally.* Or do I simply deport them and have them arrested as soon as they land in Europe?"

"There's no need for that," Jules said. "Let 'em go. They got nothing. Couldn't interfere if they wanted."

"And you?"

"They were here to ask for a loan. Willing to pay for it. I'll testify to that. You want my photos of Saint Thomas's journal, you let 'em go."

Bridget and Toby stood now. Shakily.

"That won't work for me," Colin said. "Because I am not some bargain-basement deal maker. I am a representative of Her Majesty's government in pursuit of property of the crown. You will not stand in my way, especially when you can prove so useful. At the same time, I don't actually *need* you. You're 'gravy' as the youths say these days. But *you*, my boy, you *do* need *me*."

It was a common tactic in law enforcement circles, minimizing the suspect's bargaining chip and rejecting any notion that they can be helpful to the bigger fish. Like the Reid interrogation method, it was negotiable if you spotted it. And Jules was still there despite the grogginess of the flashbang, the fighting, and the poor night's sleep.

"Then I'm with them," Jules said. "We'll spend a couple hours, maybe a couple days, banged up here while Valerio does who knows what with your Queen's book. You said you want my photos, so good luck with that. Guess that means the book was just a trophy for the royal family and of no actual value to them. Unlike the folks your people stole it from. Pics are on a phone hidden somewhere between here and that parcel depot you know about, which is almost two hours of Mongolian countryside and freeways. You ain't finding that, *my man*."

He just had to hope they didn't search him. He had two phones on him, and they'd found the one he was using to communicate with LORI, but not the dead one he'd used on the plane, which was currently nestled uncomfortably in a pouch at his groin.

"If you didn't need that," Jules said, "you'd have said something already."

Colin's deeply offended expression suggested he was taken aback, unused to being challenged in such a manner. Must have military service in his backstory.

He pursed his lips in an exaggerated pout before standing tall and stiff. "For the sake of expediency, I put this deal to you. Any assistance you offer in retrieving the items allegedly stolen by the suspect known as Valerio Conchin will be taken into consideration when the matter of charges against your..." He swiped a hand at Toby and Bridget as if they'd just broken wind. "Friends. They are taken into custody here, house arrest. Treated well, but guarded like unwelcome guests. In return, we will not pursue criminal charges *if* the Ruby Rock bangle is returned to the Mongolians, the manuscript of Doubting Thomas is returned to Her Majesty, and your dear *mama's* Aradia bracelet back in *your* thieving hands. Fair? But you have to tell me everything. Right now. In front of Toby Smith."

Jules observed Toby's cheeks redden. Bridget looked away.

The deal was a good one.

So he spilled. He told Colin the two bangles slotted together, that they opened a tomb of someone called "the first priest," and how Jules suspected this to be where Saint Thomas ended up instead of Chennai. He almost segued into the revisionist chronology of the term "Aradia," his theory that the original manuscript referred to it as such, and that it was pinned to Herodias intentionally at a later date rather than a confusion in pronunciation. As he spoke, Toby's face creased more and more, and Bridget continued to focus anywhere but on Jules. He said nothing about the effect his touch had on the stones but revealed that Valerio knew the tomb's location, that it was likely in Thomas's old stomping ground of India—

"Why only 'likely'?" Colin asked, cutting him off.

"Valerio never said. But Thomas got ill here and left Mary's bangle with the local Buddhists, then went home to die. Assuming he made it that far, his biggest congregation was in India."

"Ah, yes, Kerala. Do continue."

Jules finished up with Valerio's delusion that Saint Thomas's final gospel would imbue him with knowledge that would lead to power. He even quoted the man verbatim: *magic exists in this world.*

A fortyish Caucasian woman in a pantsuit sidled up to Colin, and the pair stepped away while she whispered in his ear, hand cupped to prevent lipreading. Colin sighed, dismissed the woman, and faced Toby.

"Mr. Smith, do you know anything about an unauthorized—"

The noise was terrific. A combined roar and scream blasted through the internal PA system, forcing the cops and Interpol agents and medics to cringe and cover their ears. Colin and Jules also fell victim. Toby and Bridget cowered but were less affected than those around them.

They'd been expecting it.

Then a downdraft thrummed from the blown-out roof. Up above, a helicopter loomed, and Harpal stood upon a skid, strapped in firmly, with a bulky pack on his back, holding what appeared to be a gun attached to the pack by a metallic hose. A flame flickered at the end.

The screeching fell silent, the power cut most likely by an agent inside the museum. By then, though, Harpal had unleashed the flames. A wide arc at first. Enough to scatter the cops and agents, Colin leaping for cover too, yelping for action. The wind threw the fire in too many directions to be controlled.

Bridget and Toby held stock-still without a hint of fear. They held hands and walked calmly toward the epicenter of the downdraft. Jules stepped toward them but caught himself.

Bridget beckoned. "Come with us!"

Toby seemed less enthused. But nodded anyway.

Them or Colin?

Who gave him a better chance of success?

He owed LORI nothing.

They weren't his family.

A line with three harnesses dropped from the chopper as another circle of fire pinned the Interpol agents back farther, dispersing before it hit anything important.

Jules had only seconds to decide.

Come on, Bridget pleaded silently. She beckoned, but Toby squeezed her hand. She'd recognized his defeat and embarrassment under Colin's gaze, and this confusion wouldn't last much longer. The flamethrower was a distraction that could only last so long.

Toby clipped the harness around his torso. "Bridget! Now!"

She complied, strapped in like someone being hoisted from the sea by a lifeguard. "Jules! Please come with us. You had no choice before. But we're out of here now."

Jules came toward them. Stopped again. He gritted his teeth behind his lips. The supposedly emotionless wreck must have been wrestling with serious emotions there, suppressing what was right with what was easier. Jules didn't take the easy route for the sake of it. If there was one thing she'd learned about him over the past few days, it was that.

But they also knew he was single-minded and belligerently focused on his mission. Hence the turmoil tearing him between Colin and LORI.

"He's made his choice," Toby said, and whirled his hand over his head.

"Wait!" Bridget reached for Jules, but it was too late. She lifted off vertically. "No! Toby, he was nearly there!"

They whooshed up, free of the roof, the fresh air hitting her like a cloak of ice, freezing her mouth, her eyes, her fingers. The line hoisted her smoothly, and Harpal helped her inside the rear of the helicopter he'd stolen from Valerio's backup team. Once Toby was also on board, the door slammed shut, and Bridget donned the proffered earphones.

Still shivering, she said, "You could have waited ten more seconds."

Toby had already equipped himself. "As I said, he made his choice."

"Screw him," Dan said at the controls. "He's done. We're wanted criminals 'cause of him."

"Dan is correct," Toby said. "We cannot return to Mongolia. Ever. Jules Sibeko must make his own way now."

Bridget stared out the window, watching first the museum then the city recede at high speed, leaving behind someone she truly believed had the potential to add a new dimension to the Lost Origins Recovery Institute. And possibly to her own world, too.

But he had indeed made his choice. And his choice did not involve her.

PART FIVE

Civilization grew in the beginning from the minute that we had communication—particularly communication by sea that enabled people to get inspiration and ideas from each other and to exchange basic raw materials.

—Thor Heyerdahl

He who knows when he can fight and when he cannot, will be victorious.

—Sun Tzu

CHAPTER
THIRTY-FOUR

LADOH, GUJARAT REGION - INDIA

Valerio's main fear now was that he'd lose Jules entirely; after the display in Mongolia with the Ruby Rock bangle, he was sure the kid was useful. Perhaps even essential. A missing cog he hadn't known was absent until he saw it in action.

Not that the cog would be hard to draw out. Jules Sibeko would keep on coming, so Valerio had no doubt there'd be another opportunity to recruit him. This time, a more forceful means of persuasion. No more Mr. Nice Billionaire Explorer.

In fact, before falling asleep on the Gulfstream for a deep, dreamless ten hours, Valerio and Horse batted around the possibility that Jules didn't necessarily need to be *alive* to activate the metal flecks within the key, and Horse promised to cut off one of the lad's fingers next time they met. An experiment of sorts.

Science.

Refreshed, showered at his house on the outskirts of Ladoh, and medicated as high as he dared, Valerio departed in the back of an armored Humvee. Accompanied as ever by Horse and a driver, they trundled from the hills along a single-lane blacktop toward the town occupied by around a thousand souls.

The streets were clean, the traffic light but chaotic, revving and honking and zipping in and out of each other's paths—as in much of India. Most of the buildings were new thanks largely to Valerio's investment in a fledgling tech startup five years ago, his entrepreneurship endearing him to a local people who believed the government had long forgotten they existed. A middle-class born out of the dirt.

"How's the cut?" Valerio asked.

Horse flexed his fingers on the arm Jules wounded first in Prague and then exacerbated in Rome. The hand turned purple at one point, but an intravenous spurt of antibiotics sorted it out within hours. "It's okay. Painkillers give me pretty much full movement. I'll rest it properly once we're done. If you don't mind me taking a couple of days off."

"Of course, my friend. You've got me this far. Take the week."

"Thanks, boss."

"Once we're done with *my* thing, of course."

No one outside Gujarat knew Valerio's location, and he existed under the alias Brandon Robinson, a name so bland he got sleepy just introducing himself. Yet it was necessary. Brandon Robinson was on his way to meet a man he'd only spoken with on the phone and via email, and the meeting at the town hall needed to go well.

They pulled up and disembarked, entering a building born from British colonial rule where they met with Ladoh's mayor in the marbled hallway.

"Sanjeev Kaur." The youthful fifty-year-old offered a handshake, which Valerio gladly accepted.

The initial up-and-down glance over his appearance was something Valerio had come to expect with every new acquaintance, but it never got easier. Jaundiced skin looked rotten, as if he were already dead, so it was a natural reaction, and he didn't hold it against Mr. Kaur.

Not much, anyway.

"Congratulations on your election, Mr. Mayor," Valerio said, breaking away.

"Sanjeev, please. If I may call you Brandon."

Jules acquiesced. First names were good for diplomacy. "I hope I can continue the relationship I had with your predecessor."

"Of course, of course. Please."

Sanjeev led Valerio into his office where two wood-framed, gold-painted chairs with green decorative padding sewn over the seats and backs waited before a table with tea upon it. In his office, positioned before the window overlooking the gardens, the scene would make a neat photo op for visiting dignitaries. This, however, was a private meeting. Even Horse wasn't invited. And after the serving boy entered and finished pouring the tea, he left too.

"So," Sanjeev said jovially, "what can I do for the illustrious Brandon Robinson?"

"You won this post on a platform of supporting local independence for the Ladoh region," Valerio said. "Which leads me to believe you have access to our friends in one of many militias."

Sanjeev steepled his fingers, maintaining his cordial mien, giving nothing away. "I believe compromise is essential. Sometimes you must talk with people you disagree with. You are a businessman. You understand this, no?"

He was leading somewhere Valerio didn't want to go. But the hand doing the leading was gentle, so he had no choice. "Yes. My investment here has brought riches to the town of Ladoh and Ladoh's surrounding region. It's this wealth that allows the separatists to campaign for independence."

"But by that same token, you would not be making... what was it? Eighty-two million US dollars last year in India alone? You would not be making that money if not for the ingenuity and hard work of our local population. Is a symbiotic relationship, no?"

Valerio suppressed an urge to press his thumbs through the man's eyes. He was getting played here. He hated being played.

What's your angle?

"Of course," Valerio said. "I don't mean to pretend I'm some sort of savior. Only that... as a gesture of friendship, I have other interests in the region. A hobby, of sorts."

Sanjeev sipped his tea. "Your company started as a factory. Cheap labor. Yes?"

"Yes."

"Taking advantage of our poverty and our lack of education. But unlike many American firms, you give your workers good facilities, you have a genuine code of conduct for the supervisors, you pay above living wages. And apprenticeships..."

Part of the agreement with Sanjeev's predecessor. "I believe strongly in workers' rights," Valerio said. "Investment in the community is essential." Big smile. The longer this summary of events both knew of went on, the more Valerio suspected there'd be some sort of sting in the tail. He hadn't even made his request yet.

"Now we have restaurants and bars, even two coffee shops. Good school, a technical college. And we are all reliant on your continued investment."

Valerio nodded. "I'm not here to ask for much, or to threaten withdrawal if I don't get it."

"Good. Because that would end badly."

Valerio bristled at the implied threat but remained cordial. "I would've gotten much higher tax breaks in Mumbai or Chennai. But I set up *here*. Because I liked the people's attitude but also because I suspect there is a site of great archeological interest located amid the ten thousand square miles of jungle out there. I mentioned my hobbies earlier."

"And you invested millions here to facilitate your hobby?"

"Here and..." Valerio counted on his fingers. "Eight other locations. Three in India. I do this because my business needs to manufacture items, design hardware and software, that sort of thing. I need locations around the world, so I pick places that can serve as a base for my pleasures as well as being sound business decisions. Does that strike you as odd?"

Sanjeev relaxed into his chair, having been somewhat tense throughout. "Not at all. It sounds most commendable. However, I do believe you need something from me."

No point in padding it out further. "Yes. The Ladoh town and region is contained within Gujarat, but we're on the coast, and this town alone makes more money than the whole of Gujarat. There are even people out here who demand independence so that we answer directly to the Indian government."

"And you no doubt picked up from my election campaign that I am a supporter of this view."

"There are people who keep the peace in the smaller villages around here. In America, we'd call them 'militia.' Armed citizens influencing the law, enforcing the law. That's on top of the regular police."

"Ah." Sanjeev stood and crossed to the window, cup in hand. "You wish me to ask them to... ease off on something?"

"Oh, no, nothing like that." Valerio stood, too. "I want to *hire* them for a job. A dangerous but lucrative one."

Valerio and Sanjeev strolled the gardens between palms and statues, the huge bright flowers and tiled benches, while Horse kept watch ten paces behind, having rejoined them at a distance.

"There are other interested parties," Valerio explained after detailing the excursion he had planned. "I need people willing to fight back should these pirates attempt to stop us. And sherpas to help with equipment. Thirty should be sufficient."

Sanjeev's pose was that of a statesman, hands clasped behind him, back straight. "You could hire professional sherpas and private security for this. For less than it will cost through me."

"I am paying for speed. A nearly immediate response. And for privacy. Better, don't you think, to keep this local? So locals benefit more than a large corporate security firm."

Sanjeev gave a brief laugh. "And because you need to pass through Ladoh militia territory?"

Valerio held up his hands. "Partly. We don't *have* to pass through, but we are close, and the main reason I want your people—"

"Not *my* people. They and I simply share a common goal."

"Then your *associates*. And if the people seeking to steal from me show up, be they... official law enforcement or not... I need a guarantee I will be protected."

Sanjeev paused as if pondering all Valerio had said. Like a bad negotiator. "I have conditions."

"Name them."

"I will ask. They will give you a price. You will pay this. Nonnegotiable. That's if they agree. I cannot guarantee this. I am not their leader, you understand."

"I do." Valerio struggled to contain his excitement. He wanted to whoop and punch the air, dance on the spot, leap to a tree branch to hang upside down, and sing. "You said 'conditions,' plural."

"Thanks to a financial portfolio I started with the free shares you gave to all townsfolk, I am really quite wealthy. A cofounder, in fact, of a business that has considerable input into a new marina in Mumbai. Coincidentally, the grand opening is tomorrow night. My final condition is that the great Valerio Conchin attends."

Valerio's heart all but stopped. "You—"

"Yes, I know. Mr. Conchin may be a renowned recluse with hardly any photographs of his face in existence, but I have my sources. *Brandon Robinson* just doesn't have quite the prestige. He certainly does not possess a yacht like the *Lady Mel*."

There were ways and means Valerio could get around this. But waiting another twenty-four hours would allow that limy curator guy to put together a plan or those others to bite at his butt again. And, with the local militia being so supportive of Sanjeev Kaur, it would require far more time and effort to circumvent the man's requests.

Besides...

Money, prestige, a spot of face time with Mumbai's rich and shameless. More important, publicity.

Perhaps making a public appearance could be turned to his advantage. He could roll with the punches, take a man exploiting him, and turn it into an opportunity. The only downside was a loss of control over how many people saw him.

Would the press be there? Probably.

But Valerio's keeping his face off the internet and away from the news was no longer a concern. He needed to put himself out in the open. To draw a cog back toward him.

Besides, Valerio would have paid much more if the man had asked. However he looked at it, this was a good deal.

CHAPTER
THIRTY-FIVE

BRITISH GOVERNMENT AIRPLANE, INDIAN AIRSPACE

The bangle was closer than ever, and all Jules had had to do was betray a bunch of people who had welcomed him into their world and wanted him to partake in their mission.

In the past week, he'd traveled on more private jets than in the previous five years combined. This was his third. The British government's Lear was far nicer than LORI's, and since it wasn't decked out in garish gold trim with the Royal Standard flag draped over every surface, as Jules had half-expected, it proved more subdued than Valerio's Gulfstream. There was no bedroom, for starters. However, the bathrooms were of the specification you'd find in a fine hotel suite, and the chairs formed beds while the cherry on top was a glass table which rose out of the floor on command, variably adjustable from the height of a coffee table to a standing desk.

That wasn't to say it was without unnecessary luxury, though. Colin's habit of trying on different watches that he kept in a safe might have been an OCD thing or vanity. Whatever, it demonstrated a whole other world from LORI's.

Colin's desk on the plane was more than a slab of glass on

stilts. It housed a touch screen akin to a giant iPad with which Jules could pair his phone—once they were en route to India. Since retrieving the phone from his underwear—and cleaning it with alcohol wipes—he had charged and then encrypted it every way he knew how, with two passwords and a fingerprint, then he password protected each photograph of Thomas's manuscript too. The jet's equipment read the screen itself rather than saving the photos, so Jules watched out for any attempt to save a screenshot, conscious that the images were his only advantage.

There were four others present: two gruff military types with firearms, scruffy beards, and Tasers; Sally, the middle-aged woman with the pantsuit whom Jules met in the museum, her hair now secured in a bun; and a man called Henry, who wore tweed and was introduced only as an expert in antiquities.

Sally examined the snapshots of Saint Thomas's journal for two hours before reporting in, with the table at a height that allowed four seats to swivel and view the progress.

"He's right, guv." She spoke with a London accent, tempered artificially to a more neutral inflection. "It's India, but these pages aren't enough."

"Valerio has more," Jules said. "You just gotta trace him and jump him when he does something illegal."

"Yes, thank you, Mr. Sibeko." Colin touched the screen and pinched to zoom out. "I have been doing this a long time. I know how to recover stolen property."

Jules watched for a few seconds as Colin tapped another page showing a diagram of one bangle, and whispered to Sally. She shook her head, and Colin sighed in frustration.

"So what's your deal?" Jules asked. "Thought you were just a curator. Don't they, like, look after museums and the stuff in 'em?"

Another sigh. He looked up from the screen. "I am not some stuffy professor keeping vases and old suits of armor free of dust. I, and Toby before me, have extensive experience in the field, but we do not achieve the post of royal curator without a lot of skills in... other areas as well."

As soon as Colin returned to the task on the screen, Jules said, "Old-school spies, huh?"

Without looking up, Colin replied, "If I were once a spy, I'd hardly tell you, now, would I?"

"Fair enough." Jules slumped back, folded his arms.

He wondered sometimes whether he suffered from what the quacks call "arrested development," a condition where one's emotional state is frozen at the point of a great trauma. So when Jules saw his parents die, his fourteen-year-old persona would be his defining characteristic of his future life. He'd grown, of course, and his life experiences had shaped him further, but there was always a niggle, that need to push a boundary or two, that left his fourteen-year-old self pounding on the door.

It's probably why he said, "Pretty lucky, huh? Born with a silver spoon where the sun can't shine, then picked up by a great man like Toby Smith—who mentored you, way I hear it. Then you gotta spend years trying to get out from under his rep."

Colin placed his hands flat on the table edges so he didn't affect the touchscreen and met Jules's gaze without lifting his head. "I spent years studying my field. I worked hard. My silver spoon would not aid *that*. When an opportunity presented itself to join Toby Smith's team, I thought it a wise move. I could not have known what a waste of a man Mr. Smith would turn out to be."

"Waste?"

"So intent on 'putting right,' as he saw it, the sins of the empire. His support for the return of the Elgin Marbles to Greece was the final nail in his career coffin." The man's expression did not falter, a stone mask of focus. Then his eyes lit up as if a fire had sparked to life. "But Britain was once a shining light across the world. Civilizing savage lands, showing them how to live better lives—"

"Religious suppression, land grabs, genocide—"

"A *benevolent* occupation of uncivilized lands. Mr. Sibeko, if those people had not rejected British rule, if people like Mr. Toby Smith had not crumbled at every request for independence, we would have shepherded this world as a force for good. The world certainly would not be in the state it currently is."

"And you think picking up a stolen book is gonna change that?"

"I think retrieving property of the crown is not simply my job. It is an obligation. The Queen is appointed by God, and she appointed me."

"So it's a holy mission."

Colin's mouth turned up, but it wasn't really a smile. "If I may..." He gestured to the screen, wanting to get back to work.

"One last thing," Jules said, warning that immature side of himself to ease up. "Why wouldn't you make your own copy of a journal that details what you can do with a fifty-thousand-year-old bracelet?"

Colin stood sharply. Sally shuffled to one side. Colin's hands waved along with the pen he was holding, which he pointed at Jules. "First of all, these items are not fifty or even thirty thousand years old. They are maybe four or five thousand, and they were manufactured by the Sumerians and passed down for several generations."

No mention of the glowing, information he hadn't shared with Colin. Did he know nothing about that side of the artifacts?

"And, Mr. Sibeko, we have proven time and again that these silly theories about ancient advanced civilizations are nothing more than fantasies thrown up by people who snag onto a question mark from years ago. Gaps in the historical record do not indicate conspiracies, and you need to get that out of your head."

The denial sounded almost like he needed to be persuaded himself.

"You really don't know, do you?" Jules said, enjoying the moment. "You honestly don't know what Valerio believes, what Toby believes?"

"I do not care what either man *believes*. They are both criminals. The difference is, we have far more evidence of Toby's activities than of Valerio's. You, on the other hand, are just a useful turncoat who is along on this ride for one reason and one reason only: *himself.*"

Jules thought of Bridget, the disappointment on her face as she rose up out of the museum in Ulaanbaatar. He swallowed, and Colin caught it.

"Yes, you see, don't you? It stings when you understand your own nature, especially when you dislike what you find there. But take comfort. A real man will do anything to achieve his dreams, to fulfill his obligations. So sit there, say nothing, and maybe you won't exactly come out smelling of roses, but you should be able to wash the stink off yourself. Eventually."

CHAPTER
THIRTY-SIX

SINGAPORE

Morgan Winter Holdings was an old company linked to the Carson Corporation, a real estate branch that served as a tax write-off for Bridget's parents when times were good, and the sprawling thirtieth-floor apartment in Singapore was a tool for that purpose. Morgan Winter Holdings owned it during those periods when no such write-offs were needed, then, if the Carson Corporation demanded a touch of leeway with the IRS, the corporation bought up Morgan Winter's properties at an inflated price before selling them all back at whatever value best served their accounts. On the day after the Carsons' darling daughter escaped Mongolia, the apartment was owned by Morgan Winter, making it difficult for both foreign governments and insane billionaires to trace.

"Let's not hang around longer than necessary," Bridget told the others after allocating rooms for a couple of hours' sleep.

"This place is just... here?" Harpal gazed about the apartment with its spacious living room, wide-open kitchen and dining room, and a view over the dark city broken up by a million or more lights. "It's yours?"

"It sits empty unless it's needed. And we need it."

"Eight hours downtime," Toby said. "Then we'll begin again."

Bridget didn't know how much sleep the others got, but it took her two hours and half a sleeping pill to drop off. After waking, she felt sluggish as she joined the team in the kitchen, perking up only when she realized she'd been out for ten full hours rather than the remaining six.

"We all needed it," Dan said.

It turned out he'd woken himself early and snuck around, deactivating everyone's alarm clocks and phones, then set to work on Bridget's notes concerning the whereabouts of Saint Thomas's tomb and figuring out how to get into India undetected. The answer to the latter question was a combination of bribery and Harpal's old contacts, but Dan said he could do no more with Bridget's work.

The four sat around the dining table, munching on bacon sandwiches and slurping coffee or tea. Bridget's printouts were scattered out of order.

"Once I put them back together," she said, "I'll try to get a closer location. Right now, I think it's in the north of India."

Dan shuffled a few sheets, attempting to reorder them. "Sorry, I just wanted to look at it from another point of view."

"There are no riddles here?" Harpal asked. "We're good at riddles."

"They're not *riddles*." Toby sounded exasperated. "They are *accounts* from the day in which they were *written*. Occasionally, people got smart and hid their directions in other forms, but that was to conceal their true meaning from those who would steal such objects. In most cases, though, we are simply working out the language, the diction, and putting it back together in a way we understand today. Thomas wanted his tomb found. His journal was intended for the other apostles. We just need to work out what he meant."

Harpal presented a phone to Bridget, an email on-screen. "Can we get these?"

"What is it?" she asked.

"Shopping list from Charlie. She's on her way."

"Here?" Toby said. "But I thought—"

"Yeah," Dan interrupted. "Something about not trusting us to stay alive without her. She boarded a plane six hours ago. But now we got some time to breathe, there's a number of things we have to discuss."

"Such as?"

"Let's go shopping first. We'll talk on the way."

The twenty-four-hour electronics store was a wonderland of tech, laid out just right, with each department allocated a set floor space and not an inch more. Except where one item complemented another, but that was only for display purposes. So where a 4K camera phone could be hooked up to a TV, it was. Bridget noted the name of the store and emailed it straight to Charlie; she would hack it and check whether their images could be found on security footage or anything internet connected. They had no idea who might be following them.

Ambling between the aisles, Dan appeared grim, tense. "Assuming we aren't giving up, we have to face the fact this isn't just a treasure hunt anymore. Agreed?"

"Agreed, but it's unclear exactly *what* it has become," Toby said. "Something's off with Valerio. He's hurt people before, killed to cover his tracks, but never randomly murdered. Not like... sport. It's as if he's terrified of losing."

"Desperate," Harpal agreed.

"He clearly believes there's more of a prize than he's claimed in the past. More than prestige, more than an ego trip."

"More dangerous than we figured him for," Dan added.

"And with Colin Waterston involved," Bridget said, "he'll be more eager than ever to throw Toby in a jail someplace. Anywhere. He still hates you."

"Yes, yes." Toby waved off her concern. "But we don't factor in my relationship with him. Only his threat to the outcome of this task. Clear?"

All agreed.

Dan remained tense as they halted beside a row of thin metal laptops. His attention fell on Bridget. "One other problem we have."

Bridget guessed what was coming, but wanted him to vocalize it.

He said, "Jules."

"What about him?" Harpal asked, reading Charlie's list as he checked the specs on each machine.

"He'll keep on going," Dan answered. "Won't stop. He can't stop."

"Which puts him in direct danger from Valerio," Bridget said.

Dan scoffed, a glance at the ceiling, then back to Bridget. "He isn't our problem, and he isn't our ally. He's in this for his own gain, and anything else is an act. I suggest we write him off now as an aggressive competitor."

Harpal tapped a new HP model, one with a sturdy metal case and a solid-state drive. He signaled the sleepy sales assistant and held up two fingers to indicate what he needed. The assistant brightened immediately and scuttled away to retrieve what would surely be a healthy commission.

"Aggressive?" Bridget said. "Please. He's hardly—"

Toby stopped her with a raised palm. "He means Jules is actively working against our interest. And I agree. He has a singular goal. One solitary item to ease whatever mental pain he still feels over his mother's passing. What I witnessed back in Mongolia was a lightning-quick mind calculating that he had a better chance of success with Colin. Whereas we need to solve this for more worldly reasons."

Harpal selected two rubber cases to fit the laptops, but was clearly listening. "He's cold. He hasn't got a social bone in his body. Right now, I bet he's got his feet up, planning how to cut Valerio off alongside that stuck-up idiot. Not a thought for us."

Bridget was about to deny that, to say it wasn't true, but Dan's pale face stopped her. He seemed worried about bringing up the subject of Jules. Perhaps her desire to avoid judging Jules was being misinterpreted as something deeper.

The lady doth protest too much?

Still, as they walked on toward the next items on Charlie's list, she could not let it lie entirely. "Let's not put him on a kill list just yet."

Dan let his head drop as if he'd been ready for this. When he met her eyes again, he acted even more apprehensive. "I don't have a kill list. I mean, I'll drop Valerio and Horse in a heartbeat, but... Jules isn't a bad kid. He's just mixed up. Charlie was right. A guy that obsessed with an outcome for so many years, without even understanding why he wants what he wants... it was a gamble."

"And we lost big," Toby said. "That's on me. I apologize."

Harpal located the new burner phones, as per Charlie's list, and as the assistant placed the boxes of laptops behind the counter to ring up, he smiled at Harpal's silent request for six cells.

Bridget rubbed Toby's back. "You couldn't have known how he'd react. After being so close, and... he did what he does. He calculated. He came to a conclusion and followed it." She turned to Dan. "Fine. He's not on our side. But we give him a chance to come back if he wants it. Okay? He needs a therapist, not a beating."

The AC hummed, blasting cold all around them, the loudest noise in the store when the voices paused.

Then the sales clerk spoke: "Sir?"

Harpal stalked toward a collection of high-end toys, and the assistant followed.

Bridget broke the silence. "Can we at least focus on the biggest threat?"

"Valerio," Toby said.

"Right." Dan almost looked happy to change the subject. "New hobby now—killing indiscriminately."

"He is taking a lot of pharmaceuticals, so that may contribute to an escalation in his natural mental issues. He's dying. His last hurrah. Either something he must achieve, or he really believes some magical tool can heal him."

"Either way, it's an endgame."

"And although Colin is better resourced than we are, he lacks our understanding of Valerio. He *will* underestimate the man."

Bridget picked up on the fear from the two men as they strolled toward the checkout, catching up with Harpal and his new best friend. When a psyche expert and a hardened soldier are afraid of someone, it pays to listen.

Dan went on, "Valerio's tactics remind me of warlord enforcement. People of means who take advantage of war and profit from it. Or like a religious fanatic faking that he follows the true faith, and recruits uneducated or easily manipulated saps. Valerio's using money and black-market mercs, but the principle's the same. Promise something big at the end. High risk, high reward."

Bridget ran her finger along a shelf of tablet computers, stopping at the final item on Charlie's list, a powerful Android device that she would wipe and install Linux on. "I can't believe he'd be so cruel, though."

"He has a *target*," Harpal said, returning to them, "and the last years of his life have all built to it."

Bridget paused by the checkout. "But *what* target? Christians believe the body parts of saints can have miraculous properties, so maybe he believes Saint Thomas's tomb will help him."

They all considered it.

Toby said, "I don't think it'll be as simple as straightforward 'belief.' But whatever it turns out to be, when it fails to heal him or someone takes away what he sees as his final chance, he will be at his most dangerous. If he expects to die, he'll take as many enemies with him as he can."

"And we're not equipped for that level of confrontation," Dan said. "Unless you want to use a chunk of Alfonse's money to recruit an army like his."

"I think we can probably come to a more reasonable accommodation."

"What I mean is..." Dan held his tongue, an admission teetering on being voiced.

Bridget took over to spare him. "We should quit."

"What?" Toby said.

"Quit," Dan said. "Part of my job is knowing when to fight and when not to. We can't win against those numbers, those odds."

Bridget placed her hand on Toby's back. "Maybe we lose this time."

"Perhaps," Toby replied reluctantly. "We investigate. We get the lay of the land. If we cannot handle it... Dan, you're our man-at-arms. If you assess a situation isn't within our ability to survive, I promise we'll turn straight back around. But not yet. Not until we know for sure we are outclassed. Fair?"

"Fair," Dan said. "But consider an alliance with people better equipped."

Toby grumbled to himself as he moved forward to pay at a counter, much like a supermarket checkout. While Dan and Harpal had the teller ring up the goods and Toby flicked through a wad of American money, Bridget wandered alone to the exit.

She pushed out into the hot night and listened to the city: engines, people talking, people shouting, the thrum of electricity in the air. It was humid too, must have rained while they slept. It was common in the region to experience a five-minute downpour most days, even outside the rainy season.

Her phone vibrated in her pocket. She checked it and found it was down to one bar of power. She should have charged it. But the odd thing was that it was Toby calling her.

She searched for him through the storefront window and pinpointed him using a phone to calculate something, probably the exchange rate in pounds sterling.

He must've swapped phones in Mongolia, charged the other, and was using it now.

He swapped it with...

She answered the call. "Jules?"

"We landed," Jules replied. "In India. And I got a problem."

CHAPTER
THIRTY-SEVEN

DELHI - INDIA

Colin did not recognize the number flashing on his phone's screen, but it was still numerals, not a blocked caller ID. He ignored it. The only people worth speaking to were those he already knew, and he could not be distracted in this. Sally had been unable to crack most of the manuscript's language, and since it had long been treated as a curiosity in the Queen's collection rather than a useful historical document, no one had even tried to translate it before. While Sally's colleagues back in the UK attempted to confirm the Sibeko boy's information, they were riding along on what the turncoat told them. Colin meanwhile set up at a military airfield north of Delhi to await the verdict, since Conchin had significant holdings and property here.

But it was damn hot. *In the middle of the night.* That god-awful *wet* hot that penetrated one's clothing as soon as a person ventured out.

They had been granted leave to use the tarmac. What had been promised as "offices" were in fact prefab cabins on bricks, such as a foreman might occupy on a building site, with no air conditioning. When Colin inquired after such a luxury, their sole host pointed at a fan in one corner.

The former military pilots didn't grumble at the chance of forty winks in there, but Colin could not rest in such conditions. As soon as the plane refueled, they would return inside, run the engines for a while, and cool off.

Outdoors, even approaching midnight, the heat was quite unbearable, so he wasn't looking forward to daylight. For now, he removed his tie and used a paperback novel to fan himself on the cabin's stoop. Sally and Henry paced gently around the deck while two former SAS gentlemen shadowed Jules Sibeko.

Not a difficult job at the moment; the boy was happy to sit on the lawn out front, using a cushion he had liberated from the plane without asking.

Colin had permitted him to roam as long as he took the close-protection officers with him. If he thought of further information to add, he should go through Colin. No one else.

It didn't seem that Jules Sibeko was fully on-side, though. He even appeared surprised when Colin sent the photos back to HQ in London. He'd been under the impression that the on-board computer worked like a common touchscreen device, requiring screenshots to acquire the images. He had not considered Colin might record the whole affair, including audio from everything said during the flight. The fact Jules tried to conceal his surprise was what made Colin tighten security around him.

Deception meant that Mr. Sibeko needed to be controlled.

Colin's phone rang again. Same number.

"Sally," Colin called. "What country starts their numbers zero-three?"

"Not a country," Sally replied, approaching. "It's a VOIP number."

"VOIP?"

"Voice over internet protocol. One routed through the internet. Like Skype or something similar."

Colin held the phone at arm's length to read the number again.

An internet call.

He answered. "That wouldn't be Toby, would it?"

The electronically disguised voice said, "What... how...?"

"Let's drop this, shall we? Talk normally? I'm not tracing or recording you. Frankly, you matter so little to anyone in the security services, I'd have a hard time simply persuading them to track your signal, let alone tap into it."

A series of clicks sounded, followed by Toby's real voice. "I do not wish to keep on fighting you."

"Because you'll lose."

"Because we want the same thing."

"No, I'm here to benefit *Britain*. My *country*. You are looking to make money. Now you lack a cause, money is all you have."

"Colin, we've had our differences, and I understand your stance on the UK's plundered artifacts. But this isn't about us. Or money. I do not wish to keep you from retrieving your manuscript, but we must intercept Valerio."

"And what, you want a truce? After Mongolia? Toby, you might evade the law with the aplomb of a ballet dancer, but as far as I am concerned, you are an enemy of the state."

Toby made a sharp intake of breath. "And you are an ass. A self-entitled kiss-up of an ass. But Valerio is *dangerous*. Even if you get cooperation from the Indian government, he won't hesitate to kill you."

Colin found his old mentor's desperation amusing. It wasn't a nice feeling, though, more a pitying hollow in his throat. He wished things had been different between them, but the man was a traitor, consorting with common pirates in search of buried gold.

"Goodbye, Toby." He hung up.

Jules watched with interest as Colin chatted on his phone, the man sweating like a water balloon with a slow leak. As soon as Colin stepped out of the cabin, moisture practically squirted from his pores. The woman and the older man, Henry, appeared less afflicted, but after half an hour, they were clearly drained. The only thing that apparently annoyed Colin more than the heat was that Jules had taken a red cushion from the jet and was using it to sit on the floor.

The last thing Jules needed, on top of everything else, was ants crawling up his butt.

Sally, the language "expert," didn't have a tenth of Bridget's ability, so while she'd managed a few simpler interpretations, she hadn't worked out a location. She recognized the name Zephon as the angel sent by God to sniff out Satan, but neither she nor Colin had attributed it to a star. That was up to Jules to relay, purely to sound smarter than them rather than cooperate, and the satisfaction that bloomed within him was short-lived. They sent the images back to a larger team with computers and access to a wider array of paid academics to work through it.

That Jules hadn't even considered the notion they might record the entire session annoyed him. It was an obvious possibility that he hadn't factored in, too eager to trust a man who was as untrustworthy as you could get. They'd figure it out pretty soon, meaning they'd have no need for Jules. That's why he had phoned Bridget.

They had taken his earbud back in Ulaanbatar, but since Colin kept it himself, it wasn't hard to pick the man's pocket after he hung up his jacket and changed his watch yet again.

So Jules reinserted the bud, and when he first sat down here, he'd slipped Toby's phone from his pocket, showed his guards the sudoku puzzle app, then quickly and quietly used the voice-recognition software to patch himself through.

He expected Bridget to hang up. When she didn't, he could barely speak, forcing out, "We landed. In India." He outlined what had happened and explained that he needed to know whether she'd decoded the rest of the manuscript.

She had, but wasn't sure about sharing, not after what Jules had done to them.

He got the sense that she was expecting him to say more. In the lull, he said, "I'm sorry."

She left the line open. It sounded like she was in a city. She said, "I don't believe you," and hung up.

So he was stuck. His choice was between fleeing now or awaiting the inevitable decision for Colin to ditch him once they established the tomb's, or Valerio's, whereabouts.

The problem was that the pair watching him were not simple rent-a-mercs. Everything about them demonstrated precision and expertise, from the way they carried their guns to the fact that they never stepped out of a subtle fighting stance.

No element of surprise with them.

A matter of seconds after seeing Colin hang up, Jules's phone rang. He heard it through the earpiece only and stretched, feigning a yawn to answer vocally. Any words would have to come in short bursts. He'd listen while his minders could see his mouth, then turn away to speak.

"Yeah."

"It's me," Bridget said. "Colin won't compromise with Toby."

Jules glanced Colin's way. "No. He's on a mission. Bigger picture type a' guy."

"Okay, then, I don't have much choice. I've worked out more of the message. An approximate region."

"India?"

"Yes, but not where we thought. It's not Kerala."

Jules felt eyes on him and made the most innocent face he could at the gruff, bearded guy. Fluttered his eyelids. The guy shrugged and performed a quarter turn, keeping Jules in his peripheral vision.

Jules said, "Toby okay with you giving me this?"

"He doesn't know. We're back in the apartment, but it's not working. None of this is working."

"Slow down. What do you mean?"

"I mean, we're not soldiers. Apart from Dan, but... even he's nervous. We don't go out looking for trouble. We're *archeologists.*

Treasure hunters sometimes. But we *avoid* conflict. Dan's killed more people this week than... well, since we started. But you need to hear this."

"Okay, hit me."

She told Jules about Valerio's "Brandon" HQ in the middle of Gujarat, the region bordering Rajasthan and Pakistan. Charlie had discovered the ID and property months earlier. Nine thousand square miles was a lot of area to cover, but Bridget suspected Valerio had more accurate directions. She'd only decoded a few pages, translating the ancient Hindi precursor through online manuals, while Valerio must've had time to process the entire book.

I will rest for all time in the light beneath the midnight gaze of Zephon.

"It's also known as *Zendor* in both ancient Sumerian *and* Indus," Bridget said, as if it were some big breakthrough. When Jules waited, hoping for more, she obliged. "Both Ze*phon*, in Indus, and Zen*dor*, in Hebrew, mean *Life Giver*. They're the same."

"It directly connects Saint Thomas's writing with the dialect and legends of the region."

"Adding weight to my theory that he's *transcribing* other works, not just writing a journal."

Okay, Jules thought, *not quite a breakthrough, but a relevant thread.*

"The area is militia controlled," Bridget went on. "Not terrorists, just fiercely territorial, and savage when they believe they are threatened. Harpal says they're suspected of dozens of killings in the region, and they're not above kidnapping for ransom. Like the cartels in Colombia."

"Then we'll start there and work out."

"'We'?" Bridget said. "You're coming back to us?"

"Valerio must have contacts. Someone inside the militia."

"We think it's a guy called Sanjeev Kaur. India doesn't use mayors very often, but in this case, there is a central point to the town, and he's been connected with breakaway groups before. If he's in with anyone, it's them."

Jules kept his voice low, his manner languid. "So he's there?"

"That's the thing," Bridget said. "Even without Charlie around to go deep on this, we just Googled Sanjeev Kaur. He's in Mumbai tomorrow night, a gala opening of a new marina. And his guest of honor will be none other than—"

"Valerio Conchin." Jules spoke too loudly, and the bearded guy tramped over. "Gotta go."

"So you'll work with us?"

Jules stood and backed away.

The guy held out his hand. "Give it up, beanpole."

Jules had seconds at most to say the right thing. To alleviate the hurt he was sure Bridget felt at his actions to date. On the other hand, she admitted that this wasn't their way, that they were ill equipped for such a mission.

Jules was too, though, meaning someone risked a fall.

As much as he'd grown to enjoy Bridget's company, to respect her and even the other institute members, some things were more important than feelings.

He said, "Stay away." Although he looked at the guard, he was addressing Bridget.

She picked up on it. "What? No. After what I just shared?"

"You said it yourself, you're not soldiers. You're archaeologists. You don't need to put yourselves in more danger. I'm getting the bracelet back, then it's done."

"Bangle," she said.

The pair of muscleheads glanced at one another with a fraction of a frown.

"I'll pick him up in Mumbai," Jules said. "Bring back both *bangles* and the manuscript. I'll take my mom's, then you guys can go after the tomb if you want. I don't care about that. Just leave me to it."

The two men lunged, and Jules chose not to fight back. He had information to impart, after all.

. . .

There was no need for cuffs. Colin had seen footage of the boy in action and knew he'd react differently if he wanted to. It was why he'd chosen Vic and Bryn as the men to watch Jules and—more important—act as bodyguards for Colin himself. He didn't need Toby bloody Smith to spell out the danger Valerio posed.

The only reason Valerio wasn't behind bars was that prosecuting him would reveal certain surveillance techniques to the general populace, and neither the UK government nor her crass cousins over the Pond wanted that. Until Valerio Conchin became a direct threat to either nation, he could gallivant around the world, raiding long-forgotten graves and mausoleums all he liked.

Toby's presumption that Her Majesty's head curator needed a worm to advise him spoke volumes about the man.

Yet Colin genuinely didn't know what to make of Jules's latest statement, given as it was with his arms forced behind his back by 300 pounds of SAS muscle.

"LORI found Valerio," Jules said. "They know where he is. But they ain't equipped to deal with him."

Colin chose to play along for now. "And they want the resources of Her Majesty's government to supplement their shortcomings."

"Something like that, yeah. Guessin' you said no."

"Where is he?"

Jules twitched his head at Vic, whose hands held him in place. Colin flicked a finger, gave a single nod, and Vic let go.

Jules stretched his neck and arms. "Can you get us to Mumbai?"

"Of course." Colin wiped more sweat from his brow with a handkerchief. "Can you be more specific?"

"About a hundred miles to the north of Mumbai, some guy called Sanjeev Kaur has a property. Valerio's holed up there. And I'm coming. Unless your buddies called you back."

Colin would verify the property, but it sounded about right. Sanjeev Kaur led a town in which Valerio thought he existed under the cloak of anonymity, and there was no way someone as unconnected as Jules Sibeko would make such a leap of logic. "Fine, you can come. But you will wait in Mumbai until we get back. Clear?"

"Clear," Jules said, and strode toward the jet without being invited.

CHAPTER
THIRTY-EIGHT

MUMBAI - INDIA

As expected, Colin ordered Jules grounded upon landing. They used Mumbai's main airport, Chhatrapati Shivaji International, touching down at four a.m., then taxiing to a private terminal. The pilots disembarked before a thin Indian man in a crisp suit greeted them, and he and Colin spent ten minutes after their initial handshake talking on the tarmac. The man, presumably a manager, made two phone calls, then swept his arm between Colin and the building that would lead them to the freeways north.

Jules's gamble had paid off.

It seemed logical that if Sanjeev Kaur was entertaining business associates in Mumbai, he must keep property here, be it via a shell or owned outright, and Jules's hundred-mile estimate gave a flexible radius in that if it was over or under by twenty or even thirty miles, he could simply state that he was rounding up or down. As it turned out, 182 miles northwest of Mumbai lay a series of industrial estates on which Kaur owned three units.

"That's around a hundred miles as the crow flies," Jules said. "Hundred and twenty?"

Colin mapped it on his touchscreen and said nothing more on the subject. It would be a five-hour drive since they had been unable to procure a helicopter.

The curator took Vic and Bryn with him this time, Henry and Sally too, which left only the airport security guys to watch Jules.

It was as if Jules had reached the limit of his usefulness to Colin and had been discarded as a loose end to keep from unraveling too far. The Indian manager didn't appear to enjoy relinquishing his guards for this duty, but whomever he spoke with next overrode his position.

Jules hadn't changed clothes in a couple of days, so he still wore the cargo pants and T-shirt Toby had supplied in Ulaanbaatar, his underwear now unpleasant to the touch. His leather jacket still looked pretty cool, yet was anything *but* cool in the heat that was sure to descend. He was without cash and without identity documents; both real and fake were all still in Rome. Unless Toby or Bridget fished them out of the rental car's trunk before leaving.

Looking around the plane's cabin, he figured cash wouldn't be a problem.

He unlocked the hatch, and once it opened and hissed to a stop, he stepped out onto the tarmac, carrying a knapsack the size of a child's lunch box, the best bag he could find. It was cooler here than in Delhi, but the sun breaking on the horizon was already warming the air.

The two security guards in their dark-green uniforms snapped to attention and rested their hands on the butts of their guns.

Jules sat on the second step, indicating that he didn't pose a threat, then opened the bag to prove he wasn't armed. From the knapsack, he selected two of Colin's watches. One was a Patek Philippe, a Swiss timepiece worth tens of thousands of dollars, with so many dials and colors it resembled a sailor's navigation device; the other was a Ulysse Nardin, close in value, with a textured blue face and gold hands and trim.

Both guards brightened, then looked fearful.

"I'll be back in an hour," Jules said. When it became plain they spoke little English, he held up a single finger and pointed at a watch. "One hour. Me."

He waggled two fingers to signal running.

The lead guard's hand trembled as he reached for the Patek Philippe. He weighed it in his grasp. In India, this item was worth several years' wages, even in a plum job like airport security.

Eyes still on the watch, the man held up a finger. "*One...* hour?"

Jules formed a wide smile and nodded. "Girlfriend." He considered making another gesture with his fingers, something lewd, but the pair laughed jovially without the need to be too on the nose. The fear seeped out of them.

"One hour." He stood and handed the other his new bounty. "Hide those. Tell no one."

Beaming, the second guard said, "Secret!"

"Definitely. See you soon!"

After passing through the private terminal, which cut out the need for immigration, Jules opened every door using the chipped IDs he'd lifted from the guards and sauntered out front to join dozens of other travelers, where he simply caught a taxi.

He felt like crap as he watched the outskirts of the city pass by. He hoped the guards found a good hiding place for those items, or they'd be confiscated and the men fired or even jailed. He made a mental note to check up on their fate once this was over and offer financial support if they needed it—once Alfonse's reward money came his way. If he kept hold of the stolen IDs, he could find them easily.

Damn.

When did Jules start caring about such folks? He'd bribed dozens of officials and low-level grunts and never thought twice about it. Perhaps because those recipients were always among the most corrupt, those who knew better. This pair appeared overwhelmed by the potential wealth on offer, in all likelihood thinking about the benefit to their families rather than simple greed.

In the knapsack, Jules had sequestered all he could from the Lear's main cabin. He had taken four elite watches from the laughably simplistic safe, two of which had already found new homes, along with a gift-wrapped box bearing a "Happy Anniversary" tag that contained a ruby-encrusted necklace, and two small bottles of thirty-year-old Scotch whisky from the liquor cabinet. Smaller items swiped from around the place included a cigar cutter, two cut-crystal tumblers, an iPhone with no power, and luckily, a charger. This time, Colin had kept hold of both Jules's phones, so it wasn't as if he could hock them.

The taxi ride from the airport cost him one bottle of fine liquor.

Mumbai was a lot like New York. No single city center but a ton of districts, similar to Manhattan and Brooklyn. He asked to be taken to where backpackers could find affordable accommodation, figuring the driver would almost certainly know one owner or another, and more important, he hoped he'd fit in better there. He wasn't wrong.

He left the taxi and ensured the driver saw him enter the Blue Palm Tree hostel. Mooching around the lobby, he waited five minutes, perusing leaflets, the drowsy receptionist not bothering him at all. Right up until he departed.

Outside, he wandered as casually as he could, the ovenlike heat building quickly and smog descending as the city awoke and its inhabitants set out to work. He carried the bag on his shoulder, his jacket in one hand, and when he heard three Americans chatting loudly outside a café, he played his favorite character: fish-out-of-water student abroad for the first time. Shyly, he asked about a market or a place to barter.

"I need to practice," he said. "Starting business school in the fall."

The three jock types assessed him, exchanged amused glances, and eventually sent him on a fifteen-minute walk to where a sprawling hangar-type structure housed an indoor market. By now the temperature had reached the high seventies, but with a roof overhead, it climbed into the nineties. It wasn't difficult to find someone willing to exchange the iPhone for six thousand Indian rupees—less than a hundred dollars. The retailer referred him to a colleague, who bought the tumblers for another thousand—around fifteen bucks—and the cigar cutter netted him fifteen hundred. Not a fortune, but it was enough seed money to get around, possibly even disappear for the day.

At a different café from where he met the Americans, he bought a meal of chicken and rice wrapped in roti bread and washed it down with ice-cold lemonade. After buying a change of clothes and trashing his old ones, he took up residence in an internet café to research Sanjeev Kaur's grand opening.

Gatecrashing the party would take dough and a backup plan and, if possible, a second backup plan. Pawning items wasn't as easy as he'd hoped, so he accessed the Tor network, or the "dark web" in layman's terms, and located a broker he'd used a number of times in the region. The broker recommended a fence a twenty-minute tuk-tuk ride away.

Operating out of one of the hundreds of building sites around the city, the man was open and easy mannered but drove down the price to a combination of local currency and US dollars, a total dollar equivalent of ten grand for what would retail at about forty thousand. Not bad.

From there, Jules legitimately bought binoculars, dark loose-fitting clothes, a short-bladed hunting knife, and a ski mask, then headed for the most upmarket retail district his taxi driver could recommend, one easily comparable to Paris or Milan.

After picking up a cap to hide from most of the CCTVs, he went on to buy an off-the-rack but expensive tuxedo plus a straight-up Wall Street–style pinstripe with matching shirts, a selection of ties, and two pairs of shoes. He probably would not need every item, but in the absence of a firm plan at this stage he wanted to be prepared. On a whim, or an additional layer of prep, he added a prestigious watch, less-ostentatious than Colin's, so set him back a mere thousand bucks. He paid for a haircut and wet shave before checking into the fourth floor of a moderate hotel by the waterfront, the nicest place he could find that took cash and did not demand a photo ID.

Laying out his bounty on the air-conditioned room's floor, he contemplated anything he may have forgotten. It was a seaport, so he could easily acquire scuba gear later.

Two approaches: undercover or burglary.

From his perusal of previous gatherings hosted by Sanjeev Kaur, the man surrounded himself with many people. An egomaniac who, like Valerio, believed himself to be above reproach.

Using the binoculars, Jules scanned the harbor from his window.

The new marina, named Visk Landing for reasons he did not care about, was busy with yachts and people. Far north of the Mallet Blunder dockyard, the multimillion-dollar development covered two square miles, boasting space for up to a hundred vessels of varying size and providing repair services, fueling, and maintenance. Cafés, bars, and restaurants lined up beside art galleries, bespoke fashion boutiques, and companies selling more boats, all secure behind a chain-link boundary, cutting off the riffraff and the working crafts that occupied piers half a mile on either side.

Unable to make out faces, it was still clear the eateries were bustling with the expertly quaffed, the bejeweled, and the stinking rich of both Indian and Caucasian descent.

Amid the forty- and fifty-meter crafts, the *Lady Mel* stood out: seventy-two meters with twin 1,070-horsepower engines, three stories with a pool on the top deck and platforms at the aft and stern. Gleaming white, its $52 million price tag oozed from every perfect angle. Valerio's yacht. Not exactly a secret out there on the standard web.

Jules lowered the glasses.

A high-profile development hosting its gala opening.

Valerio certain to be there.

Tight security.

No one would know Jules.

A failed break-in meant arrest or death, but a failed gate-crashing meant being thrown out.

And he could always return after being dismissed.

It was settled.

He had four hours to sleep and to prepare.

CHAPTER
THIRTY-NINE

The chain-link fence was not a problem for Jules, even dressed in a tuxedo and bow tie. He carried his brand-new shoes, shined to mirror-quality blackness, in a bag clenched between his teeth and climbed barefoot, having accessed the perimeter via a rowboat bought for $200. Trusting his backup scuba gear would be safe under this isolated section of harbor, it would either wait until he returned needing to access the yacht after the party, or someone would happen along the next day to give it a good home.

With no one patrolling the outer limits, he donned his socks and shoes and sauntered toward the strings of lights and the hum of voices and music.

The marina was transformed into a neighborhood fair, except the women mostly wore cocktail dresses and the men tuxedoes, with a smattering of both genders showing off the formalwear of their heritage; saris and turbans, robes and traditional tribal outfits. Designer boutiques stayed open after dark, and the bars were making a killing. Hundreds of people swarmed the eateries since even a yacht the size of the *Lady Mel* was unable to cater for all of them. Unlike similar gatherings in the States, a black man was not an uncommon sight here, many with distinctly African tones amid the Caucasian Europeans and the more local ethnicities. No one glanced at him twice except for the occasional lingering glance. But that was okay; he looked *fine*.

Not even the cops dotted around seemed suspicious of him.

He spent the next half hour mingling, faking that he was happy here, pushing the visual cues into his performance without fully understanding the underlying reason for them. At one point, he engaged in small talk with a Frenchman and picked the man's pocket, coming away with a wallet and a flyer for an aquarium. Instead of keeping them, he returned them to the man, saying he just found the items on the floor. He repeated this in four more establishments, drinking water or lime cordial, until he dipped into the handbag of an Indian woman in a blue silk sari.

In there, he found an exclusive invitation to the *Lady Mel* in gold leaf printed on heavy white cardstock. Unfortunately, it was a named invite: *Ojal Bhatia*.

Two choices: keep plugging away until he lucked across a man's name or trust that Ojal was either unisex or that the security guard wouldn't know the difference.

Reconnoiter, then decide.

On the walk along the pier where the majority of yachts and plush smaller vessels congregated, red-vested waiters handed out flutes of champagne. Jules accepted one as camouflage. They all came with berries nestled at the bottom, apparently a trendy addition among the mega-rich.

The gangplank reached the *Lady Mel* from a raised stone platform, which appeared designed specifically for larger vessels—a short walk up a staircase that came equipped with a wheelchair elevator on the side. Jules paused to assess the security guards checking invites: two Indian, two white. There was a steady stream of guests ahead of him, six to be exact, all couples.

Picking the pocket or bag of someone headed directly for the *Mel* made a certain sense, maybe even a black someone. But if that person kicked up a fuss and revealed his name, and if one of the greeters recalled admitting a guest with that invite moments earlier, Jules would have to flee. Using the name of someone who appeared uninterested in using their invite at the moment gave him more time.

He thought it through no longer, ascending the stairs with his chin high and smile wide. Two couples behind. The Indian men, who might clock Ojal as a female name, checked the invite of a Caucasian couple, while the white men attended to a black man with an Indian woman on his arm.

I belong here.

I am one of them.

These bouncers are flotsam in my shadow.

I belong here among the elite.

The white guards were freed up first.

"Hey." Jules handed the first guy the card. "How's it going?"

Both eyeballed him and nodded. One said, "Good, sir, thank you."

"Cool."

The other read from Jules's card, drawing out the words. "Ojal Bhatia."

Jules turned his head slightly to see whether the Indian men had heard, but they hadn't. Back to the white guys, he said, "It's Nigerian. Means 'babe of the sun.' My mom was kind of a hippie. Only, y'know... African."

The guard looked right at him. A cop's death stare. Waiting for a suspect to wither under his suspicious gaze.

What a dork.

You're blowing this.

"Thank you, sir." The bouncer with the invite handed it back to him with a slight bow of the head and stood aside.

His pal said, "Have a good night, sir."

And Jules walked straight through.

This form of burglary wasn't common for Jules. He never relaxed in situations where he might have to justify his presence or hold a conversation with a stranger. After all, he could only absorb so much trivia before he died of boredom. It was far easier to bribe someone for access or to scale a building and cut a hole in a window. Even the scuba gear would be more comfortable than this. Possibly easier too.

A glaring security lapse invited would-be thieves aboard the *Lady Mel* via her lifeboat access point. The launch was too big to keep it inside the hull, but the law required yachts of this size to provide something suitable to evacuate all passengers, even when docked. For tonight, that meant a larger than usual escape vessel bobbed in the water by the aft exit. Less of an eyesore and simple to access in case of a major breach.

The undercover route was less risky if caught, though.

Jules breezed through the partiers. After tipping the champagne overboard, another waiter accepted the empty glass, and Jules wound inside to a saloon with an oval bar. All was lit in light blue with sparkling electric tea lights acting as stars or bioluminescent creatures swimming underwater. A couple dozen people milled around politely, not a crush like you would endure in a New York bar.

And everything was free.

He ordered a mango juice with a soda top and explored further: the pool deck above was the most popular, where bhangra music played at a subtle volume; a reception room with a circular seating pattern found several of the more inebriated invitees lounging and chatting in slurred tones; the aft platform served nibbles of crayfish, lobster, veal, and a whole host of vegetarian options. From the plans he'd pulled off the internet for this particular model of yacht, the three locked doors he encountered throughout led to the owner's private quarters, the bridge, and the engine room.

Any safe would likely be in the private quarters. Valerio was probably down there, waiting for the party to get going before appearing, and Sanjeev Kaur too, since he should have been up here; one was the host, the other the guest of honor—even though it was his boat. They had to appear soon.

That door, though, was located down a flight of five stairs, an access point he did not attempt as the hotel-style lock flashed red. Electronic. Requiring a fingerprint, not a card.

On the plus side, it was visible from the reception room full of drunks. On the minus side, Jules had to pretend to be drunk. Another minus was that he couldn't act worth a damn, beyond the basics of social interaction. Anything more than looking stern or confident or interested or—at a push—amused, and he floundered. Those expressions got him through pretty much every situation, but faking physical inebriation was a performance he hadn't practiced.

He settled for being a sleepy drunk, silent, smiling inanely at any comment directed his way. Two Indian men with familial similarities in their faces—brothers, he expected—kept pawing, vying for his attention, trying to get him to look at some source of hilarity on their phones.

The thirty minutes it took for that door to open were the longest he'd lived through in years.

It was Valerio who stepped out first, then Sanjeev, both done up to the nines in tuxedoes instantly recognizable as being many times more expensive than Jules's, despite the fortune he spent this morning. Two knots of Indian muscle in suits greeted them, their jackets straining against large handguns in shoulder holsters, brows low and eyes focused everywhere but on the high-flying guests lest they creep out a billionaire and give rise to a party-spoiling tantrum.

They slipped out to the left to access the main deck.

No Horse.

Was he left protecting the bangles?

It was as if Valerio was—

"So you *did* think you could sneak on board my yacht! I owe Horse fifty dollars."

Jules snapped his head around to find Valerio with the two mountains in suits, hands clasped before them. They circled behind him.

He said nothing. Just spent a second assessing his options, his mind racing at his miscalculation, now switched to figuring out the prospective assailants' weak spots. Taking Valerio hostage looked the most viable option, but—

"Don't worry, Jules, we're not going to harm you." Valerio waved away such silly notions. "Come on, enjoy the party."

Jules hesitated. Watched for any sign the monstrous duo might attack. They kept still. But then, so did lions before pouncing.

With the pair in his peripheral vision, Jules straightened his jacket as he stood, ostensibly watching Valerio too but maintaining his concentration on the real threats.

As if reading his mind, Valerio said, "Don't concern yourself with them. They're more for show, anyway." He stage-whispered, "Horse would snap them in two in about five seconds. I reckon you'd probably take ten, but that flippy-chocky-socky stuff you do would win out in the end. Unless they shot you first." Then, back to normal, he said, "Yeah, they'd probably shoot you." He waited for some reaction. A laugh? Was that supposed to be a joke? When Jules gave no response, Valerio stood aside. "Assuming you're not *genuinely* off your face on booze... shall we?"

Jules spotted escape routes at every angle, even as he stepped ahead of Valerio into another passage. This led through the bar. His new bodyguards maintained a distance of only a step and a grab away, sufficient for a private conversation, but if Jules pulled a knife or gun, they'd be on him in a flash.

"I'm not entirely sure what you're doing here," Valerio said. "You really think I'd have the bangles with me? In Mumbai?"

"It fits with your actions so far." Jules eyed two fire exits and the two regular egress points. "Your personality type leaves nothing like that to chance. You'd assign your best people to guarantee their safety. But, same time, you can't let the responsibility go entirely. You showing up in Ulaanbaatar proves that. Your attack would've been more effective if you'd simply blasted through the museum and located it in the carnage. But, see, as soon as LORI fought back, you made yourself known. You had to control the situation. *You.*"

Valerio applauded as they left the bar and ascended to the first deck. "I love your brain, sir. I absolutely *love* it! You really are nearly as clever as me."

On the stern, the cocktail drinkers and smokers tipped their heads toward Valerio but did not approach with handshakes or business cards; a wary distance maintained. He stopped at the gunwale and leaned on the barrier, staring down at the water.

"I know that sounds conceited, but I first showed signs of genius aged six. I hatched a plan, along with my eight-year-old sister, to steal candy. A simple distraction tactic, but it worked. When my parents noticed the candy was missing, they only found the evidence I planted on my dear sis and assumed her guilty. At first. One thing I didn't factor into my deception: *she* was their favorite, and they took her word over mine."

He stepped back, thrust his hands in his pockets, and faced Jules.

"So, no, I don't always get it right, but I don't let unseeable variables interfere with how I do things. I issued your photo to every security point, and my CCTV does facial recognition approaching the efficiency of the US government. We employ the same contractor. So in other words, you're here because I want you here. And your distraction tactics won't work."

"There's no distraction," Jules said. "I'm alone. Sent the limy asshole on a ten-hour round-trip of a snipe hunt. I'm here to get the lay of the place, figure out a way in, get the bangles, and leave. Nothin' else."

"You don't care about their provenance? What they do? Why Saint Thomas fought so hard to keep them only in the hands of people he trusted?"

"No. I just want what's mine."

"And you still think I'd keep them here?"

"You've stashed 'em in the engine room with Horse." Jules's turn to gaze out at the harbor. This wasn't the only party, of course, but it was certainly the biggest, the most prestigious. "By the motor launch, in case you need to make your getaway. Guessing there's more folks out there with their lights off, waiting to hold off any law or... other parties who want the bangles."

"Oh-ho-*ho*!" Valerio spread his arms as he laughed. "My friend, you truly are my equal in the brains department. I mean, almost. You *did* walk in here expecting me to fall for your silly trick—"

"There's no trick," Jules said. "I get caught, I get away. Unless they're gonna pop me in front of your people here, I can be in that water and away before they even get the barrels free. What're they carrying? MP-443s? Makarovs?"

"Jules, Jules, Jules. This ruse is beneath you." Valerio glanced at two tall balding men who were approaching. Both diverted away to keep his conversation private. "Your little friends landed exactly..." He checked his watch. "Ninety-six minutes ago."

"Friends?" Shock stabbed through Jules's stomach, spread to his chest, and continued out through his shoulders. "No. I told them to stay away."

Valerio placed an arm around Jules's shoulders, mouth close to his ear. "And right now, they are being tracked. They're coming this way, to me. Or to you."

"No..."

"You wanted to steal my last chance at life, Jules. All because of your selfish, stupid obsession. And you'd hand over the Ruby Rock bangle, or 'Mary bangle,' so my old friend Alfonse can salve his wounded soul. Sorry, Jules, but you will not kill me in exchange for *money*." Valerio twitched his head, and the large men advanced, hands in their jackets. "And don't think of jumping overboard. They'll plug you before you hit the water. Regardless of how many guests leave with PTSD instead of a gift bag."

Jules assessed that Valerio's calculation was accurate. Possible at any rate. He nodded.

Then he swung Valerio around into the pair, and they stumbled, delaying their ability to draw on him.

Gambling that no one wanted a scene, he dashed sideways toward the bar again, meeting the brothers he encountered earlier, the drunk pair who'd wanted him to watch a video.

No longer drunk, no longer swaying, but rock steady.

The first touched a baton to Jules's leg, and a jolt shot through him. Electrocuted. A second shock knocked him from his feet.

His body convulsed.

Blackness descended.

And he could fight no more.

CHAPTER
FORTY

When Valerio cleared the yacht, thus ending the party early, Sanjeev Kaur threatened to withdraw cooperation if Valerio embarrassed him further. It was a lame threat. Valerio was now paying the Ladoh militia personally via an installment plan that would keep them in line and following orders. *His* orders, not Kaur's. The Ravi brothers, the militia leader's nominated deputies on this mission, certainly showed no objection, proving all Valerio needed was an introduction. His money did the rest.

After the final people were safely ensconced in one of the larger bars on the marina—and Valerio's personal American Express card had been swiped to cover the drink bill—he was more concerned about his own betrayal.

By Jules.

Sure, the lad never declared any sort of loyalty to Valerio's cause, but he thought there'd been a spark of interest. Like they bonded back in Ulaanbaatar. Jules had certainly been hesitant when LORI intervened, and now he'd dumped Colin Waterston too.

Belowdecks, Jules attained prisoner status; he was carted to the staging area, namely the exit hatch beside the engine room, where Horse and the militiamen prepped the yacht for their trip. A journey north up the coast.

"Where exactly?" Sanjeev demanded to know.

"Not telling," Valerio said. "And you can't make me."

It didn't matter whether Sanjeev knew, but Valerio was now in a mood to hold back all information until absolutely necessary. He didn't like acting this way, but even though they would soon be circling back around the militia-controlled jungle, it was still nine thousand square miles, an area they would need years to cover with LiDAR. But with the Thomas manuscript almost fully translated, they had narrowed it down to around a thousand, and once the Hindi etymology expert he hired delivered the obscure sections that Tina Trussot had been unable decode on the plane to Mongolia, they would zero in on the location.

Watched over by the Ravi brothers, Jules lay on a stretcher, sleeping off the effects of a massive electrical shock to his nervous system.

Such potential. *Who was this kid?*

A shame he was so damaged, so self-limiting. The boy—sorry, man, lad, gentleman, whatever—could achieve so much given some coaching, some inspiration, some... *balls*. And Valerio still did not fully understand what made Jules so special in relation to the jewelry, only that he was glad Jules had sought them out. Otherwise, they would have had to go looking for him.

That he came here as expected proved he was only *almost* as smart as Valerio.

While Jules lay unconscious, they tried setting both bangles in his palm, but neither glowed any more than when Valerio or Horse handled them, the conclusion being that he couldn't activate the stones unless awake. For this reason, Horse's original plan—to cut off Jules's arm, shoot him in the head, and drop him in the bay —wasn't feasible. Horse suggested it must be tied to brainwaves as much as his genetic signature, genes being their first theory.

No time for experiments now. Perhaps later...

"Are they secure?" Valerio asked.

Horse held up a waxed surfer's bag, the manuscript and both bangles sealed inside. "Watertight, boss. Just gotta get the launch secured to the *Lady Mel*, and we can set sail. Five minutes till we're gone."

Valerio placed his hands in his pocket and sighed. He looked down at Jules, then turned his attention to the marina outside.

The dark water bobbed four feet below the open hatch, the calm surface reflecting moonlight and distorting the city's illumination into ripples as a light wind picked up.

"Think it'll work?" he said.

"Has to," Horse replied. "Boss."

Valerio laid one hand on Horse's shoulder. "Thank you."

"Thank me if it works."

"No, I mean... thank you. For sticking around. I know you could probably have made more money taking other jobs, individual assignments instead of staying on retainer."

Horse turned his body to face Valerio. "Boss, if you want a financial justification, I can tell you, one of these days, you're gonna hit pay dirt with these excursions. I know we're looking for a specific place, but... it's been hidden for thousands of years. If it'd been found, even by thieves, we'd have heard rumors. But we haven't. When we find this tomb, we'll be the first people in there since Saint Thomas. It'll be worth billions. And you being the generous type... I figured you'd share."

Valerio swallowed what felt like a sad pill but couldn't help smiling. "I don't believe that's the only reason."

"No." Horse held his head low, then raised it to meet Valerio's gaze. "I believe in this, in what we're doing. Everything we've seen. We can do a lot of good with it. Makes all the bad stuff I've done worthwhile."

"If it's real."

"Yeah, if it's real. That's a bit of a gamble."

"There's more though." Valerio positioned both hands on Horse's shoulders this time. "Don't be shy. You can tell me."

Horse chuckled. A glance at the Ravi brothers. Back to Valerio. "I worked for some evil people in my time. I worked two branches of advanced military—SASR in Oz, Navy SEALs in the States. Plus a black-ops CIA program that didn't even have a name. Done much worse stuff than anything while working for you. It's been stable here. And you ain't bad. You're fair."

Valerio swelled with pride. Sadness, happiness. Like a movie star being honored for a lifetime achievement award. He never thought of himself as a good person before, just a person. A desperate one sometimes, willing to commit atrocious acts to arrive at the right place.

So not a *good* person, but perhaps a *courageous* one. A person willing to risk it all to achieve greatness.

"Thank you, my friend," Valerio said. "If we do make such a discovery, maybe you can retire. And you can stop calling me 'boss.'"

"Sure. We'll hang out."

"Are you going to kiss?" Jules asked, levering himself up to a sitting position, alerting the Ravi brothers who held their Russian hand cannons on him. He ignored them. "If you're gonna kiss, it's cool and all. Twenty-first century, guys."

Horse shrugged off Valerio's arms, disappointing Valerio a tad. No, he wasn't going to kiss the big lug, but a hug might not have been out of the question.

Valerio spun, swung a kick, which Jules dodged, and Valerio slipped, landing hard on his butt. He yelled, "Get this... *person*... out of my sight!"

Jules was wrenched up by his armpits and dragged toward the hatch. While he hadn't quite gotten his bearings yet, he was aware they were still on the yacht. The gaping hatch revealed techs working on securing the *Lady Mel*'s launch, meaning they were probably hitting open ocean soon, a less visible means of accessing the land where the tomb had lain hidden for millennia.

So Valerio already knew the location. Or was close.

And Jules was still alive because they needed something. Not a hostage. Perhaps they needed him to make the bangles light up, a feat he put down to genetics. Or did someone else put it down to that? It hinted at a half-remembered dream.

Maybe the bangles, once they formed the key, would open whatever door barred the way, but clearly Valerio didn't want to take a chance on a hitherto-unseen factor.

As he was being carted away, Jules said, "When you've done with me, what then?"

Valerio picked himself up off the floor, smoothing his hair and straightening his tux jacket. "After? I honestly haven't decided yet. But if you cause me any problems, I'll start cutting bits of you off and give the sharks a feast along the way."

Horse stood behind him. "Any more questions?"

"So I'm dead?" Jules said.

"Pretty much." Horse checked on progress. "About to haul her up. Okay, let's go."

"One thing." Jules dug his heels in, hindering the brothers' pace. "I got a grandmother."

"Yeah, me too," Valerio said. "Maybe they could've got together. A barbecue. Knitting club or something. Only... what happened?" He feigned deep thought. "Oh yes, *someone* turned down my kind offer and *screwed me over!*"

Jules had seen him manic, but never close to this, losing his temper. The way he shook and breathed and how Horse approached him with concern, it appeared no one else was used to this side of him.

"Need a pill?" Jules said.

"Get out."

Jules caught sight of a watch on one of the guys guarding him and held out once again. "My grandmother. Seriously, man. Just... let me say goodbye."

Valerio looked to the brothers, then Horse.

Horse shrugged. "Your call, boss."

"Someone recently told me I was a fair person." Valerio slipped a chunky smartphone from his pocket, a plus-size version of a Samsung, and unlocked it with a six-digit code. "Be quick. You're right. I need a pill."

Jules accepted the phone, conscious of the guns at his back, and dialed a number from memory. "Thank you." He waited for the person to answer. It wasn't his grandmother. If he'd timed this correctly, it should work. When the other end of the line opened, he said, "It's Jules. I'm on the boat. How long I got?"

"Now you've got in touch... approximately thirty seconds," Bridget replied. "Dan, it's a go!"

Horse reacted first, sweeping Valerio away from the open hatch. Then the brothers ordered Jules onto his knees. Jules obeyed, the phone still in his hand.

With no sign of danger, Horse unhooked a radio from the belt under his suit jacket. "All units report in, starting alpha four-eight."

"Alpha four-eight here," came the reply. "All clear up h—"

An explosion cut off the transmission. The floor rose several feet, and every person in this section stumbled and fell as the boat jerked back down. Then the whole vessel shuddered, and Jules had approximately five seconds to live.

CHAPTER
FORTY-ONE

Dan had never liked the water. Although the Rangers occasionally needed him to power boats and, more rarely, scuba dive, his deployments were mostly desert and jungle based, with a smattering of island and coastal missions. The Ranger left the more watery business to the Navy SEALs.

In fact, it wasn't until Toby headhunted him from his new training role with a private contractor that he even learned to sail. Since many of the treasures they hunted lay at the bottom of lakes and off the coast of former colonies and civilizations, he'd become an expert at all forms of maneuvering through and over the sea.

However, the stolen compact hovercraft he currently piloted was easily the most fun, bringing the millionaire's toy around so they could approach from the harbor's dark mouth. It acted like a Jet Ski, only smoother, and so simple to handle that Dan even allowed Harpal to take the reins while he mounted the rocket-propelled grenade and fired it at the *Lady Mel*. Well, not *at* it as such. But close enough to feel as if it were sinking.

Dan still didn't trust Jules, but he did trust Toby and Bridget, and he trusted Charlie's ability to "slip up" just enough to convince anyone watching for them that they were attempting to sneak into India without detection. That Charlie had hacked the security feed from the new marina and spotted Jules via facial recognition meant Valerio probably knew he was here, too. Dan's suggestion that they leave him to it and tail the boat left too much to chance.

What if they killed Jules?

So what? He'd abandoned them, sided with Colin Waterston, all because the odds of the asshat leading Jules to the Aradia bangle were better than LORI's.

Does that mean he deserves to die?

It didn't, of course, and since Valerio had murdered innocent civilians in Ulaanbaatar and apparently wielded enough influence and guile to evade arrest, it was up to Dan and Harpal to deliver that justice. They couldn't just assassinate him, even though that was Dan's preferred choice, so Toby demanded he come up with a better plan.

This was his plan: a *full-frontal assault.*

Sort of.

With the quiet engine, the hovercraft had been a spark of genius, which Dan took credit for.

Not luck—*genius.*

He hadn't wanted to go in at all, but after a frank assessment, and after locating and stealing this craft, he figured it was possible. He informed Toby that he was still prepared to quit this hunt, but if he was honest with himself, he *really* didn't want to lose.

He mounted another RPG and let rip, this time rocking the *Lady Mel*'s rear just as the first gunmen on the deck sought to repel him through automatic gunfire. The shockwave threw them off their feet. Harpal steered left, a temporary retreat to keep them out of range.

A smaller yacht fifty feet closer to shore was being evacuated, Mumbai's elite fleeing the attack. People stumbled. Some stopped to help, others ran on regardless. Once on the pier, all rushed for the safety of dry land with more on the quay joining them.

Gunfire from Valerio's yacht strafed the water. The shooters were plainly inexperienced as the barrage fell wide. Still, Harpal zigged and zagged until they were a reasonable distance out.

All the kid had to do now was get off the boat. He had the skill to scale rooftops, vault cars, and overcome trained military operatives, so surely he'd choose a dive into the harbor... if he was still alive.

Then, with a chug and a roar, the *Lady Mel* cast off, all seventy-five feet cutting forward and initiating the port engines to lumber away from the pier. They were already prepared to set sail.

"Where is he?" Harpal shouted.

More gunfire from the yacht.

"Can't see him," Charlie answered in their earbuds. "Hold on."

Four quadcopter drones sped overhead, expensive models with six-foot wingspans they'd picked up in Singapore. Adopting the same angle as Dan's initial foray, they climbed as they neared the *Lady Mel*. Spreading out. All equipped with camera phones and a little bonus that Charlie now utilized. The first drone dipped and kamikazed into the yacht's upper deck.

It exploded on impact.

A simple grenade with a pressure trigger strapped to a bottle of cheap vodka for extra flame gave it a psychological edge, if not a logistical one.

It scattered the gunmen temporarily, giving Dan time to assess the *Lady Mel*'s angle. Was it going to flee to open water or mow them down? In open water, its speed would outstrip the mini hovercraft and would soon be out of range of the drones. But it accelerated like a cow.

Dan still had two RPGs, though; he could take out something important, perhaps even sink her if he needed to.

"Damn it, Jules, where are you?"

"Still no sign," Charlie reported in. "Hit 'em again?"

"They regrouping?"

"Horse is giving orders."

"Aim for Horse," Dan said.

"I'm not assassinating anyone."

"Damn it, you sound like *him*."

A thunderous crackle sounded to starboard, and the hover-craft's fiberglass hull splintered with a dozen holes. Dan and Harpal hit the deck flat. Dan found the AK-47 procured from one of his longtime contacts in the region and, staying low, aimed it where the machine gun fired from.

Two Jet Skis sliced through the water, a pair of men in wetsuits on each. Black paint, black suits. They must have been waiting beyond the wall as backup.

"We really need our own spy satellite," Dan said.

"It's on my list," Charlie replied.

Dan had never liked AKs. They were efficient to a point, but they were urban weapons. Primed for close-quarters combat, not naval battles. The men coming toward them were better equipped, but it was impossible to tell exactly what they were packing. If they, like him, possessed explosive projectiles...

He opened fire in short bursts. If he hit anything, they'd be toast, but he needed range finders.

The lead Jet Ski veered left, the other right. The moon was bright enough to glimpse the setup: pilot and passenger—both with hefty machine guns, knives, and sidearms, other equipment strapped to the sides, and what appeared to be harpoons.

The hovercraft still ran, so Dan yelled at Harpal to take them toward the *Lady Mel*.

"Are you crazy?" he shouted back.

"With Valerio in the cross fire, they'll have to think twice about shooting," Dan said. "Now do it before they come around!"

Harpal obeyed while Dan alternated between the targets, keeping them dodging.

"Charlie, keep one drone over the *Mel*," Dan said. "Let's use the others to knock these guys off our tail."

"Will a water landing trigger the bombs?" she asked.

"Sure. Just slam in close by. It'll give us room to escape." He tried to scan the *Lady Mel*, but lights from the marina projected it mostly in silhouette. "How about Jules?"

"No sign yet."

"Sorry, Bridget," Dan said, knowing she was listening in. "We tried."

While the hovercraft had offered a tactical advantage in their ambush, the Jet Skis growled with superior horsepower and made it count as Dan reloaded the Kalashnikov.

"More company," Harpal warned.

Dan sneaked a glance toward the yacht. Sure enough, its lifeboat launch churned water behind, the nose rising through its acceleration.

"They're pinning us in." Dan loosed off two more bursts of five, forcing the Jet Skis to change direction and their gunners to miss. "Circle 'round the side. I'll concentrate on the asshole farthest out. Try to punch our way through."

Harpal said nothing, clearly understanding the maneuver was a make-or-break play; they'd either carve themselves out or be cut down.

"Now would be good, Charlie," Dan said.

"Five seconds," she replied.

Harpal opened the throttle as far as he could, but the motorboat still gained. One Jet Ski arrowed for them at an incoming angle. The second overtook, and although Dan concentrated his fire on that one, their speed now made accuracy all but impossible. The militiamen steadied themselves. The man on the back stood and aimed.

Dan ceased shooting. It was pointless.

Five feet from the threatening Jet Ski, a quadcopter slammed into the water and exploded. Only brief flames, of course, but the force of the blast flipped the Jet Ski and threw the assailants off.

Harpal gave a whoop of delight and steered hard to the right, the move creating a wake that swelled and spread. The other Jet Ski slowed as it hopped the waves, while the men in the water struggled to return to their vehicle, which was hopefully too damaged by the grenade to pursue.

"Hold it straight!" Dan ordered. "Slow it a bit."

"I got two more drones," Charlie said. "One over the *Lady Mel*, but you have to choose which goes boom."

While the motor launch was faster, the Jet Ski was more maneuverable. "The Jet Ski. Take it now."

In a repeat of her attack moments earlier, Charlie dived the quadcopter drone into the sea just feet from her target. But this time, nothing happened except a splash that caused a momentary diversion for the pilot.

"Sorry," she said. "I... I don't know what happened."

Dan bit back several swear words and prepped the RPG launcher. Two grenades left. "Hit the surface at the wrong angle. Trigger didn't ignite."

"I'll bring the other round."

"No time."

"I'm going to try."

Their hovercraft aimed for the harbor mouth. Commercial crafts were still using the entrance; trawlers, ferries, and now police-branded boats joined the party.

Dan mounted the RPG launcher on his shoulder and aimed directly at the Jet Ski, but that would do nothing except miss and spray them with saltwater. So he drew down ten feet ahead, visualized this driver's favored evasion tactic, which was to veer away from his quarry, meaning to the right.

He fired.

The projectile burst out, contrail tracking its progress. Sure enough, the target eased to the right, plainly hoping to skip the worst. But Dan had accounted for that. The explosive impacted almost square on, blowing the back of the Jet Ski apart and throwing the two men high into the air.

Ignoring another adrenaline-junkie cry of delight from Harpal, Dan reloaded and drew down on the approaching motorboat. "Hold her straight. This one's next."

CHAPTER
FORTY-TWO

In truth, Jules had no clue what he was doing. He wasn't adept on water. Traveling over solid ground, he could plan most feats in an instant. Even up in the sky, tall buildings, medium ones, small ones, he could see distance, feel the wind, knew his weight and size, all of which allowed him to calculate the effect of gravity on his leaps and falls. Water created too many variables, and he couldn't keep up.

The other thing he gauged correctly was human intent. In this case, that of Toby and the rest of his institute. Valerio revealed they were in town, even the time they landed. Assuming they brought everything they needed, Jules worked out how long it would take them to find him (it would be fast since Charlie and Harpal were both smarter than average), then come up with a plan and execute it.

No way did he predict, however, just how fine he'd cut it.

The explosions were enough to draw Horse from his immediate position, which left Jules with the simple work of overcoming the Ravi brothers and riding his luck all the way to snagging the surfer's bag containing the artifacts while Horse was distracted. It was close, but his escape into the lifeboat launch was aided by Dan's assault and something that exploded on the top deck.

The knife he'd swiped from one brother cut the rope easily, and tuxedoed up like James Bond, he was away.

Then, just as he thought he was free and clear, sticking rigidly to the flat trail left by the hovercraft thing, Dan went and aimed a rocket launcher at him.

"Got coppers incoming," Harpal said.

Dan held steady on the approaching boat. "Can you lose them?"

"Just shake that final bogey and I'll try."

"Guys, I'm catching up," Charlie said.

Dan could just make out the tiny blob pursuing the *Lady Mel*'s launch, gaining on them. "Okay, but I'm gonna try and take him myself first."

He leveled the RPG launcher and sighted through the notches, an old-fashioned targeting device; he'd trained with one, but never like this. The boat, though, was coming at them in a straight line. A fairly easy target, even thumping over the surface.

"Umm, ten seconds," Harpal said.

It was big, too, not just straight. And there was no gunfire.

"Charlie, how close are you?" Dan asked.

"Not close enough," Charlie answered. "It's too fast now you're going straight."

"Camera?"

"Can't get an angle."

"Five seconds," Harpal said. "Shoot him or wait?"

"Chill." Dan squinted at the motorboat, pressure on the trigger. "I got this."

. . .

Jules kept on course, understanding now that he must look like a hostile to Dan and Harpal. A fast craft aimed right at them, emerging from the same direction as the *Lady Mel*.

He had one chance: he needed to prove he was here, not swimming away or held hostage.

So he steered with one hand while rummaging in the wet bag with his other, weaving minutely, enough to maintain his speed, but not to capsize that damn thing.

Still.

There was no way of knowing when Dan would fire the rocket.

Jules finally grabbed what he was looking for. He lifted the Aradia bangle out first, its green light bright in the darkness, followed by the Ruby Rock.

Visible through the RPG launcher's sight, a green light shone from the approaching vessel, a red glow piercing beside that one.

Charlie said, "Oh my God! Wait! It's him! He's driving the boat. We got Jules. And he's got the bangles!"

Dan whipped the tube aside, recognizing she was right.

Damn, he almost blew Jules away.

Ah well. No harm, no foul.

After Jules held the bangles aloft and performed the trick only he could do, Dan lowered the weapon and began waving him frantically aside. Then Jules saw why.

Harpal took them on a hard right. The launch wasn't as maneuverable as the hovercraft, and the sharp turn sprayed saltwater over the controls. No problem; it was designed for this.

In Jules's hand, the Ruby Rock bangle snapped and crackled as never before. The energy expanded and consumed his hand, snaking around him like a glove. When more water splashed him, the light jumped and sparked. He dropped it in the bag, recalling Amir Fong's assessment.

We found it reacts badly to liquids. Mostly water. But especially to salted water. The less pure, the more the bangle repels it.

Police now joined the fray. Three speedboats pursued Dan and Harpal while Valerio's yacht grumbled and sped up, turning faster than anything that size had a right to, water churning in a huge wake.

Jules pulled level with Dan and Harpal, bringing himself to the attention of the cops. All were heading for shore.

"Turn back!" Jules yelled. "We can get out to sea."

Bullhorns blared from the cops' boats, too thickly accented and distorted to understand, although it was certainly English.

Dan called, "Negative. We got exfil backup on land."

"They'll have covered that. They got more eyes than you know."

The boat buffeted harder.

"Come on!" Jules shouted. "Trust me!"

"No!" Dan gestured violently toward the point where Jules had accessed the private marina. *"That* way!"

They didn't understand. He was clearly in possession of more knowledge than them, yet they still wanted him to fall in line. *He knew better.* And there was no time to explain it. They just had to follow him, and he'd take care of everything. Regroup later.

It made *sense.*

It was *logical.*

Surely they should have learned that by now.

Jules checked how far the cops lagged behind. Fifty feet. The short time he'd been in control of the vessel was enough to discern its turning circle, which he now engaged. He swung in a tight arc away from Dan and Harpal, beckoning at them to follow. It wasn't until he was facing back toward the harbor's mouth that he understood what they were doing with the *Lady Mel*: as the cops closed in, the yacht was attempting to block passage out to sea.

Meaning they definitely had people onshore waiting.

Despite how smart Toby and his group were, they were plainly inexperienced with operating at this level. In these circumstances. Jules had trained specifically to evade the law, to predict their behavior, their traps, their ruses; LORI snuck around war zones, skirted with diplomacy, which annoyed Jules even more.

If they'd listened to him, they wouldn't be in trouble now.

Sure, they'd come here to rescue him, hoping he would retrieve the bangles, but that did not mean Jules was willing to walk blindly into the same trap.

He pushed the engine to its limit, maximum throttle, fiddling with the now-open bag beside him. Not particularly caring what happened to the manuscript, he slipped on the Aradia bangle for safekeeping. If he went overboard, at least he wouldn't lose it. As he pulled off the sack, the Ruby Rock bangle came along with it, magnetically attached to the Aradia one by the shorn ends; a figure eight with his wrist through the larger loop.

A figure eight? Or handcuffs made of stone?

He needed both hands on the wheel to evade a police boat coming alongside. One of the overenthusiastic Mumbai cops tried to jump across, but Jules pulled away. The man splashed into the sea.

Seawater sprayed both bangles this time, the green glow expanding and fizzing where the outer surface touched his skin, boiling the water off.

Jules grasped the Ruby Rock bangle and yanked it free, his wet hand setting off its miniature electrical storm again. Jules felt nothing except a tingle that penetrated his muscles and hit his bones. Not in a painful way, no heat, just... awareness.

The *Lady Mel* now almost barred the harbor entrance. Other vessels blared their disapproval, trying to return to their home port from open water. Valerio wouldn't care. Whatever he wanted the bangles for was more important than anything else and perhaps even more potent than Jules's own desire.

And the cops were hurtling toward him, having given up on Dan and Harpal.

Dry land was definitely a trap. And LORI hadn't planned ahead for it the way Jules would have.

The Aradia bangle had consumed Jules's entire adult life, and laying his hands on it had only deepened his need to possess it. Yet, now, the way it reacted to water excited him, repelling it without harming him at all, as if opposite poles electrified and crashed together under pressure, releasing it as a physical chain reaction. Molecules were energized, twisted, then forced away at speed.

With the cops on either side of him and one behind, he couldn't slip up.

He never attempted things he hadn't calculated to some degree of probability. He needed at least 75 percent of the factors to be known for an educated guess. Right now, his only advantage was speed, the distance between the boats, and his own strength. Little precision on water, no certainty about the bangles' properties, and absolutely no way of predicting how this would pan out.

All he had was what he only ever used when left with no other option, something he hated trusting: gut instinct.

It was an unknown quantity. But here, with a trap in one direction and a dead end in the other, he did it anyway.

He linked the two bangles together, magnetically sealed along their opposite-cut grooves so they bonded to him in that figure eight again, the Ruby Rock empty below the Aradia. Then he used the cut rope to tie off the steering wheel to hold it straight and pushed the throttle lever all the way open. At the edge of the launch, Jules lay on his stomach, held on tight, and—hoping to generate enough of a shockwave to throw the cops off and squeeze through the narrowing passage—he touched the Aradia bangle with his thumb, linked to the Ruby Rock with his fingers, and thrust his forearm into the sea.

The water boiled and spat. Red and green lightning shot out from the bangles, illuminating the filthy bay. Fish lit up and turned over and died. Clouds of red and green spun like a hurricane viewed from a satellite.

Jules had never experienced such a loss of control, never explored a more idiotic experiment with no backup, no fallback. It terrified him to his very core and thrilled him even more.

Clouds coalesced under the surface, bonded by lightning, a massive cauldron of broiling mist and churning water, the hurricane fed by a cascade of twisting, crackling light emanating from Jules's wrist.

He steadied his heart rate.

Breathed.

Closed his eyes.

Then whipped this hand from the sea.

The lightning storm spewed forth, geysering twenty feet. A massive ball of energized saltwater gushed out, its power focused sideways but also forward in a mushroom-shaped wave. The police boats sprang into the air and capsized, tipping passengers as they leaped to safety.

But ahead, the wave expanded hard, growing, even as the lights beneath dimmed, until it rose higher than the *Lady Mel*'s deck.

No. The people...

The wave swamped Valerio's superyacht, collided side-on with its hull, and rammed the seventy-two-foot vessel against the harbor wall. Metal screeched against brick, and Jules could only watch helplessly.

If he were a religious man, he'd have prayed no one died, but he wasn't.

CHAPTER
FORTY-THREE

Jules eased off the throttle until he slowed to a crawl, with only the launch's latent momentum carrying him onward. It bobbed while he watched to see how badly he'd damaged the yacht. Although it hadn't capsized, it had come close, slammed by a wall of water generated by a power Jules had never heard of. Never dreamed might be possible.

The question of how he did it relegated itself to a secondary concern. If the vessel were to break up and sink, he'd need to fish people out before they got sucked under, rescue any unconscious folks—even Horse or Valerio, if it came to it.

All life is precious.

A strength and a weakness, aikido had been the best obsession he ever mastered. Not only the physical side; the salve on his inner turmoil proved essential to usher him to this point. He'd have died many times over, been lost to his demons forever, had he not respected the lives of others.

The *Lady Mel* rose and fell in the harbor mouth, twisting without power. A route yawned to open water. Cops swam in the water, clinging to their upturned crafts as the surface roiled.

Ashore, almost a half mile away, Jules could make out five

familiar people on a landing path, now floodlit by two vehicles spilling what seemed to be cops from within.

They'd all come. All five: Toby, Dan, Charlie, Harpal, and Bridget.

Bridget.

Folks who didn't know him so well thought of him as a cold fish, an emotionless thief interested only in the next score. People who knew him better thought pretty much the same. Occasionally, his lack of outward emotion lost him friends. The one girl who called him a "sociopath" had stuck for longer than he would've liked, even though it was just hyperbole.

Yet Bridget had seemed interested in him in more ways than mere curiosity.

Romance?

Maybe, but probably not. He hadn't worn a mask of normalcy around her the way he did most girls.

Still, he felt he should get to know her, too. She was easily his equal intellectually, in many ways superior. He calculated the knowns; she deduced the unknowns. An imagination Jules lacked. A compassion he shared.

Now she and the others were under arrest, and he couldn't see it not sticking this time. Certainly, Dan and Harpal were in serious trouble. Flinging explosives and firing machine guns wasn't exactly legal in many places around the world. And Jules could help, couldn't he?

Place the bangles in the water for a shorter time, steam blast the cops, and give LORI a chance to flee?

No—he couldn't control it. May end up killing police officers or his friends.

Friends.

They'd come for him, trusted he'd escape given the distraction. Yet, when the important time came for them to really, truly place their faith in him, they didn't. They continued to shore, probably cursing his arrogance, his loner attitude, not even considering he might offer a better way.

He detached the Ruby Rock bangle from the Aradia one, its crimson sparks flickering with his touch until he dropped it into the dry bag with the manuscript.

Ahead, a slim exit window lay open.

Freedom.

He gazed at the bangle, now a thin dull stone wrapped around his arm, the green flecks not touching his skin.

The *Lady Mel* sputtered. Grumbled. Its lights flickered in cabins and on deck. The light and noise died again with a cough and a belch of black smoke.

Someone was on board, attempting to resurrect it.

Meaning they weren't dead.

No bodies in the water.

Jules wet his hand and dripped saltwater on the Ruby Rock bangle inside the sack. Nothing. Again, the catalyst appeared to be *him*.

Yet, what could explain this? No ghosts, no specters bound themselves to him. He'd never done anything remotely "special." Everything he achieved, he did so through sheer hard work, through practice, through immersing himself completely in whatever he needed. The only thing that facilitated this was his brain, his ability to isolate logic and apply his observations to any given situation.

That wasn't *special*.

The red Mary bangle would fetch handsome remuneration from Alfonse, and Jules saw no problem getting out of India with the money he still carried. He would buy Bridget and the others the best lawyer available. Once he reaped the reward.

That was the most he could do for them. No prison break, no sweeping in there with his uncontrolled water storm. He had a chance... a chance to escape. With his mom's bangle.

The night loomed.

The *Lady Mel* revved again.

His window was closing.

They would think he was a coward, that he'd betrayed them

once more. And yes, he knew inside himself that to run with the bangle meant one thing and one thing only: his life could begin properly.

Beer.

Pizza.

He'd finally discover what the big deal was about Netflix.

Logic left him no other choice.

He ramped up the boat's power and cut over the still-rough water. Accelerating. Straining to dispel the image of Bridget in handcuffs, staring out at the harbor, watching as he receded with his bounty. Out to the open ocean and away. Away from her, from them.

Abandoning them.

As he neared the yacht, frantic activity dominated the deck, and shouts rang out; they'd spotted him.

So he aimed the launch out past the huge vessel and wound around a waiting ferry and trawler, their passengers and crews watching agog. They must have felt the swell but been sheltered from the worst of it by Valerio's craft.

Another flagrant example of the consequences of Jules losing control. Another reason he should separate the bangles as soon as possible. Doubting Thomas had the right idea.

The Vatican would be a good place for one; Jules's home would be the other—wherever he chose to finally settle down.

With the harbor receding now and no sign of pursuit, his mouth watered. He visualized a pizza slice—laden with tuna, red onion, and pepperoni—and his stomach fluttered. A cold beer in his hand, the bottle reminding him of expensive water but tasting so crisp, so refreshing...

Right after earning his reward from Alfonse Luca, paying for a lawyer for his friends—

No, he could not call them friends. Friendship worked two ways. Even if he wanted to be among them, to laugh and eat, to play, to put the world to rights over cocktails or... beer... they would never trust him again. Not after this.

Better he bolted and returned with real help. They could stand a day or two in a jail cell. The British and US embassies would see they were treated fairly, and heck, Bridget's parents might even use their cash and influence.

Yes, they'd be fine.

The sea was choppier out here, the land already morphed into a dark jagged line against the moonlit sky. He paused to explore the launch.

The fuel gauge remained almost full, but that wasn't his concern. He located a toolbox and opened the main panel under the steering column. He didn't find what he was looking for, so he accessed the hatch where the engine idled, chugging quietly. After five minutes poking around, he disabled the GPS tracker with a hammer. A nice boat like this would obviously have one, activated automatically as soon as he'd departed the mother ship.

He sat on the pilot's chair, perched on the edge, letting events wash over him, coming down from a rare high. His fingers trembled in the near silence, the lapping of waves against the hull soothing.

Jules possessed the bangle at last. He was free. A quick cross-country flit over the border, where a friendly contact in Pakistan required only a couple thousand bucks to smuggle him to China. There, he'd pick up one of a dozen go-bags he kept in safety deposit boxes, containing enough ID to return him seamlessly to the States.

He closed his eyes, held himself in the moment, absorbing the splashes, the birdcalls, the chug-chug-chug. He was cold, with only his tux jacket for warmth.

As he emerged from the mindful moment, he figured he should give the whole boat another once-over in case any backup devices gave away his location before pushing on.

A warbling noise burst through the night.

Jules turned in a full circle, checked every angle for attack. Found nothing.

It was in his pocket.

Valerio's phone.

Must have dropped it in there on instinct, as he would have with his own when the first explosion hit the *Lady Mel*.

He fished it out, and the screen read, "Minion Number 1."

Horse's phone, no doubt.

He declined the call and dumped it back in his pocket, then resumed his course north.

Free and clear.

If Valerio was calling him, it likely meant their only other method of keeping tabs died with the GPS unit.

Free...

The phone bonged once.

They could track him with that, of course, not just with the lifeboat's GPS. A little more work unless it was already set up, which—being Valerio's personal phone—Jules doubted. Valerio was a recluse. He valued his anonymity.

Jules lifted it out and prepared to toss it when he glimpsed part of the text message:

What can it hurt?

They hadn't found him yet, so he left it for a whole minute, plowing farther out to execute his planned right turn to the north.

Screw it.

He read the entire message:

What can it hurt? Please call back. I just want to say one more thing.

As if on cue, another text bonged onto the home screen:

I can give you the peace you crave.

Followed immediately by another:

Go on. It'll be worth it, I promise.

The man was a psychopath. Although "psychopath" was not an official medical term, it was something easy to categorize in layman's speech. "Antisocial personality disorder" was such a mouthful, but it perfectly described Valerio Conchin.

He certainly demonstrated complete disregard for the rights of others and showed no willingness to conform to the norms of society, preferring to hide his actions rather than adjust them. And he would think nothing of lying to get his way.

Meaning Jules had no reason to listen. No reason to let him in. The Aradia bangle was his, and the plans he made to disappear from the grid were tight. Valerio wouldn't find him.

Bong.

Aren't you curious about what happened in the marina? I have answers.

It was stupid. But he had to decide before he was out of range. And he decided to call.

CHAPTER
FORTY-FOUR

Without stopping, Jules told Valerio he'd listen only until the cell phone coverage blinked out. Valerio accepted.

"I can't stop you. You've made it your life's work to go unnoticed. We can hardly find anything on you beyond your juvenile mishaps. A couple of suspicious events, but nothing ever sticks, does it? Not a *complete* ghost, just a very, very good job staying under the radar. But you'll surface one day."

"Sure," Jules said, "but your disease'll have finished you off by then. That's why the urgency. Your yellow skin, your meds, your temper tantrums. You're dying. And soon."

"Yes." Something caught in Valerio's throat. He coughed it out and said, "My dying wish is to see the tomb of the first priest, to pray with him. Is that too much to ask?"

"Umm, yeah, it is. You murdered to get there. And don't give me that spiritual bucket-list crap. You ain't been aching to find it just to go sightseeing. You think there's power waiting for you. You wanna heal or some idiot idea like that. And you think I'm part of it, part of the solution. Tell me I'm wrong."

A lightness filtered through Valerio's tone. "You're not wrong, Jules. And I think someone as insightful as you must keep an open mind. *Did you see what you did?* You were like... *Poseidon* back there! Commanding the latent energies in the water. The hydrogen atoms bursting but still bonded to the oxygen ones, the sodium giving it real heft and mass... Jules, you commanded the opposite energies in the bangles to create the most stable unstable mass ever. And no one else could do it. You need to face up to that."

Jules held his course steady. "A genetic quirk. Melanin maybe."

"Oh, Jules, I'm an equal opportunity employer. Do you think I have no black people on my staff? I already thought of that. No, it's unique to you. And it's linked to Saint Thomas's journey. He discovered what they did, why they were special. It's the same reason why *you're* special. This is your *destiny*, Jules."

"You think... it's magic? Cause that's nonsense."

"Unfortunately, it seems 'nonsense' is the only explanation. *I watched what you did.* We don't know for certain if that chemical reaction is what *actually* happened in the water, but all my research, all my tests... it makes sense. I know I'm just theorizing, but what you did... it's not out of the question using modern technology. Technology that my companies have tried to develop. Electro-manipulation of molecules, of the gluons that hold matter together, changing one thing into something else."

Jules allowed a small laugh. "That's one of your attempted cures, huh? Another failure?"

"Correct again. My, you are just the *best*. But after what you've seen... ancient jewelry sparking to life at your touch, your commands creating a tsunami through sheer willpower..."

"Thought it wasn't jewelry. A *key*, that's what you said."

A pause.

Then, although Jules couldn't be sure, he could almost hear the happiness in Valerio's voice. "Yes, a key. But what does it open? Where does it lead? Haven't you ever wondered? I mean truly wondered about the item your mother kept safe all those years? She never let you touch it, but gave it such value. Died trying to protect it. Then you, all these years later... do you believe you are brain damaged, Jules? Do you believe anyone can be so obsessed with retrieving an object that he forsakes every other aspect of his life without a deeper meaning? Some other outside urge driving you?"

When Jules could not answer, Valerio went on.

"Yes, you were right, I think, about the genetic quirk. You are bonded to the Aradia bangle. Those African tribes the Romans plundered, they knew certain individuals commanded its power. When I say you're special, Jules, I don't mean like God reached down and blessed you. I mean, you have... *something*... that others do not."

"Ain't we all special in that way?"

Valerio laughed. "That's your elementary school teacher talking. In reality, you'll never know for sure what lies inside you, not if you disappear and drop the bangle in a box for the rest of your life. You need to explore this. Not shut it away."

"I can do what I want."

Valerio's tone grew strained, as if he were holding back another tantrum, but he kept it under control. "Where's your logic now? You've seen things you never thought you would. Feats that shouldn't be possible... the light, the vibrations, that ridiculously cool water flume. Aren't you interested in what makes your mom's legacy so very... *special*?"

"Man, you don't give up, do you? It's just a rock that reacts with the oils from my skin, with water. And saltwater makes it a more violent reaction. Probably laced with strontium or barium or some compound that increases those water reactions."

"Wow, someone paid attention in chemistry! You know about the earth metals. Neat. But none of them react like *that*, not that *strongly*. And what about *you*? Your ability, your brilliance?" His voice cut out momentarily, the cell service waning.

"I'm *not* special. I got higher than average cognitive skills, but I ain't a superhero. Just know a lot about a lot. And I still say the wave is a fluke. I don't care about those answers."

Another long pause punctuated by heavy breathing, an angry man attempting to sound reasonable.

"So what's next, Jules? Sure, if it was just *one* of those things, fine. But combine it all—the genetics, the light shows, the clues leading to an ancient tomb, the sheer *power* demonstrated minutes ago. Any one of those events or facts in isolation is a fluke, an anomaly."

He cut out for another second.

"Jules, a week ago you were a street rat robbing criminals of their ill-gotten gains. After all you've seen this week... you think you can settle down, start a new life? Sit at home watching football, eating Cheetos, feeling your six-pack turn into a keg? Even if you keep up with your fitness, your abilities, what then? Go to college surrounded by normal folks? Get a job? Where? In a bar? A library? A call center? Plenty in India if you want to go that route."

Jules pressed the cell phone to his ear, not comprehending why, exactly, he was listening. He eased off the throttle to slow his escape from the cell tower's signal.

"But no," Valerio said, "you've seen what that bracelet can do, and you've seen what I'll do to possess it. You're worried about why I want it? Well, you're right. I'm dying. Donors might help prolong my life, but there's no permanent fix. I am tainted at the genetic level, the way you are blessed at yours. The tomb of the first priest? His original gospel... that *might* be the answer. The book you stole from me, it writes of regenerating dead tissue. Thomas, the *doubting apostle*, he likens it to the risen Christ and again doubts Christ's divinity. If anyone can rise, does this make Christ *special*? He says yes, though, because this tomb... it cannot bring you back from the dead the way Jesus returned. No, Jesus was different, so I think we're best leaving that to the Bible. I only care about the tomb, Jules. Thomas's tomb. It *fixes* people. *Broken* people, not dead ones. All because of your 'quirk.' And maybe, just maybe, your mom carried that quirk too. Maybe she knew what it did. Maybe *the tomb* is her legacy. Not the trinket."

Jules came to a full stop.

Valerio was saying things Jules hadn't considered before, revealing secrets from the text even Bridget couldn't decipher.

"Lot of silence coming from your end, Jules. You're thinking about it. You've got the bug, haven't you? Through all your psychological troubles, all your obsessive traits, you're starting to understand what Toby and Bridget understand, what Colin Waterston understands, what *I* have understood since long before you and I met in Prague... *you need to know*. You can't just put it on a fire mantel or in a display box or wear it on your wrist like some hipster archeologist sauntering around Bushwick. You have to *know*, don't you?"

Jules lowered the phone, cutting the throttle entirely. The pitch and roll fogged his vision. No, not the movement. Tears. Tears obscured it all. His plans for the future, once so clear, were now tainted by Valerio's words. And not because the man was a manipulative psychopath, but because he was *right*.

After all Jules had learned this week, the sights, the feelings, the sheer escalation of the questions he'd long thought could never be answered... those questions resurfaced. His teenage self demanded he explore them, reaching from the past to close his throat and conceive of trusting a madman capable of killing him just for kicks.

"You got influence," Jules said. "With the authorities."

"I do."

"Then tell 'em this was all a show you put on for your guests. Got outa control. Offer to pay for the damage, a bit extra to whatever fake funds they use to accept bribes round here. You get Toby, Bridget, and the others outa jail. No charges. No records. Nothing."

No hesitation. "Deal."

"I'm gonna hole up till morning. Eight a.m., I call Bridget's phone. If they're all unharmed, free to go, I'll cooperate. Clear?"

"I could have them call you."

"Nuh-uh. I won't have a phone with me."

Jules hung up, dropped the cell over the side in case it could be tracked, and swung the launch north on a random heading to take him closer to shore. If he didn't know where he was going, no one else could guess either.

But at least, even if he was handing himself over to the devil, Bridget and the others would be okay, and Jules could die in the knowledge that he did all he could—for them and for himself.

PART SIX

It is a man's own mind, not his enemy or foe, that lures him to evil ways.

—Buddha

I count him braver who overcomes his desires than him who conquers his enemies; for the hardest victory is over self.

—Aristotle

CHAPTER
FORTY-FIVE

The random place Jules decided on was a beach sixty miles up the coast after three hours of freezing travel on a sea that ranged from lake-smooth to scarily rough. He soon spotted a cluster of electrical lights inland, so he beached the launch and dragged it up the sand. He camped under the stars on scrubland atop the dunes, sleeping on a bed of lifejackets, wrapped in a blanket, with a mosquito net he found on board propped over him using driftwood washed up nearby.

He woke with the sun, jerking to full consciousness, convinced for a second that he was covered in snakes, spiders, and crabs. No. He was fine.

As fishermen schlepped rowboats to the sea, Jules trekked the opposite way, up a dusty path toward a village. Everyone was thin, most wearing wraparound clothes of various bright colors, and the place reeked of animals and their feces. The wooden houses stood on stilts, presumably to mitigate flooding, and each person he passed ceased what they were doing and stared at the young black man walking among them in a filthy tuxedo.

He made the universal thumb-and-little-finger gesture for "phone" without success. Eventually, toward the end of the village, he found a store of sorts. Its inventory consisted of dried meats, shriveled vegetables, bottled drinks, and canned goods Jules didn't recognize. A payphone hung in one corner, but he had no coins. Just a roll of large-denomination dollars.

The old man behind the cash register was all gums, with very few teeth, grinning at Jules with the comprehension of a hamster at feeding time. Jules pointed at the phone and offered a hundred-dollar bill.

The man's eyes widened, and his gums stuck out farther. Then he looked sad, shrugged his shoulders, and opened the till with a clunk. It contained half-full cups of coins worth maybe ten bucks total. Jules indicated the heaviest-looking coins and then the phone, eyebrows bobbing in query. The shopkeeper nodded. Jules placed the hundred down and took the cup to the phone.

He lifted the receiver and found a rotary dial and four different-size slots. He fed the device and, after a degree of trial and error, he figured out the system, dialed a number, and listened to a trilling through the earpiece.

"Hello?" It was Bridget. "Jules?"

"Yeah. You all out?"

"They put us in a minivan and drove us to Surat."

"Where's that?"

"The small airport we flew into yesterday. A long way outside Mumbai. I think they're letting us go."

"Good. You okay? All of you?"

"Sure, we're fine. They even got air conditioning here. What did you do?"

Jules closed his eyes for a moment. All the things he wanted to say stuck in his chest. Not Hollywood mush or big declarations, but a desire to express sorrow, regret, perhaps a hope they'd meet again and explore whatever brewed in their brief time together. And not only with Bridget. He'd teetered on the brink of actual friendship with the whole group.

"Tell the others I'm sorry," he said. "I'll try and find you when it's over."

"When it's—"

Jules hung up on her. Fed the phone. Dialed the "Minion Number 1" phone number he memorized before ditching Valerio's cell. Someone answered after three rings.

"You tracing this call?" Jules asked.

"Of course," Valerio replied. "Now we've had the time to set it up."

"Good, because I ain't got the faintest idea where I am. There's a beach nearby. I'll be waiting. Unarmed."

SURAT AIRPORT

In the deserted café overlooking the runways, Bridget swung between boredom and utter frustration. LORI's release involved paperwork. A lot of it. The government official in the cheap suit presenting them with statements and nondisclosure agreements did not speak much English beyond the basics and exuded a gruff manner that suggested he'd rather be anywhere but there.

Bridget sat back while Toby took the lead. He even fielded a call from his former protégé, Colin Waterston.

The curator shouted and cursed, his voice clear through the earpiece. Toby tried to reason with him, offering to spill everything they learned in exchange for Colin's promise to stop Valerio. Toby insisted that Colin had the resources, the clearance, the law enforcement personnel, but was cut off constantly. Eventually, Toby relented and listened for an extended period while Colin appeared to speak calmly.

Afterward, Toby explained, "He is locked down. All foreign intelligence is under house arrest across the country. Someone with huge influence has acted here. Colin cannot help us. Cannot interfere anywhere on Indian soil."

"So, it wasn't him who sprung us from jail," Dan said.

Charlie shook her head. "Valerio Conchin isn't that powerful. Is he?"

"Money and promises," Toby said. "All he needs is a couple of politicians, and people like Colin are out of the game completely. In fact, Colin stated openly, it is up to us to stop him. If we can."

It elicited a wan smile. Bridget sensed Toby's satisfaction at getting one over on his protégé for the first time in years, but no one was feeling it. Ego-driven victories lay under a heavy shadow.

"I think Colin is more worried about Valerio than he let on," Toby continued. "He tried to cut us out, but now..."

"Now he can't break international protocol," Harpal finished for him. "But we can."

"Yet we're being deported," Charlie said.

"At least we're not in prison." Bridget found her voice weak and timid and injected what her momma called chutzpah into the next words. "Thanks to Jules."

All eyes landed on her, disbelieving.

"How you figure?" Dan said.

Bridget told them she believed Jules had made a deal with Valerio to set them free, but after witnessing the power of the Aradia bangle and its red twin, no one expressed any gratitude.

"We've held objects that appear odd before," Toby pointed out. "Even some with a curious energy to them. But nothing equal to that."

"I remember," Charlie said, and no one needed to be reminded of what had happened to her husband on that misadventure. "Which makes what Jules did all the more stupid."

"He's hurting." Bridget pressed her fingers into her palms to form tight fists. "Can't you see? He left us because he knew the cops were waiting and thought he could escape if y'all fell in with him. Because he was *right*. He was right in Rome and he was right in Mongolia. We'd be home by now."

"Home?" Harpal said. "Already?"

"Fine, we'd be on the way." Bridget released the fists and sighed. "Do you have to be so pedantic?"

Harpal held his hands open in surrender. "Sorry, but... Charlie's right. Valerio has the bangles, the full manuscript, and a translation... we have nothing except a... a best guess."

The official pointed at another paper, which Toby signed and passed down the line. Another confidentiality clause relating to the incident at the marina.

Toby said, "Maybe we could rouse Tina Trussot. She might remember something from her translation."

Dan signed the latest missive. "Why bother? He don't want our help."

"Because..." Charlie reigned in her obvious frustration, scribbled her name, and passed it on to Bridget. "Because it's not about him. It's about stopping Valerio getting hold of whatever's in the tomb."

"What if he just wants to heal?" Toby said.

Harpal's turn to sign. "What if it's a moot question? We have no clue where to start looking."

"Interpol?" Bridget suggested. "Call Colin back, explain it."

"Sadly," Toby said, "that may be our only option. Come clean. Give him everything and hope—"

Charlie's phone trilled with a high-pitched birdcall. Just once. A tone tailored for one purpose only. Everyone looked at her. They glanced between one another in confusion. Charlie slipped her phone out of her pocket. Held it up to her face. The light bathed her features in an off-white glow.

The Indian official coughed and pointed at the latest sheet of paper he'd flourished from his ring binder. His hooded eyes emitted a disgruntled boredom that Bridget clocked, but ignored. With an absent expression, clearly engaged in her phone, Charlie signed and received her stubby military knife back, still sealed in an evidence bag.

"Where?" Toby asked.

"North, up the coast," Charlie replied, snapping back to the business at hand.

The noise from Charlie's phone was fed from the Demon Server, a noise that only sounded when someone bit down on a tracking pod. And only one person not present carried a pod at the back of his mouth.

For the first time this week, the warmth of certainty swelled within Bridget. After days of guessing, chasing, living in fear, she finally found something solid on which to act. "It's Jules! He wants us to help him."

CHAPTER
FORTY-SIX

As soon as he confirmed the eight-man Indigo inflatable was his taxi off the beach, Jules swallowed the tracking pod, having rolled it around his tongue for an hour between bites of canned fruit he bought from the shop. Horse said nothing as Jules waded out to the shallows, tossed the dry bag in, and hopped on board. The Ravi brothers eyeballed him through bruising that Jules was sure had not been his handiwork. These injuries must have been either inflicted by their boss doling out punishment or suffered when the explosive wave hit.

The Indigo shot across the bay, the fishermen in their tiny boats impassive, as if this were an everyday occurrence. They reached the mother ship in minutes, not the *Lady Mel*, but a smaller craft, a mere sixty-footer, on which Valerio rested atop steps that lowered smoothly on a gimbal. Without waiting for an invitation, Jules snatched up the bag, ascended the stairs, and stood before Valerio.

The yellow-skinned mogul now wore tan cargo pants, a white cotton shirt, and a tan fedora. Like the bad guy in a Tarzan movie. "You know, I could say something very cheesy."

"What like?"

"Like..." Valerio rocked on his heels. "Like... 'You have something for me?' That sort of thing."

"Right. That would be cheesy."

"But, y'know..." Valerio opened his hand. "It's part of the deal."

"Lay off the cheesy lines, it's yours."

Valerio held three fingers up to his shoulder. "Scout's honor."

Jules placed the bag in Valerio's free hand. "Try to stiff me, and I'll fight hard. I'll lose, yeah, but you might be one of the others who don't make it."

Valerio made an exaggerated shiver, then addressed Horse, who now joined them. "See he's rested. You too. And get him a change of clothes. We have a long walk later."

The voyage north lasted eight hours, ending at a deserted bay, a rocky inlet apparently scouted ahead of time. Jules meditated rather than slept, refreshing himself nonetheless in readiness for the evening meal. Valerio spent a little time with Jules during which he explained he had borrowed the yacht from a Chinese businessman who did something complicated in finance circles, and it came equipped with a kitchen full of cooks who'd been employed for last night's festivities but were more than happy to stay on for an extended shift. They probably didn't expect to be serving gourmet food to hardened military men who'd lived the last half decade in the jungle and remote villages.

Jules doubted they would repeat the gig.

He took his own food up onto the main deck, where the sun was setting over the ocean. Valerio dined alone up here, and he waved Jules to join him at his table with its white tablecloth.

From Tarzan bad guy to British Empire colonial. He just lacked a pit helmet.

Now wearing hiking pants and boots and a plaid cotton shirt in preparation for the coming trek, Jules ate at the opposite end of the vessel; the truce deal did not include a socializing clause. The biryani satisfied both protein and carbohydrate intake while at the same time tasting like something from heaven.

An hour later, he and Valerio sat side by side in the Indigo as it swept toward shore. Valerio kept his eyes ahead, and Horse positioned himself behind Jules. It took two trips to transport the militiamen and their equipment, reaching landfall in darkness, where they unpacked and started hoofing it inland. Valerio bore a small rucksack, just enough for two bangles, the manuscript, and a hydration pack of water.

"We're heading through the jungle at night?" Jules said.

"Yup." Horse donned a helmet with what resembled stubby binoculars on a hinge. "Infrared scope."

"Sure, that'll work against snakes."

Valerio pulled gaiters over his boots. "Animals are more scared of us than we are of them. We make enough noise, they'll scatter."

"Besides," Horse added, "these guys know the terrain."

Jules stared at the darkest part of the landscape, accelerating the adjustment to his plain old human night vision. The half-moon illuminated the clear night sufficiently to get by, so if he stuck close to Valerio, he guessed any further protection would benefit him, too. "Where're we going?"

Valerio just smiled, adjusted his silly hat, and tramped into the middle of the party. Jules could only follow.

Horse remained several feet behind. Jules's vision adapted well, and his ears turned into satellite dishes, receiving every squawk, chitter, snap, and rustle the jungle emitted. The trail seemed fresh, beaten and cut by the advance group, occasionally merging with paths worn down by what were clearly large animals prowling their territory. The militiamen kept watch at varying distances, the lead party acting as sherpas to transport the equipment that Valerio and Horse guessed they'd need. Because it there was still a huge amount of guesswork.

"The location in the manuscript is not guaranteed," Valerio explained after ten minutes of silence, although Jules could have gone the whole night without uttering a word. "It describes routes," Valerio went on. "Landmarks, views that may no longer exist. Astrological references that are, frankly, inaccurate. Horse mapped the topography, and we found one location that matched. But it's only an eighty-five percent match."

"Pretty good for two millennia of nature," Jules said. "I found stuff with less than a fifty-fifty chance."

Valerio paused. "Us too. We located a stash of jewels and what was once silk that experts believed belonged to Cleopatra, something she had hidden in what we might call a 'safe house'... in Ethiopia. My archeology expert gave us a twenty percent likelihood of it being there, buried in the sarcophagus of a Christian convert in his father's church."

"What happened to the archeologist?"

At one of the Ravi brothers' urging, Valerio trudged on. "I released a trap door under his feet and let the alligators feed on him."

Jules was annoyed at himself for smiling as he kept up. "But seriously."

Valerio laughed at his own joke. "He's still with us. Older chap pretending to work for the British, but thanks to a dreadful pension, he's proved *sooooo* useful to us over the years."

"Henry."

"Oh, you met him?" Valerio slashed at a tiny branch with the machete so he didn't have to sidestep the six inches to go around. "Is he visiting with old Colin?"

"He was on the plane, yeah."

"He say anything?" Horse asked.

"About you guys? No, he was pretty quiet."

Valerio laughed again. "Horse keeps advising me to kill the poor guy. But we still have receipts and several photos that his wife and colleagues would find, uh... disappointing."

"Why keep *me* alive? Why not cut off my hand or something?"

"Because you're special. More special with a heartbeat. You might be more useful."

"Huh." Jules processed it in silence for around ten seconds. When Valerio did not break into it, he came to a conclusion. "The bangles only work when I'm alive."

They had climbed hundreds of feet, but the land was starting to even out. Not enough for altitude to kick in, yet Valerio already seemed breathless.

He paused again to speak. "You, my friend, are ridiculously quick."

"Not only alive," Jules said, thinking it through, replaying the scenario on the *Lady Mel*. He made a mistake, got zapped out cold, lying at their mercy until he came to. "*Conscious*. You already tried when I was out of it on the boat."

"We know from the world of physics that matter reacts differently when observed, although we're getting into quantum stuff here. You must have heard of the 'slit test'?"

"I read something about it. Neutrons fired through several slits in a card."

"Yes. When fired randomly at a card with vertical slits, they emerged on the other side in a cloud. Hitting the paper on the other side in a scattershot pattern. But when the test was left running with no eyes or cameras, scientists returned to find the neutrons had shot straight through the slits and hit the target in straight lines."

"So you think I need to *observe* the bangles as well as touch 'em?"

Horse nodded for him to continue moving. Like they were on a clock.

"Honestly, I *was* going to kill you," Valerio answered between heavy breaths. "Wasn't until I saw the stunt in the harbor that I was glad we failed."

Jules held up two fingers. "Twice."

Valerio gave a chuckle. "Now we know what you are, you're fairly safe."

"'*What I am?*' I'm just a guy."

"You're chosen."

"Ain't no such thing as 'chosen.'"

"I don't want this conversation again, Jules. Now fall back." He paused again. "Horse."

Horse brought the party to a halt and spent five minutes feeding Valerio pills and water. Then they proceeded onward, into the dark, where Valerio placed buds in his ears and listened to what he claimed was "a series of podcasts I've been meaning to catch up on."

That suited Jules. He preferred the noises of the jungle, anyway. How this turned out would depend whether LORI were smart enough to work out the exact location. Otherwise, this might be Jules's final expedition.

CHAPTER
FORTY-SEVEN

LEARJET, PAKISTANI AIRSPACE

"We can track him, but then we're always one step behind," Bridget said. "Charlie, you were working on a computer model for pinpointing the tomb."

"Right, it's here." She opened the laptop that had been returned by the authorities, and all gathered around, sitting on the floor of the Learjet in a semicircle. While she set up the program, she asked, "Have you translated anything else?"

They were under orders to leave India immediately, and Dan plotted a course for Pakistan, where some of Harpal's old contacts smoothed things over with the Pakistani authorities and Dan's influence secured safe passage to an air force base a hundred miles over the border. Now they circled over the base with autopilot engaged and full permission to be there. They'd land shortly to refuel, but Toby insisted on finalizing their next move away from prying ears—which rooms on a foreign military installation would most certainly possess.

"I had some time in Singapore and here," Bridget said in reply to Charlie. "I'm still working out the finer details, so let me summarize first to get my head straight."

She waited until all were watching her, ready for any snide comments or sarcasm. When none came, she continued.

"The Thomas manuscript is dated to around 50 or 60 AD, a *transcription* of the original text stolen from Herodias. Then Thomas added a journal to the original text, covering his travels after setting up his ministry in Kerala. But we don't have all of it. We don't know dates exactly, so we can't tell if it was before or after his recorded death in Mylapore.

"And it's not important to be exact on this subject," Toby said.

"Right. This is about places, not dates. According to his diary, he went to what is modern-day Mongolia, but when he fell ill, he returned to India. To be buried in the place where he found a use for the bangles."

Dan's patience wore thin. "We know all this. He sent one back to Africa because he didn't know Philip was dead yet and left the other with his pal the Buddhist."

"But part of the writing predates Aramaic. Why would some parts be Indus and others be Aramaic?"

Dan shrugged. "My butt's tingling with anticipation."

"The only reason I can think of is that it's another transcription. The Indus wise men translated the ancient language in whatever place the bangles are from, but there was no direct translation into Aramaic."

"So Thomas copied it verbatim," Toby said.

Harpal frowned. "Verbatim?"

"It means word-for-word, copied exactly."

"I know what 'verbatim' means, Professor Obvious. I just wanted to know why."

"Because it was clearly important," Bridget said. "Written down to send back with the Herodias bangle. But stating his final resting place... that's why he chose to be buried there instead of back in his homeland or Kerala. He was pointing the other apostles to his tomb to ensure they understood what the bangles represented."

"If he made it there," Charlie said.

"If he did, they never got the chance to find him," Toby added. "Until we came along."

Dan scoffed. "Until a bunch of street assholes killed the parents of a fourteen-year-old anally retentive gymnast."

"*I will rest for all time in the light beneath the midnight gaze of Zephon*," Bridget intoned. "Or *burning* beneath the midnight gaze... because that's what the original said, and he..."

"Verbatimed it," Harpal said. "Got it."

"Only we worked out the constellations wrong." Charlie showed a two-thousand-year-old star map overlaying India and its neighbors. "This is the view of how the stars would look perpendicular to the ground. *But*, the star above a certain point at midnight would be different now because our solar system constantly hurtles through the Milky Way. Over decades or even centuries, it looks almost identical, even to an advanced civilization, but the stars do move over millennia. It'd be different to today in 60 AD, although not by a huge amount. However, it'd be *very* different thirty-some thousand years ago. So we don't know exactly which star 'Zephon' is."

"Zephon," Bridget said once again. "Both names—Zephon and Zendor—mean 'life giver.' Zendor is ancient Sumerian, and Zephon is inspired by Judeo-Christian myth. The angel who Gabriel sent to earth in search of Satan."

"I agree with Bridget," Toby said. "We should assume this is the correct star. Subsequent to Jules's beacon confirming the direction."

"We couldn't use it before because we didn't have a reference point, or even an approximate place in time. Now we have that. Can we narrow it down?"

Charlie played with the mouse, and the stars beat like a heart and twisted, some moving closer together, new ones forming, until a fresh rash of silver dots covered the land map. She pointed to a red dot on the coast of the Gujarat region in India's far northwest, bordering Pakistan. "This is Jules, two hours ago." The dot tracked a path inland, a circuitous route hugging the hills' contours. "*This* is the Kerala Christians' Zephon. At least, if you looked up directly into the sky through a chimney or tube, this is where Zephon would have shone. At midnight. Thirty thousand years ago."

An inch and a half from Jules's position, a star pulsed.

"What is that?" Dan asked.

Charlie cleaned up the image without the star map, leaving only Zephon and Jules, and zoomed in to an HD model of the land.

A town. Nestled amid wild hills and jungle.

"An altitude of two thousand feet," Charlie said.

Harpal zoomed out so it incorporated Ladoh and stared for a moment. "It's a long way from Valerio's base of operations, outside the radius of his LiDAR explorations."

Toby stood and straightened himself out. "Within a small margin of error, I think we can safely say we have a destination."

LADOH BORDER REGION

Trekking into hills that morphed into mountains farther away, Jules's lungs required more breaths per minute as the altitude increased, slow-going over the circuitous route, obviously plotted taking Valerio's deteriorating condition into account.

The jungle thinned. The foliage switched to more arid climes, and the nearly constant animal noises faded into the distance, replaced by the occasional rustle, distant yelp, or hoot. At around four a.m., having climbed to what felt like two thousand feet above sea level, they rested for an hour in the increasingly cool air, ate starchy food, and drank coffee and high-performance drinks full of sugar, then continued.

The trail fell gradually until—as the sun cast a yellow glow through the mist—Jules could see a village a mile in the distance under the shadow of a huge hill.

They paused, the view filled with vivid shades of green fading out of low morning clouds. Mountains towered far beyond, much higher than their location, but the mound ahead lorded over a narrow valley that plateaued into a basin in which the village nestled—a frying pan–shaped aerie overlooking a steep drop into another valley extending farther than Jules could see.

But it was the giant molehill before them that Jules focused on: an upturned green and gray cone with paths etched around its circumference. It soared more than five hundred feet over them, and they were already on a rise hundreds of feet up from where its base originated—the panhandle valley carving a path into the village.

The village itself appeared even smaller than the one Jules encountered on the coast, although this one looked more populated. He asked for binoculars, and after a bit of wrangling and phrases such as "What can it hurt?" Horse handed them over.

Sparse activity. No modern conveniences that he could see. The thirty or so houses were constructed from rocks of varying sizes, the roofs made of vegetation from the forest and lower down in the jungle. The land seemed flat, hard-packed dirt forming streets set in concentric circles around two major features: a well with a wooden seal over the mouth and what was unmistakably a church. Big enough for fifty worshippers, maybe a handful more. A satellite dish sat on one roof.

Without seeing who, without needing to, Jules felt a hand rest on his left shoulder, easing him to the side. The other hand guided the binoculars to the hill's peak, lush with green shrubs and grass, which tapered almost to a point from this distance, but up close would be dozens of feet across. Without lowering the glasses, Jules went with it, listening.

Valerio's breath exhaled hot on his ear. "If you were to stand on that very spot at midnight thirty thousand years ago and look to the heavens, the star we know today as SDSSp I991256 would be twinkling directly above your head. The Kerala Christians called it 'Zephon.' Those who wrote the original manuscript copied by Thomas and his guides called it 'Zendor.' See the similarity in pronunciation? Perhaps it was the people who forged our bangles who gave it that name." Valerio broke away, coughed, then leaned on Jules's right shoulder. "Nearest translation we can find is 'the life giver.' How about that?"

Jules lowered the binoculars. "You think there's a cave system? Some old buildings?"

"I think it's the birth of civilization in this region. The manuscript speaks of a natural disaster. A flood, possibly a landslide—it's a fuzzy interpretation at best—but beneath that mound, maybe deep, deep down, we'll find a village, a town, maybe an Indian Pompeii."

"The well," Jules said, indicating the modern construction in the center of the current village. "Towns are built on rivers. You think down there, under thousands of years of geological movement, there's a magic cure."

Valerio inched away toward the edge of the path, gazing down at their goal. "Those people down there, those peasants... they're descendants of the Kerala Christians who pilgrimaged to Thomas's great legacy. Maybe they took him back to Mylapore, or maybe Thomas rests here, virtually under our feet. Where it all began."

"Where *what* all began?"

"The bangles open the gate to what Thomas discovered. And more importantly, the place the manuscript was describing. Right at the beginning of Thomas's section of that book. The additions he made to the copy given to him by the apostle Philip."

"Why don't you just tell me?"

A curious smile was etched on Valerio's face as he glanced from Horse to Jules. "You didn't send them the whole manuscript?"

Jules didn't appreciate the man's amused demeanor, but saw no reason to lie at this point. "Final quarter. Didn't have time for the rest."

Valerio nodded sagely. "Perhaps that's why you don't fully

comprehend why I'm here." He turned back to the view. "A passage from the very beginning of Thomas's journal. 'What the tomb holds will change everything we know about everything. And everything about the future, too.' Let's find out what he meant."

CHAPTER
FORTY-EIGHT

PAKISTANI AIR BASE

In Toby's life, he had strived to become proficient in languages, both ancient and modern, and in the skills of uncovering lost lands and tombs, but the dark arts of working with governments and appeasing the aristocracy came to him easily, probably due to growing up in those circles. It was Bridget, though, who could truly master multiple disciplines, so it was no surprise to find her continuing to study the pictograms and hieroglyphs on the tablet screen. Jules's photographed pages kept her brain occupied while Dan and Harpal made nice with the Pakistani officers in charge.

They'd been given an office and access to showers, but no one opted for the latter. They accepted the fruit and bread offered, as well as the tea and soft drinks. Bridget and Charlie had to cover their heads and arms while outside the room, but it was too damn hot to wander.

Toby tried not to watch her too closely, but conversation had dried up. He and Charlie still disagreed on Jules Sibeko's usefulness; she felt that relying on him in this instance was foolhardy.

Would Jules have activated his beacon if he wasn't sending them a message?

Charlie stated that she worried it might be a trap.

They went back and forth until a stalemate silenced them, and they returned to nibbling the food.

"Oh my," Bridget said, sitting up from her screen. When Toby and Charlie gave her their attention, she said, "This explains a lot."

"What is it?" Toby approached, tilted his head to read the copious notes she'd made.

"Anyone up for another flood legend?"

Before anyone could say "yes, please," the door opened. Harpal entered. "We're leaving. Now."

"What? Why?" Charlie asked.

"Colin's friends in Interpol are putting pressure on the Pakistani government to detain us."

"So I have to ask again..." Charlie placed her hands on her hips. *Mom pose.* "Why? Colin is the one telling us to stop Valerio because he can't."

"Not him specifically. But he was operating under the authority of Interpol. They sent him to arrest us *and* Valerio, and that's still their job. I've convinced the Pakistanis that a comms malfunction might be beneficial, but it means we'll have to pay ten grand for 'repairs.' If you get my meaning. In cash."

All found their feet and followed Harpal down a corridor and out into the searing heat. The two women pulled the scarves up over their heads, and all sped up to a jog as a mute soldier escorted them past troops drilling in the yard and out toward an area far from the runway.

"That payday is dwindling every hour," Toby said, keeping pace with Harpal. "Let's hope we don't need to bribe anyone else before we deliver to Alfonse."

"We might not be delivering anything," Bridget said as they rounded an outbuilding.

"No time for this," Harpal insisted.

Around a corrugated fence, the tarmac became a field in which a helicopter stood, its rotors turning at medium speed, engine whining.

Harpal waved them on. "All our gear's on board. We can inventory when we land."

"I hate these things." Charlie ducked under the rotors' wash as she hurried to the sliding door.

The helicopter wasn't armed as far as Toby could see, but it was sufficient for ten passengers and two pilots—a decommissioned combat vehicle.

He gave it no more thought as he joined Bridget and Charlie and strapped himself in. Harpal took the spare seat up front beside Dan, and all donned headphones and mics.

"You know," Dan said, "we might have to leave the Lear behind. Depends how much pull Colin has here."

"I'm sure we can supplement any additional administrative costs." Toby wasn't usually one for mincing his words, but he still enjoyed coming up with synonyms for "bribe" whenever the chance arose.

"Fair enough." Dan glanced back to check on the belts as the rotor screamed at full volume, takeoff speed achieved. "Hold on to your hats."

Dan wasn't used to this machine, so it was a rough ascent as he was waved off by the ground crew. His contact, a general, who had been an ally back in Dan's Afghanistan days, stayed away out of view.

"They stripped this bird of all transponders." Harpal had to shout, even with the mic and headphones. "All markings are burned off with acid. All its serial numbers and manufacturing codes. If we crash or get caught crossing illegally into India, they have plausible deniability, and we're on our own. If it is traced back, we stole a chopper due to be decommissioned and scrapped."

"Scrapped?" Charlie sat forward. "Did you say scrapped?"

"Yeah," Dan said. "This is one last hurrah for the old bird."

As the nose dipped and they accelerated hard away from the

base, Dan explained that they'd fly in under radar as well as avoid the Indian army's manual lookouts, which entailed skimming the treetops and cutting through a valley populated by small villages and farms. "We'll be fine as long as none of 'em recognize this as Pakistani."

"Bridget," Toby said, as if noticing her for the first time. "We could do with a little something to take our minds off the certain death awaiting us. You have more intel?"

Bridget stared for a moment, but appeared to get what he was doing. "I also said we might not be delivering anything to Alfonse. Now I've decoded a lot of the Indus script."

"Thought you needed an expert for that," Harpal said.

"An expert *or* time. I've had time to work through it. The original author tells the story of a worldwide flood, but not one that covered everything. Just a lot of it. Temperatures plummeting. Snow. Here in the foothills."

Toby recalled her earlier assertions. "You said you thought the Indus language was translating hieroglyphs from an earlier civilization."

"Right. It looks like the message from the olden days was describing the Ice Age. And yes, I know India wouldn't have been covered in ice, but it would have been much cooler."

"Don't forget the megaliths off the coast," Toby added.

"Oh no, don't forget those," Dan said.

"There are massive structures, possibly whole cities, submerged off the coasts of many great civilizations," Toby said, trying not to sound too indignant. "Those examined on the Asian sea shelf, not far west of Jules's position, suggest architecture that should not have existed until 3000 BC. Yet, if they were submerged at the thawing of the last Ice Age, twelve thousand years ago, these builders must have lived far earlier. It's largely cod-science, without a single paper surviving peer review, but... there's more evidence these days. And if they *did* exist, as the Ruby Rock and Aradia bangles appear to suggest... surely they were somehow capable of building much more. And writing about their fate."

"A massive flood as the Ice Age thawed," Bridget said. "The source of the majority of flood myths, religious ones and a whole host of legends like Atlantis. If they built a temple or a tomb on higher ground, that's probably where they retreated to. Where they documented exactly what happened. And why we shouldn't let anyone—Valerio, Alfonse, Colin, or even us—remain in possession of those darn things. They're trouble."

"If the floods concealed a thirty-thousand-year-old temple," Toby said, "this could be the most significant find in an age. It could mean—"

"Don't get ahead of yourselves," Dan interrupted. "We're about to cross the border. They'll shoot us down and ask questions later. So, eyes down, stories paused. You see anything on the ground that looks military, you shout. You see anything that looks like a rocket shooting toward us... shout louder."

"Reassuring." Bridget stared out her window, scouring the trees below.

"Okay. Here we go." Dan tensed up, then released his breath. "We're back in India. Strap in. It's gonna be a blast."

CHAPTER
FORTY-NINE

LADOH BORDER REGION

Valerio's advance scouting party crossed the valley a mile outside the village, and the seven-strong rearguard of Jules, Horse, Valerio, and four militiamen followed at a slower pace. Trekking down that side, they would be visible from the village, but it was still early, and the morning mist obscured most of their activity.

Jules's childhood featured a lot of movies where natives turned murderous when outsiders trampled on their holy monuments, and even though it was frequently his own ancestors portrayed in those stereotypical scenes, he couldn't help but expect a blowdart in his neck at any moment or a pack of ochre-painted fighters descending from trees with a war cry on their lips and battle axes in hand.

Then he focused. Remembered his discipline. The notions soon faded.

"Not worried about the residents over there?" he asked Valerio.

"No."

"Peace loving, huh? Won't attack? Maybe don't know what you got up here?"

"Nah, nothing like that," Horse said. "We mined the trails and sent a message to the elders to leave us alone."

"Huh, diplomacy ain't dead after all."

They plodded on, ascending irrigated paths at the lower level, allowing Valerio to set the pace, and all rested whenever he stopped. No one objected.

From the opposite side, this hill looked lush all the way up, green and leafy, but the grass he spotted at the top took over around halfway up, with only sparse trees and shrubs littering the path.

After two hours, they descended a rocky section around the blind side and arrived at a cave where the advance party gathered. They had unpacked the rucksacks and arranged ordinance by type: guns, explosives, detonators, cooking gear. A meal awaited them, but Jules was drawn to the explosives.

"Thought we had the key," he said.

Valerio accepted a bowl of spicy meat and rice and tucked in. Between mouthfuls, he said, "After two thousand years, none of us knows exactly what we'll find in there. Landslides, rockfalls, sinkholes. I want to be prepared."

"Don't you think the ancient people might've failed to predict the effects of C-4 on their door? You really need more than that?"

"I think, after all the magnificent things I've seen you do—things mere mortals can only dream of—that the people who designed these items especially for *you* to use might have installed a couple of fail-safes. So *excuse me* if I don't want to put all my faith in a block of C-4."

The village now lay far below, tiny people milling around. Jules wondered whether the elders had explained why the residents couldn't leave or investigate the strange men on their hill. Would they know something special was rumored to lie within, or did they simply live and pray, grow food and hunt, while their ancient stories faded into myth and legend?

"Thirty thousand years." Valerio produced the bangles from

the only bag he carried and held both up to the light. He offered them to Jules. "Make them glow for me."

"No." Jules stuffed his hands in his pockets.

One of Valerio's troops cocked his gun and aimed at Jules's head, shouting something.

Jules sighed, not even bothering to look that way. "Really?"

Valerio waved the man down. "Horse."

The huge bodyguard planted a hand on Jules's shoulder, another at his elbow, and attempted to lever him down.

Jules had no idea why he chose this moment to become difficult. It wasn't a big ask from Valerio, after all.

He slipped Horse's grip, dodged one way then another, taking one of Horse's hands with him, then a swift jerk threw him off balance. A kick to the ass tipped him over.

Muted laughter rippled from the militiamen but cut out as Horse regained his feet half a second later, coming at Jules in a sparring bounce. He went at it hard. Jules spun, ducked, weaved, his familiar grin pasted on, still unable to shake the swagger, the cockiness, as he aggravated a seemingly superior opponent. Whenever Horse got close, Jules eased out of position. The other men chuckled, which caused Horse to growl and add extra snap to his attempted blows. Cornered under a fierce combination, Jules leaped up one of the sheer walls and somersaulted over Horse—which proved to be a show-off move too far.

Horse predicted Jules's grandstanding and swung a fist while the younger man was still airborne.

It was as if a tree had thumped into Jules's gut. The air flew out of his body. As he landed, he dropped into a ball, gasping for breath.

"I look like I enjoy dancing?" Horse said, standing over him. He wasn't even breathing heavily.

This guy's a machine.

Jules readjusted his breathing, short and sharp, trying to recover before worse befell him. But all that happened was Valerio placed the Aradia bangle on Jules's face.

It lit up, the glow made dull through centuries of handling. Then the red one balanced next to it, sparking and shimmering on his skin.

"Thirty thousand years," Valerio said again. "Impressive."

"You think... they..." Jules hadn't regained his capacity to talk properly but struggled to a finish. "They didn't know bad people would get hold of them? You think that's why they made 'em? Why they hid this so well?" Another pause. He heaved in more air. It was getting easier. "Why did Thomas try to... hide it? Why get rid... of the bangles?"

"I don't care for '*why*.'" Valerio tapped the Aradia bangle, letting it seesaw minutely in Jules's vision. "I only care about '*what*' as in, '*What* can it do for me?' And, '*What* will *you* do for me?'"

"You're gonna shaft me, anyway." Jules shook his head so the bangles fell, their light dying. "I'm dead."

"No, no, not at all." Valerio sounded sympathetic as he picked up the Aradia bangle and swung it in front of Jules's face. "When I get what I want, this is yours. I told you, I don't kill unless I have to. Sometimes it presents a tactical advantage. In this case, everything goes back in its place."

Jules sat upright, wishing he trusted this man. If he did, it would all be so much simpler.

"Have you accepted it yet?" Valerio asked.

"Accepted what?"

"Your fate. Your destiny."

"Ain't no fate," Jules said. "But yeah, I gotta accept these things are designed for folks like me. I dunno. I'm tuned to it. Genetically. Or some quantum entanglement. But that's a quirk of nature. Not some celestial hand pointing at me and saying, 'You're the one, Jules, you're special.' This is biology. Chemistry. Nothin' else."

"Good. Acceptance is the first stage. Next... we act." Valerio stood and addressed the men. "Time to go in. Let's earn that cash."

At that exact moment, a roar shuddered overhead. The hills must have insulated its approach, but once everyone, including Jules, scurried under the cave's cover, a helicopter swept around and banked sharply toward the village.

Someone had found them.

Valerio snatched Jules's collar in two hands and pulled him close, face contorted in anger. "Is this your doing?"

"I got no clue who that is." Jules wasn't lying. If Toby was smart, he'd sent Colin the coordinates and let the authorities deal with it, and since that was a military transport, Jules was hopeful. "Let's just see what's down there. Whoever it is, I'll leave with them."

"No." Valerio released him and faced Horse. "Make sure no one follows us. Lethal force. Even if it isn't strictly necessary."

CHAPTER
FIFTY

The village below the helicopter appeared to be heavily populated for such a small area, about a hundred souls streaming into the open to observe LORI's arrival. Uniform land surrounded the dwellings, lines of a crop that Charlie could not identify from this angle, more arranged on terraced steps around the village on two sides. Toby was their resident expert in isolated peoples and insisted they not damage anything; they needed cooperation. In fact, the only clear landing spot was the very top of the highest hill, and that would require a precise maneuver. There was only one space at ground level large enough to accommodate them: the square in front of what must have been a church or temple.

Dan took them down as slowly as he could, which caused the helicopter to shake and sway. Too many people watching, not getting out of the way.

Charlie's satellite phone trilled again, her husband for the third time. She patched him into her earpiece and inserted it in her ear canal beneath the mufflers. "Yeah."

"I'm not liking what I'm seeing on your beacon, Charlie," Phil said.

"It's okay, we're landing."

"In the middle of the damn jungle. Charlie, what's going on? You're supposed to be in Singapore running computer models."

Charlie swallowed. The others would hear her half of the conversation but not Phil's, so she kept it vague without sounding as if she were pleading with him. "We tracked a possible location of a significant tomb. I needed to be on the scene. It's not dangerous."

"You're lying, Charlie. I told you never to do that. Even if I don't like it."

"What time is it there?"

"Don't change the subject."

"Must be two a.m. Or three. How are the kids?"

"Missing you. Like I am. And we'll miss you a whole lot more if you die. Or end up like me. Damn it, Charlie, we agreed. No more field work."

She wiped a tear from her cheek. "Give the kids a big kiss from me. I'll be home tomorrow. Next day at the outside."

"At least tell me you got all you need."

Charlie had prepped on the way from the Pakistani air force base. "We're using the sat-comms and running the subvocal units through that. Shorter battery life, but with the remote relays that work underground, we'll stay in contact. Unless we go seriously deep. Bridget reckons the building was buried due to monsoons and ground erosion from higher up, maybe a landslide. Plus... Dan is good at this. He'll look after us."

Dan's head twitched while everyone stared forward. They touched down.

"As good as I was?" Phil asked.

"No one is." Charlie wiped another tear. "I'm sorry it worked out like this. But I'll be home soon." She checked Phil's short-bladed knife, sheathed at her thigh, and patted it for reassurance. "I promise."

· · ·

Bridget tried to tune out the conversation and was relieved when it was over. Dan told them all to stay on board while he scouted, but as the engines wound down, they were quickly surrounded by villagers. Bridget pulled her earphones off and slid open the door and climbed out. Toby and Charlie followed, all waving the people back. The rotors were still turning.

Everyone was dressed in bright colors, oranges and greens, simple loose garments, a few in white robes. All the men sprouted facial hair, and the women's hair grew long. Curiosity, not fear or anger, clouded their faces, meaning the village was not entirely isolated from the modern world. Just a distinct lack of electricity and motor vehicles.

Dan and Harpal joined them on the hardscrabble ground, the result of decades, maybe centuries, of feet upon it rather than anything industrial. The building dominating this open space was definitely a church, shaped in a crucifix as seen from above, with just enough room between there and the well to land the helo.

Bridget led the body language; open palms patting the air were pretty much a universal indicator that they were not here for trouble. She had picked up a smattering of Hindi over the past forty-eight hours and felt like an alien as she called over the winding-down engine, "Leader."

A handful of people looked at one another. As the helicopter's racket abated, voices sounded from behind the main bulk of the crowd. It parted close to Bridget.

An old man approached through the gap, dressed in black robes that he wore like a toga, topped with a white strip in the approximation of a priest's clerical collar. He spoke too fast for Bridget to pick up anything.

Toby stepped in and pointed at the hillside. His words were in English; slow, firm, as if that might break down the language barrier. "Danger. Bad people." He gestured at the team with him. "Good people. We stop them."

The man, whom Bridget assumed to be a leader in an elder system still utilized in rural communities, replied equally slowly in his own tongue. It sounded like Punjabi, which Bridget had not studied at all. Hoping for a degree of cross-language cooperation, she used what little Hindi she knew. "We bring bad news." Two days of intermittent study was simply not enough, although she learned far quicker than most. "Uhh... people... in the tomb."

The old man's eyes wandered to the hillside. He placed one fist on top of the other as if holding a stick, then shoved the imaginary stick toward the ground and up over his shoulder. He was miming something.

"Digging?" Bridget nodded. "Yes." She mimicked the mime. "Digging."

The man stamped on the ground and made a noise in his throat like a child playing army, an "explosion" sound, and rocked back on one foot.

Dan stepped forward. "They mined the route." He also made an explosion sound, duplicating the eruption with his fingers.

The old man nodded and spoke rapidly. Bridget picked out words from his earlier sentences, matching them to their exchange.

"They can't follow," she said.

Dan and Harpal exchanged a look. Harpal said, "And nor can we."

An enormous bang rocked the hillside beyond, jerking the ground under their feet as the real explosion tore through the air.

"They've found the entrance." Toby strode cautiously toward the elderly priest, halting when the man's escorts shifted closer. "There isn't much time. Please help us."

The crowd all looked to the elder, who cast his attention over each member of the team, one at a time. His head turned to the hill, then back to Toby. He nodded once, faced away, and his two assistants escorted him toward the church.

The audience remained parted, so Bridget led the way, the others falling in behind her.

CHAPTER
FIFTY-ONE

Valerio's group discovered the blockage after a quarter mile of trekking, a wall of tightly packed rock fused with mud and centuries of creeping moisture. Because of the confined space, they set a long fuse, and every man retreated into daylight and waited for the explosives to do their job.

The dust and smoke from the detonation took longer to settle than expected. It was at least five minutes until anyone could see more than fifteen yards, and Jules predicted a further ten minutes before they could reenter, and he was correct. Ten minutes of Valerio stomping impatiently and demanding people hurry up, sending them in to check on the state of the place. In the end, they probably headed down sooner than either Jules or Horse wanted.

Within seconds of delving back into the cave with their mouths wrapped in scarves, the initial scouts turned into amorphous gray blobs before disappearing entirely. Even their headlamps vanished from view. When they reappeared, the swirl and stink of burning had all but dissipated, and a nod to the Ravi brothers brought a thumbs-up from both.

"Okay," Horse said. "We're back on track."

They retraced their steps from earlier. Everyone, including Jules, wore head-mounted LED lamps, occasionally dazzling one another, but the cumulative effect as the men spread out was to illuminate the whole passageway. Dust continued to dance, and Jules pulled his shirt up over his mouth and nose, conscious of potential damage to his lungs.

Long-term only.

It likely doesn't matter.

I'm dead anyway.

As they approached the explosion site, Valerio issued an order. "We go first. Everyone stick at least ten yards behind."

He did not give a reason. At first Jules thought he was worried about pursuit, but once they passed the blasted-away threshold, he realized maybe Valerio had other concerns. A megalomaniac such as him preferred to keep his own secrets.

The cave walls smoothed out. The deeper Jules went, the flatter the walls became until the ground could have been modern concrete, skimmed flat and laid as flagstones on a sidewalk in an upscale neighborhood.

Defining this space as a "corridor" would not be an exaggeration.

Aiming the light at his feet, Jules found a layer of dust and debris from the explosion, but it lay fresh over what appeared to be cobblestones under a skim of glass. He crouched to touch it, joined by Valerio and Horse.

"Amazing." Valerio spread his hand flat. "I saw this once before in South America. The scientists I hired said it was a sandstone bed, blasted with extreme heat. Maybe an old magma tunnel. But this... there's no volcanic activity here."

Jules lay down, head on his side, staring along the path, his flashlight beam in line with his eyes. Beyond the debris layer, it rippled slightly on a steep decline but was almost as flat as any modern office building's floor. "Agreed." He scrambled up and sprang to his feet, dusting himself off. "It's man made."

"Woo!" Valerio stood and held up a hand for a high five. "Come on, don't leave me hanging."

Jules trudged on. "Horse, you're needed."

Horse slapped his boss's hand, and both escorted Jules onward. But then Jules had to stop again.

"What now?" Horse asked.

Jules approached the wall where he'd spotted markings that he assumed to be writing. Faded but distinct etchings. Four rows of pictographs unlike any he'd seen before; nothing like Egyptian hieroglyphs and not that weird Indus writing, either. Wavy lines, boxes, straight lines, some crisscrossing.

"It's been sealed for so long," Valerio said, touching the glyphs. "This is going to be *in*-credible."

"They're uniform," Jules said.

"Hmm?"

"Look at this. Like a snake." He brushed over a longer figure, then a duplicate farther down. "They're identical."

"So?" Horse said.

"So this is solid rock. You don't beat this out with a chisel and replicate the shape. I couldn't even carve a letter *E* this perfectly."

"He's right," Valerio said.

Horse exhaled through his nose. "Of course he is."

"They used a tool. A molded tool, like a stamp. That's impressive." Valerio stood away. "Come on, this is just the beginning. Let's see what else we can find!"

They found steps. Lots of them. One staircase, twenty feet wide, digging so far down that their flashlights did not reflect an endpoint.

"What do you think?" Valerio asked Horse.

Horse fiddled with a flap on his jacket and removed a couple of sticks, snapped them on so they glowed green, and tossed them as far as he could, illuminating the stairs deeper. "We've come this far."

Jules led the way, testing each step so he didn't slip, but there didn't seem to be much danger of that. It was so dry in here; it had been hermetically sealed until Valerio's C-4 came along, so the prospect of moisture was slim. The trailing men moved slower, the gap between them increasing. The group had shrunk, six of them. Others must have turned back or been posted as sentries.

Jules's flashlight showed the bottom of the staircase, a gaping black hole that led to another corridor. It was hotter here, the pressure from so much rock creating a pocket of stale air.

Valerio virtually skipped now that they were back on even ground, overtaking Jules in order to be the first to see what came next, his headlight and a second flashlight in his hand allowing him a clearer sweep of the way ahead. In a mere thirty seconds, his excited, childlike call rang out: "Come see this!"

Jules and Horse broke into a jog and caught up quickly.

A recess in the corridor hosted a square indentation, four feet high and wide, hewn out of the rock—but that wasn't the most surprising thing. Displayed in the middle of the hole, a metallic goblet shaped as a wide, heavy wine glass stood alone in the dark.

"It's bronze," Valerio said, his fingers hovering inches away.

"Or gold," Jules said. "What's up? Worried we'll get chased out by a giant boulder?"

Valerio's light dazzled Jules as the billionaire faced him. "The people who constructed this place lived thousands of years before Jesus Christ. They created our bangles that open an as-yet unseen door, and which, incidentally, did about fifteen million dollars of damage to my favorite yacht. So excuse me if I'm a little cautious about—"

Jules reached out and grabbed the cup. Weighed it in his hand. Nothing happened. He passed it to Valerio, who looked like he'd just soiled himself. "Gold."

Jules moved on.

Horse rushed to get ahead of him, prodding his chest as he spoke. "How the hell did you know that wouldn't kill us?"

"Logic. The display case is sold rock, no place for a pressure plate, primitive or not. Plus, if we need a magnetic infinity key to get to the juicy stuff, I'm guessing it's pointless killin' us at this point."

"So what's it for? The cup?" Valerio said.

"Guess? Here." A circular basin jutted from the wall, one hole as wide as a thumb above it and another larger one below in a gutter. "It's dry now, but if there was water coming outa here, the cup's a welcome. Symbolic or literal. It's a long walk, right?"

Valerio thought for a second, then broke into a grin and slapped Jules on the back. "You would be *so* rich if you worked for me."

Jules walked on.

Valerio tossed the gold cup into the basin, and within another hundred yards, they examined yet more wall space.

"More light," Valerio commanded.

Horse jogged back to the men watching their rear and returned with enough flashlights to illuminate a larger section of wall, leaving the guards with only the glow sticks dropped at their feet.

A mural appeared clearly before them.

Although the colors bled and flaked, the representation survived: mountains, fire, rain, flood, figures of seemingly important people. Important because they stood taller and were positioned higher than the smaller humans fleeing the disasters. All the people were rendered in profile or head-on, staring directly back at anyone observing the mural.

It spanned farther than Jules first realized, covering from floor to ceiling and stretching around the next corner.

"I've read this book," Valerio said, eyes wide, hands animated, obviously dying to touch it but resisting, this time for fear of damaging it rather than of injury or death. "Societies would add to the story as the years go on. We see tapestries in Europe that do the same, cave paintings in America. Horse, you have my journal?"

Journal?

First Jules had heard of that.

The journal was a black hardback notebook full of scribblings and crude drawings, like the one Toby kept. Valerio raced back and forth over sections of the painting.

Floods.

A wide-ranging fire.

A volcano erupting.

Maps and ships.

Constellations.

Skeletal figures indicated famine more than once.

Finally, Valerio settled on one of the higher-positioned characters in profile, pointing at the sun. More people sat around him. In the direction of his finger, the ocean rose over the land, up to a pointed structure far inland with a star on top.

"They forecast this," Valerio said breathlessly. "The weather change, the floods, the... oh my."

Moving along the mural, Jules spotted something that made him gasp: a doorway in the rock wall. Perhaps once a natural chamber, now carved in right angles like the corridor itself. They stepped inside, Horse positioning the additional flashlights so they could see the whole room at once.

Approximately twenty feet square, it was covered in the same style of artwork, only this time it was carved and overlaid by dry paint. Dragons and other monsters; some kings murdering people, other kings delivering food; a benevolent figure in robes at the head of a line of crippled-looking peasants, touching one on the forehead, and a line of upright healed people walking away from him; pitched battles from which souls ascended to the sky; another flood, this one consuming a city; a bold-looking man standing tall over a sword jammed into a rock, his hand on the hilt.

"Look familiar?" Jules said.

"Myths known the world over." Valerio turned in circles as if trying to consume all the images at once. "Dragons, the result of people finding dinosaur bones. The rise of kings, good and bad; the healer figure of Christ and Buddha; and, of course, the special one."

Jules raised an eyebrow but said nothing.

"The special warrior. Only one can wield the mystical weapon.

King Arthur and the sword-in-the-stone business is older than the stories of Camelot. The Bu-Bu tribe of northern Cambodia revere a man who can wrench a battle-ax out of a block of silver. It's all the same mythos. This city." He referenced another section. "Some might call it Atlantis, but every continent has seen great civilizations fall under nature's wrath. Every modern story we have used to be someone else's. Before Jesus, we had Buddha. Before Superman, we had Moses. Before King Arthur, we had..." He signaled the man with the sword. "Whoever that guy is."

"So it's an art gallery," Jules said, pretending to be bored. Like a sullen teenager, he slipped a phone from his pocket and snapped a photo of the wall, arcing it around to create a panorama.

"Where'd you get that?"

Jules flicked his head at Horse and took another picture. "I dipped his pocket when he was lumbering after me."

"Hey!" Horse stepped toward Jules.

Jules pulled back. "Selfie?" He grinned and flipped the camera and photographed himself next to the sword-in-the-stone section.

"Asshole millennials and their selfies," Horse grumbled.

"Come on, man. History is *so* cool." Jules offered Horse the handset. "Besides, I'm not a millennial. They're, like, thirty. I'm Gen Z if you want to be accurate."

"Keep the damn phone. It's a burner anyway."

Disappointed that he hadn't riled up the big guy more, Jules put the phone away. "Fine, can we get on with this?"

Valerio shook his head in disappointment. "Always in a rush to get where you're going. Why can't you just be where you are? So desperate to get your hands on you-know-what, you can't appreciate being the first people in two thousand years to gaze upon this? They're talking about an ultimate weapon to rule the land."

"Yeah, but it's just metaphorical crap, ain't it? A myth."

"Sure," Valerio said, heading out. "Let's say that. Metaphorical."

CHAPTER
FIFTY-TWO

The conversation was slow going by any stretch of the imagination, but with their land under assault from Valerio, the elders—three of them—acted as if they trusted Toby and his friends. Two of the elders who sat by what would be the altar in a Western church were deeply creased gray-haired women, dressed much like the man: in black robes with a white Roman collar. They reminded Toby of a rather intimidating job interview he once attended.

The church itself was built in the same shape as those he'd grown up with but without glass, and sections of it appeared far older than many of the classic buildings around Europe and the Americas. He couldn't possibly age it off the cuff, but he recognized the building techniques as similar to those between the first and fifth centuries AD. It was how Thomas would have constructed houses of worship in Kerala.

They talked and used hand gestures, understood names like Jesus and Thomas, but it was Bridget who made the breakthrough. With an iPad.

She produced the retina screen and laid it before them, showing a page from Thomas's manuscript. One of the women audibly gasped. The man moved his head closer and then away.

Bridget demonstrated how to pinch the screen to zoom in and out and tapped it to turn the page. Either they were not as tech deficient as they pretended, or they were fast learners, as the man was soon flipping between images like a teenager. He rested on one in particular, his eyes ablaze with interest.

Toby craned his neck.

The male elder stopped on a photo of the Aradia bangle, one taken on a plain background before they encountered Jules. He wrapped his hand around his wrist, a question mark in his expression. Bridget shook her head and pointed in the direction of the hill.

All three lowered their heads and brought their hands together in prayer. In unison, they returned to their previous position.

Toby checked on the team; Charlie, Harpal, and Dan were hanging back, letting Toby and Bridget do their thing. Which, hopefully, they had communicated accurately: the bangles were on their way back to the tomb, they were in the possession of the people who had mined the paths, and Toby and Bridget were on the elders' side.

The elders stood and walked past them, paused until Toby moved forward, and then resumed their path to the outdoors.

The crowd understandably remained in place, a half-moon of bodies around the entrance, parting as the head of the congregation called out words the westerners couldn't hope to catch. Only Bridget grasped some of it.

"I can't understand exactly what they're saying," she told the team, "but intonation is important in this language. He's scared. Really scared. Like, end-of-the-world frightened. But he's reassuring them. Kinda. When he points at us, he's being positive. And I think... I think he's saying we'll help them."

"Great," Dan said. "Nothing like working under pressure."

The elders congregated at the well. Although they lacked electricity, they did not want for food or other commodities, such as paper and charcoal, the latter of which a ten-year-old girl duly delivered to the male elder. Using the well cover as a table, he sketched hurriedly on the sheet as large as a newspaper. It was clearly a map: a river, a series of paths, some straight, others less so. Boxes along the way... rooms, perhaps?

Toby examined it and pointed at the depiction of a river. Shrugged. *Which river?*

The elders lifted the wooden cover from the well, leaned it against the side, and all three pointed down into its depths. Then the man traced his finger from there, along the ground, until he was pointing up into the foothills.

Harpal covered his mouth, a spy avoiding lip-reading eavesdroppers. "I am not liking the look of this."

Dan retrieved everything he could carry from the helo and set up the rappelling gear and flashlights while Harpal inventoried: a couple of flares, electronics, satellite comms, digging equipment, fine-detail tools including picks and brushes. *No firearms.* It was one of the things the air base had been strict about. No Americans handling unauthorized weapons.

At first Dan felt had been insulted, but when he considered it properly, he knew he'd never have allowed a Pakistani "freelance archeologist" to roam around a US military base in with access to a firearm.

While the crowd had thinned somewhat at the behest of the elders, a sizable audience watched as LORI decked themselves out. Dan and Harpal perched themselves on the well's lip, ropes integrated to the helicopter's winch. They were to be the advance party to test how efficiently Charlie's sat-comms worked that deep, and if all was clear, the women would follow, leaving Toby up top to coordinate. And to do what went unspoken: *survive if the others did not.*

Plus, he was the least physically able and reluctantly accepted that he'd slow them down.

The pair kicked off and dropped vertically at a steady pace, descending manually, using harnesses and belay grips rather than the mechanical pulleys on the chopper; they would only be used for a swift evac.

Although each member of the team brought a specialty, other skills bridged those competencies into universally essential training for all, rappelling being one. Others ranged from the simplicity of digging a hole with care to setting a small charge and —with so many shipwrecks and sunken cities dwelling under- water—the highly complex ability of scuba diving. Even Toby was adept at rappelling and swimming. To a point.

A cool breeze signaled the water source's proximity. The rough-hewn stone ended, replaced by natural formations, a fissure through which the pair passed easily into a cave pocket less than six feet high. Dan switched on the flashlight atop his head and activated the low-light camera on his chest. As soon as he did, Toby commented through his earpiece, "Receiving loud and clear."

"Copy that," Dan answered.

The river flowing beneath was four feet wide but pooled somewhat because of the narrowing of its bed, making it easy to access using a simple bucket and rope. They swung to reach the bank and dropped glow sticks to provide consistent light. Harpal set a relay pod, which took comms from their subvocal kit via their sat-phones and transmitted the signal up into the open.

Modified army tech.

Dan said, "Okay, ladies, you're up."

Normally, Charlie managed the ops remotely, but she insisted on coming today since the comms kit was running off her proto- type pods. Plus, her affinity with engineering had proved essen- tial in the past; these ancient people sure knew how to seal their rooms, and a deep understanding of pulleys and levers might be their only way in.

The women descended, disengaged, and gazed around.

"It's an underground river," Charlie said.

"We need to head that way." Dan pointed up the passage into darkness. "We don't know what's up there, so I'll lead." A compact metal pickax snapped open in his hand, an ice climber's tool. "I'm scouting ahead, twenty feet. If I say run, you run. Toby is manning the winch. It'll pull you back up quickly."

"What about me?" Harpal said.

"If I have to hold anyone off, they'll need you to fly them out. Fast. And don't come back for me. Clear?"

No one spoke.

"These guys mean business," Dan emphasized. "If I meet 'em, I'm dead. If you try to help, you're dead too. Which is pointless. So don't get dead. Understand?"

Nods this time.

"Good." And Dan strode off ahead, hunched under the ceiling, feet sure and steady on the trail.

Toby wasn't an invalid, but he had no choice when speed was of the essence. His role was an intellectual one, with a soupçon of subterfuge thrown in alongside a scoop of diplomacy as required. Today, the waiting was especially difficult.

There was little conversation from below, so all he could do was perch on the helicopter floor beside a winch normally employed in the fast evac of soldiers. Legs dangling over the side, he propped an iPad in shadow, featuring the shaky image from the GoPro mounted on Dan's chest.

More rock.

A flash of river.

A grunt as Dan found more solid footing.

"Hiya," came a woman's voice. Next to Toby, not in the earpiece.

It was a girl of maybe fourteen, wearing a black robe with no Roman collar. Her long black hair was braided, and she wore a stud in one ear. She presented a narrow, weathered book to Toby, hands out flat, head bowed.

Toby glanced around; the three elders stood back near the church, observing.

He accepted the book, and the girl lowered her hands, turned, and retreated to the adults.

It was old but not ancient. A couple hundred years at most. Leather bound with indentations where the writing no doubt once lay. A few flecks of gold leaf caught the sun, but little else was visible.

He opened the first page, yellowed with age.

Illustrated.

Like a children's book, each page featured three or four lines of writing beneath a black-and-white sketch of events. There were ten pages in total, etched with a careful but not artistic hand.

Toby recognized the landscape. The hill before him was portrayed as more conical than it currently appeared.

A wise-looking man preaching to a crowd adorned the next page.

Water slewed through a valley.

Rain. People fleeing under the deluge.

A mountain breaking in half, the top almost amusingly snapped as if on a hinge.

Several scenes of badly drawn people running.

Then destruction: houses burning, crops turned, the conical hill smashed.

Finally, a rendering of the landscape as it now stood: the village at the foot of a shapeless mound, overlooking a deep valley, and only a narrow path in and another out.

It was the history of this settlement: a once-vital place of worship hit by natural disaster and rebuilt as best they could.

From the air, they'd seen other paths—down the drop-off into the valley ahead and around the paddy fields and crop terraces—presumably installed long after events in the book.

A single word from Dan snapped him out of his reverie: "Hold."

· · ·

Harpal appreciated Dan's commitment. It was, after all, his responsibility to look after them in aggressive situations. That was pretty much his job description as it would appear in a wanted ad: *Keep a team of freelance archeologists safe when they dive into situations they are clearly ill equipped to survive.* The "man-at-arms" as Toby labeled the role.

Harpal was handy in a brawl, as were most in his former profession, but he wasn't at Dan's level. That guy could read a fight and know whether it was worth digging in or if they should retreat. Phil Locke had been that way, too, although his confidence had turned to cockiness near the end, which is why he was now the stay-at-home dad to Charlie's breadwinner; it was why he'd likely never walk again.

That lesson was sufficient for LORI to understand they were not indestructible, no matter how good their military adviser proved.

Mortality is a tough lesson to learn.

So no one was comfortable with Dan plowing on alone. From their observations in Mumbai, it was clear Valerio was using militia from the Ladoh region as mercenary muscle. Harpal doubted Dan would have much of a problem fending off one or two of them. More was debatable. Harpal should be up there, too.

Bridget and Charlie kept their flashlights aimed ahead, and Harpal positioned his toward the river—more of a stream at this level. He brought up the rear as ordered, so shining to the front would just cast long shadows on Bridget and Charlie's path.

After twenty minutes of ascent, maintaining a brisk pace, they were clambering over the route like children exploring rock pools at the beach. The flow grew louder, an echo twisting through the passage.

"Hold," came Dan's command.

"What's going on?" Toby's voice resounded clearly, Charlie's booster relays working nicely. "What can you see? The picture isn't steady."

Harpal felt sorry for Toby. This would be killing him.

"It's... a flat surface," Dan said. "A path. Looks man-made."

"Your torch is dazzling me," Toby complained.

"Sorry."

"Is it safe?" Harpal asked.

A pause. Then, "Yeah, bring 'em up."

Bridget and Charlie pressed ahead, carefully scaling the strewn route until they met with Dan at a modest waterfall arcing from a tributary twenty feet over their heads. It formed a pool that fed the river they had just followed.

Standing to the side, Dan pointed behind the arc of water. "In here."

Taking care on the wet approach, they were all dampened by the spray, a freezing drizzle as they ventured inside what appeared at first to be a natural opening into another cave system. Dan had tossed several glow sticks ahead to illuminate what he found: a rounded passageway with a flat, smooth floor, almost polished in its geometry. Bridget was drawn to the walls, where markings showed up faintly.

"The water's diluted the colors," she said, but shook off the disappointment by skittering farther in.

Dan rushed to keep ahead of her, but she remained transfixed as she found intact writing.

At least Harpal *assumed* it was writing.

Like hieroglyphics, only less clearly defined as actual figures. No birds, cats, or strange-headed men. He concentrated on his position at the rear.

Harpal accepted he'd overstepped his ability back in Rome, so he was determined to follow orders to the letter this time. At least in Rome, they had some idea of their surroundings, a layout of the streets. Even with the hastily drawn map in Dan's possession, a lot of this was guesswork.

"Dan, hold still," Toby said. "There, right there."

Dan positioned his chest-cam to let Toby view the wall.

"I've never seen this before." Bridget ran her hand over the figures. "Carved *and* painted."

"Why would they do that?" Harpal asked.

Charlie brushed her fingertips over the same section. "Guess? So future generations could copy it. Keep it alive. Write over it. Even if they don't understand it."

Toby couldn't help butting in. "What does it say?"

"I couldn't begin to tell you." Bridget squinted at a cluster of similar etchings. "I don't even know if it's left to right or right to left. I don't think it's up-and-down, but..." She petered out, focused on a repeat of those first interesting figures. "A story, I think. Or instructions. This way."

"One sec." Charlie took another relay pod from her bag and set it near the entrance, striding past with a brief comment: "We're going deeper. Might need more signal for Toby. He can't miss this."

Dan proceeded ahead, again maintaining his scouting distance, an animated halo spearheading the route, the two women a ball of light, and Harpal the rear guard. Vigilant. Doing his bit.

Dan's next comment hit them through their earpieces, but also down the hallway. "Ho-*lee*..."

"You're on holy ground," Toby reminded him.

"Tell me about it."

They all caught up to Dan, his jaw slack, a hand on his chest, staring into a rectangular hole cut into the rock.

The hole was a doorway. Set in it, a wooden door faced them, held in place by only the sort of latch found on a countryside gate. Pitted and scarred, it displayed a crucifix, a simple cross of wood, darker than the door itself.

Toby took a sip of water from the clay cup delivered by the same girl who brought and now retrieved the history book. Pulse quickening, he observed the door through Dan's camera. It was hot in the helicopter, even with every door open. The male elder—whose name, Toby had learned, was Dasya—had grown more curious and now inspected every seat, switch, and handle. Toby barely noticed the heat anymore.

"Open it, then," he said.

"Umm... not worried about booby traps?" Dan asked.

In a lesser situation, Toby would roll his eyes and express annoyance at the frivolous interpretation of the scene, but with time pressing, he swallowed, shored himself up mentally, and said, "In all my years in this game, I have never once encountered collapsing floors or pressure-triggered rockfalls when opening a simple door."

"Are you sure, Toby?" Harpal said.

Toby checked his water. Almost empty. He'd need a refill but wasn't sure how to ask politely for one.

"Toby?" Dan said. "How sure are you?"

Toby waved to get Dasya's attention, and the man happily put down the headphones and climbed over the seat to view the screen. Dasya nodded with a smile.

Toby mimed opening a door.

Dasya nodded again and spread his hands—an invitation.

Toby pointed at Dasya and then the screen, then shrugged, hoping it translated as, "Have you been there?"

This time Dasya counted off his fingers, all the way to eight.

"Eight times?" Toby held up the screen again. "Here?"

Dasya blinked rapidly and gestured with an open hand to the door on-screen, then placed his hands together as if in prayer.

"Toby, we need a decision," Dan said.

"Go in. I think... I think it's a sort of pilgrimage route. That's how they knew the way. It's safe."

A hand extended from behind the camera's point of view and unhooked the latch. The crisscross of light beams blanched the low-light camera's sensitive lens. All Toby could make out was a series of black-and-white blurs accompanied by astonished murmurs, and occasionally a stone chest or fresco might appear, but never for long enough to ascertain its provenance. "Settle down, let me see!"

"Oh wow," came Bridget's voice. "I think we found it."

"Found it?" Toby said. "What does 'it' mean? 'It' doesn't tell me anything."

"Here, Dan," Charlie urged. "Show him this."

The screen calmed, Dan's movements slowing as he swung around to where Charlie and Bridget faced away. He wandered forward, around the women, and aimed at a slab, four feet high, seven long, and four wide. On the slab lay a human figure, wrapped in cloth pulled tight to its body. On top of this, clutched to its chest by bound hands, was a book marked by the same cross that hung on the door.

Dasya smiled. *"Tamas."*

Toby said, "Thomas?"

Bridget sounded breathless, the wind knocked out of her. "The tomb of the first priest."

"Indeed." Toby set the tablet on the seat beside him, heart fluttering, a little breathless. "You could be looking at the remains of Saint Thomas himself."

CHAPTER
FIFTY-THREE

Valerio and Jules ventured deeper, with only Horse for company. The mercs dawdled farther behind, which Jules continued to find odd, and he questioned it.

"Boss issued instructions," Horse said. "They follow instructions. Unlike some."

"Whatever we find is confidential and proprietary," Valerio added. "Look here." He gestured to the walls again: more artwork, more stories in pictorial form. "It's strange. We know they had language, writing, like cuneiform, yet they chronicle their history like this."

"Sensible," Jules said. "They probably found older writing themselves, so didn't want room for a language barrier."

"Yet here I am, not caring a jot what happened to them."

"Just what they can do for you."

"Correct," Valerio said. "And I want it kept between us, if at all possible." He gestured to the mercs. *They* are the help. Nothing more."

Drips fell overhead, the first moisture they'd encountered since the initial blockage near the entrance. A series of stalactites had formed, hundreds of years of calcified deposits mimicking a set of teeth trying to bite down and bar the way. There were only a couple of feet between the points and the floor, forcing them to crouch almost to their bellies to bypass the formation. It ran for only six and a half feet before returning to normal.

"Runoff?" Horse said.

"Maybe," Jules replied. "Or an underground stream goin' over our heads. Might even be what feeds the village."

"Again," Valerio said. "Who cares?"

Beyond the stalactites, the corridor widened. Its walls seemed rougher now, more related to their natural state. Both Valerio and Horse appeared to notice the same thing, but Jules only had the lamplight to go by.

Horse stopped and switched his flashlight aside. "What's that?"

They were looking at a door in a passage to the side. Modern by the standards they'd witnessed so far, but thick and solid.

Several yards farther along stood another. Plus one opposite, this one blocked with rough-cut bricks and smoothed over.

Moving his head closer, Jules found more writing hewn into it, hard to make out.

Horse produced a thirty-inch light bar, casting the surface in a purple glow. The letters stood out better.

"Thomas's followers wrote these," Valerio said. "They're far more up-to-date than what we've seen to date. Perhaps even written by Thomas himself."

"How d'you know that?" Jules asked.

"Because they're in Hebrew. Says we are 'approaching the point of great reward.' Well, that's nice." Valerio stood and moved on.

Jules sped up to fall in alongside. "For someone who doesn't care about history, you sure know a lot."

"It serves my purpose to know a lot. The endgame is all that matters. And the endgame, it seems, is approaching."

The corridor opened wider, doubling in size to accommodate a spacious anteroom. It wasn't until they had advanced another minute that they realized there was nowhere else to go. Not a corner, nor more displays of art.

The wall ended in an even finish, ten feet high and twenty wide, set into the contours of the bedrock and surrounded by those hieroglyph-like markings. The language of whoever built these chambers.

"Okay, Jules," Valerio said. "This is it. The final door."

CHAPTER
FIFTY-FOUR

"It can't be this simple." Bridget hovered over the mummified anthropomorphic bundle that they assumed to be the apostle Thomas. Afraid to touch anything, she arranged the flashlights that converted into lamps, allowing her to see as if a bulb had been turned on in a modern basement. "All this way, all those lines, those languages, and he's just lying here behind an unlocked door."

The room was a split-level, seemingly carved rather than constructed, the two stairs down from the crypt and altar made of one solid piece. The lower level contained fabrics in vastly differing states of decay, a musty smell pervading. Vases ranged from twelve to fifty inches tall, and two doors occupied opposite walls: one wooden, the other solid stone, more of a barrier than a thoroughfare.

"Not everything has to be difficult," Toby said, his professorial manner clear over the daisy chained commlink pods.

"But we have no proof. For all we know, Thomas is lying in the Santhome Church like the Christians say. This could be some guy who followed Thomas. Maybe a chronicler, which explains the book he's holding."

"True. But does it matter? If this is actually Saint Thomas or not, his writing brought us here. To the place he was trying to reach. The place he wanted his fellow apostles to seek out. Somewhere he wanted to protect."

"Then..." Bridget steadied herself, breathed, slowed her swirling thoughts. "Should we even be here?"

A pause. All waited for Toby's response. Sometimes it was best not to interrupt.

Toby said, "Think of it this way, Bridget. There's a whole village above you, descended presumably from Kerala Christians who pilgrimaged to what they consider their founder's true resting place. They guard it, protect it, by simply not making a fuss. The well is just an underground stream. No clues pointed to it as an entrance."

"You mean it doesn't matter what's true?" Bridget said. "Only that they believe it, and that's why we're here? That's what gives it value?"

"It means they trusted us," Charlie added.

"Why would they do that?" A moment of thought, then Bridget dropped her pack off her shoulders and rummaged to find her gloves, latex like a doctor's, only thicker, with a thin cotton outer layer.

The walls were bare except for the unknowable language of an ancient people, one—if Toby's historical musings were correct—predating the last Ice Age. From a time when, it was assumed, humans were little more than advanced primates.

If the body was indeed the apostle, Doubting Thomas—and they all now apparently thought of it this way—it was possibly the greatest find of the twenty-first century; if it could be proved that this language existed long before the Sumerians of Mesopotamia, it was a finding that *rewrote* history. It changed everything they thought they knew about human origins, and the Lost Origins Recovery Institute would be at the center of it—leading the charge into a new world of science and knowledge.

Thomas held a book to his chest. It resembled the one stolen from the Windsor archives, only much older. Perhaps the original.

Perhaps the one in Valerio's possession was a reproduction and Thomas decreed he be buried with the one he brought out of Jerusalem, the document that delivered him to the cusp of history.

Even in the first century AD, discovering evidence of such ancient ingenuity would have been a marvel. Plainly Thomas knew it.

Charlie said, "You okay?"

"Sure." Bridget snapped back to the present.

She'd been staring at the pictographic lines, faded but indisputable. Now she took in the room properly: a thick, mottled desk in one corner suggested a place of study or work, so large and wide that if it'd been in the office of an executive, there'd be questions asked about what he was overcompensating for; the fireplace indicated that ventilation must be possible; physical ornaments varied in size, age, and expertise, from exquisitely carved elephants to waist-high vases, perhaps offerings from the priests and villagers who kept watch over their founder.

"Valerio and his mob made the aggressive move," Charlie said. "We came with an open hand."

"Hmm?" Bridget again snapped back to the here and now.

"The reason the elders trusted us. I think we did it right. They blew stuff up."

Harpal and Dan hadn't moved. This wasn't their comfort zone. They plainly got a thrill from the achievement, but it was Bridget who took over in these instances.

"If this is the tomb," Harpal said, "how come Valerio isn't here yet?"

"He had a head start, and the full text," Dan added. "This isn't much of a shortcut."

"Could it be there's something else he needs?" Charlie asked. "The book talked about power, about forging history."

Bridget stood over the body. She spoke automatically, absently. "Thomas split up the bangles, sent them away."

"Yes?"

"So if they're a key to some powerful knowledge, he wouldn't have been able to get back in. The key doesn't open Thomas's tomb. The answer is in the full manuscript. The one Valerio has."

The book, the one used to transcribe Valerio's, lay on Thomas's chest, secured by hands crossed over the cover. Had it been there all this time, for close to two thousand years? A crucifix lay atop it between his fingers.

They needed to know.

Bridget pressed lightly on the surface. A brittle material, but it did not give. "Help me."

Dan stepped up and snapped on a pair of gloves. Wedged his hand under Thomas's and smiled.

"What's funny?" Charlie asked.

Dan stuttered at first, but blinked it away and said, "I'm holding hands with someone who probably held Jesus Christ's hand at some point."

"One degree of separation from our Lord and Savior," Bridget said. "But try to put your fanboy squeals aside a moment. I'm taking his book."

She used one hand on Dan's as they released the pressure on the tome, then slowly pulled it free from the dead man's hold. A tiny hiss emanated from the body as Dan gently placed the hands back on his chest. Bridget worried that it might snap something, betraying the villagers' trust in them, but the mummified corpse remained undamaged.

She shifted to the desk, its surface mostly free of dust, only a smattering of insects now growing curious about the interlopers and venturing from the shadows to investigate.

Placing her hands on either side, Bridget appraised the book with a dry mouth and a tingle down her back. "Judging by the age, the difficulty in removing it from the apostle, and the feel of the material, I'd say it's animal hide."

Per Toby's request, Dan came alongside her to film it.

She went on, "The pages appear to be something approximating paper but might be an organic weave, treated hair or wool possibly, or a material like papyrus.

"Be careful," Toby said.

Bridget lifted the cover to a forty-five-degree angle. She felt the creak more than heard it, so slowed her action. At a full ninety degrees, she could read the words. "It's not a reproduction of the journal, or the one that came with the Aradia bangle."

"How can you tell?" Dan asked.

"It's Aramaic." The ink, whatever was used on the material, was faded but mostly legible. "It's talking about this place. Like an introduction. He calls it a 'house of gods.'"

"Gods plural?" Toby said. "Not Jehovah? Not Yahweh?"

"I know the Hebrew and Aramaic words for God, Toby. This is a noun, not a personal pronoun or synonym. He's telling the person reading this to 'seek knowledge before power. Educate yourself. Power is dangerous without understanding.' It's a warning."

"What else?"

Bridget angled the front leaf farther over and turned the first page. Only she didn't turn it completely.

As she ran her hand under that page to ease it toward the cover, whatever it was made of cracked.

"No," she breathed. "Wait, don't—"

But she could not stop the page from crumbling. Its component parts disturbed from centuries of dry, motionless slumber with the priest who had brought them all here. The words inked on the surface turned to dust, and the substance of the page fell like dandruff onto the one beneath.

Tears peaked in Bridget's eyes. "Oh no... I've... ruined it."

Dan reached for the book.

She slapped his hand away, glaring daggers. "Don't try to clean it away. Don't even breathe. I've done enough damage."

"Bridget," Toby said. He would have seen the whole thing. "Let's get it vacuum packed and we'll figure it out later."

Dan withdrew, but his eyes—still on the book—went wide. He inclined his head to get Bridget to return her thunderous gaze to the page. She did so.

The tiny flakes shifted. Dancing. Some kind of vibration maybe, but then they flew sideways, congregating at the edge before fluttering to the desk.

Bridget gasped. "What...?"

"Hey, look what we found," Charlie called.

Bridget and Dan spun to where Harpal and Charlie had opened the stone door using mini crowbars. The pair shone their lights inside, a light breeze ruffling their hair.

The reason the disintegrated paper blew away.

Bridget deflated, a bit of an anticlimax after all. "What are you doing touching things you don't yet understand? You could've—"

"Toby said there wouldn't be any booby traps," Harpal interrupted.

"And we were bored," Charlie said. "But, seriously, Bridge. You have to see this."

Bridget left the book for now, and she and Dan trotted over. Throughout their exchange, neither Charlie nor Harpal had looked away from the direction of their flashlight beams, their expressions similar to Dan's giddy face when he found the crypt.

Harpal crouched in the doorway, shining a powerful bulb into the darkness. "We can't even see the end of it."

In her few years of exploring the ancient world with LORI, Bridget had seen many things she had thought impossible: monuments recovered from sunken ships, a half-destroyed pyramid in the Chilean rainforest, a literal treasure chest that once belonged to Rameses II—albeit two feet square, but it was still special. And the reward for finding it and delivering it to the authorities had kept the institute running for another year. She'd listened, rapt, as Toby regaled her with tales from his days with the British Archeological Institute and their expeditions to Egypt, Cambodia, Brazil, Ethiopia, and more. In the deepest corners of her imagination, she admitted stupid, outrageous ambitions of unearthing legendary places such as Atlantis, and her ultimate, ridiculous fantasy of discovering that the Library of Alexandria wasn't really lost, its destruction somehow a ploy to preserve its secrets.

For a fleeting moment, there in the crisscrossing beams, she thought she'd realized that latter dream. But Alexandria had first burned in 48 BC, long before Thomas and the apostles were evangelizing around the world.

This had to be far, far older.

Harpal whistled, amazed eyes scanning the scene. "Knowledge is power. You think this is what Valerio wants?"

Bridget's head spun with what she was seeing. "It's a library. My God, what have we *found*?"

CHAPTER
FIFTY-FIVE

Again, using his journal, Valerio ran one finger over the hieroglyphs and pictograms on the slab before them while Horse held a purple light to emphasize the ridges and shapes. The militiamen's number had dwindled to six, the others presumably posted to manage a staged defense of any incursion into what was swiftly becoming "their" domain.

Valerio's domain.

Jules was just an unwilling participant. Or was he?

There had been ample opportunities to coldcock Valerio, which would leave him and Horse to fight it out. The skirmish at the entrance hadn't been a real test of their competitiveness, Horse holding something back to avoid killing Jules with a stray blow while Jules pranced about to humiliate the big guy rather than beat him.

Still, he had not resisted Valerio nearly as much as he had Toby Smith. Going against instructions in Windsor, improvising alone in Rome, then betraying them to Colin Waterston in Mongolia. He'd even disobeyed their rescue orders in Mumbai. With Valerio, it was different.

With Valerio, he *agreed*.

Valerio had tempted him with the promise of knowledge. With

the promise of finally answering the one question Jules never once asked in the nine years since his parents' demise. He'd often wondered, "Where is it?" and "How can I get it?" but never "Why?"

Why did my mom and dad die trying to protect it?

Why did she keep it all those years?

He never asked where it came from or what it represented. All he knew was what it meant *to him* and that he wanted it back. Because it represented *fairness*. It was *his*. By birthright and by any stretch of human morality.

Now that Valerio had piqued those other questions, they hung as heavy as those that plagued him since his fourteenth birthday. If Jules didn't answer them now, they would drive him as hard as locating the object had if not harder. Because now, as Valerio closed his notebook and stood back from the massive rectangle of smooth stone, Jules wanted to hop and squeal, a child unable to wait for Christmas morning.

Talk to me!

His face, his hands, his feet, remained impassive, a dead stare to meet Valerio's grin, his bright eyes, his sheer... *joy*.

"In there." Valerio pointed to a section of wall to the right of the polished stone surface. He stepped forward, finger still outstretched, and placed it into a groove.

Horse joined him, the purple light shining on Valerio's hand, his digit having disappeared up to his second knuckle in the surface. He traced the line up and in a curve to the left, spilling dust and crawling insects, before it dropped down into a near circle, then out again and around to a circle beneath the first—an elongated figure eight, an infinity symbol on its end.

The exact dimensions of the two bangles when attached together.

"Batter up." Valerio offered the bangles.

Jules maintained his outwardly dour demeanor, hoping his bored manner gave Valerio the impression he'd given up, when really, internally, he was popping, recalling the first time he skydived, or the night he lost his virginity to a woman five years his senior, or that moment in Prague when he finally laid hands on the bangle and thought his life was about to start.

This, here, was the reason for all of it, every discipline and hardship he'd endured—the firearms, the free running, the martial arts, the history lessons, the code breaking, the psychology degree; from the evasion of police on four continents, the nights in police cells on two, the many failed relationships and shunned friendships, the physical and emotional hurt *every damn time* he got close... it all came down to this moment.

"Yeah, whatever," Jules said as he snapped the bangles together, their alternating edges magnetically sealed and respective glows flaring at his touch. "Why don't you try first?"

Valerio took them back, their light dying as usual. "To prove you're something different from me? Okay."

With the confidence of someone who had no doubt, no uncertainty, Valerio stood beside the infinity-shaped groove, Horse dutifully holding a standard flashlight on the surface. No need for the black light now.

Valerio hovered the pair of bangles by the lock. "If the wrong person uses this, what do you predict will happen?"

"Nothing," Jules said. "What, you think some two-thousand-year-old burglar alarm'll call the cops?"

"I'm not concerned with the rabble of savages who followed Doubting Thomas into these hills. The people I fear are the ones who harnessed the energy that powers this key. We don't know its origins or understand its effects. You saw what it did to the saltwater in the bay. Do you think that was an accident?"

"I don't know what to think. I ain't in a lab."

Valerio shook his head, humoring a simpleton. "Didn't you see the fresco? This is a civilization who lived side by side with the protohumans that populated the earth at the time of the last Ice Age, a civilization who predicted floods as the ice melted from the north. They put together these items that repel saltwater and built *this.*" He swept the bangles toward the twenty feet of flat wall like a game-show host presenting a speedboat.

Here's what you might win!

He said, "This is constructed of the same rock. Unlike the cave, which is a mix of granite and limestone, and a ton of other geological compounds. This door, that one over there with the markings, these bangles... they're quartzite, the same as the Egyptians used to build their pyramid capstones and the statues of their most precious leaders. Infused with these odd flecks, the things that glow, it seems to give the bangles a property that only you can activate. But quartzite, Jules, is found all over Africa and the Middle East. You know where you don't find quartzite?"

"India," Jules said. He noticed something on the wall above the grooves, a symbol he'd never seen before, a hand interrupting a circle, one he hoped he was reading correctly.

"Right," Valerio said. "India. So not only did these people create a pair of pretty accessories that can repel seawater with such force it all but destroys my favorite yacht, they schlep a hundred tons of it up into the mountains of India to protect whatever lies within here from the rising seas."

"But the flood waters never made it this far."

"They didn't know that. They saw the signs of a rising sea and prepared for the worst." Valerio placed the infinity-shaped bangles on the edge of the grooves, lined up as any key about to slot into its hole, the two almost-circles not quite identical, so it could only go in one way. "But they did want to install this fail-safe. A slab that will repel water when activated by a special person. A single entity chosen from the genetic mush of humanity." He shrugged. "But hey, let's take the chance they didn't build a burglar alarm into the system."

Valerio's shoulder dipped, the movement plain from Jules's years of training and experience. He wasn't bluffing. He was going to insert the key.

Jules's arm shot out so fast, Horse drew his gun. But all Jules's grasp did was prevent Valerio from pushing the stone shape into the groove. Horse lowered the weapon.

No need for words. Valerio placed the bangles in Jules's hand. They lit up, red on the bottom, green on top. Valerio stood aside.

"Don't try anything," Horse warned, backing off with his boss.

"As if." Jules slotted the conjoined bangles into the groove, pushing them in halfway before coming to a solid blockage. He held them there, the glow from within muted, bleeding out to the edge.

Nothing happened.

"Huh," Jules said. "That's something of a letdown."

Valerio frowned. "No. We can't be wrong."

"Try it the other way up," Horse said.

"Don't fit." Jules tried twisting it in case it worked like a huge doorknob. "Can I let go of this now?"

Valerio stared. "No. Stay where you are." But he wasn't staring at the bangles, or the wall. He focused on Jules. "What aren't you telling me?"

Discipline.

That was the only thing that set Jules apart from most people in this world, certainly in the West. The discipline to train, to learn, to immerse himself in a subject until he'd mastered it fully, be it conventional archeology or the science of OOPARTs—Out-of-Place Artifacts—or the physics of how an object such as a human body is affected by gravity.

But right then, his discipline abandoned him.

The odds, the stakes, the fatigue of the past week—blame what you will—but usually those outside influences barely affected him. Today, his eyes flitted to the one place he demanded they not stray.

The symbol.

The circle interrupted by a hand.

And Valerio clocked it. Studied it for a moment. Then laughed. "Oh, nice try, sir! Seriously, that was very neat. And you nearly did it." He pulled up close to Jules. His hand wrapped around

Jules's free wrist, and Jules closed his eyes in resignation. "I told you before, you're only *almost* as clever as me."

There was no point resisting. Jules was a puppet under Valerio's control as Valerio moved Jules's arm and slapped his hand on the smooth surface beside the door.

Completing the circuit.

Previously unseen symbols on the slab lit up in red and green, and muffled clunks and thumps reverberated above and below.

"See?" Valerio said. "Magic!"

CHAPTER
FIFTY-SIX

Bridget squinted through the mist of dust roiled up by its first unsealing in centuries, revealing rows upon rows of books lined an aisle wide enough for three people to stand shoulder to shoulder. The shelves on either side were flat, smooth stone bound by something they could not make out and towered twice Bridget's height. She leaned inside the doorway, leaving her feet outside, viewing the interior: two further aisles, equally long and wide and apparently stacked with tomes almost identical to the one before her.

"It's a library," she said. "Toby, this is the biggest collection I've ever seen!"

With Dan aiming the chest-cam beside her, Toby said, "Okay, let's... Bridget, we've gotta keep calm. The objective is not in here. If it was, we'd be fighting Valerio's goons right now. We need the *bangles*. If Valerio doesn't want Saint Thomas and isn't interested in books, we need to stop him getting his hands on whatever is in the main body of the structure."

"What main body? How do we *know* this isn't the prize?" Bridget snatched a flashlight and entered the space, trembling, unable to choose a starting point. She remembered the book from

Thomas's body, though, and pulled up short of touching anything. "Toby, this library is older than Alexandria."

"Bridget..." Toby's warning tone remained firm. A tone she ignored.

Just one. Just one can't hurt.

She raced down the shelves, shining the light so it finally reached the end—two, three hundred yards away—then trotted back to where she started. No book stood next to another of the same size, at first appearing like a rushed job, but Bridget sensed an intent there. Each volume was bulky, far bigger than trade paperbacks or even the bigger hardbacks of today. The smallest she could see in this fraction of the library stood fifteen inches tall and at least three wide. She selected one at random, a brown spine five inches thick and fifteen tall.

She still wore her gloves, but the texture came through as if her hands were bare—a hard, rough finish, similar to bark. Maybe it *was* bark. Treated with an oil or something as a preservative. It felt stiff and it smelled old. For a long moment, she inhaled the scent.

"Bridget, we can isolate this," Toby said. "Come back when we have more time."

"It was a sealed room," Bridget answered. "Thomas's book was subject to the elements. There's a damn waterfall just outside. Charlie, tell me I'm right."

Charlie did not reply straight away. She was Toby's ally, his first member of the team. And every time she quit, she always came back. For him.

"It was sealed," Charlie said. "But who knows what was sealed in there, too?"

She was agreeing with Bridget, but being diplomatic about it.

Bridget said, "Thanks." Then she opened the book.

The first page was illustrated, a man with a spear battling a lizardlike creature with wide jaws and a forked tongue, like a dragon with no wings. A form of writing Bridget had never encountered lined up in columns beneath the picture, closer to a

Chinese style than hieroglyphs or cuneiform, but definitely no modern language.

Her skin tingled, and she consciously informed her lungs to breathe, otherwise she'd suffocate. "I don't even know what these pages are made from. Or the ink they used. It's so... bright. So strong." She partially lifted the page and shone a flashlight behind. "This isn't papyrus, and it's not like modern paper. Less grainy. Thicker but more translucent. How—"

Charlie marched up beside her. "Get a grip, lass." Her Welsh accent always strengthened when she was being assertive. "We'll have all the time in the world to inspect this place, but for now, we have more important things to deal with."

"Yeah, and no plan at all," Harpal said.

They'd all gathered in the aisle, giving Bridget room but close enough to talk. Now everyone's attention fell on Harpal.

"We don't know what's out there," he went on. "We know approximate numbers. We know they're armed with guns and explosives. And we know they're willing to kill if anyone gets in their way. So what's the plan?"

"We'll be sneaky." Dan slapped him on the back and delved into the library proper, wafting away the occasional concentration of airborne particles, there being virtually no breeze to disperse it. "Seriously, though, reconnoiter first. Then we snatch the goods, and maybe Jules too..." He glanced at Bridget, then continued without turning back. "We'll get him if we can. But I won't risk any of you. If Valerio wins, we regroup."

"Where are you going?" Charlie called after him.

"I want to see where this leads. Coming?"

They explored for ten minutes before happening across another door. Bridget kept stopping to probe an odd-looking book —an unusual color, gold or silver binding, a ridiculously huge tome that Dan would struggle to lift...

Charlie or Dan kept her moving, though, with Harpal continuing at the rear.

She managed to snag a smaller one and turned it over in her

hands as they walked. "Again, this cover is like wood. Like the inner layer of bark this time. It's been treated. Maybe with an oil, or—"

"It'll slow us down," Dan said.

"But it's... the most amazing thing we've ever found. Is no one else interested?" Bridget's throat tightened. Why couldn't they understand? "This place... it's a source of ancient knowledge. We are going to answer so many questions. The whys, the whats, the hows. It's—"

"How do you know that isn't the Iron Age version of *Fifty Shades of Grey* or *Harry Potter*?" Charlie asked.

"I..." Bridget's gut hardened, but she forced the shock back and expressed herself in a Toby-like phrase. "I *beg* your pardon?"

"That book. We read all sorts of stuff for entertainment. You might be holding a schlocky murder mystery. A hard-boiled private detective from Mesopotamia."

Dan chuckled. "Yeah. *Detective Horus and the Case of the Missing Cat.* Could be a kid's schoolbook."

Toby's disdain bled through their earpieces. "None of you are helping."

Bridget leafed through the tome, coming across a section featuring circles inter-cut with triangles, and held it up, flashlight close. "See? This is geometry." She flipped more pages, the technical drawings matching up to a building shaped as a pyramid, only with three peaks instead of one. "It's a diagram."

"Like I said," Dan answered, "could be a schoolbook."

Bridget snapped it shut and was about to call Dan some terrible names when their military specialist raised his fist in an instinctive "Stop" signal.

All obeyed.

They had neared the end of the aisle. Dan tested the shelf with his hand—solid—and pressed himself against it. The team copied him, but slowly enough for Bridget to spot what had alerted him: another door. This one was made of stone, smoothed flat and embedded in the surrounding rock, wider than the one in the crypt, but not by much.

Like the top end, the bookshelves were not flush to the final wall, so a passage ran perpendicular to this. Dan scanned down one way, then another.

"Damn," he said, using only the flashlights, "next time we uncover an ancient library guarded by the body of a saint, we really need to pack night-vision goggles." A final check, listening too. "But it looks clear. Bridget, you're up again."

She signaled for some space. The door wasn't the same as the one they came through. This one left no gaps into which to jimmy a crowbar, no handle, no visible crack around the edge. It appeared sealed. Then she located what served as a doorframe and asked for more light. She dusted off the lines etched there and soon discovered symbols related to the ones from the corridor approaching Thomas's crypt.

Then she found the grooved pattern. Like a figure eight. "Charlie? That's like when Jules connected the bangles back in Mumbai."

Charlie leaned in for a closer look. "You sure?"

"I was watching through the binoculars. You weren't. He linked them together. This looks like it's about the same size."

"A key? Like we've been hearing about?"

"More of a pass," Toby said over comms. His voice was crackling now.

"Dead end?" Harpal said. "Do we try the other door in the priest's crypt?"

Charlie unsheathed her short-bladed knife and crouched at the symbol. She poked at it with her finger, dislodging a slew of dust. "This room has been closed off so long, there's not even a spider here." She inserted her knife. "Let's see what sort of a lock can't be picked."

"What's—oing on?" Toby asked, breaking up.

Dan angled to capture Charlie's activity, waggling the knife around the figure eight. The door shook and lifted slightly.

Charlie grinned and proceeded to trace the figure-eight path with her blade, happy to have snagged some sort of mechanism.

The door rose farther, as if her motion was working a lever.

Bridget kneeled before the door, ducked low on her hands. "I have to see this..."

"No, wait!" Toby cried.

Charlie faced Dan's chest, her blade continuing to scrape. "Pardon?"

"Charlie, Bridget, don't do that!"

A crack sounded. The floor jerked upward. Dan snatched Bridget and stepped back to where Harpal was already holding position. Dan moved back for Charlie, but it was too late.

The floor under her split, a broken line spreading all the way to Dan's post.

Charlie gazed at her friends, her look of wide-eyed resignation caught in their flashlights.

Bridget's chest clenched. The sensation of falling flowed through her, although it wasn't her who was in danger. "Charlie..."

Like a thin sheen of ice over a pond, the fissures spread too quickly. For a ten-foot radius, the whole space around the door shattered and crumbled away, taking Charlie with it.

CHAPTER
FIFTY-SEVEN

"Ain't magic," Jules said as a vertical crack opened down the center, a straight line of brilliant white light. He let go of both the bangles and the door.

"Explain it then, Logic Boy." Valerio caught himself and said, "I mean 'Boy' as a superhero name, you understand. Logic *Man* would be better, I suppose—"

"I get the reference. Relax. At a guess, it must be linked to the outside. That's daylight."

Unseen gears cranked and turned. Something squealed, something man-made. The wall parted at the central split, gears grinding, a storybook giant crunching bones in its teeth. The light extinguished as fast as it appeared. Once the gap was wide enough for a car, all movement halted, an echo of the hidden mechanism lingering in the air.

"Pulley system and counterweight," Jules guessed.

"Oh?" Valerio's voice went high. "You know a rope that can last tens of thousands of years?"

"Ain't seen evidence of this being more than two thousand years old. For all I know, it's less than that. An elaborate hoax. I ain't had anything tested. Till I do, I'm leaving my conclusions in the air."

"Ha! Doubting Jules. You and Thomas would have got along great." Valerio pointed at the division. "Time to see what's inside. Excited?"

"Sure," Jules said.

"And oh look! I haven't killed you." Valerio left a stupid smile on his face as if to say "told you so." When he received no reply, he said, "You can join us in there. See what convinced these heathens to convert to Christianity. Or..." Valerio gestured to the two bangles. "Or do you just want to take your trinket back and be on your way?"

Jules removed the key/bangles from the lock and paced to the gap. Darkness looked back. He had come this far. "After you."

Jules stayed out of it for the time being, observing only.

Horse assigned two men to watch the entrance and selected the Ravi brothers to accompany them inside. Both bowed shallowly and resumed their posture with their guns ready and their chins held higher than before.

Yeah, a great honor. Come with us and die with us.

The pair hung back a bit as Valerio led Horse and Jules through the gap.

It was virtually pitch-black, the air cool and dry. A thick, vegetative smell hung heavy, almost oily in the way it coated Jules's olfactory senses. Nature must have encroached here, as it hadn't in the outer chambers. A pinprick of daylight from a vast, indiscernible distance above indicated a spot of damage, but it was not large enough to eliminate the need for flashlights.

Valerio spotted it, too. "The light beneath the midnight gaze of Zephon."

"Quoting Thomas again?" Jules said.

Valerio pointed to the hole. "At midnight, thirty thousand years ago, Zendor, their 'life giver' star that Thomas called Zephon, will have shone through that hole. As soon as we reset the model to thirty millennia ago instead of two, the location was obvious—within a few miles, anyway."

"Huh." Jules set his ears for slithers; no way was he surviving this far only to bite it at the hands (or fangs) of a snake.

And it had to be his ears, as his headlamp barely grazed the blackness, penetrating a seemingly shorter distance than it had in the caves. Horse and Valerio flanked him, their own lights equally pathetic. Valerio produced another lamp that alleviated the murk somewhat, and Horse fired up the halogen flashlight, adjusting the beam wider. Now the path's width was clear: you'd get a couple of busses down there with ease.

Jules handled the bangles too, embracing their luminescence for once, but their red and green light did little except cast eerie shadows as they progressed inside.

The trail grew slightly steeper, paved much like the cave floor, only here it lacked the glassy sheen. Raised walls lined their route, a shade over two feet high, evidently man-made due to the cut edges, yet the impression was of a guided thoroughfare. They rose in steps, though, keeping the flat edge perpendicular to gravity, like a shelf—or close to it.

"Like an aqueduct," Jules said aloud, then pretended he meant to. "Except we're heading uphill. Not a lot. But it's a lot for an aqueduct."

"I was just thinking the same thing." Valerio swept his light from side to side. "It's evenly measured."

Jules looked up. "What *is* this place?" His lamp's beam was swallowed by the dark. "Whatever it is, it's tall... wait!"

Jules's light settled on an outcrop of cylindrical stone overhead, the bangles' glow reaching it too. Not particularly high, then; about three men standing on one another's shoulders. He maneuvered for a better angle. Horse joined in with the halogen, and Valerio with his, all crisscrossing for maximum illumination.

A creature stood over them, looming into the halo of light: an elephantine body, long neck, and elongated head tapering to a beak. The color was unclear, but the stone it was carved from appeared light in tone.

"Indricotherium," Horse said.

Both Valerio and Jules frowned his way.

"I paid attention at school." Horse held the larger flashlight in front of him and focused on the Indricotherium statue. "It's a prehistoric creature. Twice as big as an African elephant."

"And when did this handsome thing die out?" Jules asked. "Lemme guess—the Ice Age again?"

"Try twenty million years ago." Horse cast the light farther on, finding another statue, or at least part of one, its fearsome reptilian head full of teeth in an open jaw. "That's a dinosaur."

"T-rex?" Valerio suggested.

"Smaller. Allosaurus, I think. Top predator of its day. Predates T-rex by tens of millions of years."

"Genius." Jules walked on, trying to find a better view. "So these people didn't just make up stories. They pieced things together logically."

"As opposed to what?" Valerio asked.

"Dragons," Horse answered for Jules.

"Right." Jules shone his light to the left, attempting to gain some sense of scale, but located only a sheer wall face.

"Chinese found dinosaur fossils and gave them a backstory," Horse said. "Europeans added wings, fire, and drew pictures. Made up stories. These look closer to our own mock-ups, though."

"Scientists," Valerio said. "Like the forecasters in the paintings on the way here."

"Sure, whatever. You got a flare?"

"Of course." Horse jogged back to where the Ravi brothers dutifully stood to attention.

Jules and Valerio were left bathed in a wan glow, a lonely spotlight amid the blackness.

Horse relieved the brothers of a flare gun and four cartridges and returned to Jules and Valerio. Nothing more needed to be said as he armed the emergency signal, aimed away from the statues, and loosed it off. The orange projectile shot high without hitting any sort of roof. It arced over them, emitting smoke and light.

Jules swallowed and clenched his fists. His heart raced. "No way..."

In the glowing trail, an enclosed city shimmered. Statues of creatures from every era spread out as far as the eye could see alongside monoliths akin to Cleopatra's needle rising five, six, seven times its height. Behind, over the entrance, a structure had been chiseled out of the rock face, finished in huge blocks, then sculpted as a gigantic cathedral frontage. It just lacked Christian imagery.

The flare dropped, sinking the cavern into darkness once again.

"Another," Jules said. "Send up another."

Horse didn't need telling. He'd already armed a second cartridge and now fired it the same way as the first.

Jules caught more detail this time. The scenery canted at a slight angle, maybe fifteen degrees, but that didn't alter the majesty of what he saw. Great staircases rose from the ground level up to doors in the carved rock face, with buildings spread out for at least a quarter mile, possibly more; the flare's glow didn't reach it. But it did illuminate the roof.

The shadows and shimmering served to define the shape of four walls, narrowing as they met at a point hundreds of feet above them.

"It's as if we're..." Valerio seemed lost for words.

"We're in an ancient city buried inside a mountain," Jules said as the second flare dropped and was extinguished. But in its final throes, Jules remembered something that now made complete sense. "And that hole they watched the stars through... it's a chimney..."

"A what?" Horse slotted the penultimate flare into the gun.

"A chimney. 'The light beneath the midnight gaze of Zephon.' Or Zendor. Whatever. No, wait... *burning* beneath the midnight gaze..." Jules held out his palm. Used the halogen to be sure Horse could see it. "Trust me a moment."

Horse hesitated, but Valerio snatched the flare gun from his bodyguard and passed it to Jules.

"Thanks. Now get ready."

"For what?" Valerio asked.

But Jules was already concentrating. Remembering what he had witnessed, the directions, the angles. He adjusted his arm's elevation, followed both his nose and his memory.

He fired.

The glowing ball streaked across the cavern, low and fast, reaching farther. It presented flat-topped structures, boxes with sloped sides and stairs up one of them.

The flare ended its journey by hitting a wall three hundred yards away and bouncing off it to a ledge where it burned merrily but illuminated only a herd of frozen big cats, possibly tigers.

"Okay, let's have the last one." Jules reached for the final flare.

"No way." Horse pulled it away. "You screwed your shot."

"It was a range finder. Let me have it."

"No. Boss, will you tell him to leave it? I say we go on, tackle it from another angle."

But Jules stepped in, snatched the cartridge, and rushed back behind Valerio. Horse lunged as Jules dodged. A playground game of catch me if you can.

Valerio threw up his arms. *"Stop!"*

Both froze.

Valerio said, "Jules, this had better be *special*."

Using the flare petering out on the far wall's shelf, Jules aimed higher this time. "It will be."

The flare arrowed fast and true, reaching its apex. Instead of gawking at the feats of engineering and art, the trio followed the spitting ball of orange as it dropped in approximately the same direction as Jules's first.

"Great," Horse said. "He's cooked it again. I'll send the Ravis back up the tunnel for more."

"Wait." Jules watched calmly. He had no doubt. This was going to land just... right.

The dot fell behind another monolith two hundred yards from them, this one wide with a zigzag point, a hundred yards short of the other.

Horse scoffed. "You were saying?"

A whoosh of flame shot upward, marking the flare's impact site. It wasn't an explosion, but the five men ducked all the same. Fire billowed high, setting off another series of hidden clunks and resistance. The wall next to the dying flare shifted, cut over the shelf, creeping inward, a chasm opening beneath it. Air sucked that way, creating a short, strong gust of wind.

At the same time, fire traced along channels all over this cathedral-like cavern. Straight lines of flame, branching off in tributaries, those squared-off short walls actually housing a flammable substance, most likely oil or a derivative. Coverage was patchy, the structure's pitch inhibiting the light show's efficiency.

Within minutes, fires lit the entire place, all around the quarter-mile-wide construction: streets lined with statues, boxes with lids the size of coffins, freestanding structures like squat apartment buildings, none the same dimensions. Staircases led to not one but three entrance points higher than their own, spread throughout the perimeter, and ascended a central building to a towering plinth, a pavilion accessible via yet more perfectly aligned stairs. Smoke was pulled out of the air and shoved up what Jules correctly deduced was a flue to the pinprick high overhead, where it would be expelled above the hillside.

"Okay, I'll admit it," Jules said. "My mom was into some *really* weird stuff."

CHAPTER
FIFTY-EIGHT

"Charlie!" Bridget screamed.

Harpal rugby-tackled her, ending her charge toward the disintegrating floor. He tried to be gentle, hoping he didn't hurt her as they landed. He couldn't be sure the structural damage wouldn't spread to their position, but he could try. She squirmed and thrashed, even as Dan backed away, and debris billowed in a gritty cloud.

A booby trap that couldn't possibly exist had swallowed their teammate whole, but Bridget was freaking out, trying to get to her, as if that would make a tiny bit of difference. She smacked Harpal and swore like he'd never heard the southern lady do before, and it wasn't until Dan threw himself on the ground beside her that she shut up.

His face was gray in the beam of Harpal's flashlight, his eyes wide and urgent. "Bridget, calm down."

"I'm sick to death of people telling me that." Tears streaked Bridget's face, but at last, she went limp.

"I can't get to her. I need your help. But I need you to be calm... I mean, I need you... not like this."

Harpal felt as confused as Bridget looked. He said, "Get to her?"

"Yeah, she can't hold on much longer."

The tension drained from Harpal's bear hug, and Bridget sat up next to him. Dan seemed to realize what the problem was and urged them through the static dust cloud to the edge of the hole.

Charlie dangled from the figure-eight groove, her stubby combat knife embedded inside it. Her other hand supported her weight via fingertips in another symbol while her toes found purchase on the half inch of floor that remained when the rest collapsed. Her eyes were closed, teeth bared. No way to crab around to the semiopen door to her left or to safety on the fully intact floor to her right. Too far to jump with no leverage.

"*That's* what I mean," Dan said. "She's okay, but not for long."

Bridget pressed both hands to her heart and glanced upward before a tear streaked through the muck on her face. "Charlie..."

Once it was clear that Charlie wasn't dead, Toby sprang into action from his perch. He showed the tablet to what he now thought of as the chief elder, Dasya, who nodded rapidly, full of concern. Dasya hopped down from the helicopter and gathered the two women from their positions by the well, and they all watched as Dan scrambled to reassure Bridget and calm her down.

"Help us," Toby said, jabbing a finger at the screen.

Dasya tilted his head sagely and the women followed suit. Affirmative smiles.

Toby placed the tablet down and checked the ropes into the well's mouth, but having expected the village leaders to assemble a crack squad of rescuers, his hopes were dashed as he found himself alone. With no orders being barked, no rushing around from the thinning crowd of spectators.

The elders kneeled beside the helicopter. Praying.

From the scene below, crackly though it was, he heard Bridget intone, "Charlie... Thank God for that."

. . .

"Thank *Phil* for that," Charlie managed, straining to speak, referencing the odd gift her husband made upon his retirement from the group—the knife from which she was now suspended.

"Keep quiet," Dan said. "We're coming to get you. Harpal, your pants."

Harpal took a second to be sure he heard the man, but as Dan started to disrobe, he realized they didn't have time to race back to the crypt for rope. Bridget, too, removed her trousers. As she lowered them to her knees, she pulled her top down over her panties—wide black granny panties.

"Hey, they're practical," she said, apparently sensing Harpal's eyes.

"Not judging." Harpal handed his cargo pants to Dan, now conscious of Bridget assessing his own undergarments.

"Tighty-whities, Harpal?"

"They're practical."

"If anyone's interested," Charlie said, "I'm wearing a really impractical thong. I'll show you if you *just get me out of here.*"

One foot broke a chunk of rock away, the debris tumbling into the hole, out of sight. There was no noise to indicate it hitting the ground.

"Coming." Dan tied Harpal's trouser leg to one of his own, an atypical knot that Harpal assumed would hold Charlie's weight. "This is gonna hurt, by the way."

"Great..." Charlie flexed her arms, her fingers on the knife slipping an inch.

Dan secured Bridget's pants to Harpal's and tested the strength. He handed one end to Harpal and told Bridget to anchor him, too. Then he selected a book with no gloves on and opened it.

"Wait..." Bridget started, but the two men's quick, stern looks silenced her.

It's just a book.

Harpal guessed she'd be thinking about the contents, what it might teach the human race, but Charlie's life meant more than any knowledge, no matter how much it might alter the perception of our ancestors.

Dan wrapped the end of the pants rope around the twenty-inch tome and took in the slack. Harpal bound his end of the line around his forearm, and Bridget's hands tightened around his waist. Dan swung the book on the other end past his knee, clearly assessing the distance.

Charlie's fingers on the rock slipped. She felt skin break, a graze or cut, she couldn't tell, but now she dared not rely on those digits in case blood made her slip. If she'd had better purchase, she might have tried pushing upward and snagging a finger hold under the partially open door, but it was just too far and too risky.

Dan called, "I'm going to throw this to you."

Charlie nodded, groaned in pain, beads of sweat pricking on her forehead.

If Phil could see me now.

"When I say 'jump', you turn as fast as you can, push away, and grab the line. No pressure, Charlie, but it's a one-shot deal."

"What happens... if I miss?"

Dan shone his head torch into the gaping void. Back to Charlie. "Honestly? I don't know. I can't see the bottom."

"Not... helping." A snort of laughter burst from her. The voice in her head, joking with her so often, was Phil's. He'd be furious now.

I'm just their tech head.

Logistical support.

I won't put myself in danger.

If she died today, she wanted her final thoughts to be of her three children and the man who would raise them, the man she could not live without—a fact rammed home to her by a grenade in Nigeria. In a tomb in jihadi-held territory. One they'd hunted for through Ethiopia and the regions once known as Carthage, which they believed held the body and possessions of a Persian prince who perished trying to build an empire as vast and significant as that of his uncle—a certain Emperor Constantine. This unnamed prince achieved conquest and brought political change to the region—farming, irrigation, what would be termed "social justice" today, but this only worked over smaller territories. When outside rebels assassinated him, the people he conquered mourned as they would a beloved king and interred him in secret where the rebels could not desecrate his grave. A relatively unknown figure, he could have proven a great hero in the region's history.

Since no significant institutions were interested in chasing a barely referenced royal figure, LORI went at it alone and even assembled a team of mercenaries as escort, promising a cut of profits from any finders' fee. But the jihadi group holding that region got wind of a female-led expedition and took exception to it. They had no idea of what LORI were hunting, only that they must be stopped.

It was a simple gunfight that followed. The ex–British Army mercs proved too strong for the disorganized rabble, allowing Harpal to extract the team via a partially armored vehicle with more horsepower than all the jihadi jeeps combined. But not before a seemingly dead terrorist found enough life lingering within to unpin a grenade. A grenade that exploded at their backs and embedded a clump of shrapnel in Phil's spine.

So yeah, placing herself in danger in this way was a promise broken. One she didn't intend to repeat. Assuming she got out of here.

"But nice try," she said in reply to Dan. "Just throw the damn thing."

Dan eased the book back and forth, the weight needed to carry the trouser leg a sufficient distance. "Ready... three... two... one. Now *jump!*"

Charlie twisted her head.

Dan tossed the book. The trousers flowed behind.

Her movement dislodged her hand on the knife—on *Phil's*

knife—sweat slipping away the last of her grip. As if gravity paused in its effects on her, she found the strength to bend her legs against the rock face.

The book fell through the air, dropping now.

Charlie let go of Phil's knife and sprang out. At full stretch, she flung both arms forward. Her long, dark hair whipped behind with the strength of the jump.

The book fell faster than expected, just out of reach... except...

Its flat pages seemingly slowed its descent. Air resistance. Reducing its speed under Charlie's dive.

Oh, physics, you teasing minx, you.

Charlie snagged the very end of the open book, wrenching her knuckles as she grasped it. The ancient pages tore slightly, but her fingers became talons, holding on with a superhuman effort that surfaced through sheer willpower—a desperate-to-live surge of strength and adrenaline. Her fingers jarred, but she held on, swinging toward the black wall ahead.

Before she hit, she needed to switch her finger grip to wrap her whole hand around the tight material above the knot. If she didn't, the sudden imbalance would jar her loose, and she'd die.

After the initial thump over the edge, Harpal felt Charlie's weight yank out all the slack. Dan shored up the anchor, joining Harpal and Bridget to await the impact. She slapped into this side of the hole, dragging them all forward.

Safe.

Ish.

Dan and Harpal dug their feet in, Bridget hanging off Harpal's waist to add that little extra mass. As soon as the swing stabilized, Dan pulled at her, hand over hand, sweat radiating as his effort literally doubled.

A rip sounded.

Dan said, "Hold tight."

It was unclear whether he meant Harpal or Charlie, but he

dived forward, landing belly first, hanging his shoulders and arms over the edge. Harpal bent his legs, arms able only to cement the lifeline in place, not haul her up.

Dan leaned all the way over, almost to his hips, the rest of him bent into the chasm.

The rope went slack, and Harpal fell back, landing on top of Bridget, who shrieked as she hit the bookcase behind. By the time they untangled themselves, Dan was lying on his back, breathing heavily, and Charlie propped herself on all fours, gasping, grinning, verging on laughing.

"Charlie?" came Toby's voice. "Talk to me, Charlie."

She inhaled deeply, but only coughed in response.

"She'll be with you in a minute," Harpal said. "We're all okay."

Like the others, Dan knew all about Phillip Lock's injuries, inflicted while on duty with LORI. He also knew Charlie and he had been lovers beforehand, and she married him soon after he left the hospital, promising to settle down. But Toby and Harpal were Phil's friends, too, so even with a fledgling family to look after, he couldn't demand that Charlie abandon LORI when they needed her.

After learning of this incident, perhaps he would. And Dan would back him on that.

When Dan took over Phil's role in the group, Phil made him promise to study everything they did wrong prior to his injury, because it wasn't only the point man, the military and tactical expert, who could suffer if things went sour. And, of course, Dan's promise extended to protecting his charges with his life.

Now, with his pants back on—having torn a little on the seam —Dan sat, with Charlie hobbled beside him, using his shoulder for support, and he ran that scenario through his head: explaining to Phil why his wife, mother to their three kids, would never be coming home again. Why it was unlikely there'd even be a body to bury.

"We can jump," Charlie had suggested of the six-foot gap between the library and the door that stood open enough to crawl under.

"The ledge on the other side is only a couple of feet wide," Dan said. "We can make the jump, easy, but landing there, we'll fall back into the hole. Nothing to hold on to."

Bridget agreed, as did Toby, which left Harpal's vote void, but he voiced no objection, so Dan figured he was on the same page. They decided to attempt a different route.

Reaching the exit into Thomas's room, all sat on the floor exhausted. Crashing from the adrenaline as much as the physical drain. Although Charlie came off worst in that respect.

"You should go back," Dan said. "Stay with Toby."

"Yeah, okay," Charlie replied, although her tone made it clear she wasn't going anywhere.

Dan exhaled through his nose and said, "Seriously, Charlie. You nearly bought it back there. I didn't predict it, and we barely pulled you out."

"But you *did* pull me out." She leaned in to him and placed one hand on his knee. "And we need to get something else out of here. It's more important than any of us. Clear?"

Dan shifted his attention to the other exit. "Think we can get door number two open?"

Door number two hung opposite the library entrance within Saint Thomas's crypt and was constructed of wood. A heavy slab maintained by people with more advanced skills than first-century priests. The settlers from Kerala, their descendants, clearly looked after the person they believed was their founder.

Following a swift session with the crowbar, the wood panel, almost a foot thick, opened. There must have been another mechanism behind it, something with a counterweight, because after the initial breach, Dan and Harpal lifted it, backs against the surface. They propped it open with a wooden chest, and Dan ordered all flashlights extinguished; there were unfriendlies about, and their locations were unknown. A beam of light would be more than a tip-off.

Dan led the way, not even allowing Harpal to accompany him. "If I don't make it back, drop the door and lead the team out."

Harpal hadn't liked it any more than he liked his role as the rear guard, but it was even more important now that the others survived. If Valerio escaped, someone would need to track him down.

Dan flicked off his own headlamp, waiting for his eyes to adjust somewhat, and crawled under the raised door. In the tiny room, reminding him of an entry hall, he stood to his full height. Ahead, the walls narrowed, but remained just wide enough for him to squeeze through.

Beyond this, a passage presented itself, a corridor of sorts, illuminated by a weak light source. As he reached the edge of the aperture, he heard voices. Not a language he recognized, but they were deep, rough sounding, muted.

They didn't want to be heard too obviously.

Which meant they were close.

Dan pricked his ears; determined their direction was to his right, toward the light source; and slid his head out to spy out who he was up against.

The two men crouched with guns aimed up the corridor, guarding against any incursion from the same direction they entered. Their main light source was glow sticks, although they also wielded gun-mounted flashlights.

To his left, deeper into the dark, the path sloped down, underground. The militiamen were his prime concern, though.

Dan estimated the daylight was half a mile away, a blob uncovered by the explosives they heard earlier. He also spotted a pack at the men's feet; cylindrical, tightly wrapped, the length of Dan's forearm, with a rectangular box on top.

Explosives?

Surely they'd be better off setting charges in places to cause maximum damage like... like crevasses in the wall.

Dan then looked at his feet. The faint illumination outlined another package down there.

Right.

He retreated through the passage and back into the now-darkened room. He flicked on his headlamp and got Harpal to help him lower the door silently. Once done, they turned on the bigger bulbs, returning light to the room.

"I think I can confirm they're not interested in Saint Thomas himself," he said. "The whole place is wired. But we're on the right level. We can't follow the same route Jules took. And it's heading down into the hill."

Bridget stared at the closed door. "If we can't go that way, how do we carry on?"

Dan pointed into the library. "This way. We need to make a bridge. One way or another, we're learning what's out there."

PART SEVEN

Heroism is not only in the man, but in the occasion.

—Calvin Coolidge

The battlefield is a scene of constant chaos. The winner will be the one who controls that chaos, both his own and the enemies.

—Napoleon Bonaparte

Where is all the knowledge we lost with information?

—T. S. Elliot

CHAPTER
FIFTY-NINE

Logic dictated the most important business occurred at the center of... whatever the heck this was. Jules still hadn't allocated it a name. Valerio had been calling it a cathedral, but Jules now accepted it predated any religion modern man had ever heard of. Besides, it was far bigger than any church, cathedral, or temple. More comparable to an underground city. If designed to lord over the dead, perhaps it was a giant acropolis.

Thanks to the blazing light, their path no longer depended on electricity, and whatever fuel burned did so at a far cooler temperature than gas or alcohol. The flames were blue in places, tipped with yellow and orange. That's not to say it wasn't warm—like a sauna, but not close to wandering through a burning building.

Or a burning city, for that matter.

They admired the twenty-foot statues and needles, the slabs and pillared boxes that may have been habitable once upon a time.

"It's like different folks built each of these," Jules commented.

"Offerings," Valerio agreed. "Some advanced carvings, others architecture, all of it unique from the next."

Horse remained on alert as if someone threatened to scurry from a building or a statue might come to life and bite someone's head clean off. He stopped by a column standing alone. "This looks Greek."

"And that's Egyptian." Jules referred to a man-size humanoid with the head of what may have been a dog or a squat lizard.

They made it to the foot of the stairs leading to the central pavilion three stories above. It looked almost Aztec in nature, a simpler, miniature Machu Picchu-type pyramid. Horse and the Ravi brothers scouted around the base, then all three ran up the stairs, guns aimed ahead as if breaching some terrorists' safe house.

Valerio sweated profusely.

"You okay?" Jules asked.

"A bit out of breath. This exercise..." Valerio coughed, hacking from the base of his lungs. "This smoke isn't helping. Ingenious ventilation, but... nothing's perfect." He coughed again.

Jules tried not to feel sorry for the guy. Murderous rampages tend to stick in the mind even when a person is laid low, barely able to lift his head.

Horse returned, calling from halfway up. "All clear."

Once again, Valerio set the pace, a mooching plod when Jules wanted to run, sprint all the way up, like Rocky Balboa during a training montage.

A wheeze, another coughing fit.

Horse came to help, Jules unwilling to touch the man who'd brought him to the verge of answering every question he'd been able to summon.

On the top step, Valerio sat, gazing out over the flickering cityscape. The Ravis stood sentry at either end of the platform while Horse stuck close to Valerio. Jules remained standing, a 360-degree view, enough to note that Horse must have issued an order to take the high ground.

A gunman was now posted on each of the three staircases leading to a door at the pinnacle of the higher balconies. He was taking no chances with further ingress points, no matter how unlikely.

Below, the layout resembled a maze, a crisscrossing labyrinth of streets lined with art and engineering feats. A collection of sorts, reminding Jules of a...

It can't be.

No way.

Nothing's that simple, is it?

The ground seemed to sway ever so slightly, and like Valerio, Jules had to sit to catch his breath. He checked his logic again, fired it through all he'd learned—the pictograms, the frescos—and assuming Valerio only got a fraction of his interpretations right, Jules found his own conclusion sound.

. . . awarding the finder untold power. The knowledge of the world.

Ultimate knowledge.

Forging history... or forged *in* history.

"The Mongolians dated the Ruby Rock bangle to between thirty and fifty thousand BC," Jules said. "The curator you murdered, Amir, he was certain, but... it sounded like crap." His head buzzed, thick with conflicting notions—what he knew, what he learned, what this place indicated. "If those frescos are right, they predicted the flood from melting ice—"

"Yes, at a time when humans were supposedly struggling to use flint to cut animal hide." Valerio was perking up. "The only possibility, if true, is that they explored the north, which had been covered in ice for all their lifetime, observed melting, and when they saw the sea encroaching on coastal cities, they worked it out. Doesn't need satellites or fancy instruments. Just willpower and brains." He coughed again—five big, dry hacks—then thumped his chest before resuming his calm outer shell. "Are you starting to believe?"

"What if this place is a record?" Jules's frown pressed deep into his skin, unable to trust his own words. "Like a museum. If they knew civilizations'd be swamped but couldn't know the extent of the flooding on its way... a stupidly huge door that repels saltwater when the right person touches it... the different architecture... all of it."

His head spun. This was too much. He couldn't accept it blindly. Where was the actual *proof*? The empirical evidence? Plus:

"How'd they get it up here, smartass?" Horse asked.

"It doesn't matter," Valerio answered quickly.

Too quickly.

"You *know*," Jules said. "You *know* how they did it. Don't you?"

Valerio stood shakily. "Let's see what we have here."

Jules wasn't getting an answer, so he simply complied and followed Valerio to the pavilion where four pillars held a square slab aloft, as wide and long as a family car. Beneath, a pool shimmered in the firelight. The water sat in a deep, roughly hewn depression. It was gray with a faintly colorful film, a stagnant pond. Dead insects bobbed on the surface, a blanket of beetles, spiders, millions of flies and mosquitoes.

Horse scratched his head. "I don't get it, boss. How is that still here? After even a year, it'd evaporate or bleed off someplace. If no one's been here for centuries..."

"Maybe the instruction manual will tell us." Valerio crouched to a knee-high plinth where a stone tablet lay upon it like a Bible before a priest. He wiped a layer of dust, then produced a soft-bristle brush that fit in his palm, and dug out the last of the dirt without damaging the surface.

It was infused with etchings depicting the language they'd witnessed a couple of times now—columns rather than rows, scratches and shapes instead of pictographs.

Valerio beamed. "Their own language."

"Just how much did you have translated?" Jules asked. "And how?"

"A bit of guesswork, a bit of human input, and a supercomputer back in Ladoh did the rest. Those Indian graduates really are very smart."

"A supercomputer." Jules stuffed his hands in his pockets. "Why does that feel like cheating somehow?"

Valerio dipped his hand in the pool, then withdrew it and

shook it off. "Here." With his dry hand, he tossed the stone plate to Jules, who caught it.

Surprised how light it was, Jules expected it to glow, but nothing happened. "What do I do with this?"

"Give it to Horse."

Jules obeyed. "What now?"

"The healing powers of this pool reflect many of Jesus's own miracles, so with the artifacts in hand, it wasn't hard for Thomas to persuade the local scholars or incoming pilgrims that this place and Thomas's religion shared an origin: God. This is God's pool."

Jules pulled back and swallowed. "You wanna drink that? Be my guest."

"Oh good lord, no, it's not for drinking." Valerio rubbed his chin. "Now take off your shirt, handsome."

CHAPTER
SIXTY

Bridget felt terrible about dismantling an artifact as important as Saint Thomas's desk, but its top section would allow them to progress—it was sufficient to reach over the hole, light enough to transport without industrial machinery, and able to hold their weight. This latter condition was subject to much debate, mainly surrounding the notion that two-thousand-year-old wood could survive that long. It had been treated with oils, though, a blend of Bronze Age varnish, and did not appear to bend when they propped it against the wall and each person pressed their body weight onto it.

Having carried it through the library, they laid it across the chasm that had almost swallowed Charlie, more than wide enough, with a foot of purchase on either side.

"I'll go first," Dan said.

"No argument here." Harpal stood aside.

"Bridget goes first," Charlie said.

Bridget turned cold, but said nothing. They lit the scene with the camping-style lamps that had brightened Thomas's crypt. The effect here was less, but they could see all they needed, from this part of the library to the door Charlie had cranked.

"There's a foot of grace on either side," Charlie added, referencing the amount of wood that met the ground on both ends. "That's six-to-seven feet of relying on the molecules to hold together. After centuries of lying inert, I reckon giving it the biggest shock is the wrong move. Introduce weight to it slowly. Bridget's the lightest, then Harpal, then me, then Dan."

"I'm not heavier than you?" Harpal sounded insulted.

Charlie smoothed her hands over her hips. "I'm still fitter, Harps. But you squeeze out three kids and try to weigh the same as a twenty-year-old."

Harpal held up his hands. "I'll take your word for it."

Dan grumbled but didn't argue. He kneeled by the desktop bridge and added his grip to both corners.

Bridget stood at the edge.

"Spread your weight," Charlie said. "Hands and knees."

Without speaking for fear of bursting into tears or running away screaming, Bridget kneeled on the solid section. She leaned over. Her fingers curled around the edges, preventing her body from pitching sideways into the void.

"You can do it," Dan said firmly.

She didn't want anyone speaking to her, just needed to work this out in her own way, so set her brain into the mode that had gotten her through roller coasters and skinny-dipping in the River Thames for a dare during her university days.

I have to do it.

She moved one hand forward, then her corresponding knee so it stood over the hole. Next hand, next knee.

She was now hovering over a seemingly endless chasm with only four inches of wood for support.

If I don't do this, they'll think less of me.

She recalled a time at Disneyland, her dad urging her to go on one fast-paced train or another, a goldmine, she recalled; she survived that. And the River Thames, freezing at night, her class-mates fearless through freshers-week alcohol, screaming for her to join them... if she hadn't done so, her years there might have been different.

She inched forward another cycle: right hand, right knee; left hand, left knee.

This wasn't ego or a dare or letting her dad down after hyping up the visit for months. It was her *life*.

She reached farther this time, her knees moving faster, the blackness unavoidable in her peripheral vision.

The wood creaked and bowed minutely in the middle.

Three intakes of breath from behind did nothing to stop the tremble in all four limbs.

Bridget closed her eyes, pleading with the universe to spare her, with God, with whoever was up there watching over the people he/she/it created.

Please...

She opened her eyes and, in the absence of divine intervention, kept going. Hand, knee, hand, knee.

Repeat.

She reached the other side and lay on the ledge between the partially open door and the gaping fissure. Her head spun, arms and legs jelly, as adrenaline surged back inside her.

A shuffle sounded, and before Bridget fully recovered, Harpal matched her route and technique. She sat up to watch. Then, with no idea how much it would help, she put her weight on her side, as Dan was doing the other.

Harpal made it to the middle in three shuffles, where—again —the wood protested under the pressure of a human. But unlike Bridget, he carried on without hesitation.

The wiser option.

Bridget shifted aside to let him off, and he, too, lay on his back for a moment.

"So, that was scary," he said.

Charlie didn't hesitate. She was already moving. She kept her eyes forward, boring into Bridget. She smiled as Bridget pressed down again at her side. Probably did nothing for the integrity of the link between there and here, but it made Bridget feel less useless.

As Charlie reached the middle, the wood cracked. Her face slackened momentarily, then her pace increased.

A louder creak, a longer rent of wood splitting.

Charlie cried out as she shifted from her knees to her feet and pushed forward. She landed on the ledge where Harpal and Bridget secured her with grabbing arms. When they looked back, the desktop still spanned the gap, but the middle had buckled, forming an elongated V.

"My turn?" Dan said.

Dan's confidence was high, and to be honest, he preferred it this way. He was less nervous about traversing the gap than if he'd had to use the desk's surface.

"Don't be stupid, Dan." Bridget pointed unnecessarily at the snaggletooth of a crossing.

"It's only six feet. I jumped farther than that in tenth grade."

"But—"

Dan cut her off by heaving the wood to one side and letting it drop.

The broken slab turned end over end, spinning until it was lost to the darkness. All listened for the crash. Sure, small rocks might not have resonated, but surely this—

The impact, when it came, was as quiet as a car door closing.

Dan shrugged. "At least it'll be a gnarly ride down."

"That's supposed to be my line," Harpal said.

Charlie glanced around at their perch, the two feet of floor before the solid door and its gap beneath. "We haven't got enough room to catch you."

Yeah, Dan had worked that out already.

He picked up the lantern and tossed it across, the shadows dancing and shimmering. Charlie caught it. Dan said, "Leave that by the edge so I can see. Everyone, get under the door. It's my best chance of making it."

Bridget rubbed the back of her neck and stuttered at first, but managed, "Dan—"

"No more debate," Dan said. "I gotta play Superman."

Charlie guided Bridget backward. "I think I know what he has in mind."

He had to argue a few seconds more to persuade Bridget to leave him, but Charlie took charge and shepherded her under, both women fast-crawling on their bellies. Harpal stayed.

"You too," Dan said, backing up.

"Nah, I'm watching this." He fished out his cell phone and fiddled with it. "You make that jump, it's going viral. And not because it's a long way, but cause it's gonna look hilarious. I'll get Charlie to make sure—"

"No more talk." Dan set off running.

His legs pounded, his eyes focused on the lip of the void, unsure which foot he'd be pushing off with, but that question was soon answered: his right.

He leaped in a straight line, throwing himself flat—like Superman. Landing feet-first on sand might not be a problem, but one error in his balance on the edge of that drop and he was toast.

He slapped onto the smooth surface head-first, arms ahead of him, momentum carrying him on and under the door, where he rolled to a stop in a dim passageway. Charlie and Bridget pawed all over him.

"I lost visual," Toby said.

"It's dark." Dan sat up and brushed off the attention. He checked the camera. "Sorry, I busted the lens, too."

Harpal followed him under with the lantern. "Can you do that again? I didn't hit 'Start.'"

"Maybe on the way back. Right now..." Dan pointed along the short corridor where it ended in a more conventional set of doors. "We're beyond the barrier that the bangles unlock. I wonder what's behind there."

. . .

Although they thought he was only joking around about the video, something about it really hacked Harpal off. Probably a hangover from his "gnarly" sporting exploits. Whenever someone performed a stunt that was video-worthy but no one captured it, they called those events "unauthentic," a variation on "photos, please, or it didn't happen."

Missing what Dan did shouldn't irk him so much. No way Toby would allow it out there, but for personal use, it'd be a gold mine of entertainment. The centerpiece of Harpal's planned Christmas party montage. That's probably why he was so intent on his phone right now.

His thumb hit the "Record" button, hoping to capture someone's reaction as these doors opened.

First, the approach: the doors towered two stories over their heads, yet possessed static handles.

Second, the examination: metal frames—"Probably iron," Charlie speculated—with rock inlaid as the main body. A faint light lined the point where the two met as well as the bottom join.

Third, the debate: all their lights had to go out, including Harpal's phone, but he just set it to manual and flicked the LED off. Dan then tried the door. Presumably the booby-trapped slab was considered sufficient security since the huge barrier eased open. Harpal aimed his phone through the gap.

Fourth, the twist: outside this door, a militiaman was standing with his back to them. He must have heard or sensed something, because he turned and reached for his gun. But Dan sprang on him, silenced his voice with a jab to the windpipe, and flipped the man over his hip. On the floor, he thumped the man's head with the heel of his hand, knocking him unconscious.

Fifth... fifth was the slow, steady realization that anything Harpal had ever witnessed paled into insignificance compared to the scene that unfolded beneath.

A sprawling complex of buildings, statues, and any number of regular shapes cut in massive relief all seemingly blazed away. On closer look, like many of the monolithic carvings, the flames seemed to form a steady pattern too, stemming from a single point that must have been the source—a pool of flammable liquid feeding the channels.

From their elevated position, all stared out for several seconds, maybe minutes; it was hard to tell.

Dan pointed out similar aeries on which guards were positioned. He ushered his charges to crouch by the ornately carved barrier to hide their presence.

It was Bridget who voiced the reason why they weren't spotted. From all their positions, with dozens of stairs leading to the lower level, they all focused on the central structure where five men went about their business: two more militiamen, plus Horse and... was that Valerio undressing? And Jules watched on, hands in his pockets.

Valerio shouted, *"I'm serious. Take off your shirt!"*

CHAPTER
SIXTY-ONE

Jules reluctantly pulled his shirt over his head, folded it, and handed it to Horse. "Look after that, yeah?"

Horse frowned and dropped the garment on the floor.

"Real mature." Jules placed the bangles on the T-shirt and approached the now-topless Valerio.

It was impossible to tell in the flickering orange light, but the man seemed a deeper yellow and far skinnier than when he was wearing clothes. His chest was pretty much concave, and blueish veins spider-webbed his torso. Skin hung from his arms as if the muscles had shrunk rapidly.

"I know," Valerio said. "Beautiful, right?"

Jules said nothing.

Carrying the tablet he referred to as the "instruction manual," Valerio stepped into the pool up to his ankle. He shrieked. "Ooh, that's fresh."

Jules watched.

Valerio said, "Come on in. It's lovely."

"Sure I can't just watch?"

Valerio held out his hand. "Positive."

Jules forewent the hand and stepped in, disturbing the insects and spiders. It was thicker than water. Viscous. Not quite like oil. More like cream. But still as clear as water.

Dirty water.

"Ready?" Valerio asked.

"No."

Valerio stepped farther down. Jules followed suit, the icy liquid now up to his knees. Then up to his thighs. A final step saw them standing waist deep.

"Put on the bangles," Valerio said.

Horse waded knee deep and handed them over. Again, Jules obeyed.

If this was the big show, the reason for Valerio's crusade, his murders, Jules's own mom's killing, he had the front-row tickets he needed. The only thing that might ruin it was watching from the top of one of the staircases leading to the back wall: LORI.

Jules spotted movement up there seconds earlier, but hadn't looked for fear of alerting Horse or Valerio. Someone was actually filming using a cell phone, their hand held over a barrier, and now someone else—presumably Dan—stood to attention, the pseudo-army jacket, doubtless taken from the original sentry.

The presence was concerning, but not unwelcome. Jules just hoped they waited for his signal before interfering.

"Hold this." Valerio gave him the tablet.

Holding it at the top, the lettering glowed green gently, a toy with weak batteries.

Valerio kept hold of the bottom end and locked eyes with Jules. "I'm just guessing mostly, by the way. If this doesn't work, we'll try something else. But our supercomputer thinks that's what the text said. An equation: the bangles plus the tablet and the pool can only be activated by a chosen one."

"*A* chosen one?" Jules said. "Not *the* chosen one?"

"I guess it pays to have spares."

"And this is your big moment?"

Valerio guided the tablet toward the pool's surface. "The biggest."

As the stone touched the fluid, it glowed brighter. A fizz around the edges. Some sort of reaction, a compound like the bangles that reacted with this substance. But little else.

"Burst your bubble a bit there?" Jules said.

"Now is where we try the alternate scenario. Have faith. And trust me."

And Valerio hugged Jules to him, both their skins pressed against the tablet.

"Cozy." Jules glanced at Horse. "Don't get jealous, big guy. I ain't enjoyin' this."

Valerio laughed and pitched himself backward, taking both of them under.

By the time the water began bubbling and spitting, Bridget had worked out that the complex was a repository of knowledge. The books, the various artworks, the architecture...

She relayed it in a whisper to Toby and asked whether the hill was smoking.

"Like a low-powered volcano," Toby replied, Charlie's boosters working well. "I wish I could be there."

"You will be," Bridget said. "But right now, I don't have a clue what Jules is doing with Valerio."

With Dan in place, posing as the guard, he'd been able to see more than the snatched images the others made do with, popping up for moments at a time to observe. He confirmed there was a lower entrance, probably where they would have come out on the original route, the explosive-lined passage being a downhill gradient. Now, though, they gave no thought to staying hidden. Their heads—and Harpal's phone—spectating live as Jules's situation distracted them from the myriad questions posed by the discovery.

Who built this?

Why?

How did they build it?

How old is it?

Is that a chimney or an entrance?

All questions to answer later when they could sift through the knowledge base, maybe keep it hidden from the likes of Colin Waterston. Perhaps it'd be worth letting Valerio Conchin go to do whatever if it meant Bridget and Toby could feast upon this place even for a short time.

It was too much for their small institute, but they could get a head start, maybe learn that language and make themselves useful to whoever took possession of the tomb. The Indian government, no doubt. The Americans would want in, naturally, and the Brits would be apoplectic if excluded. She guessed the Indians would get the final say, but for now, only this select few even knew of its existence.

Then the two men down below surfaced, and a whole host of new questions burst into being.

The waters bubbled and hissed as if they were boiling. The heat intensified, emanating from the stone slab between Jules's body and Valerio's. Jules's lungs reached capacity, but thrashing about in this washing machine resulted only in Valerio's grip strengthening—a crocodile hauling an antelope to drown. Then, when Jules thought he might pass out, Valerio pushed him away.

Jules stood, gulping at air, coughing and spluttering and trying to orient himself. Staggering to the edge, he sat on the steps and searched for Valerio. He didn't have to wait long.

Valerio rose up out of the filthy pool, brushing the dead creatures from his skin. And it was a skin transformed. White, not yellow. Even under the glow of fire, his sunken eyes were strong and bright, his chest firm, the sagging skin now taut.

"Hoo, yeah!" Valerio held out his arms to the sides, embracing something unseen. "That was amazing!"

"Amazing" undersold what Jules thought. Despite the feats so far—the sparks from the bangles, the wave, the glowing doors—

he hadn't seriously expected this to work. Those other events were explainable using current scientific theory. To regenerate diseased matter, to heal completely, was beyond the scope of serious scientists.

It was impossible.

Valerio waded to the side and strode up out of the water. No hobbling, no hesitation. Just a strong, committed gait.

Jules stood and lifted himself out, joining Valerio, both dripping onto the pavilion.

The Ravi brothers covered Jules from opposing angles. Horse pointed a gun at him. "We done here, boss? Can we kill him now?"

"Horse, Horse, Horse," Valerio said. "I gave this young man my word." He scooped Jules's T-shirt off the ground, strutted over with his back straight and head held high, and passed it to Jules. "Go now. Take your precious bangle and enjoy your life."

"Seriously?" Horse said. "I thought we were just joking around."

Valerio remained focused on Jules. "Now you know what your mom was protecting. More importantly, you know magic really exists."

Recovered from the submersion, Jules accepted the shirt and allowed his gaze to start at one end of the structure. He turned a full circle, not only to assess LORI's position without giving them away, but also to give him time to think, to work out whether his second epiphany rumbling to life was paranoia or terrifyingly real.

He stopped and faced Valerio, pulled on his T-shirt, and spoke as loud as he dared. Enough to carry the hundreds of yards to Bridget and the others, but not so much that Valerio or Horse would suspect.

Very simply, he said, "I ain't going *anywhere*."

CHAPTER
SIXTY-TWO

"People have called me 'special' for a long time," Jules said, his voice carrying up to the nest where Bridget continued to crouch—a balcony fit for a Roman emperor spectating as gladiators fought their bout. "I never was, not really. I just worked damn hard. Maybe on some level, I gotta concede, it could be my brain's wired different. I learn quick. I don't forget stuff that might be useful."

He paced, monologuing, and Bridget got the impression that he wasn't only speaking to those in his immediate vicinity.

Had he spotted them?

"But I work hard," he repeated, the guns following his path. "Ain't no pool of crap and light ever healed me or rebooted my cells to their optimum state or whatever the hell happened here. I studied history, psychology, language. I trained with masters of burglary, parkour, aikido, firearms. And don't get me started on diet and gym work."

"But you know!" Valerio hunched over, pleading. When he returned to full height, he seemed bigger, less wasted. Even his skin looked fresher. Verging on radiant. "I am now free of disease, of all ailments. I feel healthier than when I was twenty-one. I am a *god*, Jules. Because of you, because of your genes and whatever quantum business goes on with your consciousness. It's wild, isn't it? But you don't accept it. You don't want to head out into the world, take your prizes. You know things no one else does."

Jules held up both hands, the bangles on his wrists. He lowered them. "Lemme tell you what I *know*. I know my skin reacts with these stones. I know now that we had civilization before the accepted record, and these folks, they used the special properties in the rocks to build great things. Like this place. To answer Horse's question about how they moved all this stuff from the port up through the hills, must've been connected to magnetism, to properties in these stones." Jules shook the bangles. "Like a monorail, right?"

"My theory exactly," Valerio said.

"But despite their genius, they got wiped out by war or environment—the Toba eruption was round here, wasn't it?"

"Toby, boss?" Horse asked.

"Toba was a supervolcano," Valerio answered with a swat of his hand, implying it was no big deal. "*Seventy-five* thousand years ago. Wiped out the human race to maybe ten thousand souls. The bangles are much younger."

"I know that," Jules said. "Maybe we'll never know exactly what made them abandon this place. Maybe it was the fire we saw."

What fire? Bridget thought. *They can't mean the one raging right now, could they? No, don't be stupid. Something else...*

"We'll never know," Valerio said.

"Damn, that's what I figured." Jules was pacing again. "See, one of the problems we got as humans is we don't know what we don't know. Meaning we ain't always sure what questions to ask. Me, I just figured I wanted my mom's bracelet home with me, a memory to keep hold of. Some shrink told me once I was trying to resurrect her through an inanimate object and urged me to give it up. But you... clever guy... you pushed my buttons good. Got me asking *why* instead a' *where*. Not 'Where is it?' and 'How can I get it back?' but 'Why did she hold on to it?' and 'Why did she die to protect it?' So I'm asking myself, 'Why is Valerio here?' and 'Why is he letting me go?' Answer is pretty obvious. And you confirmed it for me just now."

Bridget couldn't see Valerio's expression, but his body held stock-still.

"We saw those paintings, the carvings, all predicting floods and disasters. Or maybe they're recording history as well. There were two sides to that 'forecaster' dude."

Forecaster dude?

Bridget really needed Jules to survive this. She needed Valerio gone so they could defuse and explore those explosive-laden tunnels. A historical record from *pre*history. She literally tingled all over.

"Two sides." Jules held one forefinger inches from each side of Valerio's head. He wiggled the first. "One with fires, violence, that kinda thing." He wiggled the other. "The second side was the flood downing a city."

It sounded magnificent. She checked Harpal was still filming.

"So I started asking? the question again. *Why?*" Jules dropped his hands back and stepped away from Valerio. "I know for certain you didn't set up a whole town in Ladoh and install a supercomputer just to decode whatever ancient languages you pulled outa the ground for your hobby. You didn't risk robbin' the Queen of England and plan that ambush in Rome for a book that *might* lead you to some tomb. You didn't kill dozens of people in Ulaanbaatar, then recruit all this muscle and set the place to explode behind us... yeah, I figured out the mercs planted bombs... just to heal yourself and let me go on my way."

Bridget whispered to Dan, "What's he talking about?"

"What Toby was scared of," Dan answered, holding his pose.

"Maybe you getting better is a bonus," Jules continued. "Might even've started out looking for this spring or pool, whatever it is. But you can't get away with the scale of destruction and murder you left behind. No amount of money can make that go away. To make all this worth it, there's more at stake."

"He understands," Toby said over comms, now breaking up every five or six words. "A little late, but he finally understands."

"Understands what?" Charlie asked.

"The sort of man Valerio Conchin truly is."

Jules lingered near one of the Ravis before wandering on in his circle. "Those pictograms, the hieroglyphs, and that... writing-writing... it all predates Hebrew, predates Sanskrit. And you knew enough to follow the writing. You just needed the woman from Rome to figure out the key, the basics, and you used that to program the computer, to lead you here. But not to heal."

The newly invigorated Valerio nodded and laughed. "I really do like you, Jules. I mean, I've killed people I like before, but if you don't stop talking and start heading out, I'll figure myself a way to live with the guilt."

"Toby," Dan said, "evacuate the village."

"No choice now," Charlie agreed.

Toby's voice cracked again, this time nothing to do with a poor signal. "That might be wise."

Harpal held his phone steady, twisting to join the discussion. "Why?"

"I ain't leaving," Jules said. "Just come clean. Just do what you gotta do. What you planned to do all along."

Valerio wagged his finger as if he should be making a tut-tut noise, but the acoustics didn't carry. What he said next did, though: "You should have taken the bracelet and run."

"Then I'd be dead."

"Yeah, you got me. *Horse.* It's time."

Horse took a cigarette pack–size box from his pocket and held it aloft before pressing his thumb to it.

An explosion boomed through the lower part of the structure. The ground shook. Another explosion, a third, fourth.

"He's blowing the place," Dan said.

"But his men—" Bridget started, but then a final ear-splitting bang plumed clouds of smoke and dust out of the ground-level entrance, shaking the balcony and staircase.

She couldn't help it. Before she knew it, before she could consciously stop herself, the scream was out there. Which meant, of course, there was no hiding anymore.

The three men on other aeries aimed guns their way, as did Horse and the two on Jules's level.

"Oh!" Valerio shouted happily. "Now it really *is* a party!"

CHAPTER
SIXTY-THREE

Jules drop-kicked Horse in the side, whipping the gun out of his hands as the big man tumbled down the stairs.

He then turned his attention to the Ravi brothers, the main threat right now, and tossed the machine gun toward the most prepared. This stunned the other momentarily, Jules's odd choice giving him pause. By the time the gunman refocused, Jules was upon him.

A flat hand to the man's chest sent him off balance, a tug of the gun, a sweep of the feet, and Jules used the momentum to throw him into his brother. Then it was a case of a solid heel to the brother's head, knocking him out, pinning the first and smashing that guy's face into the floor.

Bloody.

Bruised.

Unconscious.

Times two.

No *lasting* harm.

It all took less than five seconds. By the end of those five seconds, Valerio was screaming, "Kill them all!"

Jules kicked all three automatic weapons into the stagnant pool, aware that sidearms were still in play. Also in play, though, were the sentries following orders to take out the interlopers. Their guns rattled, echoing through the cavern.

As he faced Valerio, Jules couldn't help wondering how the men felt about the recent explosion. Was that the plan? Did the men expect to sacrifice themselves to protect their paymaster?

Horse raced back up the stairs, past Valerio, charging at Jules with a fury he'd not displayed to date. He'd been so calm, so measured, even when plainly angry. This was a new side to the man.

A personal grudge?

Let's find out.

Jules ducked the first blow and sidestepped, dropped into a low stance, and kicked at his assailant's leg. Horse dodged and weaved. Their styles competed for dominance. Jules slapped Horse aside several times, the larger man's weight giving Jules an advantage, easily maneuvering him via the momentum from his attacks. But Horse was still fast and well balanced, striking precise, hard blows, each missing for now, but Jules's gut still ached from the last time Horse made contact.

With LORI pinned, there wasn't much chance of help.

Outside the cave, Jules had been showing off—a teenager riling up an old man. Not anymore. This was the real thing, and although Horse would have made training a priority at one point, for the past six years, Jules had *lived* it. A shorter time on the planet, but utterly dedicated, consumed by the need to be better, stronger... prepared for anything.

So Horse couldn't cope with the switch in strategy.

Jules moved in close, fast and sudden, utilizing Krav Maga now rather than aikido, raw power exploding through his elbow, up into Horse's chin. A crack sounded from inside the big man's mouth. Jules followed up with a knee to the groin, the side of an arm to the head, an open hand to Horse's battered jaw.

Jules's direct approach slammed him this way and that until— finally—Jules ended this bout with a sidekick to the man's already damaged head.

Down. Out for the count.

Valerio was running down the stairs.

The exchange of gunfire continued—Dan with the automatic weapon, Harpal with a handgun. They weren't in a bad position, but they made no progress either. And they were on a clock.

"We can't hang around," Dan said. "Those explosions gave this old place a real beating."

"It's already hurt," Charlie added. "It's on a slight angle. Subsidence, earthquake, I don't know."

"Then this'll be a problem." Harpal pointed out one of the sentries advancing down a flight of stairs, mounting an RPG launcher on his shoulder.

"Oh, not in here," Dan said. "As soon as he fires, you move. Ready?"

Bridget hit him on the chest. "Of course I'm not ready!"

"Tough. Cause here it comes."

The militiaman released the rocket-propelled grenade, its contrail spewing white behind, drilling hard through the air.

Harpal and Charlie reacted quickly. Dan pulled Bridget with them. Harpal literally dived for the stairs, rolling, while Charlie chose to slide on her ass. The two seconds the grenade spent streaking across the cavern allowed them to duck and cover on the walls to the side. Landing a touch high, it blew the doors apart and sprayed rock and twisted metal.

It also gave the other bad guys an opening to advance on their position, leaving one now out in the open—reloading his RPG— while the others snaked through the "streets" below.

"Okay," Dan announced as Bridget pulled away from him. "I'll hold 'em. It's evac time."

Dan laid down a burst of three, wounding the man on the steps. The attacker's stomach, hip, and leg streamed blood, agony visible on his face from several hundred yards as he dropped the launcher.

"Not a chance." Harpal aimed his gun at a runner. Fired. Missed. "The girls can go."

"No," Charlie said. "Someone needs to prime the helicopter. That's you or Dan. Which means it's *you*."

"But—"

"Plus, why do you even have the gun? I'm a better shot." Charlie snatched the weapon.

"You don't do fieldwork."

"Needs must." Charlie fired at another runner, pinning him back. She held out her left hand, the Russian Makarov pistol weighing down her right. "Come on, you know it's the right call."

"She's ex-army, Harpal," Dan said. "She can shoot as well as you."

"Better," Charlie emphasized.

Harpal relinquished the two spare mags taken from the man Dan killed up on the balcony and beckoned to Bridget. "Okay, fine. Come on, Bridget. We'll meet them up top."

Bridget shook her head rapidly. "I can't make that jump to the library."

"It's less than six feet."

"Standing start," Bridget said. "You can't throw me, so I'll need a run up. That means I need someone who can open the door."

"She's right too," Dan said.

Harpal swallowed hard, glancing slowly at each of them. "Just once, I'd like to be the one who's right."

"Plenty of time for that," came Toby's voice. "My plea with you, Harpal, is to do as Dan says."

Harpal nodded, his lips tight. "See you topside." He ran upward, two steps at a time.

Dan and Charlie both lay on their stomachs, using the rise as cover. They fired single shots, evenly spaced, protecting Harpal from the militiamen, each of whom tried to plug him. But they knew better.

"Bridget, wait here." Dan checked on her: back against the

wall leading up to the library entrance, currently shielded from the men trying to flank them. "We'll bring Jules back."

She held up a fist and pumped it. Dan assumed that meant she was on board.

"Charlie, we're gonna alternate," he said. "I'll move to draw their fire, while you get a better angle. Clear?"

Charlie slapped in a fresh magazine. "Like riding a bike."

Then Bridget yelled at the top of her voice, *"Jules!"*

CHAPTER
SIXTY-FOUR

The cry came over the sound of gunfire, Bridget's voice, calling his name.

Jules remained atop the pavilion, assessing Valerio's route. Definitely heading for the main fire pit.

"Jules, we have a way out!" Bridget shouted.

Choice time: escape in the direction Bridget urged, or pursue Valerio.

They're here for me.

But they didn't know what Jules knew. They didn't know Valerio had far bigger ambitions than simply healing himself.

So Jules did what he did best: he ran the opposite direction from Bridget, although not straight toward Valerio; with his newfound physical prowess, the billionaire achieved too big of a head start.

Jules accelerated on a downward angle. Once at the right level, he wound up enough speed along the flat step, calculated the added weight from the two bangles, and launched himself toward a sloping roof atop a house-like building.

Up and over, through the air, that familiar sensation of controlled falling rushed through him.

He landed on the tiles. But whatever passed for cement during its construction had long rotted away, and the tiles themselves were brittle, made from a compound of mud and wood. Just as he felt the roof give way, Jules spread his weight and rolled to the edge where the structure was stronger. He ran up to the peak, jumped left, swung around the point of one of the shorter needle-type erections, and propelled himself onto the back of an elephant. Its length was sufficient to gather the speed to jump to another building, this one a flat-roofed Greek-type configuration.

Then to an Egyptian man with a wolf head.

Over a line of fire, its heat scorching his legs.

Then a simple sandstone cube, perfectly proportioned as far as Jules could tell.

All in a straight line, chasing Valerio as the crow flies, gaining ground.

Approaching the clear target point—a recess almost hidden by the end of the main fire pit—Jules found himself climbing. The structures, the statues, the monoliths, all increasing in size the nearer he got. It wouldn't normally be a problem, but he was tiring now. The exertion of the trek up here, the lack of sleep, the crappy food.

He didn't stop, though. Plowing onward, overtaking the boss man as he swung through a black, horse-headed warrior's mouth and up again, over a horned beast like nothing he'd seen outside of depictions of Satan, on which Jules rested to take stock of his progress.

A gunshot sounded, blowing a chunk of horn off the blueish devil-like sculpture, a type of stone Jules couldn't name. It changed color depending on his angle, from translucent with a blue tint to an aquamarine hue.

Jules dangled over the other side, taking cover behind its head, and found himself directly above the main fire, the pool fifty feet below him feeding the rest of the cavern.

Yellow and blue flame raged, its heat shimmering in the air. Still nowhere near the temperature it would have been had the fluid been gas or oil or even alcohol. This was something else.

Something that burned slowly, that kept its heat close to the surface.

And it didn't help him one bit right now.

Another gunshot. Closer.

Struggling to find a view, he shifted to the left.

Twenty feet down, another of those solid cubes waited, the biggest so far, adjacent to the fire.

Clambering on top of it, Horse seemed to have recovered.

Reaching the library, Harpal left the camping light on the short side of the chasm to aid anyone else fleeing this way, activated his headlamp, and leaped the gap as Dan had done in reverse; a tough feat given a mere two feet of purchase on the door before the void. But it was doable and far easier than *landing* on the short ledge. Harpal managed to hit the other side and roll, and when he shone his headlamp around, its narrow beam captured a new cloud of dust and a blocked path.

Outside the crypt, the path Dan had seen sloped down into the structure. It was logical that one or more of the bombs may have gone off beneath this floor.

One of the seemingly solid bookcases, having towered three people high, had now toppled into the next, leaving a triangular tunnel through which to pass, the impact having smashed off one side.

"Guys," Harpal said, hoping they were still listening. "The explosions must have affected the library. It's pretty much upside down."

"Go," came Dan's strained reply.

"Okay, but I've got one thing to do first."

He bent at the knees and heaved the slab that once formed the vertical edge of the bookshelf. His fingers and shoulders protested with sharp pain. The stone scraped against the floor, but Harpal pushed it toward the deep, black canyon, keeping his weight on the back third. A few inches from the opposite side, it began to tip.

Harpal moved to the back, preventing an accident, and shoved it more slowly.

It hit the other side. But didn't rest on the lip. It just bumped into it.

A matter of millimeters too low.

"Ahh."

Harpal sat on the end with his ass, jiggled it a bit. He shuffled as far forward as he dared and bounced.

The slab shifted slightly.

He bounced again and jammed his hands under the sides to stop it from falling flat. The slab's mass pressed down on his skin, his bones, as agonizing as trapping his fingers in a car door. But he continued to shove with his feet on the floor, his arm muscles straining, sinew stretching against tendon, and—eventually—the slab settled on the other side.

A better bridge than the desk had been.

He took ten seconds to suck his sore fingers, replaced the tiny half-moon flaps of torn skin, then sprinted over the fallen bookcase, out into the crypt, and returned to the corridor that took him to the waterfall.

The rest of his dash was of Olympic quality, rushing back up the well after telling Toby to winch him up.

When he surfaced into daylight, Harpal pulled himself clear to see Toby's evac was thoroughly underway—and with good reason.

The ground had collapsed in places, sinkholes caving in from the hillside and spreading all the way down here. Like an unsafe mine sucking the settlement away. The villagers were gathering possessions from their homes, a steady stream heading for the drop-off that overlooked the rest of the valley. A town of refugees fleeing for their lives. The elders prayed on the hearth of their church.

"Jesus," Harpal said.

"I'm afraid not," Toby answered, abandoning the winch and

rushing to see the state of Harpal. "But we may well need his help soon."

"Guys," Harpal said. "You need to hurry."

"I'm gonna kill you, boy!" Down on the plain cube, Horse bled from several places, most prominently his mouth.

Jules's philosophy was one of Zen, of peace. He was ashamed that he'd enjoyed fighting Horse—just a little—but now, seeing the mess below him, that enjoyment turned bitter, a curdled drink in his gut. Horse's mouth contained broken teeth to be sure; he had a busted eye socket, which now swelled approximating an apple; and he limped even as he drove on toward Jules.

He fired again.

Jules found a foothold on the blue flint devil statue, easing the pressure on his arms. He could not leap down onto Horse without the bodyguard shooting him. Equally, he couldn't fall into the fire.

Let's try something...

He rocked.

The statue gave, shifting a couple of inches before settling back in place. It was lighter than it looked.

While geology was not a field Jules troubled himself with, he inevitably had to study certain rock types, and this felt similar to flint, only lighter, less hard. You certainly wouldn't carve a tool out of it.

Jules held on, dug in his heels, and shifted his weight again. The statue almost tipped over.

"I see what you're up to." Horse loosed off two more shots. "Won't work. I'm gonna kill you before it even hits the ground."

Those calculations that used to dance in the air before him came racing through his mind. Taking it all in—the angles, the weights, the trajectory.

The cube Horse is standing on is thirty to thirty-two feet high.

Its surface is twenty-five feet square.

I am between fifty-one and fifty-three feet up.

Where is Valerio?

"Your pals," Horse called. "They're dead too."

From his vantage, Jules could now see Valerio standing before a blank wall perpendicular to the wide, flaming pool, manic as he paced back and forth, eyes straight ahead, oblivious to the surrounding conflict.

Switching angles, Jules made out the gunfight, the urban warfare at which Dan was highly experienced, and Charlie was plainly no slouch.

"Ain't a problem," Jules said. "Two on two, I'd bet on Dan any day of the week."

"Except it isn't only two."

Jules adjusted his grip, moved enough to stay hidden from Horse, but also to view the central pavilion.

Empty. The Ravi brothers were mobile again.

"Dan!" One hand slipped as the realization hit him. He immediately regained his grasp. "There's two more! Watch yourselves—"

Three gunshots came his way, each as close as any to date. The stone chipped, sharp fragments spraying Jules's left cheek.

"Okay, let's stop messing around." He let his feet fall free, swung them back, and hurled all his weight at the statue's torso, sending it teetering but not falling. "Here we go, Horse, get ready to catch me."

"Give it your best," Horse said.

One more thrust with Jules's legs, and the demonic carving surrendered to gravity, a tree expertly felled.

Jules whipped himself up and slid down the flintlike surface to the halfway point, like a fireman's pole, below the cube's lip. Then he jumped to his feet and ran back up, spinning the timings through his head, ignoring the steep odds of pulling this off and just acting as if it were a given.

Running faster than the statue's fall, Jules reached the cube's level.

As hoped, Horse must have assumed Jules was turning tail,

trying to hide, and with his angry head working harder than his tactical mind, he ran into Jules's hands.

Jules dived off at an angle, swung his feet forward, and slammed into the oncoming juggernaut's shins. One of the bones snapped under the attack, Horse's scream far girlier than Jules expected.

He also lost all sense of himself. No balance, no control. He dropped his gun, bounced, and somersaulted before flying over the edge toward the mass of flames.

Jules closed his eyes, unable to bear witness to the first life he ever took. One he didn't intend, but even there, amid the chaos and destruction, his overwhelming thought was that this death would haunt him forever.

As the devil statue crashed to the ground, it breached the edge of the fire pit, and shattered into a million chunks as if it were glass. The barrier around the fire suffered damage, a V ripped out of its front section, and the clear fluid within flowed over. It oozed onto the floor with the consistency of spilled custard, diverting around the small buildings and monoliths first, headed for the statues and offerings from around the world. The shifting pitch guided it directly downhill.

Toward Dan and Charlie.

A deep-throated growl rose from the cube's edge. Jules dashed forward.

Horse hung from another wedged sculpture by his fingertips. He bared bloodied teeth at Jules, eyes narrow with hatred and rage.

Jules's whole body flooded with relief. Although *logic* dictated that losing Horse would have been both accidental and self-defense, he could not bring himself to write off a human life that way. He knew *logically* that Horse would strike to kill him at the earliest opportunity, yet this was his one commitment that *logic* alone could not override. It could in others. But not him.

You go ahead, but it's not for me.

Jules stuck out a hand. "Grab it."

"Go to hell." Horse glanced back down at the fiery pool leaking away. More surface area burned now.

"You sure?" Jules said.

Horse looked back at Jules. "On second thoughts... fine, pull me up."

Jules crossed his arms and crouched on his haunches, reaching right over the edge. Horse released one hand to grip Jules's forearm just above the Aradia bangle, then the other above the Ruby Rock. Jules pushed with his legs, heaving the 250-pound gorilla up. The gorilla howled again as his broken leg scraped the cube's corner.

Once safe, Jules let go and rolled away, springing up into a low stance, close enough to tackle Horse if he produced a backup firearm.

But Horse lay there on his side, both hands in plain sight. Jules chanced a quick pat down, and Horse didn't try to fight. No weapons.

"I don't need to do anything else." Horse panted for breath, gritting through the pain. "The boss is clear. Your pals are dead." He pulled himself across the cube to the point where he climbed up the remaining section of blue-green devil, slithering and pushing himself with his one working foot. "And you got no way out."

Jules had the perfect comeback, a retort that would make Horse feel silly in the extreme, but he never managed to deliver it.

Charlie's scream cut him off.

CHAPTER
SIXTY-FIVE

Still using the monuments and sculptures around the wide staircase for cover, Dan spotted the two additional guys, his vantage better than Charlie's. Good sense said he should pick off the militiamen from up high while Charlie guarded the imagined perimeter he had relayed to her.

The one he took out by the library entrance was as troublesome as a mild cold while the pair rushing them from the other aeries acted conservatively and knew how to hold cover. Potshots exchanged, nothing more. Now, with a survivor from the explosions in the entrance below, two others who'd had real training stalked them too.

When the gunfire went quiet, Dan figured they were communicating somehow.

A four-way barrage ensued. Machine gun–fire blasted from the ground level while the two experts fired handguns from atop a yurt-shaped building with spires and domes.

Dan made a beeline for a naked bronze man holding a spear, one higher than his current spot and almost in line. The gunfire followed him. Slugs impacted behind, but he made it, the ricochets pinging off the metal.

From there, he observed Bridget's hiding place—behind the plinth of a silver-looking pregnant woman, naked, of course, holding her round belly and gazing heavenward. Dan patted the air, indicating she should stay down.

A huge crash rang across the cavern, and he was certain the flames licked higher over the far end. Sparks danced, and the flaming channels shifted and shimmered.

His movement, though, had exposed the pair at ground level. Emboldened them. Dan aimed through the warrior's legs. Not trusting the single-shot function, he set the gun to a three burst. "Charlie, give them something to think about."

"Copy that."

She hunkered between two plinths, home to identical male nudes in white stone, holding hands above her, more a victory celebration than love. At the first minor letup, Charlie's Makarov boomed four times. The two men, just outside her range, instinctively ducked and shifted.

Dan blasted twice, taking the pair out. Neither moved on the ground.

"Got 'em," Dan said. "Just need the rooftop, guys."

"I can see both." Charlie pointed, then flattened her hand to chop the air.

"I got no clue what that means. Some Brit signal?"

She sighed. "Run like hell to the right, head for that big bear statue. Fire a couple of rounds if you can."

"Hey, tactics are my domain."

"You going or what?"

Dan checked his breathing, clutched the stolen machine gun—a nice AK-400—then set it to single rounds, and ran. Doing his best to aim properly, the gun bucked with each shot, coming closer and closer each time.

"Now pretend to fall," Charlie said. "Trust me."

All or nothing.

He stumbled on purpose. His momentum sent him sprawling

in a more gangly fashion than he intended, which induced genuine panic.

But it worked.

Both militiamen steadied their positions, static in their shooting stances.

Charlie sprinted from her spot and improved her angle. Kneeled. Aimed. Fired twice.

The two heads atop the yurt-come-temple burst into red mist, and all that remained of the gunfire was the familiar echo in Dan's ears.

He stood. Held up a fist Charlie's way. "Nice."

Another report split the air.

And Charlie cried out, clutching her stomach.

Blood streamed from between her fingers. She dropped her gun and added the second hand for pressure. She sat, lay back on the steps, reducing the need for circulation.

Where...?

The guy with the RPG was across and to the right. He wasn't dead. He lay in his blood with a rifle aimed their way, struggling to find a bead on his second target.

Dan had no such problem. He fired five single shots at the man, each thumping home. If he wasn't dead this time, he was powered by whatever magic was driving this place.

Charlie wasn't magic, though.

Bridget crept out to see, and when she did, she hurried down toward her friend.

Dan joined them, ripping his top shirt off as he went. He pressed it on Charlie's wound, the gun to one side, more frightened now than he had been throughout the entire firefight. "Bridget, keep an eye out. Anything moves, you yell, okay?"

Bridget pulled off her pack and rummaged inside. Came out with a roll of electrical tape. Dan wiped his hand on his own white shirt and accepted the tape. He removed the makeshift staunch while Bridget ripped open Charlie's shirt at the bottom, then Bridget reapplied it. Dan tore off a length tape and stuck it to the cleanest part of Charlie's skin, unspooling it across the wadded shirt. He passed it through the gap formed by the stair under her back and guided it over and around again. He kept on going, tighter each time.

"I... I think you got it," Charlie said, her face pale.

"You're not surviving some bottomless pit only to die from a boring old bullet." Dan lifted her like a baby. "Gonna get you in that pool."

"You can't," Bridget said. "It needs Jules and that tablet thing, and we don't know where they are. Take her back to the helicopter. There's a first aid kit there. It's less than half an hour to the border."

Charlie's arms hung around Dan's neck, but they were weak.

Bridget jabbed a finger at the exit. "We can't know that it'll fix a *bullet wound*!"

Charlie said, "Bridget's right. We don't know... where the hell Jules is. Plus... look."

They all saw it now: the slow creep of more fire, oozing throughout the channels and makeshift streets. The repository was being consumed.

"*Take her*." Bridget pointed at Charlie, then the door to the library. "Harpal said there's a new way across."

"That kinda sounds like you aren't coming," Dan said.

"I'm bringing Jules out."

"How you plan on doing that?"

Bridget picked up the AK-400. "No idea. But I'm guessing there's a way through those fires."

No time to argue. Dan handed her the final magazine and pointed to show her how to eject the old one. She struggled to get the new one in place, but once it was, she armed it like a pro.

He said, "You've fired other weapons back home?"

"Everyone's fired guns in Alabama."

"Select your rate of fire, point, and shoot. And you know not to bluff, right?"

"I'll do my very best. Now go."

As much as Dan feared this was a mistake, it was a simple triage choice: stay and Charlie dies for sure, go and maybe she lives. He could only hope Bridget knew what she was doing.

CHAPTER
SIXTY-SIX

Bridget had no clue what she was doing. Yes, she'd fired rifles and shotguns and six-shooters with "Smith & Wesson" embossed on the side, but a machine gun was something else entirely. Nor did she know exactly where she was going or where Jules was currently located.

Her decision: scout the structures, don't get cut off by the spreading flames, preserve her own life as best she could. If Jules came with the bangles they'd come for, great. If not, they would write off the bangles as a loss, and she'd insist they never attempt anything on this scale again.

With Dan taking Charlie to safety, she was now the only wild card. If they didn't count Jules. Which she figured they didn't.

Yet she wanted to give him one final chance.

Was that all, though? How much of what she was doing was linked to the bangles? To the history? To the desire to linger just a little longer in the most extraordinary find since... since when? Since what?

The wonder of opening Tutankhamun's tomb?

The rewriting of human evolution through unearthing the bones of the hominid known as Lucy?

The scientific breakthrough of mapping the human genome?

This was a moment like no other. And it was falling down around her.

Yes, spending those additional moments here meant the world to her. If she could save Jules and survive the day, that would be a real bonus.

By the time Jules had traversed halfway to the pavilion, he could see the staircase where the gun battle played out and that Dan carried Charlie in his arms, leaving Bridget behind wielding a machine gun that was way too big for her.

Jules bounded forward, down to ground level. Having mapped out the fire's flow, he gave it a wide berth, hoping none of the materials here were flammable, or worse, combustible. The people who built it seemed at least as intelligent as modern humans, but explosive rock wasn't beyond his imagination.

He reached the far side, where Bridget picked her way at a jog.

He said, "Hey, Bridget."

She responded by hefting the gun, a slow process due to its weight, but he held up his hands anyway.

"Is that all you got to say? 'Hey'?" She lowered the gun, stashed it on her back with the strap, and ran toward him, sweating now in the rising heat.

"You wanna 'how do you do'?"

Behind her, back at the staircase, the stream of fire pooled and branched off toward the entrance Jules had come through. She reached him and placed both hands on the bangles. "You got them both! That's great. Wait till you see the library we found!"

"A... library?"

"Huge! Like... like finding all the books from Alexandria, only... so much better. Come on!"

He resisted her pull. "I can't."

"What?" She furrowed her glistening brow in disbelief. "I stuck around for you. I came to find you. That's what you wanted, isn't it? You activated the tracker."

"I thought you'd send the cavalry, not come yourself." Jules struggled to keep his voice even. The dumbness of coming alone was unspeakable, but voicing that would do no good here. "And there's something else. Something important."

"What? What's more important than your *life*? This place could cave in at any moment."

"And yet here *you* are."

"Yeah. Trying to make you see sense. To preserve what I can."

Jules's expression must have conveyed that he didn't understand.

"The charges that went off," Bridget said. "They're collapsing the land around this... thing. It's the same as a ship going under, dragging debris with it. Jules, we need to *move*."

"I can't—"

"Sorry, dear, that's my fault." Valerio strolled into view, approaching them, Horse slumped behind him on the floor, seemingly having been helped along by his boss. Topless, vain, Valerio's peacock strut was even more pronounced. "Look, I have abs now. Aren't they great?"

Bridget raised the machine gun, faster this time, sweat dripping from her. "Ignore him, Jules. Whatever he says, you gotta come with me."

"Oh no, no, no." Valerio came closer, almost within touching distance, forcing Bridget to step back. "He doesn't *have* to do anything. He has his trinket back. He knows his momma's deep, dark secret. That she possessed knowledge no one—especially someone like *me*—should have. He's free from his drive to find it. Free to do as he pleases."

"He's coming with me."

A new channel of fire lit up nearby. The pooling at the destroyed entrance was pushing the fluid back. Eventually it would congeal at that corner, but for now, the resistance diverted it elsewhere. Depending how large the reservoir was that fed the fuel lines, it was only a matter of time before there was no way out.

"Let him choose," Valerio said.

Jules could have fought him. Despite his physical improvements, it didn't seem likely he'd be able to compete with Jules one-on-one. So what the hell was he doing here?

"You wanted to kill me," Jules said.

"What can I say?" Valerio opened his arms. "I'm contrary. If changing one's mind is a crime, shoot me."

"Okay." Bridget adjusted her grip, the stock at her shoulder.

"In cold blood?" Valerio shook his head. "Unarmed? I don't think so, my perfect little rose."

"I ain't *your* anything, asshole."

Valerio applauded her. "Jules, I made a mistake in hurting you. I'm sorry. But I need a partner. Someone to share this with. Horse is... incapacitated, and since you're the one who beat him..."

"You want a new bodyguard?" Jules said.

Horse strained to shift himself on his butt, dragging himself to his feet, the stone tablet from the pool in one hand, where he teetered on his good foot. "Boss... I'll be fine."

"He needs you, Jules," Bridget insisted. "He needs you to open whatever he's trying to steal."

"She doesn't know anything." Valerio held out his hands again.

Jules eyed him carefully, about to launch a combo of punches to disable him, when Valerio simply grasped hold of both the Aradia bangle and the Ruby Rock.

Both bangles glowed under his touch.

Valerio beamed maniacally. "You see, Jules? That pool altered me on a *genetic* level. I don't need you at all. Because I'm just *like* you now. *I'm* special too."

CHAPTER
SIXTY-SEVEN

The whole chamber shook as if a bomb had dropped, but Bridget kept the gun trained on Valerio Conchin. Several statues toppled into the flaming rivers, but she remained focused on the man with the glowing objects in hand, still wrapped around Jules's wrists.

Jules had insisted he wasn't special and that his ability with the bangles was nothing to do with fate or destiny. A genetic quirk, he suggested, and now that appeared correct.

"Jules, it's over," she said. "Whatever he can do, whatever this means, none of it will matter if you die. Come with me. Please. Before it's too late."

"There's so much more." Valerio's face seemed to glow like the flecks embedded in the bangles themselves.

Jules stared at Bridget. "What if he's right? What if there's more to discover?"

"Show 'em the writing, boss."

Bridget's attention shifted to the tablet Horse now offered.

Valerio clearly enjoyed the shock flowing over Bridget and Jules, and the darkening of the bangles as he let go excited him even more. "Oh yes, the tablet. Lookie here, you two." He took the stone from Horse and held it behind his back. "Before I show you, Jules, please tell your friend what language was written on this."

Jules hadn't looked at anyone since Valerio let go of the bangles, clearly still stunned by what he saw, but he managed to answer, "Dunno. Didn't recognize it."

Valerio held the tablet out in two hands so Bridget could see. "Recognize it now?"

She did. And the sight of it scrambled her thoughts and made her head spin. She lowered the gun. "Are you sure it was unreadable before?"

"Yeah," Jules said. "Why?"

Bridget pointed at the stone. "Because that's not some ancient unheard-of language. And I might be a bit rusty these days in the vocabulary of God's chosen people. But that's Hebrew."

The hasty retreat out of the underground lair was hot and hard. As Charlie's grip on Dan's neck slackened and the adrenaline spike from the initial urgency receded, she grew heavier in his arms.

He'd carried many a fallen comrade like this out in the open in the aftermath of one IED or another. He sensed the phantom blood on his hands today, the desert heat on his neck, the need to not glance at the ragged stump of a leg blown off, and the young soldier's weight increasing step-by-step as Dan and his remaining platoon raced toward an LZ. He couldn't make out whether the memory was of someone specific or if it was an amalgam of several incidents as he tried to keep Charlie's body steady, desperate to prevent tearing the wound.

It was a relief to come across the lamp and bridge Harpal had left, which held their weight without complaint. He took his time over the mounds of books and collapsed shelves, ready to dodge anything falling from above.

And there was plenty of rubble to slip on. The whole room had altered, angling to his right much more than before, with fresh chunks of rock from wherever the ceiling commenced.

"It's all coming down," he said, hoping Bridget could hear

him, that she would heed the warning. If she didn't show soon, he'd get Charlie to safety, then return.

The obstacles left Dan unable to use his own hands for balance until he took a moment to pause, to catch his breath and… Yeah, he could spare a moment. It could be important before pushing on.

After a couple of seconds, he checked Charlie's position wasn't adding undue strain to the wound, then made it over the fallen bookcases to the crypt. He barely glanced at the body of the saint who brought them all here as he ducked out into the passage, where he was thankful for the coolness of the waterfall's spray.

The remaining trek was downhill over rough terrain, which he sped over like a heavy gazelle until he reached the bottom of the well and found the harnesses in place. "Harpal, Toby, you copy?"

"I'm here," Harpal answered. "Toby's helping with the evac. How's Charlie?"

Dan checked her face. "Conscious but hurt. On my mark, winch us up. Slowly." He strapped himself in and held even tighter. "Stay with me, Charlie. I don't need Phil's foot up my ass if we lose you."

A smile dawned on Charlie's lips, and Dan's heart fluttered as he planned in his head what to say to the medics.

The harness tightened around Dan's chest, and they rose steadily. Without a pulley system, the rope hung directly on the bricks, so Harpal must have halted them when Dan's face showed. He summited the well's mouth in seconds, and Dan passed Charlie up to Harpal before pulling himself out. Both carried Charlie to the helicopter, where they strapped her to a stretcher. Once she was in, Dan allowed himself a moment to assess the scene.

The half of the village bordering the hillside had been obliterated, a series of sinkholes having swallowed swathes of the place into the concealed cave system. Great sections of the rise itself had vanished too, smoking with dust and debris.

An explosion tore through the air.

"The mines are going off," Harpal explained. "Every time the ground shifts."

Dan understood. "Which damages the substructure even more."

Toby jogged over from the church, where the elders kneeled and prayed. Outside, sensibly. "It's no use. They're praying for deliverance."

"They might not lose the whole village," Dan said. "The tunnels don't extend that far."

"The ones we know about," Harpal pointed out. "That place is so big. Who knows how deep it goes?"

Toby stared at the hill, at the smoke pouring from the top. His arms were pinned to his sides, eyes moist. "And we're going to lose it all."

"Not necessarily—"

But more grumbling from the land cut Harpal short, and a mere fifty yards away, a smaller hole opened, dropping a line of soil underground that led away from them like a plowed field. The depression must have caught a mine as another explosion rang out.

"Damn," Dan said. "Bridget's bringing Jules up. I'm gonna help."

"No." Toby placed a hand on Dan's chest. "They need us here."

The elders stood from their prayers and hurried from the church.

"Even they know it's no use," Toby said. "Bridget made her choice. If she doesn't make it out, you won't either."

"But I have to," Dan said. "Bridget, you hear me?" No answer. "The relays must have bought it. I can't raise her. Toby, she needs me. I have to—"

"She doesn't need you, Dan. Do you think she'd consider the children here less important?"

Dan clocked what he meant. These were large families, and

they needed guidance. Kids were being herded toward a trail at the far end of the village.

Toby said, "Bridget and Jules will get out. We all need you here." Without a reply from Dan, he repeated, "It's *her* choice. *Her* decision."

"Fine," Dan said. "Get the chopper going. But if she dies, Toby, it's on you."

"Remember the fresco?" Valerio said. "The forecaster, the storyteller."

Jules didn't much care where he was going with this. They'd been static too long. And when another earthquake hit, the dust and chunks of rock were accompanied by half a dozen boulders smashing artifacts and artwork as the hole at the peak destabilized.

"Let's talk on the way out," Jules suggested.

"Do you really think I didn't plan for this?" Valerio said. "There's more than one way out of here!"

Bridget backed away. "And you have no clue if that's collapsed, too. Come on, Jules."

Valerio placed his palms together. "One more minute, I beg you."

"No. Jules, let's go."

Jules was about to leave when Valerio said, "The weapon."

Jules halted in his turn. Slowly returned to Valerio, who nodded, pleased with himself.

"Jules…" Bridget forced a warning tone into her voice.

Valerio paced a full circle, beholding the ruins collapsing around him. "A weapon that can only be wielded by special people such as you and I. Imagine what someone like me could do with it. With you by my side to keep me in line."

A pause to take in Jules's reaction. It must have been affirmative, even though Jules made no conscious indication.

"A sword, perhaps. A battle-ax, a spear, an arrow. Throughout history, we have examples of these things, wielded only by us—the special people. Damocles. Excalibur. Solomon. Who cares about the legend's origin? The result is *power*, Jules. And this tablet, the one from the pool, it's been *amended*... changed... with *Hebrew writing*... a language you know, correct? Not me, Jules. It changed... for *you*."

"Why not English?" Jules said, dying to run, compelled to stay.

"I don't know. Maybe the... pool doesn't know English. Maybe it dug inside you to find a common tongue, something you both understand. But that isn't the point right now. The point is we're the same. And there are two ways out of here. Back where your red-haired fox wants you to go or through the first priest's tomb."

Bridget shook her head. "Don't listen to him. Thomas is back that way. We found him."

"Thomas isn't the first priest," Jules replied without thinking. "He was the most *recent* priest. But not all priests follow Jesus. This place isn't even remotely about Christianity. Just happens it was a Christian who discovered it." That wasn't an outcome he'd consciously thought about, but all the facts, all the things he'd seen coalesced into one simple truth. "Thomas found this place. He was one of the descendants, one who carried the gene all the way back from the time these people built it."

"Not starting to believe in *fate*, are you?" Valerio said.

"Fate is just coincidence given retrospective meaning. And Thomas learned all he could about it. Enough to scare himself silly, and he tried to seal this place."

Bridget glanced between the two men. "Jules, you can't know this."

"Except I do," he said. "Thomas discovered the power that's held here. But he didn't know about genes or quantum physics. He believed in messiahs. And holy people. He believed the right person'd find the tomb someday and open it up."

"A savior," Valerio added. "*We* can be saviors to the world, Jules. You and me."

Bridget turned her head back and forth, stepping one way, then the other. "It... makes sense. Thomas *couldn't* be the first priest of the ancient writing. It *predates* Thomas. He just *copied* it."

Valerio nodded along, exhilaration radiating from him.

"The tomb is farther in, deeper underground," she said. "In the real center of this structure."

As a milder tremble dislodged more rocks, sending them plunging, Valerio whooped with delight, tossing the tablet back to Horse. "If you want to be with Jules so much, my dear, come with us. Come meet him. Meet the first priest. What waits beyond those doors makes a thousand tons of crumbling boulders utterly irrelevant. What's there will make me the most powerful human being to ever walk the earth. We will be *gods*."

The four stood in silence. Jules worked it all through his brain, desperate to see how much more his mother's legacy might entail.

But Bridget seemed convinced.

Refusing to give in to Valerio's temptation.

"Come with me," she said. "Please. Come this way. It's the right thing to do."

"The tomb..." Jules could barely speak, the calculations coming at him so fast.

"He's wrong," Bridget said, calm but firm. "You don't belong with Valerio. Or his delusions."

"Decision time." Valerio tapped his wrist where a watch should have been. "Now or never."

CHAPTER
SIXTY-EIGHT

"I'm going with her." Jules snatched the tablet from Horse and turned his back. "You wanna come?"

"Me?" Horse said.

"Him?" Bridget said.

Jules stood between Valerio and Horse. "His leg's broken. He's got no place with Valerio."

"Not true," Valerio said. "I look after all my employees. Even the lame, err, horses. Heh-heh."

"He'll get rid of you," Jules warned. "We'll help you get out, find you medical treatment."

"And get me put in jail," Horse said. "No thanks. I had faith in the boss for a long, long time. Can't lose it now. I'm following the money."

"And the power," Valerio said.

"Then I'm sorry." Jules turned his back again. "Another time, eh?"

Bridget led the way. As more sections of rock fell all around, smashing pieces too old to imagine, they fled, jumping the encroaching flames, dodging boulders.

To the left side of the complex, daylight cracked through. The jagged gap widened, then brightness from the outside world poured in. A huge rending of earth echoed across the cavern, and the biggest section of roof gave way.

Wide as a football field, twisting inward, the back part remained attached to the hillside's outer layer as if on a rusty hinge. It was huge, wide enough to annihilate a quarter of the floor space. The ruptured slab of land and roof slammed into the repository, louder than any explosive.

Plumes of dust and shrapnel followed them, and Bridget ditched the gun, its weight plainly holding her back. She ran with Jules through the door to the library at the top of the stairs, shielded from the shockwave of debris just in time.

The tunnel was dark, and both had left their headlamps behind at some point, but a wan glow ahead lit enough of the contours to navigate by. Jules kept Bridget a couple of yards in front.

Once they reached the source of the light, she ducked low and crawled under the slab of a doorway. He followed, stunned by the sight that greeted him.

A room so long he could barely see the end—he estimated 600 feet or more—with books and shelves scattered all over, the shelves felled like dominos. A chasm guarded the place, right in front of him, too dark to measure, with a stone slab allowing them to cross. But there was only so much light because of flames licking through from multiple fissures below.

"No," Bridget breathed as she stepped onto the crossing.

"We gotta go back," Jules said.

But Bridget ran over to the fallen tomes. "That last cave-in must have cracked the floor. Help me. We need to seal it. Maybe we can come back, save them."

Jules stuffed the stone tablet in the back of his belt and dashed over to join her, but not to save the books. "We can't. I know it's huge, I know it's tough, but come on. Be realistic."

She rounded on him and thumped his chest. "*You* be realistic.

You're the one who was thinking about going with Valerio." She hit him again.

Jules held her wrists, firm enough to stop her from hurting him, gentle enough so she wouldn't be harmed. Their eyes locked, hers moist, flickering in the firelight, while he leaned closer. "But I didn't go with him. I went with *you*."

Bridget relaxed her arms, tears spilling. Their faces drew closer. She trembled in his hold.

A group of books went up with a dry crackle, the fire spreading fast, cutting off their route.

Jules held her hand, and they both dashed back over the bridge, ducked under the door, and ran down the dust-choked corridor, returning to the chaos of the repository.

The *museum*.

Because that's what Jules would remember it as. A three-dimensional record of civilizations long forgotten, undetected due not to their stupidity or lack of advanced skill but simply through their inability to commit to the written word. Only one of these peoples seemed able to write back then, the ones who constructed the museum, the bangles, the doors and mechanisms forged to generate a chemical reaction and keep all this safe.

Whatever they were, *who*ever they were, their achievements now appeared doomed, too.

The cavern's peak, the ventilation hole, had widened, but the best way out was up the collapsed saucer-shaped expanse of roof. Constantly checking for threats, the sprint involved a leap over the fire, onto a breastfeeding mother made of bronze, then over to a plinth that was home to the approximate rendering of a stegosaurus, the result—most likely—of coming across fossils and imagining its true form.

Jules helped Bridget where needed, but she was fit and fast and seemed adept at scrambling over the mostly fallen ornaments and sculptures, the still-standing buildings. It was as if the whole hill was angling farther, and the collection fell sideways. At the final point, before reaching the rock, soil, and grass that acted as a ramp to the outside, a trail of flaming oil cut them off.

It was no wider than five feet, but the fire licked as high as their heads.

"Gotta jump," Jules said. "Go high. Ain't as hot up top. Which is weird, but there you go."

"No. I can't. There's got to be another way around."

Jules sweated, his arm waving to the increasing destruction. "Suggestions?"

"Fine." Bridget ran at full pelt and jumped through the flames, crying out as she did so.

Jules followed, leaping higher, a moment of searing heat, then he landed.

Bridget was on fire. Her left leg. She slapped it on the floor, but the oily fluid had splashed her as she landed. He smothered it with his own body, robbing it of oxygen, but she was in tears.

She lay there, hands by her knee, the patch of burned cloth smoldering on her calf muscle.

Jules assessed the task ahead—the football field–size escape route.

Thirty-five-degree angle.

Increasing to forty-five, then sixty near the top.

Uphill.

Risk of more damage to the structure.

One-hundred percent certain death if we stay.

"Come on, we gotta move quick." Jules heaved her up, ignoring her cries at first, but as she hopped rather than hobbled, he stopped and faced her.

She was tear streaked and shaking.

He said, "Put your weight on that leg. It'll hurt like hell, but you need to do it. I can't carry you at this angle. And the flames are spreading."

She checked back to where they'd jumped. It was now ten feet wide; no way she'd have made it if they'd waited even a minute longer. Jules guessed she was thinking the same.

"Where the hell is it coming from?" she said as they hobbled up toward fresh air.

"Got no idea. Must be a reserve deeper in the complex. But can we keep that sorta question for later? Need my brain power to help my feet go."

A smile flickered through her pain, and she dug in harder. Jules pulled her as the climb reached the forty-five-degree angle, but then a flash caught his attention to their right.

"Faster!" His heart hammered as he got behind Bridget and grabbed her butt with both hands.

"Hey!"

He pushed hard, virtually launching her into the air as their climb steepened. She shut up as she saw what prompted Jules's desperate move.

A swell of flaming oil surged down the valley formed by the roof meeting the ground level. It must have built up at an obstruction nearby, the dam finally bursting and unleashing the torrent, a tidal wave of flame.

Jules jumped the final phase, hurling Bridget clear, up out of the hole. The fluid missed his feet by inches as he scrambled farther up.

His hands reached the outside, so much cooler than the fire below, so much fresher, far more welcome on the skin. Below, the river subsided, its initial surge waning as it found other avenues to explore.

Bridget sat up, tentatively examining her leg. Whatever that substance was, it stuck like napalm and was still plainly causing her considerable discomfort. But as usual, there was no time for such an examination.

They were half a mile from the village, somehow turned around and approaching from a direction Jules hadn't expected; they were on the opposite side of the hill from the entry cave and would approach the helicopter—whose rotors now circled in its warm-up—from behind the church.

He pointed at a worn path leading from their current perch.

Bridget seemed to get his meaning, but she limped harder than before.

"It hurts so much," she said. "It's getting worse."

Jules sat her down, squatted before her, and lifted her leg to his thigh. Ripped her pants leg. She threw her head back and screamed.

The cloth was fused to her skin, and the burned area was almost black. The red corona around the damage was swollen and angry, as if seeking fuel to feed upon.

"A little better," Bridget said through short, sharp breaths. She squeezed her eyes shut tight. "I have to tell you something."

"On the way."

Jules helped her up, and sure enough, she moved easier.

Was the substance feeding off the cloth? Melding it to her skin as acid might?

Later.

Cross-country was the direct route, but the path made more sense. Bridget found a rhythm that enabled her to travel faster and said again, "I should tell you something."

They were on the same level as the main part of the village now, running, limping, for the channel by the church. The helicopter was in sight, its rotors up to full speed.

Harpal waved excitedly.

"That tablet," Bridget said, "the one that changed to Hebrew. That's why I knew we had to get out. Did you read it?"

"No. Keep going." Jules's lungs labored under the effort, something he hadn't experienced in years. He could only imagine how hard it was for Bridget. A touch of arrogance, sure, but he knew his capabilities. "Nearly there. Wait till we're on board."

Mere yards from the church, ready to sprint the final straight, a mighty rending of earth blared from beneath.

The pair pulled to a halt as a crack detonated and the church itself imploded, a canyon spreading wide before them.

Coming their way.

They reversed direction and found some reserve of strength,

something to keep them going. Back up the path. To the high ground.

Then the opposite happened: a significant mass below must have shifted, a pressure change, and the land rose before them, jutting high and sheer. The bedrock, cold and black, blocked their escape from the earth imploding behind.

CHAPTER
SIXTY-NINE

With the cathedral doomed to collapse, Valerio allowed Horse to accompany him back to the tomb's entrance, the big man's weight nowhere near as hard to support as he expected. His body had undergone a total reboot, regenerated into peak condition. Thankfully, his brain was not dulled by the transformation.

It had taken him a while to interpret the markings he found here, but when he did, it really was ridiculously simple.

Beside the fire pit, the sheer wall before them matched the door that required the infinity key made up of the two bangles, yet there was no keyhole here.

The fire was the key.

Now pretty much useless, Horse watched on, a faithful acolyte awaiting his master's gifts. And why not reward him? He'd stuck by Valerio even when he had the chance to escape, could have taken Valerio's place with ease at any point today. But no, he kept to the script, honored his contract.

Valerio respected that.

After the roof opened and crushed what looked, from their position, to be half the cavern, they found a portion of semi-destroyed statue—an arm of hollow iron—that Horse leaned on as a crutch along with Valerio's shoulder, and they made it back here. On the way, Valerio promised he meant to tempt Jules as an *addition* to Horse, not a replacement.

"The fire," Valerio said, stroking the wall, feeling the marks under his fingertips. "The fire sets him free."

"Boss?" Horse said. "You want to burn it open?"

"No." Valerio strode over to the fire pit.

Even as it leaked out, as the structure tipped more and more to the side, the pool never seemed to empty. Either it was fed by a huge source such as an underground reservoir, or the builders designed it to circulate via a system of arteries.

The warmth grew into heat as he approached. He stood right at the edge, the flames licking high over him. The clunk of Horse's crutch announced his movement.

"Boss, are you okay?"

"I suspect the original designers provided a means to apply the fire. I torch or bowl. But that seems to be long gone. Decayed or lost today. But we don't have time to work out something more suitable. I am about to become a god."

Valerio reached and, keeping his face clear, dipped his hand into the flaming pool.

Horse's mouth fell open, eyes wide in shock. "Boss!"

The burn was excruciating. All the way up Valerio's forearm, the fire gripped him in agony. He remained calm, though, as he withdrew, cupping a measure of the oily substance in his hand. Tears streamed. He'd never known such pain, even at the lowest, most vile point of his illness.

Horse looked on aghast. "Boss, your arm!"

More thunderous collapsing signaled their time was almost up, so Valerio wasted no more savoring the moment and threw the liquid at the wall.

Flame spread to the etchings as if it were alive, as if tiny insects dragged it piece by piece, infiltrating every nook, every etched word, until the whole wall spoke to him. Only a soccer ball–size blank circle remained free of fire.

Valerio bit his tongue. Hard enough to draw blood, and spat it at the stone circle.

Horse said, "Eww."

"Don't worry, my friend," Valerio said. "Blood and holy fire. That's what it takes." He could barely lift his scorched arm; his nerves fried like it was still burning. "It'll all be worth it."

And the slab of wall parted, rumbling in a mechanism that had not operated in at least two thousand years.

Did even Saint Thomas get this far?

Had Valerio outdone an apostle of Christ?

He suspected… yes. Of course he had.

Inside the tomb, a glowing gutter illuminated the small, simple space with art on all four walls and a central feature: an ornate silver sculpture raised on a podium, a man in repose, resplendent in robes, a beard on his sleeping face, and—clutched to his chest in his slumber—he held a sword. Its grip was longer than a medieval longsword, close to a samurai design, but its cross guard showed in profile, both sides tapering to points, while the blade was two straight edges, four feet in length, with a tiny curve toward the end.

Valerio wandered inside, marveling at the reward of a decade's work. "It's mine." He ran both hands over the reposed figure, his burned palms cooling to touch it, leaving a smear as he sought out the opening he was certain would be here. "This is a sarcophagus. Bound to the interred priest, molded around his form. Only to be opened by someone worthy."

As the whole world shook, raining stones and boulders and now mud outside the door, Horse grimaced and hopped into the tomb, his faith plainly rattled.

But Valerio did not falter. He found the practically invisible join, the tiniest flaw on the surface. "Thomas wasn't the first priest at all. *This* is the first priest. And I'm gonna meet him at last!"

He dug in his fingers and opened the sarcophagus.

CHAPTER
SEVENTY

With Charlie strapped in, her bullet wound sealed with glue from the helicopter's field medic kit, and Toby and Dan satisfied the village was empty, all Harpal needed was to lift off. They'd all seen Jules and Bridget racing toward them, and the engines revved up to full speed. Then the earth gobbled up every bit of land surrounding the church, and their path was cut off.

That was okay, though. The pair would run around the edge, and they could rendezvous in the other direction.

Unfortunately, they couldn't wait.

The ground under the town square had buckled, meaning this was next, so Harpal opened up the bird, and they were rapidly airborne. An intercept for Jules and Bridget was preferable to making them run farther anyway, especially since Bridget looked hurt, favoring her right leg.

Airborne, with the side door open, Harpal banked to get a better angle, the rotor wash whipping up even more dirt and earth, so he climbed higher to figure out where they went.

"It's getting wider," Toby pointed out.

"I see it." Harpal rose, pulling away from the creeping destruction. Sure enough, the fissure that consumed the church was spreading. "There! Got 'em."

But it wasn't what he expected.

Before the pair, the growing hole blazed with that weird fire a long way below, the sides climbing into the hillside, while a cliff face appeared to have burst from the ground to cut off their planned avenue.

"We can't land there," Harpal said. "Dan, feed out the line."

Without hesitating, Dan unbuckled his belt and stepped over Charlie, checking her as he moved. She was conscious, aware of movement, it seemed, but fading.

Dan unhooked the winch and fed out the line. "Take us down!"

As the helicopter hovered for way too long, Jules detected the warmth from below, the earth giving way more with each passing minute. Up high, the hill's conical peak was wider, and no longer just toppling inside but ejecting rubble down the sides, showering Jules and Bridget with bits that seemed to grow larger every time a fresh crack gouged to life. They trooped onward, backs to the risen rock, trying to climb higher.

Then another exponential stretch of ground disappeared, plunging into the halls below, now more flame than art, leaving Jules and Bridget with less than two yards of walkway.

The helicopter's nose dipped and swung toward them, harness dangling, with Dan at the controls. His hand jabbed at the air, and the transport swayed sideways before coming closer.

Bridget laughed.

"What's funny?" Jules yelled over the rotors.

She held Jules's arms, firming her position. "Two things, actually. First, I know we're going to make it up onto the chopper. Second..."

"One sec." Jules reached, but the harness flew past. Way too fast. He beckoned and Dan whirled his hand, shouting something, and the helicopter wobbled, glided backward, the straps bypassing them again. "It's the updraft. They can't keep it steady."

"You wanna hear the other precious, hilarious thing?"

"Save it."

"Why?"

"I'm concentrating."

A helicopter that can't keep steady.

A harness flapping by at variable speed.

It's 6.4 feet ahead.

Altitude is level with me.

Jules threw himself out over the pit. Nice and high. Arms spread wide. Allowing for as many eventualities as possible: the speed, the downward force, the updraft's effects on the cable and harness...

And grabbed the line.

Both palms sliced open as he slipped down it, his sideways momentum forcing him out wider than he'd hoped.

He held on, though, and took advantage of the error. Now, physics in his favor, using his legs like a pendulum, he returned toward Bridget faster than he departed. He let go with his left and extended both arms.

Bridget, still grinning, her red hair billowing behind, pushed off with her unburned leg, fully stretched over the pit of raging fire. Jules's hand met hers and—

The blood was too slick. She fell from his grasp. Dropped straight down...

Where she held on to Jules's legs, the sudden shift jarring his shoulder, threatening to tear his skin from his palm. He wrapped his legs around her, joining his ankles. Which made her heavier. With his free hand, Jules reached for the harness itself. His knee joints twisted to wedge Bridget in place, as if caught in a martial arts locking move.

The helicopter altered course, causing him to slip farther, holding on with only his fingertips. He strained, the leather strap and buckle right there.

Just within reach.

He slapped it against his bare arm above the Aradia bangle, set the clip to hold him in place, and let go.

They were secure.

The chopper banked, the winch wound upward, and the flaming hole sped by until Dan wrapped his arm under Jules.

Jules clung on to Bridget and she to him, her teeth gritted with the sheer effort.

Both were hauled up into the helicopter's body, where they lay, breathing hard for several seconds.

Jules was pretty sure his shoulder had dislocated, but he managed to sit up. "So what's the big thing you wanna tell me?"

Bridget propped herself upright, inhaling too deeply to speak, exhaling too fast. She leaned into Jules, Dan supporting her. Toby twisted in the front seat.

"Well, first," she said, finally able to talk, "I told ya we'd make it." She swallowed, gulped deep, hoarse breaths, watching the land. "Second... I read that tablet. The words changed from instructions to a warning. I don't know how, but Valerio was right. Saint Thomas, or someone, converted it to Hebrew once it was used. Valerio must be more than rusty. I mean, sure, it told us that Thomas saw the power, all the wonders, the artifacts that might be used as weapons, and the actual weapon inside the priest's tomb... and he sensed the presence of God within. But Valerio must have missed the meaning of 'scattered' in the writing. There's no direct translation, but as I understood it, Thomas summoned his new disciples and announced that these things were never meant to be gathered in one place. It was always supposed to be temporary. So he *scattered* them all. Not throughout the repository, but outside. Away."

"All of them?" Jules said. "You're sure?"

"Yes." Holding Charlie's hand, squeezing it with reassurance, Bridget allowed a tear to fall. "After all his killing and destroying all those books and artwork... there's nothing there for Valerio to find!"

CHAPTER
SEVENTY-ONE

It wasn't the best feeling in the world. In fact, it pretty much sucked worse than anything Valerio had ever experienced. And he'd once suffered food poisoning in Yemen.

"Why is it empty, boss?"

It was a question that would have caused Valerio to shoot his faithful bodyguard in the head if he'd been in possession of a gun. Luckily for Horse, Valerio was unarmed, but Horse's increasing concern and insolence were becoming somewhat grating. And Valerio's skin seared worse than before.

An empty box.

"A trick," Valerio said. "A final test."

That shut Horse up even though it was a spur-of-the-moment lie made up to deflect what might be a significant failing on Valerio's part.

Admitting failure was weakness.

The rising din from outside had been driving him crazy, so he closed the doors by placing both hands on their surfaces. He could control them with precision, with growing ease, despite the burns. Then he tried to concentrate on the paintings, realizing quickly that the colors were not painted at all.

They were jewels.

Unlike the frescos on the way in, which must have been repainted hundreds if not thousands of times, these were inlaid stones, chipped apart and set into the walls to create images. Understandably, they were simpler than the others, but since they told a simple story, that's all that was needed.

"A volcano erupted," Valerio said.

Horse examined it. "Could be a meteor."

"Whatever. Catastrophe. Death. Look."

The deaths were depicted after the eruption, creatures of all kinds, the apelike half humans resembling hominids along with taller, more graceful types. But stuck in the ground next to this, a sword stood. A naked man reached for it.

"A sword, risen out of death," Valerio said, tracing to more pictures. "The rise of great cities before the sword cuts them down."

Destruction, fighting.

Floods, fire.

A mountain drawn around the sword, with winged humanoid figures hovering like guards.

"Angels," Horse said.

"Or their precursor. The sword hidden here."

"Except it's not here."

A deafening boom thundered through the tomb, shaking the room like a magnitude-seven quake. Valerio leaned on the empty sarcophagus, which reflected fire from its gutters, dancing over its surface. He laughed. Rising in pitch until his hyena cackle echoed back at him.

"What the hell are you doing?" Horse demanded. "We need to get outa here. You said there was a back door, now—"

The next shudder threw them both aside. Horse stumbled, landing on his broken leg, and shrieked before tumbling to the ground. The whole room tipped on its side. The coffin spilled over. Valerio dodged it just in time, the thrill sparking him to life.

The doors split, and the far wall cracked open.

Horse dragged himself over to Valerio, who simply could not stop laughing.

"You killed me," Horse said.

"Yeah, that's true," Valerio replied, clutching his employee as the roar of rending stone grew and grew and the ceiling and floor folded in on themselves. "But don't you feel just *so* alive?"

And then the whole room crushed in on itself, and everything turned instantly black.

CHAPTER
SEVENTY-TWO

With everyone strapped in place and his dislocated shoulder reset with brutal efficiency by Dan, Jules watched from the sky as the villagers gathered on the ridge overlooking their former homes. The path had taken them down a ways, then wound up to a granite outcrop disconnected from the hillside in which Saint Thomas had been interred. They kneeled in prayer, all but motionless as the final remnants of the hill's cone tumbled in on itself, taking the entire town with it.

The implosion followed a long pause in which nothing new happened. No mines went off, no new sinkholes. All was quiet. Then wider holes formed and swiftly expanded, first across one side of the hill, which disintegrated, collapsing like the controlled explosion of an office building. It smothered the fires, replaced by acres of dust clouds and ash.

Although it couldn't possibly all settle before they fled, through the plumes and mist, the vague shape of the original structure faded into view: jagged and misshapen but familiar the world over, four broken sides of a pyramid jutted from among the wreckage, standing for just a few seconds, then like the rest of the sprawling edifice, it was gone.

"They lost everything," Jules said.

Bridget wiped away a tear. "And the library, too. All that knowledge, history from *pre*history. We'll never find anything to match that again. I..." Her voice cracked as she forced herself not to cry openly.

"You can't know that," Toby said. "If there was one repository, there may be more. And let's not forget... Saint Thomas scattered many of these people's art and culture. Their achievements."

"The weapons," Harpal added.

Toby nodded, but seemed to be ignoring the implications. "We'll find it, Bridget. If it's out there, we'll find it."

Jules swallowed back his own sadness at the events of the day. "Those men Valerio brought with him."

"They knew the risks," Dan said. "All mercs do."

"That's not the point." Jules's eyes were hot, his vision blurred. "It was all pointless. He executed them so they'd keep his secret. But there was no secret to keep. We could've just... gone home. Let him do this."

"Result'd be the same," Bridget said. "He'd have killed them, anyway. He'd have had all the time in the world to examine the temple, the books, the frescos. Then he'd have demolished the place so no one else could find it and carried on looking for that priest's weapon. We'd be none the wiser. You wouldn't have your bangle."

Jules looked down at the Aradia bangle in his lap, and his mouth moistened. Having reclaimed what was his, he could now give up the world of constant training, travel, fighting, theft. The easy life beckoned. His cut from Alfonse Luca's reward would help.

Pizza.

Beer.

A couple of weeks off while he considered what to do with his life. Maybe he'd learn to cook. Be a chef.

Even now? After everything he'd seen this week?

"He valued me more than the militia because I believed in

him," Jules said. "I entertained him. He saw me as a kind of equal."

"And because he needed you," Toby said.

"Even after he healed and changed his genetics?" Jules continued to observe the wrecked scene, though there was no time to properly scout for any who didn't make it out, who might have survived. He accepted that Charlie needed medical assistance ASAP. "He kept me on. He said he wanted me dead, but I don't think he believed it. He knew how it'd turn out."

"These people," Bridget said. "Can we help them? Rebuild, I mean?"

"Let's go," Dan said. "I'll alert the Pakistanis as soon as we're in range."

Once Harpal leveled the helicopter in a straight line, Toby unbuckled from the front seat and traded places with Dan. He sat beside Bridget, placing himself between her and Jules. "Do you think they'll want to remain here? After they lost the relics?"

"It's sacred land," Bridget said. "Destroyed or not."

"There'll be an investigation." Toby's voice sounded strained, low in tone. "But we will help them rebuild wherever they want. We'll force Colin Waterston to commit to it if he wants our silence over this, as I'm sure the British will demand."

"What if he doesn't play?" Jules asked.

"Well, since Charlie set up a program long ago that records all our phone activity, we have Mr. Waterston on tape requesting our help. Everything we did today was at the behest of Her Majesty's Government."

Jules finally detected a smile creeping into the world. "Like special agents. Deputized."

"I'm just sorry we couldn't preserve that library." Toby shook his head. "Such a waste."

Silence in the chopper. Jules leaned over to check on Charlie, who blinked and swallowed to prove she was conscious and aware.

"Where we headed?" Jules asked.

"Pakistan," Dan replied.

Oh.

"Listen, guys," Jules said. "I might have some sorting out to do when we land. There was a... misunderstanding a few years ago."

"Something to do with a stolen bust of Marco Polo?" Toby said.

"Maybe."

Toby smiled. "Don't worry. I'm sure we can come to an understanding with our hosts."

"Then I guess now's as good a time as ever to hand this over." Jules untucked his shirt and reached behind his back. "In the library, I figured this was more important than the stone tablet."

When he produced his hand, he handed Bridget a book. Rough and brittle, but intact.

"Ditched the stone," he said. "Saved a book instead. Could only manage one, though."

Bridget accepted it in both hands and laughed. "Oh wow... *thank you!*"

"Hey, Bridge," Dan said, passing his pack to her. "Make it two."

She hurriedly gave the first book to Toby, who secured it on his lap. Digging into Dan's bag, the tome she pulled out appeared bigger, and she struggled to peel the Gore-Tex outer from around it. This looked softer, made from a whole other material, perhaps from a rubber tree.

"Two." Bridget allowed the tears this time. "Thank you. Both of you."

"Ready for the main event?" Harpal asked. "Check mine. Stashed by your feet."

Bridget handed Dan's book to Toby. She yanked the backpack out from beneath her and opened it. "Two more!" She carefully but hastily took them out, one large, one small, very different covers.

"I could only fit two in," Harpal said. "Better than nothing, though, right?"

Bridget clasped the books to her chest, and her eyes sparkled as she thanked them again and again. Four books saved when she thought there were none, and her friends had all taken a second out of running for their lives to think of her.

Including Jules.

Amid all the death and loss, it might not have been magic Jules was seeing, but there was certainly plenty of goodness left in the world.

PART EIGHT

For every minute, the future is becoming the past.

—Thor Heyerdahl

You may be always victorious if you will never enter into any contest where the issue does not wholly depend upon yourself.

—Epictetus

CHAPTER
SEVENTY-THREE

BRITTANY - FRANCE

Alfonse Luca was a happy man. So happy that he flew his subcontractors back to France first class, paid for a private medic to supplement Charlie's repatriation to the UK, and retrieve the Lear Jet from Pakistan on Toby Smith's behalf. In fact, Alfonse could not wait to get his hands on the Mary bangle, so he traveled a day early to make himself comfortable in Chateau Caché.

Their elderly housekeeper was seemingly disgruntled at having to accommodate him. When he told her that he planned on donating the institute's latest artifact to the Vatican, though, she transformed from miserly harridan to sweet old aunt, one who hadn't seen her errant nephew in far too long, and she proceeded to spoil Alfonse with her best coffee throughout the day and with fine cooking and sugary treats. Then, once evening fell, she supplied as much alcohol as Alfonse desired.

All in all, a *splendida* reception.

She did not know of her employers' exploits, of course, or if she did, she chose to ignore them. Alfonse didn't really know that much himself, and it was not until the gang gathered in the drawing room at ten a.m., surrounded by coffee and croissants, that he got the full story.

"Four days," Toby said. "Four days of interrogations and accusations."

All appeared tired. Even the young African American fitness freak looked drained, wearing sunglasses and a baseball cap indoors. In addition to multiple cuts and contusions on his face, neck, hands, and one forearm, his other arm was strapped up completely, a shoulder injury apparently. Bridget displayed a bandage on the leg that suffered a burn, while Dan and Harpal boasted minor lacerations and bruises. Everyone's eyes were dark, with bags forming, and each of them looked ready to sleep for a week or more.

They were only entertaining him due to the electronic transfer of funds he had already processed, preferring not to schlep a bag of cash through French customs. It gave them little choice but to receive and debrief him.

"Charlie is recovering at home," Toby went on, "and this... is yours."

Although the British wanted the two bangles for themselves, Alfonse had negotiated on LORI's behalf with the Pakistani authorities, insisting they treat the objects as a red line with MI5, largely due to the Christian dynamic of Alfonse's interest.

Did they really wish to risk a feud with the Vatican? And in a Muslim-majority country—a significant vocal minority of whom fell into the "extremist" category—did they want to retain such blasphemous items while mobs who demanded the destruction of all non-Islamic symbols gathered and protested?

They saw sense.

In addition to his own arrangements, the British government themselves had smoothed things over with the Pakistani and Indian authorities, downplaying incidents such as crossing the border without permission—twice—as accidental incursions, and the British figured such a favor was worth losing a couple of rocks over. Similarly, Colin Waterston agreed to play nice with the

Mongolians, who accepted a handsome sum in exchange for what was listed in their inventory as a minor trinket of limited interest. The cash would go into a fund for the bereaved loved ones of Valerio's victims.

Alfonse wished he cared more about the people who died on this mission, but any empathy he once held commenced rotting with the first life he snuffed out in exchange for profit and deteriorated over the many years after. Now, having felt God's touch, understanding that his sins angered Him, today was the initial step toward reclaiming his soul.

Maybe one day he would weep for strangers.

Toby presented the kind of silver case that Alfonse still associated with firearms and opened the clasps. The red-flecked rock jewelry lay amid the foam-lined inner, perfectly preserved.

Alfonse lifted it in both hands. "Mary, the virgin mother of Our Lord Jesus Christ..." Warmth spread throughout his body, starting at his fingers and spidering to every limb. As with his confession, he accepted the touch of God. "She wore this. I am holding pure holiness in my hands."

"Yeah, you got it." Jules Sibeko removed his sunglasses and waved his own wrist on which he carried a nearly identical item. "I don't mean to be rude, but are we finished?"

The Aradia bangle. Just there. Not in a safe, not hidden. A pagan artifact infused with power that could only be utilized in conjunction with the Mary bangle. A yin and yang situation if he ever saw one. And it was better that the pair remain separated by continents as well as Vatican security.

Alfonse replaced the bangle and closed the lid. "Thank you. All of you. And I will let you get some rest. It is just that... there are many questions. The books you brought with you, for example."

Of them all, Bridget acted the least frazzled, and at mention of the books recovered from the site, she sat up straighter on the leather couch. "One we've preliminarily dated to eighteen hundred years old, so a short while after Thomas died. But it's made of a thick paper like we have today. Not quite the same as our paper, but the process looks similar under a microscope. It's treated with something that preserved it. We don't know what yet. But its presence there means pilgrims still visited, revered it as a holy site. Probably the ancestors of the villagers who... who watched their home get destroyed." She gave Toby a brief smile. "The secret wasn't sealed with Thomas. Others knew. And that book, it talks about the journeys, the places the author had been. I read it cover to cover on the flight over. We have plenty to be looking into, a ton of potential sites where other objects might be hidden."

"Interesting. And the others?"

"The second book is around three thousand years old. Again, it's been treated with some sort of resin. Maybe the same as the other. It's as if, when they got delivered, the people who ran the library, or whoever took it over, they were determined to preserve the writings. And that's remarkable. And just fabulous for us." She was almost glowing with the news, her Alabama twang clear even to Alfonse's European ears, excited to announce it to him. "But the third is closer to *five thousand* years old. Which is just incredible."

"How so?" Alfonse asked.

"It's right on the cusp of the birth of the written word," Toby replied. "And this is amazing because the oldest text humanity has ever recovered is Sumerian, and that's in the form of clay tablets, carved and restored. This book, sealed at the moment, is not Sumerian."

"It's a complex language," Bridget said. "Scratched-out syllables, like a Chinese dialect, but nothing we've seen before, nothing on record. There's no key either, so it'll take some time to decode. If we ever can. I just don't know. We only decoded Egyptian hieroglyphs because of the Rosetta stone, which gave archeologists and linguists the clues they needed."

"And the fourth book?"

The gang all exchanged glances, as if unsure whether to share.

"Inconclusive," Toby said. "Carbon fourteen testing is only so reliable. The older the test subject, the less exact it becomes. Something that's five thousand years old is fairly simple. Ten thousand, it's accurate to within a few decades. When you get to fifty to one hundred thousand years, the margin of error is centuries, and so on, exponentially rising to millennia and even millions of years as we go farther back. Which isn't a problem when we're talking dinosaurs and early mammals—"

"Your best guess?" Alfonse said.

Bridget clasped her hands and stared at them. "Initial indications, when we take the paperlike substance and scrape off the preservation resin... is forty-five thousand years."

Alfonse knew little about decay and erosion, and even less about the science of carbon dating, just that it was meant to be the best indicator of age widely used in conventional science.

"A radon or argon test will confirm," Toby said.

Alfonse nodded, assuming he was referring to a test along the same lines as the carbon 14 examinations.

"If true," Bridget said, brightening again, "it will be the single most important artifact in the study of human development. Actual *writing* from a time when we thought humans were just learning to use paint and tools."

Alfonse suddenly wanted to hold it, to shake its secrets loose, but they had all been secured in the airtight vault in the chateau's basement, where they would remain until Charlie recovered and was fit to return.

"Who knows about it?" Alfonse asked.

"No one," Toby said. "We took the sample ourselves. The Pakistanis allowed access to their national museum's lab for a couple of days while they negotiated with Colin and his mob. We registered it as the bangle, which already knew was at least thirty, possibly fifty thousand years old. So it's a secret. And the circle is this room. And Charlie. Probably Phil too by now."

Alfonse stood and paced to the window, gazing out over the

grounds. "You have the books and you have Harpal's video that he shot."

"It's shaky, but Charlie will tidy it up."

"This is the find of a lifetime, my friends. Who were these people?"

"Well," Toby started. At Jules's pointed cough, he said, "I'll be brief. We only have hypotheses at the moment. More study will be needed to map out an actual theory, but... we used to believe all humans developed at the same pace, tribes branching off once they reached a certain level of intelligence. The Toba catastrophe is one factor. Before then, it was all about brute strength, but after, you needed brains to survive. The cleverest humans lived to pass on their genes, which is why we see such a big spike in art and ritual a few hundred years later."

"That does not explain so many things in your First Priest's Tomb," Alfonse said.

"Ah, yes. Well." Toby ignored the fake snores from Dan, Harpal, and Jules. "We think it is possible humans across the globe developed at different rates. In some areas, the strongest and most virile passed on their genes, while in others, it was those whose brains served them well. It could have been that these people avoided the fossil record by living higher lives, burning the dead instead of leaving them in the mud. All guesswork, of course, but we hope there are more clues. After the ice melted, as the tribes were brought together, the single line of what we might think of as 'higher humans' must have merged with the more primitive ones. Eventually, they scattered far and wide, and their history descended into stories and legend."

"Guesses?" Alfonse said.

"Logical," Jules answered from the couch, sunglasses still covering half his face. "But yeah, I'm sure Toby'll get into the history first chance he gets."

In his former life, one of the factors that had stood Alfonse above his competitors was his ability to spot an opportunity. A lucky meeting with a man who worked the docks at an as yet uncompromised checkpoint might mean mobilizing a team to follow him home, to learn all about the man's family. A bribe would be administered too, a way of casting doubt on his story of threats and coercion if he was caught and attempted to divert blame.

Learning of a politician's taste for domineering prostitutes was an opportunity, too.

Discovering that a senior policeman's sexuality was not as clear-cut as his wife believed: *opportunity*.

The CEO of a pharmaceutical company addicted to her own product: *opportunity*.

And a firsthand journal written in the near-immediate aftermath of biblical events, detailing locations that could be the apostles' missions and paths, so far only guessed at by historians... *that* was perhaps the greatest opportunity of Alfonse's life. An opportunity to unite the world in knowledge.

Alfonse turned to find Dan and Harpal literally asleep, with Jules slouched, and only Bridget and Toby eyeing him.

He said, "I have a proposal."

CHAPTER
SEVENTY-FOUR

After Alfonse departed, Jules didn't blame Dan and Harpal for fleeing to their rooms. Bridget and Toby would soon follow, but Jules didn't want to hang around longer than he had to. A train for Paris departed in an hour, and he'd be on a flight to the States by nightfall. He was on his feet as soon as the housekeeper interrupted them.

Margarete cleared the breakfast things away and offered more coffee, which everyone politely declined. Then she inquired as to when Alfonse might return.

"Probably quite soon," Toby said, waiting for her to leave. When she was gone, he and Bridget stood, too. "Jules, you're more than welcome to stay longer. You can defer your flight."

"Thanks." Jules shook his wrist. The bangle felt like a thick watch strap. Not irritating, just... *there*. "But I got what I came for."

"It's dangerous," Bridget said. "Can you protect it from other people like Valerio?"

Jules forced a polite smile. They were delaying him. "It's mine. It belongs with me."

Bridget stepped ahead of Toby and threw a glance over her shoulder. Toby returned a rueful smile, rocked on his heels, and walked out of the room, leaving them with the words, "It's an open invitation. Listen to Bridget."

Once Toby was gone, Bridget said, "It'd be nice to give you a proper send-off. I mean, I know you don't want to be a part of what we do, but... maybe a couple of days? France doesn't just do good wine. The beer isn't too shabby either."

Jules found himself liking the idea. "They got pizza too?"

"Sure."

"Backgammon Pizza? Cause that's kinda my plan."

"Plans can change, Jules."

"I know they can. But not this one. Get my mom's property back, order my birthday pizza, and drink my first beer. I'm gonna do that. If I don't... what've the last nine years been about?"

"Answers." Bridget held both his hands in hers, the movement jarring his shoulder and shifting the bangle so it rested on the top of her hand. "You have your answers. What we saw asked more questions. If you don't stay, if you keep on running away, when will it end? When will you be satisfied?"

Jules didn't need a psychology degree to self-examine that one. *Obsession*, they called it. And he was aware of that. Had always been aware. But it was a barrier he couldn't surmount. One he needed to break down with the achievement that had repeatedly eluded him. Even now, after learning more than he ever expected, he could not let go of this notion.

"I'll get in touch when I'm settled," Jules said. "I'll be back to visit... one day. Okay?"

Bridget let her head drop. She sniffed. "When you figure out where you belong and when you get things straight with yourself, you do that. You come back."

"I will."

They stood there for a long moment. He wasn't sure whether it was the right time to show that he regretted leaving, or if he wished he understood himself well enough to be sure of his feelings for her. But since he was on his way out of her life, it was probably impolite to kiss her.

So he was relieved when she rose to her tiptoes and initiated the kiss. Not a big romantic gesture, but a firm, unmistakably genuine one. Her lips warm on his. Mouths closed. The moment morphed into a hug, and for the eight seconds they stood locked in each other's arms, Jules fiercely debated the wisdom of leaving.

These people had taken him in, believed in him even when he betrayed them or endangered their mission. They helped him and saved his life, and he theirs.

But the embrace ended before he could reach a conclusion, and Bridget simply wiped her eyes, turned her back, and walked away.

Even after she left the study, Bridget hoped she'd changed his mind. She didn't go in for the sloppy romantic nonsense portrayed in many films, where the guy rushed back to sweep the girl into his arms and kiss her while the music rose and the vision faded out. She wasn't exactly sure she wanted that from Jules.

One thing she definitely wanted was friendship.

She had few true friends. Some university alumni she met with occasionally for coffee or cocktails, a handful she stayed in touch with back home in Alabama. But, of course, the only people she truly trusted were present in this house... plus one who was in a whole heap of trouble with her husband in Britain.

With Alfonse sponsoring them via a generous retainer and access to his entire shipping network, all they needed to do was furnish him with any artifacts of Christian interest that were discovered as a result of deciphering the ancient texts. They now had access to cargo planes, diplomatic back channels, and sea-salvage operations, among many other advantages. Although Toby said they'd "think about it," the answer was not in doubt. A resurgent phase in the Lost Origins Recovery Institute dawned, and that alone should have convinced a new recruit to join them.

Yet, as soon as Jules said he'd be back one day, that he'd stay in touch, Bridget's head dropped, a conversation returning to her from what seemed months ago, years even, but was barely over a week. A conversation over—fittingly—pizza.

Yeah, people say a lotta stuff they don't mean.

Anything you need.

Let's stay in touch.

I'll be back.

Until that moment, she really thought there was a chance he'd stay. But he didn't. He just trotted out the platitudes and left.

Bridget lay on her bed, listening to the noises in the old house.

Her leg stung. The doctors in Pakistan and then Germany on the way home had treated the wound, and she had enough painkillers to keep Hollywood going for a year. When her parents heard, they dispatched a surgeon, who would arrive the next day and recommend a procedure. For once, Bridget did not try to hold her distance from their wealth.

She popped another pill and waited for it to take effect.

She would have to deflect their questions about what happened, convince them she did not break their agreement that allowed her to keep LORI going. Even with Alfonse's backing, she still had to rely on them for this base, for the vehicles they used, the modest allowance from her trust fund. If she broke laws that threatened her folks' reputation, or they heard she'd placed herself in mortal danger, they would cut her off and she would be obligated to pursue a more businesslike college degree. Then, she expected, she'd be stuck in the family business instead of pursuing her true calling.

For now, she was willing and able to deceive them, and diplomatic gymnastics would keep her activity from sullying the business.

The door to Jules's room three down from hers opened and closed once, then silence fell as he gathered his things. Outside, a car pulled up, followed by his soft footsteps padding by her door, and Bridget could not resist heading to the window to watch him leave.

To perhaps watch him turn around and see her and change his mind.

No, she wouldn't do that. She wasn't a silly little girl, pining for the boy to notice her. If that boy wanted nothing to do with her, if he chose to run away and reject her from his life, so be it.

She couldn't sleep, though. Not now. There wasn't enough coffee in the world to keep the others up, and it wasn't the caffeine driving Bridget. It was the unfairness of Jules's departure.

He had his answers. He had his closure. But she never found the answer to her own *what if*.

Although she had never been a big drinker, her body clock didn't care that it was before noon, so a stiff brandy wouldn't go amiss.

She threw open her door and strode back along the corridor, the soft carpet absorbing what would be her stomping footfalls in a different home. But she grew annoyed at another thing Jules had done: he'd left his door ajar.

Scruffy as well as selfish.

Good riddance.

She reached for the handle to pull it shut.

But she paused, spotting an object on his bed.

She hadn't expected the room to be laundered and perfect, but she certainly didn't think he'd forget anything. This was a clean break for him, after all.

So Bridget stepped inside and over to the bed. A sheet of paper lay over the item, and the words were written in capital letters:

IT'S ONLY ON LOAN.

Bridget flicked the note aside and snatched up the Aradia bangle.

She dashed out of the room and sprinted along the corridor, down the stairs two at a time, and almost knocked Margarete over with a result of much cursing in French. She whipped open the front door and burst out into the sunlight.

The taxi was already turning at the bottom of the road.

But Bridget just ran in a circle, not caring whether she looked like an idiot to anyone watching. She didn't even know why she was so happy. The painkiller kicking in, the euphoria of learning that not all platitudes were lies, or simply the lack of sleep sending her mad.

All she knew was this wasn't an end.

It was a beginning.

EPILOGUE

GUJARAT - INDIA

Prihya Sibal had been a construction foreman on fifteen projects before this one. She was Indian, originally from Goa, but she'd relocated to Mumbai five years ago. Work was hard to come by, though, so with her fluent English she'd spent years in various call centers with an alter ego known as "Kylie" but, more recently, construction work paid far better. And in the aftermath of tragic accidents such as collapsed bridges and tunnels, she'd made a small fortune.

Female foremen were rare in even the most cosmopolitan districts, so it had probably been her gender that brought her to the attention of first the local councils and later—in light of much female empowerment across the country she loved—the government itself. She was a literal poster girl for three different campaigns to recruit women: in construction, search and rescue, and her true love, archeology.

She worked her way up the ranks of construction sites on her merit, though, and soon went to night school to learn more about ancient history with a view to a full-on archeology degree in England—when opportunity and funds allowed. Yet it was the search and rescue ops of first the Gindo Bridge and then the collapsed Yaleh Tunnel that cemented her reputation and earned her that rare foot in the door. In fact, she only agreed to let her image be used so widely on the condition that someone in the government find her work with a genuine dig.

A week ago, that call finally came.

Prihya arrived in Gujarat, handpicked by some unspoken-of government agency, so even though the almost exclusively male crew obviously wasn't that happy with her, someone had clearly set out the ground rules for addressing her.

Ma'am.

Ms. Sibal.

Oh, she could get used to that.

So yes, she was handpicked by the government. But no one would confirm exactly which other governments were involved. She heard the leader of the NGO funding the operation speaking, and he sounded the same as the colonial masters her grandfather had regaled her about.

She was so excited, and a little suspicious, that she even called up her night school professor, and he was happy to hear from her, recognizing her immediately and asking how her "historical philosophizing" was going—a term he coined to describe Prihya's penchant for questioning the source and manner of every assertion that didn't jibe with the conspiracy theories she was addicted to on YouTube: the Annunaki, holes in the Arctic leading to an underground world, aliens having built the pyramids, and OOPARTs aplenty. The professor claimed to have never heard of the man who led the dig, a false name, most certainly, which added to her paranoia.

The only thing that distracted her from that suspicion was the nature of the work, her simple-sounding task: retrieve what artifacts and writings may remain under the ground of a pyramid-type construction discovered in the foothills of an innocuous mountain range.

A pyramid.

Here, in India.

Okay, there were pyramid-like buildings around the country, dating back to the eleventh century Chola dynasty, but those were mostly temples, functional and practical, while this find obviously predated the famous Egyptian monoliths. It stimulated both her philosophical and scientific sides.

The collapsed structure was a straightforward design, and she'd understood her professor's explanation for pyramids being found on several continents: namely, it was the simplest formation to build using primitive materials and methods. In fact, it would have been odd had they *not* turned up in multiple places.

So she brought forth as many chunks of flat wall as she could, ordering her men away whenever new writing or illustrations were discovered. The NGO must have been incredibly well funded, as each time she flagged a significant find, it was whisked away by helicopter to a place the man in charge promised she would learn about in due course.

But on the tenth day, as the sun was dipping behind the mountains, something put a monkey in the works. They'd found a weak spot, one they'd secured with scaffolding, a point of focus because of the bull's head the size of a motorcycle which they'd managed to extract fully intact—more or less. They drilled deeper, the loose debris allowing for some of the best finds of the whole project.

But the sounds were unmistakable. A rhythmic knock-knock-knocking meant only one thing.

Someone was alive down there.

Prihya ordered all work halted and shut down everything that could cause the slightest vibration, then ran back up the crater to where the NGO project leader had set up a flamboyant tent with a kitchen, bedroom, lounge, and even an office.

He sipped tea outside under a canopy, wearing a beige shirt and beige shorts with too many pockets. His mosquito spray remained within reach at all times, despite the camp being too high for such biting creatures, and he carried an old-fashioned fan with him. He would probably have requested that an assistant waft him with a larger instrument had he been able to get away with it. But, somehow, the British man with the birdlike nose had been placed in charge of this Indian government-sponsored dig.

Expertise was their one-word reason.

Breathlessly, she said, "Excuse the interruption, sir. But we think someone is alive down there. A survivor."

The man placed his cup and saucer to one side, next to his mosquito spray, and pressed his fingertips together, smiling over the top of them. "Excellent. Clear the site of everyone except the most essential personnel. When you've made the survivor safe, bring him to me."

PUERTO VALLARTA, MEXICO

It took Jules several days searching online for a beachfront property within the delivery radius of a Backgammon Pizza, but he finally located a two-room-plus-bathroom shack on the west coast of Mexico. It was technically a vacation rental, part of an all-inclusive resort marketed to upper-income middle-class couples, and although he shared his stretch of beach with dozens of neighbors, each deck was built so it did not encroach upon anyone who might value their privacy. Therefore, couples could hold hands or kiss or simply cuddle up to watch the sunset and listen to the waves lap at the shore while local fishermen hauled their boats up the beach in the middle distance, half-hidden by the haze whipped up by a gentle breeze.

Jules was especially glad of his fluency in the Spanish language today, having ordered online and received a return phone call querying his choice of pepperoni, red onion, and tuna, which he quickly allayed, insisting it was a delicacy in New York. The delivery kid made his way through the five-star pools and apartments, accompanied out to the shack by a security guard who reminded Jules that all dining was included in the resort's price. Jules indicated that, having read the contract before signing, he was aware of the amenities on offer, so he thanked the guard very much and tipped the Backgammon guy handsomely.

Slumped in a beanbag on his deck, Jules flicked the top from a bottle of complimentary cerveza and opened the pizza box lid. He separated a slice and tried not to imagine the portions of fat, salt, and whatever chemicals held it all together.

The triangle's point entered his mouth, and he clamped down, ensuring he included at least one portion of all three main ingredients, and ripped away a mouthful, severing a pepperoni circle as he did so.

He chewed.

As his jaw worked, water filled his mouth, a biological reaction that mixes enzymes into the mushed-up foodstuff and aids digestion once swallowed.

If he swallowed.

The concoction tasted like the swill at the bottom of a toothbrush cup left too long without cleaning, or maybe garbage water dribbling from a bag neglected until overflowing.

It'll probably taste better with beer.

He forced the pizza down, then chugged from the Corona. This fizzed in his mouth and throat, and as he sent this the same way as the pizza, his stomach hissed and inflated. He switched out the beer for a cola drink he once read could dissolve a tooth in two days and found it marginally more refreshing.

Having desired this for so long, Jules finished the slice down to the crust, and tried the beer a few more times.

Corona was, so he heard, one of the finer drinks of its ilk, so he guessed he just wasn't used to it. And still, the pizza didn't quite carry its deliciousness forward from his childhood.

The second slice was marginally less disgusting. By the third, it was bearable.

But still not *nice*.

He had drunk as much beer as filled the bottle's neck but favored the cola drink that was more sugar than water.

That was all he could manage.

He closed the box and wiped his fingers, then poured the beer down the bathroom sink, all the while picturing the items he just consumed rotting away his gut and hardening his arteries as they dissolved and became a part of him. Unable to shake the image, he downed half a pint of Evian, changed into his shorts and a sleeveless T-shirt, and ventured back out onto the deck.

The sun hovered over the horizon, a yellow disc lighting the sky and ocean in orange. He wished not for pizza and beer, not for an ancient bangle genetically bonded to him and his mother, but for something else.

He wasn't sure what that something was, only that he didn't have it. And driving the images, smells, and feelings of his recent past from his mind, Jules set off for a run, hoping to dissuade the junk inside him from instigating heart disease.

At least, not before he had a chance to say "hey" to Bridget and the others again.

Some secrets get buried for a reason…

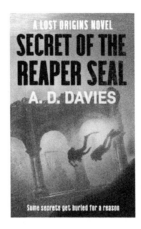

When Toby Smith attempts to repatriate artefacts from the tiny Eastern
European nation of Striovia, he is imprisoned as a spy. What, exactly, are
they trying to hide? The Lost Origins team turn to the one person reckless
enough to help: Jules Sibeko.

With Jules on board, they embark on a furious international adventure,
follow ancient stories from the permafrost of Eurasia to the cradle of
North American civilization and beyond ... where they must unravel the
secrets held by generations of Sumerians before Toby's captors do.

Scan the QR code or search your online retailer

AFTERWORD

Thank you for reading to the end of this eBook. Jules and the Lost Origins team will return for a new adventure in *Secret of the Reaper Seal* .

If you would like to leave a review, please go to Amazon, GoodReads, BookBub, or wherever you like to leave reviews, and search for "Tomb of the First Priest"

Sign up for updates at:

http://addavies.com/LORI-News

Or follow A. D. Davies on your local Amazon store, BookBub, or Goodreads.

ACKNOWLEDGMENTS

This has been a work of fiction. However, if you wish to know more about any of the historical notes mined for the novel, the following were invaluable in my own research, allowing me to clear up those gaps and fuzzy accounts that allow fiction to flourish:

The Story of Writing by **Andrew Johnson**

Sapiens: a Brief History of Humankind by **Yuval Noah Harari**

The Gospel of Witches by **Charles Godfrey Leland**

This is a genuine book, and its history is longer and more interesting than I had time to outline here. Jules's summary is correct, though: a woman named Maddelena passed a transcription of *il Vangelo*, the supposed gospel, on to Mr. Leland, written in her own hand, and Leland waited seven long years before publishing his translation. Leland's version was very much aimed toward condemning the subjects of his work, which (it is alleged) Maddelena's original text did not.

However, we cannot know the contents of that original manuscript because shortly after Leland published, Maddelena disappeared along with anything she passed on.

It is not known whether Leland forged the whole thing, or whether Maddelena herself simply wrote a story based on the traditions of her own circle, or if it is the genuine account, passed down through the centuries by the witches of Tuscany.

It is a rare example of the history of the book itself being as interesting, if not more so, than its contents.

The Feast of Herod painting by Peter Paul Rubens

This is a real painting, depicting the head of John the Baptist on a platter presented to Herodias and her husband during a feast. Many sources tell the story of this painting. The abbreviated version is that Herodias took exception to John's criticism of her marriage to her brother-in-law (as mentioned in the novel, he referred to it as incest), and persuaded her daughter to perform for the guests at the feast. While they were captivated by the girl's performance, Herodias had John snuck away and beheaded before anyone could object. Leaders and those of high standing who cannot take personal criticism tend to react by lashing out in extreme ways.

Flavius Josephus

Although he is a genuine chronicler of that era, he did not, as far as I know, pen an eyewitness account of John the Baptist's fate although he was most certainly around at the time and commanded respect in high places. Rumors abound regarding the writings he did produce, as many of these were lost or are locked in Vatican archives, accessible only by the most privileged scholars.

He was genuinely a student of Jesus of Nazareth and detailed a number of events in the context of that period. Any mention of the jewelry worn by Christ's mother, however, is a result of my imagination, a spur required to ensure that the apostles treated the secrets appropriately.

Flavius's real offerings may have been somewhat biased in favor of the Roman accounts, but his writing is a good source. It is a shame so much of it is locked away.

The Saint Thomas Christians in India

Christians are technically a minority group in India, but they number in the millions. They are spread far and wide, not just in Kerala, but they are among Thomas's most well-known followers. There are many fine churches worth visiting, whether you are a Christian or not.

The Fates of Thomas and Philip

The apostles Thomas and Philip ministered as outlined in the novel although I did not have space to reference all their achievements.

Philip was executed—crucified upside down—after converting the wife (or perhaps mistress) of a significant Roman nobleman while ministering in Carthage, which is in modern northern Africa.

Thomas did establish churches across the Middle East, engage and debate with Buddhists and other religions, and founded many Christian sects in India, including the Kerala Christians. He was most likely killed by a spear wielded by a local soldier in Mylapore although the reasons are sketchy to say the least.

His actual final resting place is believed to be beautiful Santhome Church in Chennai although, like many relics and bones of apostles and saints, it is impossible to verify this, and there remains a great degree of doubt among historical scholars.

These gaps in the verifiable record are where fiction like *Tomb of Aradia* finds its breathing room.

The Saint Thomas Manuscripts

While Saint Thomas's writings secured by LORI in this novel are no more than a rumor (and fleshed out in imaginative scope for narrative purposes), much of his genuine verifiable work is still in existence today. In fact, there is a project ongoing in Syria to preserve huge numbers of Christian manuscripts, and at the time of writing (mid-2017), it was still viable despite the troubles in that region. It is called the Project for Preserving the Manuscripts of Syrian Christians in India and can be found at this short and snappy website: www.srite.de.

Catacombs beneath Windsor

I have never witnessed such things, so many will say it is not, strictly speaking, true. But it might be. There are always rumors about secret passages and storage beneath significant buildings, including Buckingham Palace.

I have no actual proof of this, though. So for now, it remains a piece of my imagination.

The Mongolian Natural History Museum

My heartfelt apologies to the staff and patrons of this museum. Not only for having a number of them killed but also because, while the museum in real life is indeed a beautiful, interesting, and very worthy place to visit, alas I had to take many liberties with the exhibits present.

Gandantegchinlen Monastery

This is a temple outside Ulaanbaatar, and there was a real project to restore it, and yes, they did find many treasures in long-forgotten storage rooms. A bangle that glows when certain people touch it? Not that I know of.

Locals do shorten the name to Gandan. Not just for the benefit of fiction writers or their readership.

Physics

The slit test proving that the exact same atoms can react differently when observed is *fact*. Look up "slit test" and you'll find a great number of articles.

Flood Myths

It is mentioned in the story that all civilizations have flood stories. Historians seem to largely agree that these floods are huge in nature and occurred regularly during times when oral history was the only way of passing down information. When the land was flooded for miles around, people of those days could very well have seen this as the entire world drowning. Imagine, during a recent flood you saw on the news in the developed world, if it was not for helicopters or even satellites, would the people of those places know it was a localized event?

These stories made their way into the modern day after writing developed, and they have inspired many stories across cultures from every continent. Sometimes it's the whole world, sometimes just a lot of it.

This is not an attempt to debunk whatever flood you might believe in, be it biblical or otherwise, just a note of the evidence gathered.

Toby talks about how monuments off the coast of India are older than they should be, and although this isn't accepted science at the moment, underwater monoliths around Africa and Asia do suggest a higher quality of building occurred much earlier than the famous Giza pyramids, possibly by tens of thousands of years.

Unfortunately, the technology (or more likely the funding) does not currently exist to examine them properly. So if you happen to be a bored billionaire struggling to spend your cash, get in touch. I'll help you throw it in the ocean in search of archeological fame.

Because history really is cool.

ABOUT THE AUTHOR

In addition to his Lost Origins series, A. D. Davies is an author of crime and thriller fiction. His work covers the subgenres of police procedurals through hard-boiled private investigator novels among others.

These are grittier, affairs than the Lost Origins series, but if you do not mind violence and a bit of bad language, do check them out too.

Antony (A. D. Davies) is well traveled, his favorite destinations being New Zealand and Vietnam, and his travels have influenced his writing tremendously. For now, however, globe-trotting is taking a back seat to raising his two children and writing, although he hopes to one day combine all three.

NOVELS BY A. D. DAVIES

Co-Authored:

Project Return Fire – with Joe Dinicola

Lost Origins Novels:

Tomb of the First Priest

Secret of the Reaper Seal

Curse of the Eagle Plague